Homoerotic Tales of Intrigue and Suspense

"A top-notch collection of erotic fiction that is highly original from beginning to end. Within these stories you'll find surreal description, imaginative experiences, and dangerous attractions between men. *Men of Mystery* is satisfying on all levels for a fan of the genre—quality fiction with an erotic edge on a topic that intrigues—the sexual outlaw. Bad Boys, Great Writers."

—Paul J. Willis, Founder,
Saints and Sinners Literary Festival

"Surpassing the predictable nature of the modern, homoerotic collection, *Men of Mystery* blurs the boundaries between the dark corridors of the queer mind and the appetite for lust that dominates a culture without remorse. The collaborative efforts of editors Sean Meriwether and Greg Wharton are bold and easily unrivaled. The storytellers provide a daring, engaging, and altogether tour-de-force ride into a world created of the darkest desires—such is the grueling power of this collection. *Men of Mystery* is an erotically driven masterpiece that leaves nothing left for the reader's mind or body, save for a cold shower with all the lights turned on!"

—Andrew Wolter, Author,
Nightfall and *The Rules of Temptation*

NOTES FOR PROFESSIONAL LIBRARIANS AND LIBRARY USERS

This is an original book title published by Southern Tier Editions™, Harrington Park Press®, the trade division of The Haworth Press, Inc. Unless otherwise noted in specific chapters with attribution, materials in this book have not been previously published elsewhere in any format or language.

CONSERVATION AND PRESERVATION NOTES

All books published by The Haworth Press, Inc., and its imprints are printed on certified pH neutral, acid-free book grade paper. This paper meets the minimum requirements of American National Standard for Information Sciences-Permanence of Paper for Printed Material, ANSI Z39.48-1984.

DIGITAL OBJECT IDENTIFIER (DOI) LINKING

The Haworth Press is participating in reference linking for elements of our original books. (For more information on reference linking initiatives, please consult the CrossRef Web site at www.crossref.org.) When citing an element of this book such as a chapter, include the element's Digital Object Identifier (DOI) as the last item of the reference. A Digital Object Identifier is a persistent, authoritative, and unique identifier that a publisher assigns to each element of a book. Because of its persistence, DOIs will enable The Haworth Press and other publishers to link to the element referenced, and the link will not break over time. This will be a great resource in scholarly research.

Men of Mystery
*Homoerotic Tales
of Intrigue and Suspense*

HARRINGTON PARK PRESS®
Southern Tier Editions™
Gay Men's Fiction

Elf Child by David M. Pierce
Huddle by Dan Boyle
The Man Pilot by James W. Ridout IV
Shadows of the Night: Queer Tales of the Uncanny and Unusual edited by Greg Herren
Van Allen's Ecstasy by Jim Tushinski
Beyond the Wind by Rob N. Hood
The Handsomest Man in the World by David Leddick
The Song of a Manchild by Durrell Owens
The Ice Sculptures: A Novel of Hollywood by Michael D. Craig
Between the Palms: A Collection of Gay Travel Erotica edited by Michael T. Luongo
Aura by Gary Glickman
Love Under Foot: An Erotic Celebration of Feet edited by Greg Wharton and M. Christian
The Tenth Man by E. William Podojil
Upon a Midnight Clear: Queer Christmas Tales edited by Greg Herren
Dryland's End by Felice Picano
Whose Eye Is on Which Sparrow? by Robert Taylor
Deep Water: A Sailor's Passage by E. M. Kahn
The Boys in the Brownstone by Kevin Scott
The Best of Both Worlds: Bisexual Erotica edited by Sage Vivant and M. Christian
Tales from the Levee by Martha Miller
Some Dance to Remember: A Memoir-Novel of San Francisco, 1970-1982 by Jack Fritscher
Confessions of a Male Nurse by Richard S. Ferri
The Millionaire of Love by David Leddick
Skip Macalester by J. E. Robinson
Chemistry by Lewis DeSimone
Going Down in La-La Land by Andy Zeffer
Friends, Lovers, and Roses by V. B. Clay
Beyond Machu by William Maltese
Seventy Times Seven by Salvatore Sapienza
Virginia Bedfellows by Gavin Morris
Planting Eli by Jeff Black
Death Trick: A Murder Mystery. A Donald Strachey Mystery by Richard Stevenson
Third Man Out: A Donald Strachey Mystery by Richard Stevenson
Ice Blues: A Donald Strachey Mystery by Richard Stevenson
Drag Queen in the Court of Death by Caro Soles
Men of Mystery: Homoerotic Tales of Intrigue and Suspense edited by Sean Meriwether and Greg Wharton

Men of Mystery
Homoerotic Tales of Intrigue and Suspense

Sean Meriwether
Greg Wharton
Editors

Southern Tier Editions™
Harrington Park Press®
The Trade Division of The Haworth Press, Inc.
New York • London

For more information on this book or to order, visit
http://www.haworthpress.com/store/product.asp?sku=5885

or call 1-800-HAWORTH (800-429-6784) in the United States and Canada
or (607) 722-5857 outside the United States and Canada

or contact orders@HaworthPress.com

Published by

Southern Tier Editions™, Harrington Park Press®, the trade division of The Haworth Press, Inc., 10 Alice Street, Binghamton, NY 13904-1580.

© 2007 by Sean Meriwether and Greg Wharton. All rights reserved. No part of this work may be reproduced or utilized in any form or by any means, electronic or mechanical, including photocopying microfilm, and recording, or by any information storage and retrieval system, without permission in writing from the publisher. Printed in the United States of America.

PUBLISHER'S NOTE
The development, preparation, and publication of this work has been undertaken with great care. However, the Publisher, employees, editors, and agents of The Haworth Press are not responsible for any errors contained herein or for consequences that may ensue from use of materials or information contained in this work. The Haworth Press is committed to the dissemination of ideas and information according to the highest standards of intellectual freedom and the free exchange of ideas. Statements made and opinions expressed in this publication do not necessarily reflect the views of the Publisher, Directors, management, or staff of The Haworth Press, Inc., or an endorsement by them.

This is a work of fiction. Names, characters, places, and incidents either are the products of the author's imagination or are used fictitiously, and any resemblance to actual persons, living or dead, business establishments, events, or locales is entirely coincidental. This work may contain scenes of graphic sex and/or violence. It is not the intention of The Haworth Press to condone any particular behavior depicted within this fictional work.

Cover photo by Jack Slomovits Photographs, www.jacknyc.com.

Cover design by Kerry Mack.

Library of Congress Cataloging-in-Publication Data

Men of mystery : homoerotic tales of intrigue and suspense / edited by Sean Meriwether, Greg Wharton.
    p. cm.
    ISBN: 978-1-56023-663-4 (pbk. : alk. paper)
    1. Gay erotic literature. 2. Erotic stories, American. 3. Suspense fiction, American. I. Meriwether, Sean. II. Wharton, Greg, 1962-

PS648.H57M458 2006
813'.01083538086642—dc22

2006037810

CONTENTS

Preface — vii
Sean Meriwether

Requiem for a Punk — 1
Thomas S. Roche

Any Means Necessary — 13
Fiona Glass

Fireflies — 23
Jeff Mann

A Perfect Scar — 39
Trebor Healey

The Rubens Gamble — 53
Patrick Allen

The Boys of Fu Manchu — 73
Simon Sheppard

Never Trust a Pretty Face — 87
Michael Stamp

Lions and Tigers and Snares — 97
Vincent Diamond

A Different Trick — 117
Steve Berman

Fade to Red — 139
Max Reynolds

Too Many Questions *Gregory L. Norris*	159
Hollywood Blvd. *M. Christian*	171
Bruised *David-Matthew Barnes*	185
Augury *Mark Wildyr*	203
Breakfast in the House of the Rising Sun *Caitlín R. Kiernan*	235
Above All the Lights *Patrick Califia*	253
Afterword: What If . . . ? *Greg Wharton*	273
About the Editors	275
Contributors	277

Preface

Queer sex has always been dangerous. The physical act shared between men has been punishable by humiliation, imprisonment, and death (and still is in some countries), but as we move closer toward mainstream assimilation and acceptance, we're losing a certain edge to our sex. There was once something heroic in our copulation; your libido overruled your fear of discovery and drove you into sodomy with a friend, with a stranger, despite everything you stood to lose. Getting off was a subversive act with a tangible risk, and that weight added an intensity to the moment, heightening the experience and giving each person equal power over the other. The shared secret bound men together into more than just sex partners; they became co-conspirators against a society that turned up its nose at their illegal desire.

I am not suggesting we return to the dark days before Stonewall in order to spice up our bedroom lives, but there are some of us who want to recapture the gritty glamour of being a sexual outlaw. In retrospect, although our gay predecessors lived in various modes to conceal their sexuality, they were members of an exclusive community that required a serious commitment in order to join. They speak of meeting men clandestinely, of underground clubs and private sex parties, entire networks of other gay men who kept a closely guarded code of membership.

In lieu of those faded days, some of us seek out sketchy men in sketchier situations for the dark thrill of committing a crime with our passion, an act that makes us feel endangered and alive. Sex with risk is more intense, just like that first time you held another man's cock in your hand knowing it was what you wanted all along, despite what everyone else told you. Risk flavors the down-and-dirty coupling with a sweaty bite, making it more than sex—making it *sexcrime*. It's not the hookups of backrooms or bars, but erotic gambles where you stand to lose as much as you gain.

There are those of us who forgo the sanitized version of homosexuality and drive down darker alleys, seeking the adventure of hard sex with a threat in it. We want dirty cops who harass their suspects, shifty criminals who offer a violent fuck that will leave you aching for more, Mafioso who live with the daily threat of death, even dominant specters from beyond the grave who challenge us to define a whole new way to please them. We want to be taken down, and hard, by rough guys who make us feel more masculine as they pump into us: hard-talking, chain-smoking men with guns; thieves who dodge bullets and questions.

What makes these shadowy men of mystery so attractive? It is more than the lack of background, not knowing if he'll hurt you or throw you the hottest fuck you've ever had; more than the rough-hewn masculinity he exudes, a pheromonal challenge to all takers; beyond the *fuck you* attitude he gives the world in his stance. It's the threat he holds over you, the shared secret of your crime, the potential for violence. Living outside society's boundaries gives him a freedom to do with you as he pleases, and that's what our authors have captured.

We've gathered sixteen stories about our obsessions with these mystery men. Some tales take us back before Stonewall, to an age of secret lives and hidden sex, when every tryst was still a crime. Others bring us the shadowy figures of the underworld; mobsters and hit men, chop-shoppers and classic villains. There are private dicks here, nosing their way into the tawdry underside of society, feeding their own desires while they service their clients, along with cops who are as hard on each other as they are on their suspects. Even tales from beyond, the sensual spirits of men teasing us into paranormal submission.

Cross over with us to the underbelly of society where our dark men live. Turn down the lights, take off your shorts, and prepare to conspire with our lineup of sexual outlaws.

Sean Meriwether

Requiem for a Punk

Thomas S. Roche

"I'm a dead man," Kenny moaned, raw terror in his voice. "I'm a fucking dead man."

He was wearing a torn white T-shirt and he looked like he'd slept in the street. His black leather jacket was cracked and mottled with dirt and corrosion, and he didn't look like such a badass in that jacket now.

"Hey, relax," I told him, patting him on the shoulder and handing him a glass of Old Crow. He drank it all down in one gulp, his hands trembling. The sharp smell of his fear filled the tiny apartment. I sat down on the coffee table and squeezed Kenny's arm. "What the fuck is up? Why would Lucky Joe want to kill you? You're one of his best runners, Kenny."

Kenny was out of it, sobbing hysterically. I'd always known that kid would crack under pressure, but God help me, I'd vouched for him anyway. When I brought him in I knew I was gonna be sorry one day, but I just couldn't say no to that fuckin' kid. It wasn't just those fuckin' dopey, shit-stupid blue eyes that I could spend a whole year looking into; it's not just those big full lips or that tight ass of his or those tight jeans he wore. It was the way the whole package fit together into the finest punk piece of ass this side of the Hudson River.

Not that I'd had him, mind you. First off, the motherfucker acted straight as an arrow, not that I don't, but I saw not one hint that he swung the same way as me. And besides, I don't mix business with pleasure unless absolutely necessary. And with Kenny I'd always figured it wouldn't be necessary. Now I was beginning to think that through again.

He just rocked back and forth and kept repeating, "Lucky Joe's gonna kill me. He's gonna fuckin' kill me. You gotta help me, Nick, you gotta fuckin' help me!"

I smacked him good, across the face.

He blinked at me, stunned, with those dumb-as-dirt blue eyes. I smacked him again, grabbed him by the shoulders and shook him. The kid just rattled back and forth in my grasp like an old rag doll. "Get a fuckin' hold of yourself, you pansy motherfucker!" I shouted into his face. "What the hell did you do this time, you fuckup? Did you screw around with the receipts?"

Kenny was silent for an instant, like he was getting his wits about him. "Just a little," he finally mumbled, looking embarrassed, his face turning red. "I didn't think anyone would notice. How the fuck did he figure it out? It was only twenty dollars, Nicky. How did they figure it out?"

Another smack, this time with my fist. Kenny groaned softly and sprawled out on the couch, blood leaking from his lip. I stood over him, raising my fist, then thought better about it and just leaned down and screamed in his face, "You fucking stupid fuck! A dollar here, a dollar there, that's how Lucky Joe built his fucking empire, motherfucker! Micks and Polacks puttin' down their pocket change! You think he doesn't know that if you get away with it, pretty soon everyone'll get away with it and then he'll hafta fuckin' change his nickname?"

I stopped yelling at him, staring at his pathetic, shaking form on the couch. I instinctively felt in my pocket for my smokes, but since I was wearing that ratty old bathrobe my mother gave me, there were none in there—not even a pocket. Cursing, I stormed over to my little metal desk and looked in the drawer—pay dirt. Unfiltered Pall Malls. I shook one out and lit it. I was fighting the urge to wring Kenny's neck, but I had to admit it wasn't 'cause I was just mad. I was fuckin' scared for him. So help me God I still liked the little fucker; however many times he fucked up I wanted him worse than anything.

My own hands trembling with rage and fear, I took out a second Pall Mall, lit it, and handed it to Kenny.

"You know how deep in shit you are this time, don't you, Kenny?"

Kenny just sobbed there on the couch. "I'm sorry, I'm sorry, I'm sorry.... You gotta help me, Nicky. Please help me!"

"Take the fucking cigarette before I burn my fingers, punk." I said it with quiet menace in my voice.

Kenny obeyed, huddling on the couch, bogarting the cig like it was his last link to sanity.

"I didn't mean to take it, Nick, honest I didn't. It's just . . . it was a mistake, yeah, that's it, a mistake! Just an honest mistake!"

This time I smacked him so good the cigarette went flying across the room and landed on the carpet. I walked over and stomped it out.

"Come on, Kenny! I don't believe that shit any more than Joe's going to. Why'd you take the money?"

"It was . . . it was this prostitute, see . . ."

"Jesus fucking Christ," I groaned. "You stole a twenty from Lucky Joe Rossi so you could see a fuckin' chick?"

"Not a chick," he said sheepishly. "It was a guy."

That's when I started laughing, and pretty soon I was hysterical. Kenny just curled up on the couch and said "I'm sorry, Nicky, I'm sorry."

I sat down next to him and patted his ass. "Well, whatever the fuck you're sorry for," I finally coughed, blinking with tear-filled eyes, "don't be sorry for that. Perfectly good reason to place yourself in grave jeopardy. I've done the same fucking thing for a few street hustlers myself, specially when I was young and stupid like you. Now if it'd been some fuckin' tart . . ."

Kenny stared at me, his eyes red-rimmed and incredulous. He sat up.

"Look, Kenny. Tell you what. You get some sleep. You're gonna have to lie low for a while, but that's okay—I got it all figured out. There's this place I got up in the mountains, about six and a half hours away. Nobody knows about it, not Joe, not Rocco, not anybody. I'm gonna set you up there, while I come back to town and smooth things over with Lucky Joe. We'll have you home by the end of the week, okay?"

Kenny leaned back on the couch and he looked plenty damn fine in those torn jeans. "You mean it, Nicky? You'll help me out?"

"I'll fuckin' save your sorry ass, is what I'll do, pal! Meanwhile, try and get some sleep."

A curious look passed Kenny's face. It was one I recognized.

"I'm not much in the mood for sleep," he said, looking me over.

I'm a weak man, okay? I know it was exactly the wrong thing to do in that circumstance. But I reached out and grabbed Kenny's long, feathered hair and pulled him against me. Then I pressed my mouth to his, tasting his tongue and reaching down to grab a great big hard-on through his worn, faded jeans. Kenny was hung like a horse, a fact I'd noted plenty of times when I'd seen him around the back room of Lucky Joe's restaurant.

"You know, some guys get hard when they're scared," I told him when our mouths finally parted, a string of saliva glistening between them. "I'm surprised you didn't come in your fuckin' pants."

"Me too," said Kenny, leaning forward and kissing me again. He reached out and undid the tie of my robe, letting it fall open. He reached out for my prick, which was getting rapidly hard.

"Jesus," he said with a little shiver. "You sleep naked?"

"Ever hopeful," I told him, and stood up, pushing his face down onto my cock. He went right to work and took it in his mouth, pumping back and forth on it. As it hardened all the way, Kenny whimpered and took it down his throat like it was all he was meant to do in life.

"Oh yeah," I grunted as I pistoned my hips against him, thrusting my cock harder as the pleasure built. It looked like that hustler of his didn't do all the work. But I wasn't going to let that little cocksucker get the best of me.

"Get your clothes off," I told him. "But leave the jacket on. I've wanted to fuck you in that fuckin' jacket since I first laid eyes on you."

Kenny looked a little embarrassed for a moment, but he obeyed me, grabbing his belt and unfastening it, unzipping, pulling down his pants. He was in such a rush to get undressed that he pulled his jeans off over his sneakers and climbed onto the couch with his sneakers still on.

He struggled out of the jacket and shucked his T-shirt, then put the jacket back on. I tossed off my robe and stood there naked behind him, working my cock. I looked up and down the rough outline of the worn leather jacket, loving how tight it was around his lower back, the way the black leather melded with the curve of his ass. I ran my hand up his inner thigh and reached between his legs, grabbing his balls and squeezing. Kenny gave a little whimper of pain as I squeezed harder and harder. Then I started slapping his balls, listening to the moans as Kenny's cock jerked in time with my abuse.

I wrapped my hand around his meat and stroked him while I formed a good ball of spit and let it dribble onto my hard organ. I climbed onto the couch behind Kenny and worked the spittle all over my prick. Kenny gritted his teeth as I nestled the cockhead into his cleft. His ass felt good and tight as I penetrated him, and as it went in all the way Kenny let out a low, rapturous moan. Then I gripped his waist, feeling the tight belt of the leather jacket and feeling my prick surge in response to its texture. I fucked Kenny good and hard, pounding him in long strokes while I reached around his body to work his shaft. He was the first one to come, shooting long streams all over my ratty orange sofa, and I got as much come as I could on my right hand and grabbed Kenny's hair with my left, leaning forward so I could rub that come all over his face. He lapped at it, groaning as I kept pounding into him, and the sight of that boy with his face all glistening and covered with jizz was enough to send me off the edge. My cock spasmed and I shot deep into Kenny's asshole, shuddering as I released everything I'd ever had into that boy's lithe, well-muscled body.

By the time Kenny and I had finished a few more whiskeys in the darkness, both our cocks were hard. So Kenny sucked me off, tasting the musk and shit of his own ass as he rubbed himself. We both came and Kenny lay there on top of me. By that time it was almost light, and Kenny dropped off to sleep.

I eased myself out from under him and went into the bedroom. I sat down on my bed and drank another whiskey, running over it all in my head. Then I got out a fresh pair of pants and a shirt, put on a sports jacket and slipped on my shoes. I went into the top drawer of my dresser and took out the twin .22s I kept in there. I made sure each was loaded and put one in each jacket pocket.

I had to pass Kenny on the way out, and his eyes fluttered open. His eyes suddenly got big and scared.

"Wh—where're you going, Nicky?"

"Hey, relax, I'm just going out to get more smokes. We're gonna need them on the drive up."

"Hey, you shouldn't have to do that—why don't I go out for you?"

I rolled my eyes. "Relax, Kenny."

"Then mind if I come with you?"

"Look, you stupid motherfucker. If Lucky Joe's looking for you he's got my place covered. You're just fuckin' lucky you didn't get yourself sprayed with a Thompson when you showed up here last night! You are not going to set foot outside this fuckin' apartment until I bring the car around for you, okay? Be ready to go in fifteen minutes."

"But—" Kenny started to mumble, and I shot him a particularly vicious look. He fell silent.

"Stop being such a stupid fuck," I growled at him affectionately. "You're gonna get yourself killed, and I'm starting to like that tight ass of yours."

I left him sitting there looking glum on the couch. I went down to the liquor store on the corner and bought three packs of smokes. As I walked, I looked around for a familiar black Buick, or maybe a Packard.

I found it.

I stopped in the diner across the street, which was just opening for breakfast. My stomach was rumbling, but I didn't stop for food. I went to the phones in the back and called Lucky Joe.

I brought the Caddy around back and parked it with the hazards on. The meter maid in the neighborhood is on Lucky Joe's payroll so it was no big deal. I went up the back stairs to my apartment and let myself in.

Kenny was sitting on the couch with his jeans on and no shirt or shoes. He had my .45 in his trembling hand and he was pointing it at me.

Goddamn it, I knew I should have brought the fucking thing.

"You called Lucky Joe," Kenny moaned pathetically. "They're coming right now to kill me."

I spoke in my most soothing voice. "Kenny, Kenny, put that fucking thing away. You ain't shot a gun in your fucking life. You aren't going to shoot me now."

"Oh yeah?" he choked, and raised the gun. His eyes were red and tears were forming. "Try me."

"Kenny, relax! Put the gun down! Those fuckin' Colts have a way of going off, okay? Why the fuck would I call Lucky Joe?"

Kenny didn't put the gun down. "Maybe now that you've fucked me you don't give a shit!"

I laughed, inching closer to him. "That's bullshit. I'm not going to hurt you, Kenny!"

"Damn right you aren't," he sobbed. "'Cause I'm gonna kill you first!"

That's when I hit the ground and reached up for the gun. He pulled the trigger, but the stupid fuck had the safety on. I came up and kicked him in the balls, yanking the pistol out of his grasp.

I flicked the safety off, knelt over Kenny's squirming form, and stuck the muzzle of the gun in his mouth.

"You gotta take the safety off," I told him. "Now if I was gonna deliver you to Little Joe, why wouldn't I just blow your fuckin' brains out right now, motherfucker, and say you gave me a struggle? Then I could fuck your dead body for all anyone would care, asshole!"

My finger inched closer to the trigger.

Kenny quivered underneath me, his eyes flashing "I'm sorry."

I pulled the gun out of his mouth and said, in the softest, most compassionate voice I could manage: "Get your fuckin' clothes on. We've got some driving to do."

My little show of dominance must have convinced Kenny to roll over, because he didn't give me any more trouble on the way up. I even let him piss on his own, half-hoping he would run away into the woods and get his sorry punk ass eaten by a bear. But he didn't.

Instead, he acted like we'd been best friends since childhood. By now I was convinced that Kenny was totally schizophrenic. But he gave me a blowjob during one of our pit stops, so that kept me kindly disposed toward him—up to a point.

As we got closer to the cabin, I could feel the weight of the .22s in my jacket pockets, the bulk of the .45 Colt stuffed into my waistband.

I thought about Kenny dying in the cold dirt of the mountains. I could almost smell his piss and shit and blood.

It was late in the day when we pulled off the remote mountain road and parked in front of the cabin. I fished in my pants pocket for the key and walked up the stairs. At the landing, I waited for Kenny.

"Come on, punk, I ain't got all day." Kenny climbed the stairs wearily and followed me into the cabin.

Inside, it was dark. Kenny had just closed the front door when Rocco Morelli's voice, rough as sandpaper, said, "Hello, Kenny." Tony Brakes grabbed Kenny's arms as Rocco hit him hard on the side of the head, and Kenny went limp in Tony's arms.

"Afternoon, Nicky," said Rocco. "Pleasure to be working with you again."

I shook his hand. "Likewise," I said. "Listen, I want to be the one to do this fuckin' punk, okay? I got a bullet with his name on it."

"Be our guest," said Rocco. "For us, it's business—not pleasure. So be our guest." He laughed.

Kenny wasn't out for long. By the time he came to in the trunk of the Caddy, we were deep in the middle of nowhere and the sun was going down. We could hear him pounding against the trunk, trying to get out, but we didn't bother to knock him out again.

"He's thrashing around like a dying fish," chuckled Rocco with a cruel twist to his lips. He tossed a cig out the window of the Caddy and lit another one.

"Yeah," I said. "Just like a fucking fish."

Kenny was sobbing as we made him dig his own grave. "Why are you doing this to me?" he kept asking. "Nicky, Nicky, make 'em stop! You promised you'd smooth things over with Lucky Joe for me! Please, you gotta give me a break! You can't just fuckin' kill me like this!"

About the hundredth time Kenny said that, Rocco started shooting. Chunks of dirt sprayed up inches from Kenny's foot, but none of the shots hit him. Rocco always was one hell of a shot.

"Come on, you fuckin' punk, shut the fuck up and dig faster. We ain't got all night!"

I was afraid Kenny might start spewing shit about what we did the night before, trying to beg for his life. And I knew that might cause me more than a little discomfort with Rocco and Tony. But for whatever reason—and I never really did figure this out—Kenny didn't say a thing about that. As much as he blabbed, he never did say anything about the fact that he had my cock in his ass less than twelve hours before.

So when it came time to do him, to put him in the ground, I guess I felt more than a little guilty.

"Just like I told you, boys. I want to put the bullet in this fucking punk's head."

"Be our guest."

Kenny stood sobbing at the edge of the hole in the ground, waiting for the impact of the bullets to push him into the grave. I lifted the .45 as Rocco lit a cigarette.

I sighted Kenny's head with the Colt, let the tension build as Kenny shook and blubbered.

"Just kill 'im already," grunted Tony.

I pulled the triggers of the .45 and one of the .22s at the same time. Kenny gave a yelp and disappeared into the grave. I heard him hit as the midnight wind whistled through the trees.

Blood was splattered all over me. I could smell the piss and shit. Bone fragments were scattered over the ground. I looked down with what I would have sworn was more than half a hard-on, and felt Rocco's hands grasping at my ankles.

I looked down the barrel of the .45 and emptied it into Rocco's prone body. Tony was already dead.

Kenny, that pansy fuck, was lying in the bottom of his grave sobbing hysterically. I don't know if he thought he was dead or had just gone completely fucking nuts with the stress. I climbed in after him and pushed his face into the soft earth. I grabbed his jeans and yanked them down, then undid my own and wiped the slick blood and brains from Tony's head over my cock.

Maybe on any other night it would have disgusted the fuck out of me. But I was running a little short on mores tonight. I rammed into Kenny's asshole with all the force I could muster, and soon I was moaning and our loads were mingling in the soft dirt of Kenny's grave. He stopped his sobbing as his hard-on, covered with jizz, slowly dwindled.

I looked down at him with that weird mixture of contempt you can only have for someone when you've completely fucked up your own life for them. For no good reason.

"Get out of the fuckin' grave," I told him. "We've got work to do."

"He's communing with nature, all right. Only one thing, what the fuck ever happened to Rocco and Tony? I had to do the job alone. Yeah. Yeah. No, I never got word from them. Jesus, you don't think…you don't think that, do you? No. No. Look, I'll keep my eyes open. No, it was easy; he died like a punk. All right. All right. I'll keep my eyes open. I just hope they show up. If those fuckin' East Side motherfuckers whacked Rocco and Tony, I promise you I'll fuckin' make them pay. I'll find out who it was if it's the last fuckin' thing I do. You understand me, Boss? If it's the last fuckin' thing I do, I'm gonna get the motherfucker who whacked Rocco and Tony. Yeah.

Yeah. I know. All right, look, I'm gonna get some sleep. Maybe they'll show up. I'm sure they're fine. All right. I'll be in touch."

I eased the receiver into the cradle of the pay phone and went back to the Caddy. Kenny was almost done putting the gas in.

I settled back into the driver's seat and opened up the map.

Kenny finished up with the cashier and slid into the passenger's seat. He looked nervous.

"You okay, kid?"

He shrugged. "The sooner we can dump those packages in the trunk, the better I'll feel."

"You and me both," I told him, and found the spot on the map. "About a hundred miles away. Just hope Lucky Joe doesn't decide to dig up your grave."

Kenny gave a shudder at that one.

There was no way to predict what shit was going to hit the fan first. I didn't know if I could make one of the East Side bastards look guilty, give them a motive they never had, incriminating evidence that didn't exist. Or if Lucky Joe would see right through my trick of mirrors and one night soon I'd be digging my own grave in the forest while Sammy or Johnny Numbers or Max the Knife pointed a .45 at me and laughed about how I'd pissed my life away for a faggot punk.

But until that night came, that fine sweet ass of Kenny's was mine. And it was almost like he'd grown up in the moment he fell into that grave. He had a different confidence now, a coldness he hadn't had before. Like visiting his own grave had made him different somehow. He didn't act like such a punk now. Maybe this is his requiem, then: his story, and my own, told in my scattered thoughts to the purr of a Caddy's engine, motoring down the interstate toward and away from twin destinies of sudden death. Requiem for a punk.

I pulled out of the gas station and eased onto the freeway, keeping the Caddy right at the speed limit through the endless fields of gold. The sun was starting to come up again, and the roosters were crowing.

Any Means Necessary

Fiona Glass

"Sammy? Nah, not Sammy, Mr. Hughes. Ancient history, Sammy is—has been since Christmas." The old man rambled on, words muffled round the permanent half-mast cigarette spilling tubes of ash down his grubby mac. Words that included "Colman" and "new kid" and "pretty boy," but Hughes had already stopped listening to the flood.

"You sure, Paddy? It's important." Important wasn't the word. More like vital, or desperate, or devastating. More like his bloody career on the line, and Mackay's too if the old guy was right. If only they'd checked their facts first, instead of storming in mob-handed. If only they'd played the good guys for a change.

"Course I'm bleedin' sure. Aren't I telling you? You only got to go round the clubs come Friday night—soon see for yourself." He removed the fag-end long enough for a noisy swig from his beer and wiped his mouth on his sleeve. "Surprised you didn't already know, Mr. Hughes. Been common knowledge on the streets for months. Colman never keeps the same boy more than six months. Thought you knew that."

And we should have known, Hughes thought. Should have known, should have checked, should have bloody *thought* for a change. They'd been tracking Colman for months, convinced he had a finger in virtually every dirty pie in the city, from fraud to racketeering to full-blown organized crime. But the wily bastard was too smart for them, moving on, never leaving a trail, laundering every last tuppence through a maze of offshore accounts convoluted enough to baffle a homing pigeon with GPS. But he did have one weakness, did Colman—he liked boys. Rent boys, usually, in any shape or size as long as they were clean and pleasing to the eye, and legal, if only just. And young Sammy had been the latest in a long unsavory line and they'd been so intent on using him to trap his powerful friend that they hadn't stopped to check the facts. He kicked savagely at the leg of Paddy's bar stool, slopping the old man's pint halfway to his mouth.

"Oi! What d'you go and do that for? Said I'd help and I'm helping, aren't I?"

"Yeah, yeah." He didn't have time to coddle the old soak, or for anything except a hasty exit and a call to HQ. And Sammy had even less time than him. Not that they'd kill him, of course. That was still against the law no matter which cloak-and-dagger outfit you worked for. But leave the kid to Mackay's tender mercies for an hour and he'd have suffered a fate worse than death. Hughes knew better than anyone just what his thug of a partner was capable of. He'd been on the receiving end often enough, the only difference being that he liked it—liked the loss of control, and the stolen sinful pleasure that bordered on pain, and the heavy body that held him down with nothing more than its own weight. And Mackay enjoyed it too, for all the opposite reasons. Give Mackay a body to work his brutal magic on and he'd be there with his tongue hanging out, reveling in the power. There was a word that described Mackay to perfection, and that word was *psychopath*. As Sammy might be about to find out for himself.

He left Paddy to his spilled beer and dashed back to the car, shrugging his collar higher and pocketing his hands as he hit the rain-slicked street outside the bar. Darkness had descended and neon signs striped the sodden pavement in flickering backwards imprecations to "eat, sleep, breathe Coca-Cola" or "see the topless girls dance for you." Ignoring them with the ease of familiarity, he lowered his head against the rain and ran. The car, by some minor miracle, was still intact and still where he'd left it. He wrenched open the door and was already reaching for the mobile before he remembered—bloody things weren't working, were they? That new satellite dish on the town hall had seen to that and the boss's complaints had achieved bugger all. The dish stayed put and their phones stayed fucked. He'd have to find a pay phone instead.

Needless to say, the first two he tried were vandalized to hell and back—daubed with graffiti, stained with stale and stinking urine, and with all the wires pulled free. The third still worked, but it didn't help him much. "Boss is in a meeting and can't be disturbed," was the laconic reply, and when he asked for Mackay instead the same bored voice said "Him too." There was nothing else for it—he'd have to deliver the message himself. And hope to God that said "meeting" didn't involve young Sammy.

The hope was vain. He knew that the instant he rounded the corner of the corridor and saw the guard outside the interview-room door. Statue-still the man stood, arms folded across his chest, an immoveable barrier to whatever was happening in the room behind. And Hughes could see movement through the obscured glass of the door. Not the ugly, urgent movement of a beating, thank Christ, but that didn't necessarily mean it was all right.

"Okay if I go through?" he asked, expecting to have to argue the point with the goon.

But the guard just said, "No problem, Mr. Hughes. The boss said to let you past." And the policeman-plod feet shuffled aside to grant him passage.

So, he was one of the favored now, was he? One of those few hardy souls trusted to witness the real way the department worked? That was a new development; Mackay must have put in a word. He could hear the lazy voice now. "Yeah, Hughes is all right. One of us. Not too fussy how he gets results—saw it myself on that blackmail case." Most of the time, his partner was right. Up to a point. And that point had just been reached. The interview rooms were supposed to be soundproof but the groan still percolated right through the glass; without further thought he turned the knob and strode inside.

Things were exactly as he'd feared, stark fluorescent lighting and a lack of furniture leaving little to the imagination. In a plastic chair in the corner sat the boss, reading a file, watching over his specs and making notes, for Christ's sake. Young Sammy, or what could be seen of him, was bent unceremoniously over a table with his pants shoved down his legs. And Mackay, with his back three-quarters turned, was plastered up against the kid's backside, ramming into the shadowed cleft between his legs, so hard the table feet were squeaking on the floor. Mackay's own arse bunched and relaxed in syncopated rhythm and the big dick emerged with regularity from the darkness, glistening with the spit he'd used for lube. Hughes felt a moment's thrill at the sight and had to clamp it down. Sammy might be nothing more than a cheap street whore, but he didn't deserve this.

"Better get off him," he gravelled. "You've got the wrong bloke."

Mackay turned at that, a grin ghosting through his exertions. "Fucking hell, Hughes, you've got lousy timing."

And was echoed by the boss. "Don't be ridiculous, man. He's an important suspect and we need to question him."

"Doesn't mean treating him like dirt. Sir."

The boss remained unimpressed. "You know as well as I do that we'll use any means necessary if a suspect isn't cooperating."

"Yeah, come on, mate. What the hell were we supposed to do, pat him on the head and send him on his way?" Mackay panted, still thrusting although his pace had slowed. Hughes wasn't sure if that was a good sign or not.

"Anyone thought that maybe he wasn't cooperating because he doesn't know anything?" he said at last, allowing the bite and disgust to color his voice. "I already told you. He's the wrong man."

There was a pause as the repercussions of that sank in, and then Mackay pulled out of his victim, tidied himself away without a word, and sat with his arms and ankles crossed to await further orders. The sudden shift from arousal to patient composure unnerved Hughes. Psychopath, all right.

The boss, though, was inclined to bluster. "Are you sure? Our information was that—"

"Your information was wrong," Hughes interrupted. "I just finished talking to old Paddy at The Bar. He says Colman dumped Sammy at Christmas. Paddy's seen him doing the rounds at the clubs with a new lad since then."

"That's right!" the object of their discussions piped up, one hand reaching for his pants. "He's seeing Carl now. Carl Claverson. You know, Mr. Hughes—that black-haired bitch what works down Bridge Street. I 'aven't seen Mr. Colman in months. I don't know nothing!"

"We'll see about that," the boss said, but he was just fishing now. They knew, all of them, that without the link to Colman they had no reason to keep Sammy here. Best let him go before he got onto some hotshot lawyer and started screaming wrongful arrest.

"Here," said Hughes, handing him his sweatshirt, and they stood awkwardly, not meeting each other's gaze, watching while the kid dressed himself again.

"See that he gets home," said the boss then, and with a jerk of his head indicated that they were dismissed.

In the corridor he and Mackay locked eyes. Psychopath he might be but they were still partners. "I'll see to this," he said gruffly. "You go and get yourself cleaned up."

"Yeah, thanks. Think I will." Slinging his jacket over one shoulder, the big man strode off whistling, apparently suffering not a moment's twinge of conscience for what he'd just put Sammy through. And Sammy? Hughes regarded the kid with his hands on his hips, not liking the sideways sneaking stare he got back. Too much triumph in that gaze by half. His hands itched to smack it off the pretty face. Just because he'd got them off his back—literally and figuratively—didn't mean he could crow. Just because . . .

"Come on," he said abruptly, snapping his own chain of thought. "Let's get *you* cleaned up and all. You can come back to my place. I'll check you over for any damage."

"Okay, Mr. Hughes. Ta very much."

Back at his bomb-site of a flat he gave the kid free run of the bathroom without bothering to mention that the door didn't lock. Halfway through the splashing ablutions that followed, he walked in. The kid was in the shower, naked, and hadn't drawn the curtain. Was that hurry, or the deeply ingrained urge to work no matter what? Hughes wasn't sure, but he watched Sammy anyway, the wet young body shivering in the draught from the open door. Fetching little thing really, all eyes and hair, if a bit old for a rent boy. Must be on the wrong side of twenty by now and probably finding it hard to get work—especially now Colman had left him to it. *If* Colman had left him . . .

Holding out a towel—his excuse for barging in—he said, "Thought you might need this."

"Oh. Yeah. Ta." The kid eyed him for a moment, and Hughes noticed the exact instant when the eyes flicked below his belt to check him out. Definitely still at work. Not that there was anything for him to see. Although there might be if he stayed here much longer, watching the water run down the kid's back and part the twin halves of his bum like a cascade through domed rocks. It was hard to look away, especially with Sammy pouting over his shoulder like that, a challenging, sensual pout that had nothing to do with gratitude and everything to do with lust.

"Get yourself dried off and hop it into the bedroom. I need to see if Mr. Mackay hurt you," he growled.

Sammy grinned, seeing straight through the subterfuge like the canny street urchin he was. "Give us that towel, then." He rubbed himself down deliberately, stroking the length of each limb in turn, leaving his back to Hughes and teasing him by propping one foot at a time on the bath to dry between his toes. The move showed his arse off to perfection, as he doubtless intended. Hughes could see the play of muscle, the lean thigh stretched taut, the rosy pucker winking from its lair amongst the few stray hairs. It beckoned, and Hughes found himself wanting to touch, to run a finger round the wrinkled flesh, to push inside just a little, to feel the muscles grab and squeeze.

If the kid looked now there'd be something to see all right. He could feel his cock lengthening and filling inside his pants, the material starting to stretch. "Bedroom," he said briefly, and turned and led the way. There was a patter of footsteps on lino as Sammy followed, and the springs of the bed dipped to his weight, and squeaked.

"This okay?"

"No, on your back first. Need to see if he bruised you slamming you up against the table like that." He patted one slim thigh in encouragement and the kid flipped, half-erect cock standing free. Hughes was reassured; if the kid was responding like that there couldn't be too much wrong. Better safe than sorry, though . . . He took the shaft in his hand, unconsciously weighing it against the memory of Mackay's, and found it wanting in every way. Slimmer, shorter, lighter, and his balls were smaller too, with only the softest coating of down, and he was cut so the head felt different, more thickly skinned.

But a cock was a cock, and this one was hardening nicely as he stroked it up and down. He bent and took it in his mouth, and was disappointed to taste only soap, not the strong flavors he was used to. And that cut head felt strange to his tongue, calloused and harsh. He spat it out again, and slapped the boy's hip to turn him over once more.

It was better when he couldn't see the kid's face, or the impudence—accusation?—that challenged from his eyes. It was better, too, that he couldn't see that different cock, or the thin ribs and thinner arms and legs. From behind, most blokes looked the same: long back, knobbly spine, the powerful jut of buttocks, the single dark eye between. Concentrate on those and he'd be okay.

Unzipping, he drew out his own cock and held it for a moment, warm and heavy in his hand. He pulled his foreskin back and rubbed the very tip against the kid's rim, feeling every last hummock and indentation against the sensitive tip. God, but that felt good! He could feel the shivers of anticipation all the way to his toes. He paused and rubbed, paused and rubbed and shoved, and his cock slid in where Mackay had ploughed a furrow of his own. A thought intruded: If he'd delayed his interruption longer, back there at HQ, it could've been Mackay's spunk easing his way. His cock twitched. Powerful turn-on that was, following in his partner's footsteps—or the stretch marks of his dick. Mackay's cock had touched this rim, had stroked against these fleshy walls, had nudged the boy's nub and left behind his own distinctive snail trail of saliva and pre-cum. Touching and stroking and nudging in turn, he rode the slender body, knees tucked into the hollows behind knees, chest molded to small of back, balls slapping against one thigh. He plunged in hard and pulled out slow, giving in to the clutch of Sammy's arse. Was this how it had felt for Mackay? Had his partner been squeezed just so, like a hand grasping through a rubber glove?

One thing for sure: the kid was enjoying this fuck more than the last, if the succession of grunts was to be believed. In fact, the kid was enjoying it more than *he* was. Business before pleasure, Hughesy old son—and this wasn't, after all, Mackay. Wasn't his weight, or his voice in Hughes' ear, cajoling him on. Wasn't his arms, corded with the strain, braced either side of his head. Wasn't Mackay's rough stubble catching on his chin, or Mackay's thick-veined cock ramming him into next week. A fuck was a fuck, though, and not to be turned down. He continued to thrust until Sammy cried out.

Half-muffled by the pillow, it sounded like "Mack." For a moment he was baffled. Surely the kid couldn't be crying out for Mackay after what his partner had done? Slowly, very slowly, various snippets of information met and meshed. Not "Mack," but "Max." Max Craig, Colman's Mr. Big. The top boss himself, a link in the chain so high that the air he breathed contained less oxygen than that of everyone else. Well, well, fucking well. No wonder Sammy had looked so triumphant. He'd taken them all for a ride.

But now the ride was over, in more ways than one. The realization cooled Hughes' ardor, and he couldn't be bothered to finish the charade. Work was more important than sex, unless it was Mackay, and sometimes even then. Easing himself out of the kid's body, he rolled over, waiting for the haze of almost-pleasure to clear.

"Oh well, if I'd known you wanted him for yourself..." The caustic tone cut through the haze like wind on a foggy day and he tried to remember when he'd given his partner a key. Oh yeah. Christmas. He'd hoped—don't laugh—they could make something together, something more than the slam-bam-thank-you-man action that was all they'd tried so far. So far, it hadn't worked. He sighed.

"What the fuck are you doing here?"

Cool blue eyes regarded him from the doorway. "Came to see if he was all right."

"You're kidding."

The faint grin vanished. "I'm not a complete bastard, whatever you might think."

"But you'll do anything you're told?"

"Was only following orders."

"And if those orders had killed him?"

Wide shoulders rose and fell in a shrug. "It's my job. Yours too. You don't exactly pussyfoot about when it suits you."

And that was closer to the truth than he wanted to think. Scowling, he said, "Maybe not, but if pussyfooting about gets better results then I'll do it. Like this time. Amazing what you can get out of a bloke with a bit of kindness." Point made, he was quite enjoying this, enjoying turning the tables on Mackay, enjoying the knowledge that this time, his methods had worked. Any means necessary, all right.

"Yeah?" The blue gaze had turned wary, as though his partner wasn't sure what was coming next.

"Yeah. He's all yours. Take him back in if you like."

"What? But I thought you said Paddy said . . ."

"Paddy told us what he saw, but he didn't tell us why. Colman's got a new bloke all right, but he didn't dump Sammy. Sammy dumped him."

"You what?" Shocked eyebrows swooped upwards, twin crows' wings, to merge with Mackay's hair.

"Yeah. Got someone new himself, hasn't he? Someone bigger than Colman—Colman's boss! And guess who's organizing this latest scam? We play this right, we could nail Max Craig while we're at it."

"Jesus!" Mackay breathed. "So he knew about it after all. Little bitch!"

The little bitch in question had been quietly getting dressed, for the second time that day. Hughes let him get on with it; they could scarcely take him back to HQ stark naked, whatever the entertainment value of such a move. He had to admit, though, that he hadn't expected the sudden cyclone of movement, the flinging of arms and legs and the protesting shriek of springs as their quarry launched himself up and out and into the sanctuary of the bathroom.

"Oi!" Mackay yelled and charged past the bed in outraged headlong pursuit.

Hughes lay back and watched the inevitable as the door banged shut on the end of his partner's nose.

"Fuck!" said Mackay before shaking the woodwork with the staccato beat of his fists. "Come out of there, you little shite!"

But the only response was breaking glass and mugs being knocked off the sill. Young Sammy was climbing out the bathroom window.

"Well, don't just sit there. Come and get this door open. The boss'll have our balls if we let him get away."

Hughes shrugged. "Let him go." And couldn't repress the wince as Mackay span round, anger darkening his face. Sarcasm to blazing rage in thirty seconds flat—a psychopath, all right.

"Are you mad? I'm not letting him get away. Take us hours to find him again, days if he goes to ground. And he could run straight to Craig and warn him off and all."

There'd been times in the past when he'd been downright scared of Mackay and his moods, but this time he had the perfect answer, and this time the thrill was turning him on. "Don't worry; he's not going anywhere. This place is on the third floor and the fire escape's round the other side. He's got three choices: he can jump to his death, climb back in, or dangle there till we're good and ready to fetch him. He won't be doing much warning in any of those positions." His partner's face had cleared, a small but appreciative smile lurking in his eyes. He risked adding, "Hey, you got your handcuffs on you?"

"Yeah, always have. Why, think he'll cause trouble?"

Hughes had been slithering his jeans down his legs. Now he kicked them off, and hauled his T-shirt over his head. "Wasn't him I was thinking you could use them on," he said, and made a Mackay-sized space on the bed. "Do the little sod good to dangle for a while, don't you think?"

His partner was grinning now. "You're all right, Hughes," he said. "One of us. Not too fussy how you get results—saw it myself on that blackmail case."

He grinned back, even as he licked his lips at the powerful body being exposed to his gaze. His partner was right. Up to a point. Any means necessary, all right.

Fireflies

Jeff Mann

> The wind doth blow tonight, my love,
> With a few small drops of rain.
> I never had but one true love,
> And he in the cold grave has lain.
>
> "The Unquiet Grave"

There is only one photograph of him. An old daguerreotype which hangs in the front parlor of the inn. The proprietors point to it and sheepishly smile, whenever a tourist who's brushed up on local folklore asks about the resident ghost. He was a Confederate soldier, they uncomfortably explain. His blood still stains the hardwood floor at the top of the stairs. His presence still haunts Room 203.

I was sixteen when I first saw that photograph, when I first fell in love with Stephen Ferrell. My parents had brought me into Melrose, the county seat, to celebrate my birthday with an expensive meal at the Highland Inn, amidst elegant surroundings none of us was accustomed to. I had grown up nearby, on a hillside farm twenty miles from Melrose, but had only once before been inside the inn, during a fifth-grade field trip to historic sites in southwest Virginia.

That night, after lobster bisque and prime rib my father could barely afford, after a coconut cake complete with birthday candles and the obligatory embarrassment of being sung to by off-key waiters, I was waiting in the front parlor while my mother chatted with a distant well-to-do cousin and my father paid the bill. Bored, I tapped my fingers on the arm of the settee and scanned Civil War photos on the opposite wall. McCormick County had had its share of battles during the War of Northern Aggression, as we Virginians like to call it, and every historic building in town still displays faded photos of the local Confederate heroes.

Sighing with impatience, I sank back into the settee. Then he caught my eye. My fingers stopped their restless tapping. I stared. I rose. I stood beneath the photograph. Alone in the room, I was free to gawk unashamedly.

"Sergeant Stephen Ferrell" said the small plaque beneath the daguerreotype. "April 1860."

"Allen? Time to go!" My mother's face appeared smiling in the parlor door.

I said little on the drive home, watching fireflies rise from pastures, mountains flow by in early August haze. Only recently had I begun to realize that what I felt for certain muscular teachers and classmates was desire, desire I knew to keep to myself. But none of them, men or boys, had seized me like that face on the wall of the Highland Inn.

When we got home, I thanked my parents for the birthday celebration and went to bed early. In my humid bedroom, I turned on the window fan, pulled off my clothes, and stretched naked across the unmade bed. When I closed my eyes, I could see him still—vaguely, as if glimpsed through mist or cloudy water. His proud, dark, almost cruel eyes. His dark curly hair and black goatee framing full lips. His gray cap and Confederate uniform, stretched over a beefy physique, a sword hanging from his hip.

How many decades dead? Somewhere, I knew, all that was left of him, all that remained of that handsome face and strong body, were boxed bones, niched perhaps in some sunken unmarked grave. Still, what I saw beneath the proper military pose of the photograph was the muscles of his chest and arms, the hair spreading across his chest and belly. Over the sparse, adolescent fur around my nipples I ran my fingers, then on down the light trail of belly hair to grasp myself, a release I had learned only recently.

I woke, a few hours later, the stickiness dried on my thigh. A single firefly winked over my bed like a flirtatious haphazard star. *How did it get in?* I wondered sleepily. For several minutes I watched it drift and blink about the room before falling again into sleep.

The very next morning, I started my research. I asked around as discreetly as I could, all under the pretense of a project for history class. Who was Stephen Ferrell? Where did he come from? How did he die? There were a few pertinent historical records, and, much more revealing, some hesitant word-of-mouth tales that heightened my fascination even more. Local storytellers claimed that his ghost haunted the Highland Inn, and I wanted to know why.

After that evening, every time I got to Melrose and could manage some time away from my over-solicitous parents, I slipped into the front parlor of the inn and stared at that daguerreotype. If I thought I could have gotten away with stealing it, I would have.

Instead, one day I furtively took a picture of it. Photo of a photo I kept hidden inside my diary. So many frustrating removes from reality, so far from the real, long-dead man I wanted to touch more than any living man I'd ever seen. More than Doug, with his big football player's arms, showering near me in Phys Ed class. More than Mr. Honaker, the barrel-chested science teacher. More than Billy, the buddy I skinny-dipped with in Lick Creek on summer afternoons, whose hairy ass I tried not to stare at. More than Mike, my older cousin, whose thick black beard I studied as we tramped through the hillside snows with our hunting rifles.

Stephen Ferrell haunted me—the unsmiling face in the photograph, the imagined muscles of his body, the stories I'd heard, the few facts I'd read about him. Throughout those last remaining years of high school, I lay on my bed whenever I could find the time, watched the leaves come and go in my window, watched rain fall or sunlight glitter over the surrounding hills, and touched myself as I wanted to touch him, wishing that Confederate hero were there with me, naked, long black hair falling over my face, a solid weight atop me, his beard brushing my cheek, his hands brutal one minute, tender the next.

Local history books gave the bare details. From a family of Irish immigrants. Joined the 20th battalion. Died in Melrose in 1863, at the age of twenty-five. No mention of the location of his grave, else I would have visited it to pay my respects and satisfy my slowly growing obsession further. The relevant folklore I gleaned from locals was maddeningly vague and contradictory. He was discharged from the army for some unnamed immorality. He was caught with an officer's wife and summarily punished. He was a war hero in the Shenandoah Valley Campaigns. He was killed in a skirmish in Patrick County. He died in the Highland Inn, in Room 203. His ghost often appears in that room or at the top of the staircase, where he received a mortal wound and where, beneath carpet, his blood still stains the floor.

The few times I managed to get up the guts to ask the proprietors of the inn about their resident ghost, they laughed off my interest and told a few of the same sketchy stories I'd already heard. It was only during my last weekend home, just before I headed off to college at Virginia Tech, that I heard a new piece of the tale, one that seized me most of all.

I was visiting my grandmother for a few days at her little home near Marion. She was preparing a pecan pie when, one evening over coffee, I asked her if she'd ever heard anything about the Confederate soldier whose ghost was said to haunt the Highland Inn.

"Son, hand me the corn syrup," she asked, as she beat the eggs to a froth. It was hot in that kitchen, even after sundown. Outside, tree frogs chirped. She looked out the window screen for a few seconds, as if weighing her words, before she said, "What my mother told me was Stephen Ferrell was a crazy mixture of contraries. Best-looking man ever came from this county. Brave in battle. But he ended up the worst kind of sinner. Only reason the army didn't throw him out was he was such a fine soldier. Died saving his sister when Yankees tried to burn the Highland Inn."

"Sinner? What kind of sinner?" I asked, simultaneously hopeful and afraid.

She shook her head. Silent, she poured the pie mixture over the pecans before replying.

"What a waste," she sighed. "Boy that handsome a morphodite."

I left McCormick County, and, for a long while, I left behind Stephen Ferrell. College years at Virginia Tech. First love affairs. Graduate school on the West Coast. A PhD in history. Then a succession of academic jobs, a succession of cities, a succession of lovers, none of whom stayed around for long, none of whom lived up to the rough and passionate intensity Stephen Ferrell's face seemed to promise. At the same time that I was achieving some small bit of professional prominence, I seemed, on the personal front, to be making a sad career out of falling in love with the wrong guys. From the Kinders, my mother's side of the family, I'd inherited a tendency toward depression, which didn't help. In the aftermath of each romantic disaster, I ran through my share of suicidal thoughts, antidepressants, and expensive therapists. Love, for me, seemed to be the way into isolation, rather than the road out of it.

Two decades passed. My grandmother died, my parents died, the farm was sold to pay back taxes, and then there was no reason ever to return to McCormick County, to the front parlor of the Highland Inn.

Until the professional conference held in Melrose, the autumn after I turned forty. I was recovering from the end of a foolish, agonizing affair with a married man, I was sick of teaching, and I needed some kind of escape. I needed to go home, even though there was no one there to greet me.

Lavender-gray rain, October dusk, after several hours of mountain-edged interstate, I pulled the rental car into the parking lot of the Highland Inn. As I tugged my bags from the trunk, I thought of my father, who had kindly paid for that expensive birthday dinner so long ago. Now, comfortable on a professor's salary, I could afford to spend this conference weekend at the inn. Needless to say, the room I had booked in advance was Room 203, the room where, according to the tales, Ferrell had died. A room I'd never entered. A room where I might at last be near him: as near as the gap of a century and a half would allow.

The daguerreotype still hung in the parlor, faded significantly further. This time, oddly, that stern face with its lush lips and black goatee seemed to smile. I smiled back, and suddenly the memories of those high school nights alone in my bed came back to me. Then, my imagination had been limited by ignorance and inexperience, but now, after two decades in and out of leather bars across America and overseas, I knew exactly how Sergeant Ferrell and I would make love, if only we had been born in the same century. It seemed to me, as I dropped my bags on the thick carpet and stared once more at his image, that I'd spent the last twenty years looking for some replacement for the way I'd felt staring at that photo at age sixteen.

Room 203 was near the top of the staircase. As the bellboy showed me down the hall to the room, I couldn't help but imagine the crumpled body of my fallen soldier being lifted and dragged down that same hall, the blood leaving a trail all the way to what would become his deathbed.

"Is this the original furniture?" I asked, once inside the room, as I handed the expectant bellboy his tip.

"Yes, sir! Our inn prides itself on its antebellum authenticity," he blurted, proud, apparently, of both the establishment and his vocabulary.

"So this is the bed that Stephen Ferrell died in?" I gestured toward the huge four-poster.

His eyes widened, then dropped to the carpet. Most visitors didn't know that name, and, I guessed, the owners of the inn were likely to have coached employees not to play up the ghost story. Bad for business, I'd imagine. Who wants a bunch of weird curiosity seekers and scruffy ghost hunters staying at your inn?

"Yes, sir, I think that's what people say," he replied nervously.

"Have you seen his ghost?"

"Uh, sir, sorry. We're not supposed to talk about the superstitions," the bellboy muttered before giving a sort of sideways bow and retreating down the hall, his black shoes silent on the carpet beneath which, I felt sure, laid a long brown stain of blood. In a wild image arching through my mind like the electric flash between opposite poles, I could see myself on my hands and knees at the top of the staircase, cutting up the carpet with a hunting knife and licking thirstily at the long-dry stains.

Unnerved by the unwelcome vision, I locked the door behind me. Slowly I unpacked, admiring the elegant room and its period furnishings. From a decanter on the dresser I poured myself a glass of sherry.

Rain ticked on the window like impotent buckshot, like an impatient teenager's fingernails on the wooden arm of a settee. For a few minutes I contemplated dinner: lobster bisque and prime rib, perhaps, to remember my parents and that sixteenth-birthday dinner. Menus at places like this, far from the restlessness of urban trends, far out in the tradition-bound Southern countryside, rarely changed. But ever since the breakup with Thom, I'd been more interested in drinking than eating, and besides, I'd had a substandard but filling dinner on the plane between Detroit and Roanoke.

Pulling a pewter flask from my briefcase, I slugged back some Maker's Mark. Much better than Zoloft or Prozac. In between swigs, I tugged off my clothes. I stood at the window for a few minutes, flask in hand, watching the rain glittering on the grass and stippling black puddles in the street below. It was good to be back in this town, even without family. It was good to be back in the mountains.

In the bathroom I washed the oil and grime of travel off my face and studied myself in the mirror. Not bad for forty. Hair thinning, yes, and beard streaked with silver. But I'd kept myself up, hoping, as I had for twenty disappointing years, that big arms and a solid set of pecs would make me worth loving for longer than a weekend. The sparse fur on my adolescent chest and belly, which I'd stroked those young evenings as if I'd been reverencing a lover, had thickened into the sort of dark mat I'd always imagined spreading over Stephen Ferrell's torso.

I closed my eyes. Between my thumbs and forefingers I worked my nipples till they hurt. Then I turned out all the lights, gulped the last of the flask, propped my head on pillows and stretched naked on the bed, listening to the October rainstorm, musical and soothing on the roof of the inn.

If I'd believed in the supernatural, I would have muttered some invitation into the darkness, would have tried to sense his spirit in the room. Instead, I tried to feel him on top of me, holding me down, his beard pressed hard and hungrily against mine. In the bed where he died, I spat into my palm, stroked myself, gasped and soon shot into my fist. In the bed where he died, I licked it off my hand, rubbed it into my beard, pretending it was his semen, his blood. It was the only intimacy available to us.

I woke suddenly, in the middle of the night, the way I often do when I've had too much to drink. The rain fell harder than before, gurgling in the old gutters, rolling down the glass. I lay on my back, spread-eagled atop the bedspread, gazing up into the dense darkness of the bed's canopy.

Something was wrong. A great weight rested on my chest. Drowsily, halfheartedly, I tried to move, tried to move my splayed arms and legs, roll over onto my side. No success. I might as well have been bound to the bedposts.

Above me, a tiny point of light flicked on, then off. On, then off. A second light joined it, then a third and a fourth. Like the firefly in my room, that night when I first saw the photograph, first fantasized about Sergeant Ferrell.

Odd, I thought, again trying to move and again failing. *Fireflies in October. Doesn't make sense.* The erratic flights slowly regularized, until the lights were silently circling, a small phosphorescent cloud, over my naked body.

The weight atop me shifted, as if a lover I couldn't see were finding a more comfortable position. Then, as if lips hovered only inches from my right ear, I heard a sigh.

Fully awake now, I panicked. I tried again to rise. As if in response to my struggle, the weight increased. Terrified by the sense of increasing paralysis, I cried out, and immediately a warm, moist weight pressed itself against my mouth, as if a sweaty hand gripped my jaw.

Helpless, I lay there. Above me, the fireflies circled. Then something pushed between my thighs, forcing them further apart. Gentle pressure against my balls, like a nudging knee. The scent of wood smoke, like the boy-scout campfires of my childhood.

Another sigh. I closed my eyes and groaned against the invisible hand. What felt like a beard brushed my ear, gently brushed my forehead, tickled my chest.

Then the pressure increased, a scratchy nuzzling around my nipples. I grunted and bucked up against the darkness, but the feeling only intensified, as if those lips had parted to allow teeth their turn. Teasing nips, then harder and harder bites, as my nipples hardened beneath the torment.

This was the rough lovemaking I'd long ago developed a taste for, the sort only the best and briefest of my lovers had given me. When the unseen mouth had bitten and chewed my chest to its satisfaction, it moved down my belly, teeth ranging cruelly. Finally it covered my cock, and within seconds I had shouted beneath the hard hand that gagged me, and shot spurt after spurt into the darkness.

I lay there panting, and the weight atop me gradually dispersed, as if heaped stones were removed one by one. Above the bed, the winking circles of light broke apart, the fireflies faded. When I reached down to wipe up my semen's sticky mess, what had felt like a voluminous load, I found nothing but sheets damp with sweat. As if the night had swallowed it.

For a good fifteen minutes I lay on the bedspread, stunned, excited, disbelieving, and exhausted. When I finally turned on the bedside lamp, there was no evidence in the room of anything unusual, no sign of another presence. The only evidence was printed on my flesh.

My nipples were crusted with drying blood. Tiny bruises speckled my chest and my belly, ran in parallel rows down the shaft of my softening cock.

All day historians droned on in the stuffy little rooms of the Melrose Conference Center. My own presentation on the Wilderness Campaign I gave listlessly, despite the caffeine buzz I'd garnered from several rushed cups of the Highland Inn's coffee. During interminable sessions on topics that normally might intrigue me, beneath the handout-scattered table I gripped my hard penis. In the restroom stall, in between sessions, I tugged at the hard points of my nipples, throbbing painfully beneath Band-Aids, beneath my professorial dress shirt.

I'd overslept that morning, missing the first round of presentations. After climbing reluctantly out of bed, I'd checked my body in the bathroom mirror, only to discover that the bruises I'd fingered with astonishment the night before still remained, like someone's indelible signature, beneath the hair of my chest and belly and all along my cock.

I skipped the late-afternoon sessions. Instead, leather jacket over my shoulder, I wandered the picturesque streets of Melrose, along its brick sidewalks made uneven by tree roots. In a gift shop a distant cousin of mine once owned, I bought some reasonably priced Civil War paraphernalia that caught my eye—a rusty dagger, a few old coins, some photos of the town during antebellum days. In a low-ceilinged bar where my old hunting buddy Mike used to bartend, I knocked back several Warsteiners before moving on to the Civil War cemetery, an easy walk at the edge of town. Twenty-some years ago, soon after my obsession with Sergeant Ferrell had begun, I'd searched the headstones for his name, with no luck. But it was a beautiful October day, sunny after last night's hard rain, so I sat on a bench with my recently refilled flask and watched the sugar maples drop their sharp-edged flakes of fire.

Gently stewed, strangely content, using my jacket as a pillow, I stretched out on the bench, the warm slant of sun surrounding me. As soon as I closed my eyes, I could see what I wanted most to see: his face, the face I could not see last night.

The bourbon, the warmth of the afternoon, my exhaustion—all combined to slip me uncomplaining into daydream, into a world I much preferred. Ferrell's strong hands held me down. His teeth worked my chest again. The smell of him broke over me: unwashed, the musk of a field laborer, the scent of rain-wet wool, of freshly tilled earth readied for spring seeding. When he pushed his tongue into my mouth, I tasted bourbon. I tasted steel, as if I held between my teeth the very bullet that had felled him.

Then he released my wrists, only to cup the back of my head in his hands and push his thick cock between my lips. His flesh tasted simultaneously sour and sweet, like an apple just barely ripe. Sucking eagerly, jaws already aching, I looked up the length of him. Just as I'd imagined: a pelt black as a country night swirling over his belly and over the thick shelf of his pecs. Grinning, he looked down at me, eyes wild, full of a weird complexity vacillating between cruelty and tenderness. Then he threw back his head, shoved himself against the back of my throat, and roared.

I woke, blinking into the sun. When I rose unsteadily, I realized that, beneath my jeans, my briefs were sticky with cum. The moisture trickling down my chest was not sweat, I soon discovered, as the front of my shirt stained dark, but blood, from the reopened wounds on my nipples. Pulling on the convenient concealment of my leather jacket, I picked up my shopping bag of Civil War souvenirs, shoved my flask into my back pocket, and hurried back to the Highland Inn. Before me, at the end of Main Street, the sun sank behind a line of white pines. In front of the inn, fallen maple leaves whirled madly about in a dervish of wind.

On my belly. Tonight he wants me that way. Legs spread, paralyzed again, hands wrenched behind my back and tied there. Blinded, as if a black leather strap were bound tightly about my eyes. Mouth stuffed full, as if he'd pushed a rag in my mouth. I grunt into the sheets as he slaps my buttocks—sharply, abruptly—then bites them, licks them, bites them harder, till I'm sobbing.

Now he stretches out on top of me. That sigh again, half-aroused, half-bereft. I lift my head, struggle under him, till his strong hands shove my shoulders back down onto the mattress.

Something wet and burning hits my back. Tears, blood, or spit? Wax from the candles I've lit tonight? He wipes it up, then spreads my ass cheeks, moistens my tightness, and begins to pry me open with a finger.

Again he sighs, a sound sodden with grief. His loneliness breaks my heart. I have come here to give him whatever he wants.

I bite down on the darkness filling my mouth as he pushes himself inside— another finger, a third. Then the thickness I've taken only in dream. The thick head, then the thicker shaft. I shout against the pain, fighting ineffectually beneath his bulk. His hand's clapped over my mouth now, his bearded lips brushing my temple, trying to soothe me. One big arm around my chest, he rolls us over onto our sides, and then he begins a steady rhythm, pushing in and out of my ass, kissing my shoulders, his belly hair tickling the small of my back, his sighs filling my ears, his fingers twisting my nipples till they bleed.

Spots of blood all over the ecru cotton sheets, as if I'd slept in some bedbug-infested roadside dive instead of one of the most elegant inns in the mountains of Virginia. Rope burns around my wrists and ankles. Tiny pinprick marks all over my buttocks, bruises shaped like handprints, my hole so sore it hurts to sit down. And again, no evidence of the semen I'd shot into the sheets.

Room service brought up a meager breakfast of sweet rolls and coffee. I hung out the "Do Not Disturb" sign, skipped the plenary session, the last day of conference presentations, and stayed in bed. The rains had come back, and I lay all day on the elegant four-poster, where Sergeant Ferrell had died, my head lolling on overstuffed pillows. Dreamily I watched rain streak the glass. At noon I shifted from coffee to Maker's Mark. All afternoon I drowsed, too weak and apathetic to rise. When I touched my chafed wrists or scabbed nipples, the memory of that midnight intensity instantly returned. I got hard, jerked off, then drifted back into sleep.

At dinnertime, some semblance of an appetite woke me and I dressed. The dining room was crowded, too noisy for my taste, so I headed for the bar in the back of the building, where only a few tables were occupied, by elderly couples quietly chatting.

Tossing back a few bar nuts, I asked for a menu and, tired of bourbon, ordered a martini. The letters of the menu smudged beneath my gaze. The pretty brunette bartender placed before me the usual inverted cone of clear gin, but within seconds, right before my eyes, the drink had turned crimson.

"Ma'am?" Startled, I rubbed my eyes then waved her back. "I believe you've used sweet vermouth instead of dry in this drink." What other explanation?

"Oh, sorry, sir! I've never made that mistake before," she said, reaching for the glass.

It was then that I noticed her nametag. *Nancy Ferrell.*

I gripped the glass. "Wait." I took a sip. Taste of wild grapes, sourwood honey, rusted steel.

"This is fine. Just leave it." I smiled then gestured toward her tag. "Are you related to the ghost?"

I expected the awkward equivocations I'd always gotten from the inn's employees, but this time I got a different response. She smiled.

"My first week working here, and already someone asks! My mother told me this would happen."

I gulped the red drink. Blood on the floor at the top of the staircase, hidden for generations by musty carpet. Blood on my shirt. Blood on the sheets.

I stared at her. She smiled again.

"Yes. Stephen Ferrell was my great-great-great uncle. I'm descended from the sister he died trying to save."

It was my academic credentials that convinced her to give me all the details her family had kept to themselves for generations. That, and the several drinks I bought her once her shift ended. A monograph on the Civil War in McCormick County, that's what I claimed to be writing. I swore to leave out the scandalous parts if I ever published the article.

According to the family stories Nancy Ferrell had heard, her ancestor Stephen was indeed a war hero, a true berserker on the battlefield. He'd fought with valor in several of the major battles in Pennsylvania and Virginia. During his infrequent trips home, Melrose women fell in love with him in droves. A handsome, strongly built soldier with an impressive war record—who wouldn't? However, he encouraged none of his admirers, keeping to himself, maintaining the family farm as best he could before returning to the war.

Only a few months before his death, he was discharged from the army and came home disgraced. The reason for the discharge the Ferrells kept to themselves. The community of Melrose was painfully curious, then shocked, as the quiet, upstanding soldier they'd known became a hot-tempered vigilante. Stephen Ferrell returned from his war experience in a fiery rage. He ended up in many a bourbon-soaked bar brawl. He shot a neighbor who claimed to know some unsavory truth about the mysterious army discharge. He recklessly rode the outskirts of the county alone, on the lookout for Yankee raiders.

On the afternoon he died, a crew of ten such raiders entered Melrose. They began to pillage the Highland Inn, which had been converted into a makeshift hospital where Stephen's twin sister Ramona still worked as a nurse, despite her pregnancy. Stephen made a timely and unexpected appearance, entering the inn from a rear entrance. A crack shot, he killed four of them, wounded four, drove all the survivors out onto the porch, and barred the door. When the infuriated raiders tried to burn the inn with whatever flammables were at hand, Stephen ushered the nurses toward the back door, then shot dead four more Yankees from the inn's upstairs windows before they could torch the building.

The two raiders remaining rushed the porch. Finding the door barred, they smashed through the window of the front parlor, determined to avenge their cohorts' deaths. From the top of the staircase, Stephen Ferrell brought one of them down before, at that crucial moment, his ammunition ran out.

The last surviving raider shot Stephen in the belly. He had, however, little time to relish his victory. Hoping to help her brother, Ramona Ferrell had hidden in a closet, rather than fleeing with the other nurses. As the Yankee gloated over Stephen's mortal wound, she took an old iron and swung it against the back of his skull. When townsfolk finally arrived on the scene, the raider's head had been bashed into chunks, and Ramona was cradling her dying brother in her arms.

Sergeant Ferrell was taken to Room 203, as the legends had accurately reported. He lingered for several days, praising his sister, cursing Yankees, cursing the officers who had discharged him. In his last delirium, he'd muttered the name "John" over and over again. His remains were buried in the tiny Ferrell family cemetery, in an especially mountainous area of McCormick County.

And who was John? My grandmother had been right. The Ferrell family, trying to hide a truth that would have been monumentally shameful in the mid-nineteenth century, spread the rumor that Stephen had been discharged because of a love affair he'd had with an officer's wife. But here and there the truth leaked out, despite the family's efforts, to be whispered unbelievingly about kitchen tables and over corn in need of hoeing.

"Stephen fell in love with Colonel John Kinder," Nancy Ferrell whispered over her whiskey sour, in a dark corner of the bar. "They were caught together in a barn. The colonel, terrified, claimed that Stephen had tried to rape him. Kinder, a married man and of superior rank, they believed. Stephen, despite his record for valor, was unmarried, of inferior rank. They gave him a sodomite's punishment. They bucked and gagged him, left him that way for days. They strung him up and flogged him repeatedly, and then they cut him down, threw him a hunk of hoecake and told him to walk home. He did. All the way from New Market to Melrose. My great-grandmother once told me that when his sister Ramona was laying him out for burial the scars on his back were so horrible she miscarried."

He rests beneath the limbs of a black spruce, in a little graveyard atop a mountain on the southern edge of McCormick County. Crickets are chirping as I push back the gate. To the west the sun sprawls in a pool of its own blood, then sinks, as if sucked down a drain.

I have brought a flashlight, but I won't need it. I wanted to take a picture of Stephen's grave for my upcoming monograph, I claimed, and so Nancy Ferrell kindly gave me directions here: down Route 12 to Forest Hill, up Greenville Road, then a fork to the left, past the ruins of the Ferrell farm and up the grass-grown hillside to road's end.

Chill descends with nightfall. October in the Appalachians is often balmy during the day, frost-sharp at night. But I take off my clothes nonetheless, neatly folding my jeans and Virginia Tech sweatshirt on top of my leather jacket in the grass by the gate.

There is still sufficient light to find his grave, one near the back, a black obelisk upon which some unnamed admirer or descendant has taped a tiny Confederate flag. I run my fingers along the weathered name and dates then lie on the grave, sunken as those old graves often are. The pine box has rotted; the earth's heaviness has nestled in around the bones.

In Room 203, he came again last night, as he has for the past two weeks. I have quit my job, I have not returned to my lonely adobe house in Pasadena. What are those compared to the intensity I've found with him?

Last night, naked, I sat on the floor of my room. I bound my feet, tied a bandanna between my teeth, slipped between the crooks of my elbows and the crooks of my knees a wooden dowel I'd bought at Melrose Hardware, wrapped rope about my wrists, then clenched my fists and bowed my head. Bucked and gagged. What he went through. I wanted to feel what he went through.

He came to me then. Sighing, he chewed my neck. Sighing, he whipped me hard. This morning my back was striped with welts. Every night he uses me, and every night his violence turns to tenderness, his anger slowly subsides.

Love is about diminishing distance, and that I will do tonight. Naked, I stretch out in the grassy cradle of his grave. On my hairy chest I rest the antique dagger, the one I bought that first sunny afternoon back in Melrose.

I now know what he wants, and I offer it. I finish the flask, toss it into the weeds. Then I cut myself. I grit my teeth and the knife sinks deep. Rope-chafed ankles and wrists first, then the side. Drunk as I am, the pain pushes through nevertheless, and I am about to scream, about to regret, when the fireflies appear.

Once there was one. Then there were four. Now there is a multitude, circling above me the way the entire sky appears to revolve about the North Star. My blood pours into the grass, leaches into the soil like autumn rain. Soon my blood will reach his bones.

Now the sighing begins, and the weight upon me, heavier than ever. Again his night-black beard brushes mine. His mouth tastes like bourbon and tobacco. His body smells like resin and smoke. His lips nuzzle my neck. The fireflies descend in a great glowing cloud around us. Across his warm broad back I run my hands, over the ridges of his scars.

A Perfect Scar

Trebor Healey

It always begins with cigarettes. I don't even smoke. I don't even respect smoking. I don't think it's cool. As if what I thought would ever matter with Tran. Smoking is sexy, yes. But cool, no. Sex isn't really cool, either. I found that out, courtesy of Tran. Sexy perhaps, but cool, no. Need is never cool.

It wasn't even about him, really. It rarely is. I got him like religion all the same. Same difference. After all, what's Christianity got to do with Christ? I came up with rationalizations like all religious types. But in the end, it was about faith. And faith can't be explained. Tran was the man, plain and simple.

What we had in common was religion as it was. And that was it. Catholic Tran. Why is it that so many Catholic cultures breed gangsters like lice? Not that Vietnamese is a Catholic culture any more than I'm a gangster, but I wasn't reared in Belfast either. Which didn't prevent me from being a drunk. But let's not blame the Irish for that. I was generations removed, and though this tale might whore itself to a handful of stereotypes, they hide as much as they reveal. Homosexuals don't need to be Irish to have drinking problems, that's for sure. But you could say I knew the territory all the same. Had a knack for it.

I could find my way to the corner liquor store blindfolded. At 8 a.m. for a newspaper and a cup of coffee; at noon for a sandwich and a six-pack to get me through the afternoon and lay a foundation for an early evening nap that would prime me for club-hopping by 10.

This story first appeared in *Law of Desire: Tales of Gay Male Lust and Obsession* (Greg Wharton and Ian Philips, eds., Alyson Books, 2004).

They say it begins with one drink, blah, blah, blah. Sure thing. It began with a cigarette in this case—and it sure didn't end there. Turning it over? The higher power? Tran was the higher power.

Tran, his pale milk-white hairless skin; the appendectomy scar, so pink and narrow, fine as a crack in a windshield. A perfect scar. What a mess of hair he had on his lithe shins, the only indication at all of the truly earthbound monstrosity that lay coiled at the root of his soul. But his body was all Asian cliché innocence. I didn't create that idea of purity, but it sure turned me on in depraved criminals. There's no greater aphrodisiac than a full-blown paradox.

I should point out that I despised Tran from the moment I met him. Tran with his low-slung Acura rice-rocket, his black Armani blazer, the gelled hair, the dangling cigarette. Tran was the worse kind of cad: a crook; a ruthless, greedy racketeer who gathered and disposed of people like so much food. But Tran had charm, and more balls than anyone I've ever met, and say what you will, the world parts seas for such a one—and did. Who was I to be the exception?

He looked at me with his what-the-fuck-are-you-looking-at glare that first morning in the corner store. Tran's first impression for everyone.

"Excuse me," I softly implored, hoping to defuse his aggression as I handed my fifty cents for a newspaper over the gum rack to Yusef, the cashier.

"Yeah! Sure thing," he half-shouted, his face erupting into a smile as he gathered his newspaper, cell phone, car keys, and wallet off the counter, the cigarette bobbing amidst his cackling braggadocio.

Sarcasm? Sincerity?

He walked out and I followed him with my eyes. *Asian trash,* I concluded to myself. Every ethnicity had their trash. The white variety might be in pickups and trailers, the Mexican might be fat, poorly tattooed, and too focused on Honda Accord rim accessories, but it was the gangsters who occupied that sorriest of stereotypes in the Asian community, with their trashy vamp girlfriends and their toy cars, the ever-present cigarettes, like some kind of sorry-ass anachronism from the golden age of Hollywood.

How could I have known (how would it have occurred to me?) that he was sizing me up, and while I wallowed in my inane prejudices, he was downloading the skinny on me?

I'd in fact completely dismissed him by the time I walked out, and so no wonder I was surprised when he addressed me from ten feet up the sidewalk, leaning rakishly against his suped-up car.

"Howdee!" he barked, cigarette dangling—and that smile. I just looked at him, vexed. *What does he want?* It crossed my mind he could be cruising, but I laughed at the thought. He was far too brazen to be a closet queen. "What's your name?" he half-commanded through his manic cheer.

I kept walking, looking perfunctorily over my shoulder. "Ben," I murmured. *He must be selling something.*

He slapped his thigh, but didn't get up. "Like Franklin!" he guffawed. "C-note. Toilet paper. Ha, ha, ha." And he laughed fully and heartily. "Go for a ride?" He told me more than asked me.

"Not today." *Maybe he's a Christian, or worse, one of those Cao Dai dudes who worship Victor Hugo. Time to lose the creep.*

"It's a good day to die, all that shit. Come on." He motioned me with his head. *What the fuck?,* I thought. *Now he's quoting Crazy Horse.* Who is this guy—who laughs at my dismissive rebuffs and then offers me a ride in the guise of a thinly veiled threat? But by then, without being fully aware of it, I'd stopped and turned and was staring back at his wide grin. God, what a smile—weirdly irresistible like a clowning little kid's.

He held his keys in the air with his left hand, and gesturing with his head toward the car, he dramatically pressed the key button, releasing the door locks, which clicked resoundingly. An invitation; a casual command. I found myself opening the door as the suped-up Acura engine whirred to life, thinking briefly of small children who foolishly climbed into vans with beefy, bald child molesters. And I hadn't even lost a dog—or been offered candy. Not yet anyway.

I climbed in simply because of his smile and his authority and the fact that—to be completely honest—I'd have rather done just about anything than return to my apartment and my bullshit, failing-business Web design work. In a moment of uncanny clarity, somewhere between Ben Franklin and Crazy Horse, I'd intuited an odd feeling that he knew something I needed to know.

He peeled away from the curb and through the yellow light that was red by the time he was in the crosswalk. Honking ensued, matched by Tran's guffaws. "Dumb motherfuckers," he said more affably than anyone I'd ever heard use the term.

I looked at him. Tran wasn't someone I'd take a ride from, nor even talk to. What was I doing in his car? Listening now to some kind of Viet rap. "Ben Franklin!" he announced, cracking up like it had been a damn good one, and as he laughed, pulling in front of a BMW ten feet before a red light. How he glared into the rearview mirror.

I disliked his showmanship; I wasn't into his looks or his extortionist's charm. But I had never held my legs so wide, so fervently, before Tran. I was so fixated on watching him enter me. Watching him in general. At liquor stores, the way he charmed Arabs, Indians, blacks, Koreans, rednecks and racists. Every gesture, every word, perfectly laid down like calligraphy; the way he reached into his pockets; the way he giggled with his head down at jokes I know he hadn't understood, nor did he care to; the way he opened his chest, his hands at his hips like a gunslinger, completely confident and yet pistol-less, thus defusing any aggression aimed his way. In bed, it was the same, just more esoteric. The thin alabaster hips, the long blue-black wiry hairs cresting over his cock, the tight knot of his belly button, the goose-pimpled skin of his scrotum bouncing against me—and the scar, the scar that never quite touched me as his hips bounced repeatedly against me. He banged me mercilessly, holding and massaging my wrists with his big veiny hands, all the while sporting that wide grin on his face. Ben Franklin. Lightning.

"Fuck your ass," he'd say sometimes. "Fuck your white faggot ass." And he'd laugh. Laughed like a goddamn monkey—like he did in traffic when he pissed people off. Like how his cock laughed up my ass.

And he'd pay me. Though I told him not to. I didn't understand at first. I told him I wasn't a hustler and that I did it with him because I wanted to. He looked at me, with a different grin then. The one that said: You dumb motherfucker, you think I don't know a hell of a lot more about what's going on than you ever will? You think this happens because *you* want it to?

Then the smile would just as quickly soften and he'd revert to his old high-school-chum jibing: "Fuck you, C-note, you need the money." And he'd lay another bill on top of the one he just put down, doubling my take. Then he'd laugh some more.

I worked for him the day I met him, as did we all. Tran was the kind of crook that paid you more and more if he felt you were slipping out of his grasp or if you didn't want to be paid. He buried people with money, smothered them in it, emasculated them into drooling junkies for it. His money was like his cum: you'd take it and like it. Tran's largesse was like the weather. A simple fact.

Tran ran a gang of Cambodian and South Vietnamese chop-shoppers. Mostly they stole cars, but they weren't above stereo equipment and all manner of jewelry and fur coats from the right house in Hillsborough. They only stole from Asians—Chinese mostly—and Tran was a stickler for always trying extortion first and afterward. Thievery was below Tran. A bit of a joke even. He wasn't that into "stuff." He liked to see people's fear. He liked to laugh and smile at things people couldn't smile at.

I never even knew his name. He used the name Tran, which, in my stupid white-boy way, I took to be friendly, diminutive—like Tim or Tad. I didn't even know it was, in fact, a last name—and not *his* either. Imagine begging "Smith" to fuck you—when his name was Miller or Ramirez to boot. "Fuck me, Smith." No wonder he laughed.

That first morning he'd taken me to a Travel Lodge. He never even asked. Six blocks from the stale yellow light, Tran had said coolly, "I been watching you," and nodding his head with enthusiasm, he'd winked at me. He was chewing gum now, which made the smile more comic. I felt my cock stir and uncoil. I hadn't really expected that. In fact, I hadn't really been thinking anything except that I'd made a strange choice. Like I say, it was all about faith.

"Room 206," he imparted flatly, pulling suddenly and sharply, and way too quickly, into the motel parking lot. He got out of the car without heading to the office. I watched him climb the stairs, stop and turn. He held the key chain up again, gave a couple of big alarm clicks and let that smile of his spread like sunrise. I got out, and as the door shut closed, I heard that familiar finality of the locks clicking into place.

By the time I pushed open the door to 206, Tran was nude and half-hard, looking casually into the mirror. He turned as I shut the door, swaggered over to me at half-mast, the smile filling the room like the overpowering scent of something musty; something that made my knees weak: dirt and wood and water. He stripped off my clothes and pushed me with one bouncy shove onto the bed. Then he hopped on me and went wild, grinding and licking me.

There was never any need for, nor option of, negotiating sexually with Tran. It was wholly unnecessary. He took what he wanted and the world gave him change for it. Tran didn't have to ask or worry about stepping over any lines. Tran's sexual movements had the same charm as his smile, and one simply turned one's will over to him. It was odd, how it just happened, without any thought, any consideration of any kind. Tran was in sync and the world rolled with him, plain and simple.

And Tran made me realize how out of sync I was: broke, drunk, aimless and unhappy. Which made me want him all the more. It wasn't envy so much as a kind of hero worship. A strange hero. But that's what he was in the end. He had the karma, the kryptonite, the confidence . . . the *something* that I craved.

Tran put it in slow that first day, smiling, talking ("yeah, yeah") as the grin grew. He must have fucked me for a good forty minutes, holding my feet up, fascinated at "my engine" as he called it, which referred to my whole middle: ass, belly, cock, balls.

He chattered about his "business" when he slowed down his long thrusts. It was like he wove me, on and on. Or rather, I was the loom, and what he wove—I don't know what it was, but I was his tool and he was the craftsman, and all of it tied me to him somehow. And while he wove, he told me things he shouldn't have told strangers.

"Motherfucker told the cops about one of my shops. I broke his nose." And he giggled triumphantly.

"How'd you break his nose?"

"Brass knuckle, martial arts pop. None of these sorry-ass people know how to fight like Asians," he said with disgust. Then the smile filled his face again. "Then I went by his house and played in the yard with his kids."

"And you smiled, right?"

"The whole time. Ha, ha." And he gave me a knowing look, and thrust harder into me a couple of strokes.

"Fuck, Tran, that did it, huh?"

"Fuck yeah. He never did anything after that, but I still had to pay the cop off. Then he had to work for me for a while."

"Doing what?" I watched his cock while we conversed. We both watched his cock moving in and out of me. We never looked at each other when we fucked or talked of crime.

"Dismantle."

"Cars?"

"Yeah, cars, dumbass motherfucker. He was a mechanic. I should have whipped it out at him. No one doubts my jack!" And he laughed.

That's what he called it. He was proud of it. It was good-sized, a fat seven and a half inches, and uncut, well-marbled with veins that clung to it like vines on a column. Considering he was 5'5"?, his cock cut quite a figure. Maybe that's what the world recognized in him, unknowingly, subconsciously. The superior, fine-ass cock. And men bought it more than women did. The straight ones especially. They knew who the boss was.

"We're gonna cum now," he finally said, and momentarily we increased our rhythm before long strings of arcing cum shot out of me as he filled me, groaning gutturally. It wasn't until then that I felt the dread of it all. I'd been lost in the fantasy, but once I'd shot I was in that old familiar place of maneuvering an extrication. Lovey-dovey boys who wanted to spend the night were one thing; straight boys who looked offended and startled at what they'd just done were another. But ruthless gangsters who related actionable crimes in detail seemed far more problematic and dicey.

Tran got dressed, smiling at the floor as he methodically buttoned up his white shirt. Then he picked up his coat, dropped something on the TV table, and walked out.

Not long after, I heard the whining rev, the peel. He wasn't going to be giving me a ride home.

I pulled myself together and left. It was *just one of those things*, I figured. A lark. He wasn't queer-identified (that's about the only difference left between gay guys and straight boys these days) by the looks of it, and he'd just had an experience with a stranger who knew nothing about him. Who'd given him a chance to talk, without repercussions. I'd been like an old-school prostitute, down to the c-note he'd left on the table before leaving. I'd gained a story.

I who'd collected stories for a decade. Every boy was a story. And the less you knew about him, the better the story. I should have remembered that as I strolled home. Most boys left their numbers; most boys I dispensed with after the third or fourth date when the story wound into suburban reminisce and career skills. Most boys filled the lies I told myself with truth fast enough so that the story I was making up didn't ever get the chance to grow into a big fat dragon of projection.

Not Tran. Tran left me nothing but a sore ass and possibly the best fuck I'd ever chanced upon. Some heady seeds for any tale. He'd left a few million of those.

Then came the dreams. Dreams of Tran. Tran as a nice college boy in a v-neck sweater; Tran as an artsy graphic designer in a mod glass house on a hill, drinking fine wine; Tran as a young soldier; Tran as a grease monkey at the body shop two blocks south; Tran slinging coffee; Tran dancing with his shirt off; Tran boxing; Tran wrestling. And at the end of every dream: Tran fucking me to nocturnal emissions that woke me with a start; that made me break a sweat and take a deep long breath like you do when you're scared to death.

I took to lingering at the corner store all the same. I asked Yusef if he'd seen "that Asian dude."

"This isn't an Asian neighborhood," he answered, obtusely.

"I know, but he was here once—he'll come again."

"Lots of people pass through just once," he said. And he looked at me portentously.

I wished I had a picture of him because suddenly this strange guy I'd never look twice at had become a form of epic beauty in my dreams. Tran was suddenly beyond handsome to me. He was more beautiful than any surface could ever hope or have a right to be, because his beauty was not in one or two dimensions, not even three. He was like five dimensions of it. A sort of overpowering beauty—almost vaguely horrific—that made my breath catch. A sort of Möbius strip of lust for him came over me.

I needed a drink.

I told Lou the whole story at the Lucky Bar, lost in my cups. I'd bragged at first, bluffing. "Guy just picked me up, Lou, wanted me something fierce. I can't shake him now. I'm dreaming of him. I want to do him a few more times, get him out of my system."

Lou'd rolled his eyes: "Fat chance, Ben. Let it go, man. This is bullshit."

"No, no, Tran is not bullshit. I don't know, Lou, it was like the most doubtless hour of my life when I was with him. From the minute I saw that damn smile. I didn't think once for an entire hour. I just knew."

"What the fuck are you talking about—doubtless? Maybe you just need to do crystal more often."

"Ah shit, Lou, this was real, man. Fuck crystal . . ." I could have continued, but I didn't completely understand it myself, and I sure didn't want to cop to any mystical mumbo jumbo around Lou. Lou was a regular guy, a modern man, what I'd been until a week ago. I felt now like someone who'd been abducted by aliens, or met Jim Jones. There was no point in talking about it; they'd just laugh at you. But I knew. We knew. Those who know Jesus are just different.

"Do this for me, Lou. Come out to get Pho with me."

"You're kidding, right?"

"It's the only way I stand a chance of ever seeing him again."

So Lou came with me to Clement Street, to Pho 87 in the Sunset, and a week later to Pho 99 in Daly City. By the third week, at Nam

Dinh, he'd taken to relentlessly telling his prize joke about me and my "Trans-gression" as he called it. "Pho-get about it, Ben. We're Tran-spotting."

It wasn't funny. Not to me. Religious people can never take jokes. He was using the lord's name in vain. The lord who, not ten minutes later, walked in. Who smiled in his huge way when he saw me. Who made my throat catch and heart jump and my whole body click, click, click to attention like Tran's door locks. I felt tears well up even.

And he saw me like Tran would. Tran, who took in a whole room in two seconds flat—he missed nothing. I don't know how I ended up on my feet but I was moving toward him, though I stopped abruptly when three more wiry Asians in black suits came in on his heels. He barked at them in Vietnamese, turned toward me, re-smiling, and reached out his hand to shake mine, placing his other hand on the opposite shoulder. He winked, said, "206-10," let go of my hand, turned his back, and proceeded to his table.

I'd be lying if I didn't admit I was somewhat frightened to meet him again, but it was like being a child entering water: I didn't want to drown, per se, but I was a little fascinated by the danger of it. And as with a full-blown paradox, the full-blown insecurity of danger was erotic too.

Lou was glib. "You've fucking lost it," and he dropped his chopsticks. That was the last time Lou ate Pho.

The awful things he told me were shared as he slid his prodigious jack in and out of me. And how meticulous and fascinated he was as he did so. He took such an interest in entering me, sliding it in this way and that, trying different angles and thrusts, consumed with the various placements of it. He'd literally go for hours, and he'd chatter, telling me things about his business as he moved it around in me. Crime was clearly erotic to Tran. He'd recount beatings and various swindles while he watched himself fuck me into driveling submission.

But he wasn't confessing. I'd been wrong to think I was his whore with the heart of gold. He bragged to me, in fact. So much so that I was never really sure what was true. He'd recount robberies, beatings with his "silver deuce" as he called it—a long stainless steel-tube he wielded like jack sticks—and, of course, the endless litany of extortion schemes and threats.

I was as sickened as I was fascinated by the satisfaction he took in scaring people. And I was sickened and fascinated by the satisfaction I took in him—in the fact that he could kill me, but didn't; could abandon me, but didn't; could even love me, but didn't.

He used to just say it to me, during sex, in coffee shops. "I love my cock. You love it?" I did love it, but it wasn't a cheerful, happy love for small talk. I loved his cock like one loves their country, a country like Israel or Bulgaria that costs you something dear for the love of it. Not like here. I loved Tran's cock like I loved Tran's scar. I loved his cock like I loved life. Life with its pain and misery and constant disappointments. Not that his cock ever disappointed. But it was all about the difficulty of all-consuming love. Like for a child. It owned me. I belonged to what I loved. Sure, I loved his cock. But being that I despised him, what did that make my love? And what did that make me?

Tran really had no ethics, no tenderness, nothing humane in him. The smile was the most elaborate charade of the whole picture. I never completely disbelieved it, but I taught myself to with whatever flickering spark of self-preservation I had left in me. I'd seen him turn it on and off. I saw how he smiled at V, his girlfriend, when she'd walk in to the coffee shop and see us there.

He made up outrageous stories on a dime. "V, this is Ben. He's in computers, imports from Japan, knows all about customs shit." V didn't care, but as it gave me criminal-cred she could dismiss me and not get any ideas. Not that Tran would care. If Tran wanted to fuck boys, V would have to accept that. And it was likely she would. But more importantly, if Tran chose not to acknowledge it, then it wasn't there unless Tran decided it was. That was fine with V too. Tran was God: He doesn't have to explain the Big Bang or cop to dark matter unless he wants to.

V was just like me really. She had her faith too. I wondered if she watched him the way I did.

Tran was indisputably a good thing to have around. Tran took care of everything. Tran kept troubles away. Tran intimidated trouble. It didn't even bother after a while. V had immigration troubles that ended abruptly when she met Tran. V had family troubles because her parents didn't want her dating a gangster. Tran lavished them with gifts and planted acquaintances who vouched for his legitimacy. And he smiled of course. Until they loved him. He got a home loan for her old man and found a way to half the rent on her mother's nail-manicurist shop. Tran even ended up getting me a job. A good job. I didn't have an easy time finding work and Tran just pulled it out of a hat. I never figured it out. The place was one of these dot-com organic-beer-Fridays hipster places. Completely white and by the book. How the hell would Tran have an in? Tran wouldn't tell of course. Just smile. God, Tran works in mysterious ways. But he works. Every time.

Tran was charming and Tran was necessary. And Tran was a presumptuous and precocious little punk, who at twenty-nine was riding very high among the crooks of his circles. Too high, in many people's opinion. I'd met his little lieutenants, whom he abused. Not a few of them were tight as a spring with repressed anger. You could tell they had ideas. Like all too-powerful people, Tran would have to go. The world likes balls until it doesn't. Steers outlive bulls; just look around.

I realized it one night, as he had my feet planted on the wall behind the bed, violently coming inside me: This too, this too is erotic; is what I crave. That Tran is clearly doomed; a marked man. Like MLK, JFK, Gandhi—riding just too high. And smiling to boot. Unstoppable. It made people want to lay him low, or see him laid low. Crucify him and then make a religion out of him. He was unstoppable, all right. You wanted to see him die and then you'd cry like a baby at the loss. You wanted to be one with Tran, and since it couldn't be—whose fault was that? Not yours. It was his. He'd betrayed you in a sense. He was the hero, the law of nature. And as such, it had become his job to take on the final and most ominous foe. Go Tran!

Tran was a superhero is what he was. A real-live one with all the compromises that required. There was no Krypton, there was just Saigon, a depraved city that had fallen to the communists and gotten his parents killed. But like Batman, Tran had prevailed, taken to sea with his brothers and the boat people. Found his way here. I don't know if Tran had it figured that way—that he could exact revenge for the ruination of his family and childhood. I doubt it. Tran would have laughed at Batman.

Tran laughed when I told him I'd like to fuck him sometime. No one fucks Tran. I developed a fantasy after that of fucking Tran and throwing him out to be gunned down in the street by Duc, his next-in-command. Go on and kill that which you love.

He got sick fast. He'd run a red light in the Richmond and plowed into a bus. The MRI revealed a tumor the size of a fist in his head. The hospital was hell, loads of people. Fucking "Don Tran," like some mafia kingpin. Hideous flowers and endless gifts, and way too much red and yellow Chinese and Vietnamese good luck shit. And never a moment with him alone. And having to explain over and over again the lie of who I was. And V; V carrying on crying, helpless without Tran. Tran dies, God dies. I wanted to read her Nietzsche; she was getting on my nerves. I suppose because she reminded me so perfectly of my own sorry state. One day she just vanished. Duc told me she saw the writing on the wall, was looking for someone else. Tran had betrayed her, and she got with the program: Death, steps 1 through 12.

As he slipped away from us, the smile stayed. A weird comatose smile. It made me doubt my earlier assessments that he was a con man through and through. I don't think Tran ever killed anybody. I don't think he even robbed anyone, middle-class or poor. I began to see him as a Robin Hood of sorts. In those last few days, I realized I did love him—in a different way than I'd thought. Fiercely, with all my heart. I admired him for his power, but as it ebbed, there was a sweetness to his fragile, wounded body that was as multidimensional as his beauty.

I pulled back the sheet late one night, just me and Duc in the room. Duc nodding off. I didn't care if he saw. I pulled back the sheet and looked at Tran's naked body, how beautiful he was. How pure and virile. And I held his cock in my hand, felt it limp and heavy, the skin slack and smooth. I wept for how his cock had made me feel safe, and for its simplicity. For what it told of Tran. Always it had been that. His cock was innocent, completely guileless. It was the way I loved him. It was how he showed himself to me. Maybe to V. I don't know.

I kissed his scar then, before holding up my hand in benediction—Catholic to the end. I didn't kiss his cock. It was too holy now. I kissed only his scar, his perfect, ephemeral scar.

And when I went home, I marked myself with him. With a kitchen knife. To let him out, to unwind the weave.

The Rubens Gamble

Patrick Allen

I was released in the morning, but it was late afternoon by the time I stepped through the iron gates of Crowhaven Minimum Security Prison for what I swear on my mother's as-yet-unoccupied grave will be the last time.

There was no one to meet me. I hadn't expected anyone. Any friends I might have had were long gone.

I clutched my oversized jacket (I'd lost weight) around my shoulders and faced the prospect of a two-mile walk into town. The thirty dollars in my pocket wouldn't stretch to cover motel and cab fare, and the fine state of Maine hadn't seen fit to make sure I got there safe.

A late-afternoon squall struck. I turned the collar of my jacket up; I might as well have tried to stem Niagara.

The rain muffled the sound of the car. By the time I heard it, the bumper was on my ass and I nearly wound up in the mud-soaked ditch sidestepping it.

I swung around, freezing when I realized it was a custom-made Bentley limousine, and the guy stepping out of it was the best-looking piece I'd seen since I last cruised Chelsea looking for dick.

He was around my age, mid-to-late twenties, clad head to foot in a deadly combination of leather and denim. He had spiky blond hair and his baby blues held mine. His mouth was the most fuckable thing about him. I could easily imagine stuffing my seven inches down it, and my dick responded predictably.

Now you're probably thinking, whoa, boy, a guy who just spent the last two years less a day incarcerated was getting it pretty regularly. Well, nonconsensual sex with a guy called Bubba never did appeal to me. And the hard-core butt fuckers get sent up to Attica or the like anyway. Crowhaven was for the tamer, executive types who get caught borrowing company funds and socking it away in the Caymans. Most of them have wives who came for conjugal visits, so to say I hadn't been getting any for a while is an understatement.

"Dmitri Alexandrovich Zalupkoff?" the hunk said, not tripping over the patronymic name my parents foisted on me.

Just the way he said it sent shivers of desire through me.

"Why don't you come in out of the cold," he said.

"What do you want?"

"I have been sent to ask a favor of you. Please." He indicated the limo's open door. "Let's talk inside."

I was going nowhere fast and the rain had picked up. If he didn't care what my sodden clothes would do to that fancy upholstery, who was I to turn down a warm ride? Besides, I was curious. What kind of favor?

I slid onto the butter-soft leather seat, shaking when rivulets of water shivered down my ribs.

My handsome rescuer adjusted something and a blast of heat washed over me. I sighed and leaned back, closing my eyes. When I reopened them, he was holding out his leather jacket.

"Take those off," he said. "You will catch your death of pneumonia."

He spoke with an old-world courtliness I haven't heard since I was last on the Continent. France, to be exact. Picking up a commission for an Etruscan bronze I'd liberated from its former owner. Almost all that money went to pay the lawyer who had failed to keep me out of jail. The job that had landed me there hadn't paid a dime. Hardly surprising, since I hadn't delivered the goods.

I skimmed out of my clothes. His jacket smelled enticingly of his scent. I wrapped myself in it and inhaled.

"Who are you?"

"A man with a job offer."

"Job offer," I repeated. "What do you want?"

"It is not what I want, but what my employer wants."

"Your employer?"

"Mr. Torstead."

He waited. I realized he thought I should know the name. Torstead? It had a familiar ring, but . . .

"Torstead a cop?" Maybe they wanted me to rat out my last employer. "Sorry, like I told you guys the last time we talked, I don't know nothing—"

His mouth twitched in a smile. "I am not with the police, Mr. Zalupkoff. Neither, I assure you, is my employer. He has a . . . business proposal he wishes to make."

"Who are you?"

"My name is Kyril."

No last name. Go figure.

"Kyril? Russian?"

Again the enigmatic smile. "At one time."

No trace of an accent, just that formal way of speaking that said English wasn't his first language. I was intrigued.

"Where?"

"Leningrad."

The fact that he called it that rather than the repatriated St. Petersburg told me Kyril had been over here a while. Probably immigrated with his parents as a boy, which explained the lack of accent.

Kyril picked up a phone and gave some low-voiced instructions to the driver. Minutes later we pulled into a strip mall containing a coin-operated Laundromat and a diner that featured a blue-plate special for $3.99.

"Paul will take your clothes in to dry them." Kyril handed me a soft green throw. "Cover yourself with this. I will get us coffee while we wait. Would you like something to eat?"

I was starving. Kyril took my order for corned beef on rye and a jumbo coffee and climbed out of the limo after I handed my clothes to the stoic driver.

The sandwich was ambrosia. Prison food might meet the daily food requirements but quality it's not. I scarfed it down, even licking my fingers.

Kyril looked amused. "I did bring napkins."

My face grew hot. "Sorry. It's been a while since I had anything this good."

"I could get you another—"

"No, that's okay."

He nodded and sank back beside me.

I took the napkin and cleaned my hands and face. Lying back against the soft leather seat, the heat and the food combined to make me sleepy. I cracked a yawn and didn't have the strength to apologize.

I must have dozed. When I woke it was to find the car in motion and my clothes neatly folded beside me on the seat. Kyril's dark eyes watched me.

I was all too aware of my erection under the blanket. So, it seemed, was Kyril, judging by the way his gaze kept drifting over it.

"You are rested?"

"Where are we going?" I stole a glance out the window. Through the tinted glass I could make out the leafless forests slipping by in the growing darkness. Black limbs dripped in the ongoing rain; it looked cold and desolate. I was glad for the warmth of the car.

"That, I'm afraid, is something you cannot yet know."

"What the hell is that supposed to mean?"

He did two things then: pulled a leather briefcase off the floor and drew a heavy piece of red cloth out of his pocket.

I forgot everything when I glimpsed what was in the briefcase.

Money.

Four rows of crisp bills, still in their bank wrappers. Hundreds. My mouth dried. He flipped one stack out and held it up for me to study.

"Five thousand," Kyril said softly. "For services rendered."

"What services?"

He put the stack back and closed the briefcase, sliding it between his legs on the floor.

"That is for my employer to explain."

"The one whose whereabouts I don't know?"

This time he picked up the red cloth. "Can't know. As a condition of this meeting—for which my employer is prepared to pay you five thousand even if you don't take the job—you will agree to be blindfolded the rest of the way."

"Blind—how long is this trip?"

"Approximately an hour."

An hour blindfolded. For five gees. As the punks today say: *Duh, a no-brainer.*

I studied Kyril again. No pain there. His eyes were a riveting blue, dark as nightfall on a Mediterranean coast. A full mouth opened to display perfect white teeth and the occasional glimpse of a pink tongue that I wanted to taste. He wore only a thin, denim shirt, which molded itself to his form like it was custom made. He possessed tight, well-sculptured pecs and abs over a flat stomach and narrow waist. His dark denim pants hugged his thighs and displayed a basket I ached to explore. He didn't look particularly dangerous.

"Taking a picture?" Kyril asked softly.

For later, sure. I smiled and raised my hands, palms up, to indicate he could go ahead.

The blindfold was made of a heavy material. It had clearly been in Kyril's pocket a while, as it smelled like his jacket. Which didn't help my erection any.

I was plunged into darkness. Almost instantly I became more aware of sounds—the hiss of wheels beneath us, the soft rustle of Kyril's clothes as he moved, and the sensual squeak of leather behind and under us. Kyril's breath was warm on my face as he leaned over to tighten the blindfold. His fingers brushed my cheekbones, and then his thumb slid over my mouth.

"You're quite the sexy one, aren't you, Mr. Zalupkoff? I hadn't expected that."

"Please," I said huskily. "Call me Dmitri."

I could smell him now. I tentatively put up my hand and touched his face.

"Kyril?"

"Would I be taking terrible advantage of you if I was to do this?" His lips brushed mine with the lightest of touches. If I hadn't been blind I might never have felt it. My heart hammered in my chest so hard I felt the vibration in the seat behind me.

I trailed my fingers down his throat, tracing the outline of his Adam's apple, brushing his collarbone. He shivered.

"Are you?" I said.

"Am I what?"

"Taking advantage of me?"

"I hope so . . ." He groaned when my wandering fingers found his nipple.

I skimmed my hand up his shirt front and got the first button open. I popped the second in my eagerness, but I barely missed a beat as I shoved my hand inside and tugged on the fleshy nub. His heart was trip-hammering against his ribs as I played with first one then the other.

Then it was my turn to groan when his mouth returned to mine. His lips closed over mine, and his tongue came out to delve deep, plundering my mouth. Without sight my other senses were alive with him. His lips on mine were warm and firm, his face felt slightly rough with a five o'clock beard. He tasted of the same corned beef I had eaten. His fingers were agile and sure as they teased aside the blanket and traced a heated path up my thigh, sliding like hot silk over my rigid dick. It filled his hand like velvet marble.

He pushed back the foreskin, running a finger around the glans, over the piss slit, collecting a drop of pre-cum, which he smeared over the thickening head.

"Very nice," he murmured against my mouth. "Mr. Torstead will be pleased."

I wanted to tell him I didn't know Torstead had to be pleased but what Kyril was doing with his clever fingers made words impossible. He pushed my legs open and delved between them, first rolling my nuts around in their loose sack, then diving deeper, delicately stroking the perineum before slipping one fingertip into my dark hole.

I cried out and thrashed on the seat. The blanket fell away as his heat infused me. I twisted my blindfolded head back and forth, my breath coming in sharp gasps.

"Lovely," Kyril whispered, then his hot mouth left mine and he laid a trail of fire down my belly, flaying me with his tongue.

Then he wasn't touching me anywhere. I could feel his presence, his breath on the skin of my belly, ragged and uneven. I thrust my hips up, blindly beseeching him not to stop.

"Kyril—" I grunted when his furnace-hot mouth closed over the head of my dick.

My hands clamped down on his head. I thrust into him and he swallowed my fat cock. He tongued me, his lips and even his teeth toying with my bulbous head. My fingers twined through his short hair. I wished I could slip off the blindfold just long enough to watch him eat me, but my hands were too busy.

My dick swelled in his mouth. My balls tightened.

"Kyril . . ." I moaned a warning. His only response was to suck harder, his tongue lashing me into a wet frenzy. I humped forward, shoving my hips upward. "Oh, fuck yes, fuck yesssss!"

The muscles of my thighs locked as I thrust up, pushing my dick down his throat so deep I wonder how I didn't touch his stomach.

Cum blasted out of me, streaming down his throat. When I finally sagged back in the leather he released my still-hard dick and straightened. His lips came down on mine. When they opened I slid my tongue inside and tasted myself.

It was too much. Even as I groped in his lap, exhaustion took me. Under the blindfold my eyes slid shut despite my best efforts to stay awake.

I awoke to find the limo bumping over cobblestones, part of me wondering if we had somehow been transported to Paris. Kyril's warm breath washed my cheek and I heard the laughter in his voice.

"We are come, Dima," he said, using the diminutive of my given name. "You must wake now."

I sat up, realizing that I was still naked, though I had been covered again by the blanket.

Kyril seemed to realize my predicament the same time I did.

"Let me help you get dressed," he said. "Though I much prefer you this way."

My fingers groped at the blindfold, but he caught them.

"Not yet, Dima. Soon."

"But—"

"Trust me."

Not normally reassuring words in the criminal world, but for some reason I did. Trust him, that is.

"For a while longer then," I said grudgingly. He raised my hand to his mouth, caressing my fingers. The rigidity of my dick made getting my pants back on a chore, but eventually I was fully clothed again.

Almost immediately the rear door opened, letting in a blast of icy air. Kyril took my hand and guided me out. I swayed in the wind that drove frozen fingers straight through me.

"Let us get you inside where it is warm."

I couldn't have agreed more. Paul, the driver, took my other arm and together they got me up a flight of stone steps into a foyer that was redolent of lemon polish and roses.

Instantly I was surrounded by warmth. Somewhere a fire burned. I could smell applewood and hear the pop and crack of flames dancing on wood.

"This way." Kyril still held my hand. "We will await him in the library. There is a fire there."

Underfoot the floor changed from tile to wood to carpet as we passed through several rooms. He guided me into an easy chair and within seconds pressed a glass into my hand.

"Vodka," he said. "It will warm you."

I could have told him he did an admirable job of that, but now that we were in the house, his manner had changed. He was no longer the man who had sucked me off so exquisitely in the car. Instead he was aloof. Preparing for his boss?

"Thanks," I murmured. I'm not normally a drinking man—I've found it clouds the head and rarely lives up to its advanced billing—but on this occasion it seemed appropriate.

"When—" I began. Beside me, a phone rang.

Kyril answered it.

The exchange was a stilted mix of "Yes, sir," and "No, sir," and "At once, sir," before hanging up. "Unfortunately business has kept Mr. Torstead longer than expected," he said. "He asked that you make yourself at home in his absence."

"Okay," I said dryly. "But normally I don't sit around in a blindfold."

"Of course." The laughter was heavy in his voice. "What was I thinking?"

He stripped the cloth from my eyes. I blinked up at him in the sudden invasion of light and drank in his beauty again. I stared at his talented mouth for a heartbeat, remembering what had gone on between us, then let my gaze wander the room.

I still wasn't exactly sure who Torstead was, but the name was one I had definitely heard before. I began to understand why as I looked around.

The walls were covered with exquisite art. In a glance I saw a Van Dyck, a pair of Rubens, an early El Greco, a Gainsborough, three Cézanne, and a Matisse I swore had been reported missing only a month ago. There were also some Etruscan bronzes, a smattering of Greek pottery, and a pair of Chinese horse soldiers flanking the door the same way they would have guarded a Chinese emperor's tomb.

Without examining everything closely I had no way of telling if anything was real or just excellent copies. Given the setup and secrecy I'd just gone through I suspected real, but it wouldn't be the first time I'd been wrong.

The fireplace was big enough to cook a steer in. The blaze was held back by a pair of black screens. Heat washed my face and the last chilly remnants of my exposure faded.

"Do you approve?" Kyril murmured.

"Very much." I grinned. "Torstead doesn't need a live-in art expert, does he?"

"Mr. Torstead has all the help he requires at the moment."

"Then why am I here?"

"The job he has in mind for you is a one-time deal," Kyril said. "In his absence he has authorized me to tell you of his wishes. Then if you agree to pursue it, we can begin."

"Okay, 'splain away, Lucy."

"Pardon?"

"Never mind. Just tell me what Torstead wants."

"Mr. Torstead has acquired an invitation to a private party being held by one Conrad Gorman. Are you familiar with the man?"

"I've heard of him." I sipped my vodka. "What kind of party?"

"Mr. Gorman has recently acquired a Rubens from a rather unscrupulous dealer in Amsterdam. The painting was supposed to have gone into Mr. Torstead's collection—"

"Don't tell me: Torstead paid for delivery but the piece went missing the day of arrival and has not been seen since? Was the Amsterdam dealer's name Van Sytha?"

"You are familiar with the man?"

"Oh, Hans and I have a long history."

Kyril frowned. "Not a good one, I gather."

"The man would scam his own mother. He personally owes me over a hundred grand." I sipped my vodka. "So tell me, how did you learn Gorman had bought the piece?"

"Mr. Gorman himself bragged of it."

I grinned, swirling vodka around before taking another sip. "And now you've decided you want it back."

"It should by rights have been ours to begin with."

"Possession is nine-tenths of the law—"

"Agreed," Kyril said sharply. "And we mean to possess it. That is where you come in."

"You want me to steal the painting?"

"That is what you do, is it not?"

"That's what I did," I corrected him. Kyril looked dubious. "I'm going straight."

Whatever reaction I had expected it wasn't what I got. Kyril burst out laughing.

"Hey, I am, you know. I have no intention of going back to that place."

"Oh," Kyril said between bouts of laughter. "I am sure next time they will send you someplace much worse."

"All the more reason to go straight."

"And how will you finance this lifestyle of innocence?"

I hated to admit it, but he had me there. I had no skills to land me a legitimate job. No training I could put on a résumé. I raised my chin.

"I'll manage."

"You would manage much better after this job." Kyril leaned forward. "We are prepared to pay you one hundred thousand dollars for the return of the Rubens."

"One hundred—" I nearly choked on my drink. "And if I get caught, who takes the fall? Me, right?"

"If you get caught, what can Mr. Gorman do? The painting is not his to own. It belongs, I believe, to the Dutch. He will not go to the police. I know for a fact Mr. Gorman has several questionable art pieces in his possession. He cannot afford the scrutiny of overeager authorities."

"You said something about a party," I said, as much to gain some time to think as to learn his plans. "Tell me about that."

Kyril nodded. "Mr. Gorman is expecting us. We will—"

"Wait a minute. Expecting us? I told you, I never met the man and I have no reason to think he knows me, let alone that he'd welcome me into his home—"

"I'm sorry; I misspoke. Mr. Gorman is expecting Mr. Torstead to arrive with his latest . . . boy."

There was something about the way he said it. "What kind of boy?"

Kyril looked pained. "Mr. Gorman believes Mr. Torstead shares his taste for certain practices . . ."

"What? Golden showers? Scat? BDSM? What is it I'm supposed to be? His slave?"

Kyril actually blushed. "It is the best way to get you into the house, with your presence there uncontested. In fact, Mr. Gorman is looking forward to meeting you."

"Torstead offered my services for the night?"

"Mr. Torstead has spent considerable time building up your reputation just for this purpose."

I looked down at my shabby, dated clothes and shook my head. "How the hell do you expect to pull that off? No way I can pass as some rich man's boy toy."

"You underestimate yourself, I think." Kyril shrugged. "A new haircut, the proper outfit—Mr. Gorman will see what he expects to see."

"You've really thought this all out, haven't you?"

"We were just awaiting the right person to assume the role, someone with the necessary skills. Are you interested?"

I was, but habit made me hold back. "How long is this charade supposed to last? And how far do I carry it? Do I let Gorman fuck me?"

Kyril winced. "We can hope it does not come to that. He is, I fear, a bit of a pig and I understand he enjoys inflicting a great deal of pain in his play."

I thought of the hundred thousand Kyril had promised me. Money like that buys a lot. But there are limits.

"Mr. Gorman's parties are predictable," Kyril said. "Once he has shown us his latest acquisition we will be invited into his theater. Things will degenerate quickly and it is at this point we will slip out. It is up to you to work out how to remove the painting from the premises. Paul will be waiting outside."

"Will you be with him?" My hand stole up his thigh, cupping his hard dick through the denim of his jeans.

He grabbed my hand. "It is time for you to meet the hairstylist."

I pretended to pout. "Maybe you could help me get into the role. I've never been anybody's plaything."

"Later, Dima."

And I had to leave it at that.

I have to admit, once the stylist was done with me I looked and felt years younger. For once even the prison tan worked for me. I'd let them talk me into losing the moustache I had so carefully cultivated in Crowhaven and I looked positively waiflike in the mirror the stylist held up for me.

The clothes delivered the next day were Tommy Hilfiger. I would have preferred Versace, but Kyril pointed out that Versace didn't suit a naive twinkie who was going to let Gorman abuse him just for fun. The Hilfiger made me look even more boyish. I began to think we just might pull this off.

I really enjoyed the appreciative glances Kyril kept sending me as we met for a late lunch. When I asked him when Mr. Torstead would be joining us, he shook his tousled head and said, "Later."

Then it was time to go.

The limo met us at the front door. Paul held the door and nodded formally as we descended the steps and slid inside.

Kyril was stunning in his Versace suit and camel-hair overcoat. I now wore the leather jacket he had worn when I first met him. He said it suited the image I was trying to project. I told him a real slave boy would probably wear nothing but a loin cloth, ready for action whenever his master wanted some.

"In Greece, maybe," he replied with a laugh. "Not in Maine. Though I must say, you would look hot in a loin cloth."

I slid over next to him, my hand nestling over the thickening bulge between his legs.

"Tell me where and when, and I'll be there," I said huskily, then planted my mouth on his and whispered, "for as long as you'll have me."

We kissed deeply for several minutes, then Kyril broke away.

I licked his chin and snuggled in his arms. "So, where is Torstead meeting us? At Gorman's?"

Kyril took my hand. "He's not."

"Not what? Meeting us? But this—"

"He's already here."

"Wh—" Realization dawned. *"You're* Torstead?"

"I confess." Kyril—or was that Roger—still held my hand. He wove his fingers through mine. "I did not lie to you. My birth name is Kyril, Kyril Ivanovich Gorsky. Roger Torstead is the name I adopted as an American collector."

"But why the fake-out? Who called you in the library?"

"I had Paul place the call from his quarters. I needed to know your intentions before I revealed my identity. As long as I was only Kyril, the hired help, it did not matter if we became intimate. But once I became Roger Torstead . . ."

"I might be trying to bed you to get your money?"

"Something like that."

"I won't lie and say it's not tempting, but you want the truth?" He nodded solemnly. "I like Kyril better."

"Good," he said, before ending all conversation with a kiss that left me shuddering with desire.

Ten minutes later we pulled into a gated estate ablaze with lights. A line of cars crept toward the front door where half a dozen red-coated valets waited. Minutes before we were to disembark Kyril drew something out of his coat pocket.

"Will you wear this tonight, Dima?"

He held up a diamond-studded collar and a pair of matching slave bands.

"To convince Gorman?"

"And to remind us both who you really belong to."

I've never been into subjugation, but I swear when he fastened that collar around my throat I got rock hard and wanted nothing more than to please him. Kyril changed too. His eyes darkened as he clipped a thin gold chain to the collar and tugged on it gently.

"Come here," he said softly.

I leaned forward and he strapped the bracelets around my wrists.

"Now kiss me."

I did, with great enthusiasm, and only broke away from him when Paul opened the limo's door and let a wash of light and cold air inside. I blinked at the faces peering in at us.

One, a fat, porcine man, took in the collar and chain and my flushed face and smiled, showing tobacco-stained teeth. Gorman.

"Torstead, glad you could make it. This must be the boy you've been telling me about."

I scrambled out at Kyril's command and stood in the lighted courtyard of Gorman's estate, being appraised like a bull on its way to the breeding sheds. Or the slaughterhouse. Just being eyed by Gorman left me feeling slimy.

I suddenly prayed it wouldn't be necessary to let this grotesque pig touch me.

Gorman led us into the house and a uniformed maid took our coats while another one handed us champagne. The house impressed me. But as my gaze swept through one room after another as we were led on a whirlwind tour, my respect faded. I counted a half a dozen bad fakes, including a Michelangelo that wouldn't have fooled my second-grade art teacher, and she'd been blind as a bat. Whoever Gorman used to vouch for his collection didn't know his ass from a pietà.

Kyril kept a short hand on my leash and occasionally would tug at it just to remind me of its presence. Like I could forget. Nor could I forget the boner I sported. Kyril looked indifferent to it, as though it was only what he expected, but I caught the odd glance under half-closed eyelids that told me he was perhaps not so blasé.

On the other hand, Gorman couldn't seem to take his piggish eyes off it, or me. I shivered every time his reptilian gaze crawled across my scantily clad body, knowing what he wanted to do to me. Knowing I might have to let him.

The painting was everything Kyril had said. *Tarquin and Lucretia*—I recognized it from my art history studies—depicted the mythological rape of the chaste Roman wife, Lucretia. The Rubens painting had vanished from the home of Joseph Goebbels, only to reappear sixty years later in the hands of the Russian mafia. It had vanished again, shortly after. Now here it was, in the home of a piggish sadist. A situation that desperately needed correcting.

There must have been a dozen of us, clustered around the massive painting hanging by itself with a single spotlight exposing its beauty. Several of the other "boys" wore outfits similar to mine; this was clearly a meeting of like-minded men.

As I stood there, trying not to look too interested, I felt a hand slip between my legs from behind and grab my balls. I gasped and tried to spin free.

Gorman leered down at me.

"Pretty boy," he whispered in my ear. "I will enjoy teaching you what it is to be fucked by a real man."

"I haven't decided if I'm sharing him, Conrad." Kyril stepped between us. "He pleases me yet and I am loath to break in another."

Gorman shrugged and released me. "Perhaps later, then. Come," he said. "It's time for my special treat."

This turned out to be a series of badly made S&M films. Kyril led me to a seat near the exit and soon I could tell by the sounds around us that several of the other guests were indulging in their own show. Time to make our move.

Up front I could see the back of Gorman, flanked by two young men. We waited until Gorman appeared involved with his latest trick, then we slipped out into the hallway. In case anyone stumbled upon us, I stripped off my shirt, leaving the fly of my pants half-opened, revealing the tiny thong Kyril had insisted I wear. Now we would look like we'd been caught making out.

He eyed me appreciatively. "Very fetching. I think we'll adopt it as the new house uniform."

I glared at him. "And how fetching is Paul going to look in it?"

Paul weighed at least two-fifty and didn't stand an inch over five ten.

Kyril winced. "Okay, but you have to promise to wear it sometime when I can truly appreciate it."

In response I grabbed his hand and dragged him toward the Rubens room.

I had made a point to check out Gorman's security from the time we entered the house. Lucky for us, like his choice in paintings, it was abysmal.

While Kyril took up position inside the door, I stood in front of the painting and studied it. There were no obvious alarms on it and aside from a single unset alarm on the door, I saw no overt security at all. Gorman's laxness was making this too easy.

I ran one hand over the bottom of the frame, lifting it away from the wall. Then I stopped, frowning. A quick glance showed Kyril still on guard. He kept darting nervous glances at me.

Ignoring his silent entreaties to hurry, I leaned in, almost pressing my nose against the canvas. Then I stood back, studying it from another angle.

I burst out laughing.

"What is it?" Kyril hissed. "Someone will hear—"

The door burst open, nearly knocking Kyril back against the wall. "What the hell is this?" Gorman stormed into the room. "This room is off limits—"

I smiled up at him. He froze.

"I just love this painting," I gushed. I leaned toward him, forcing myself not to shudder. "I simply had to see it again." I pouted back at Kyril. "Do we really have to leave?"

He rallied quickly and looking stern, took my arm. "Yes, we must."

"Oh, very well." I flounced from the room.

As we passed the outraged man, I couldn't resist: I reached down and pinched Gorman's flaccid dick.

"You really should take something for that, Gorry. Gotta keep the boys happy if you expect to keep them around."

He sputtered. We ducked around the corner, where Kyril grabbed me. "We can't leave now. I will not let that pig keep my painting."

I started laughing again.

Clearly not expecting that, Kyril drew away from me. I shook my head, still laughing, not wanting him to go. Finally I found my voice.

"No, you don't understand," I said.

"I understand you are giving up—"

"It's fake."

"*What?*"

"It's a forgery," I said between gales of laughter. "And not a very good one."

Kyril gaped at me, then he too exploded. Behind us, Gorman appeared in the hall, looking thunderstruck. Not wanting to explain what had us in gales, we turned and fled, barely pausing to collect our coats from a startled maid.

Thirty minutes later we pulled up in front of Kyril's. We were still giggling. Once inside, I hugged Kyril and he briefly hugged me back. I thought for sure he was going to dismiss Paul and finish what we'd started earlier. Instead he said he had business to take care of and disappeared.

Stunned, I let Paul fix me a plate of fruit and cheese and then crept to the room I had slept in the night before wondering what had been screwed up. How could I have been so wrong about Kyril's feelings?

Reluctantly, I showered and went to bed, where I lay awake, hoping Kyril would come. The door remained stubbornly closed. I thought of trying to find him on my own, but given the size of the place, knew it was futile.

I awoke when the first velvet cuff went around my wrist.

"What the—" I sat up in bed, only to find one arm already secured to the ornate metal bedpost. A figure knelt on the bed, facing me, a second cuff in his hand, ready to go around my other wrist.

Kyril leaned down, kissing and licking the skin of my chest, throat, and face. "Indulge me, Dima." He whispered against my mouth, "You will not be sorry."

My resistance melted. I wanted the man so much I didn't object when he put the other cuff on. I didn't even object when he slid the blindfold around my eyes again and the collar around my throat. Once more my world plunged into darkness, ripe with erotic tension.

He laid a trail of feather-light kisses along my eyelids, cheeks, and jaw. He buried his nose in my armpit, while his hands skimmed my chest and shoulders. He moved up to my elbow then back down, ending with a throbbing nipple in his mouth.

I groaned and tried to hump his leg, but he held me down with the weight of his deliciously naked body. His hard dick nestled achingly between my thighs; our cocks slid over each other, sharing an ample coating of pre-cum.

He moved onto the other nipple, scraping his teeth and stiff tongue over it until my breath came in sharp gasps. He slid his hot mouth down my chest, licking and sucking every inch of skin along the way. He teased my navel, but just as I thought he was going to take my pulsing dick in his mouth, he moved down to the end of the bed and caressed my feet, sucking on my toes and biting at my ankles and heels.

I moaned his name again and again, lost in desire, beyond thought. Beyond anything but the raw need that possessed me. I wanted his mouth on me. I wanted his dick buried deep inside me.

He nibbled the skin inside my knees, inching his way up my inner thigh, his mouth tracking a volcanic path along my supersensitive skin. I humped empty air, tugging at my restraints with desperate need.

He pried my legs apart. I cried out when his mouth closed over first one then both balls, rolling them around with his lips and tongue before moving down, sliding over my perineum with excruciating slowness.

When his tongue first probed my hole, I rose off the bed with a shout. I've been rimmed a few times in my life, but nothing like what Kyril did to me that night. He ate me out with an enthusiasm that left me panting and gasping his name, writhing on the bed, my blindfolded head whipping from side to side in a frenzy. My balls tightened and I knew it was only a matter of seconds before I blew my load. I groaned a warning and he quickly shifted position and swallowed my throbbing dick in one gulp.

Cum blasted out of me with shotgun ferocity. I drove my dick down his throat. My orgasm crashed over me and I emptied myself into him.

Finally I sagged in my restraints, barely aware of being covered by his naked body. His mouth pressed against my ear.

"I am going to fuck you, Dima." He tugged at the leash around my neck. "You are mine, tonight and always."

In answer I wrapped my still shaking legs around his hips. The head of his fat dick probed gently at the entrance to my hole. I would have thought he had sucked everything out of me, but as he slipped his thick, mushroom-shaped head past the tight ring guarding my hole and made his first slide over my prostate, my body came alive to him again. He roused sensations in me I had never felt before.

I could smell his arousal as his sweat-slicked body covered mine. I heard his quickening breath as he penetrated my ass, gently at first, then driving into me as lust overrode caution.

He pounded into me, his wordless grunts filling the room. I wrapped my legs tighter around him, pushing him deeper into my bowels. My own dick grew hard again as he rhythmically stroked my prostate. I rose to meet him, thrust for thrust. Under us the solid oak bed rocked against the wooden floor as the fury of our lust consumed us.

He was chanting my name now. His mouth swooped down on mine and I swallowed his cries as he thrashed on top of me. Deep inside me his dick swelled and throbbed and I felt the first explosion of cum hit the walls of my fuck hole. He froze, straining against me, every muscle in his body rigid as he drove into me. Again and again cum poured out, a torrent of molten essence searing me inside.

His hand snaked between us and he grasped my dick in his fist. He pounded at me; despite my earlier workout, it didn't take me long. I came, splashing my jism across my stomach and ribs, smearing us both as he collapsed atop me.

Gently his lips touched mine. "Baby, you are magnificent."

"Look who's talking."

His laugh was shaky. Quickly he undid the blindfold and released my wrists from their velvet chains. I wrapped him in my embrace.

"Will you stay awhile?" he asked. He tugged at the short leash around my neck. "Please."

Now how the hell could I say no to that?

It turns out Maine isn't really that cold when you have a hot man to hold at night. Kyril tells me it's even colder in St. Petersburg, where he plans to take me next winter to see some of the treasures of the Winter Palace. He's made me promise I won't embarrass him by trying to steal anything.

Like I'd ever.

Although I hear those Fabergé eggs are something pretty to behold.

The Boys of Fu Manchu

Simon Sheppard

The campaign speeches had been made, the pots of jasmine tea had been drained; the $200-a-plate banquet at The Shanghai Palace was winding down. White-jacketed Chinese busboys were clearing away willow-pattern dishes bearing scraps of egg foo yong. Candidate Owen Carstairs, though more than ready to leave, was surrounded by well-wishers eager to shake his hand.

"Mr. Carstairs," purred a matron in a silk gown bearing traces of a misaimed bite of orange beef, "San Francisco could really use an upright, forthright mayor like you. It's about time someone plunged in to clean up this city's corruption and . . . and . . . perversion."

Carstairs thanked the woman and several more like her, but all the while his pale eyes were darting around the scarlet-and-gold dining room in a distracted little dance. "Let's get the hell out of here," he hissed to his bodyguard, sotto voce.

Once in the backseat of his chauffeur-driven Lincoln, the mayoral candidate stripped off his evening clothes and changed into a rumpled, nondescript outfit. The Asian driver, knowing what was expected of him, left the lantern-lit tourist thoroughfares, steering the car into a dim, sordid alley, pulling up at a trash-encrusted curb.

"One hour," said Carstairs. He slid from the car's posh leather seat, stepped over a pile of trash, and knocked on a door with peeling paint. A view-hole opened, the door swung ajar, and Carstairs found himself, as he had on many another night, in the ornate sitting room of Wing Ho Lee's.

"Ah, Mister Carstairs," said the wizened proprietor, wreathed in clouds of joss smoke and opium fumes, "you will be pleased to know that your favorite boys are available for your pleasure."

"I should hope so, considering what I'm paying," the pale-eyed white man muttered, but he was already being led through a curtain of crystal beads, down a candlelit hall, and into a darkened room, its walls hung with brocaded silks, its floor covered with large embroidered cushions. In the four corners of the dim room stood grotesque golden idols, each in a different posture, each with a third eye in the middle of her forehead.

"Please," said the proprietor, an insincere smile creasing his wrinkled face, "make yourself comfortable. The boys will be in to serve you shortly." The elaborately carved door shut heavily behind him.

Carstairs stripped naked, leaving his clothes in a messy little pile in one corner of the room, then pulled a turquoise silk robe from a hook on the wall and wrapped it around himself. He lay back on the cushioned floor and reached over to a low, black-lacquered table glittering with semiprecious stones. On it, a long-stemmed pipe already bore a bowlful of opium. He was inhaling his first puff of the sizzling drug when the door opened.

Two beautiful Chinese boys, looking no older than eighteen, entered the room. The young men were in traditional Oriental garb: crimson jackets embroidered with dragons, loose-fitting black pants, and little black velvet slippers. One boy closed the door and shot the bolt. While Carstairs held the bowl of the pipe over a sputtering oil lamp and inhaled the sweetish poison, the other young man knelt between the white man's hairy, outstretched legs. Carstairs' dick, already protruding half-erect with pleasure from beneath the silken robe, soon swelled to fill the boy's warm, skilled mouth.

The other young man had peeled off his red-and-gold jacket, revealing a lean, smooth torso punctuated by dark, prominent nipples. He watched the man's dick, shiny with spit, being caressed and teased by his fellow whore, and awaited Carstairs' command. It soon came.

"I'm parched," said the drugged white man. "Quench my thirst." He watched from beneath half-closed, iron-heavy eyelids as the young man walked over and stood straddling Carstairs' torso. Slowly, the young man pulled open the fly of his Chinese trousers, reached inside, and fished out a dark, slender cock. Carstairs' mouth gaped open. The boy aimed his half-hard penis.

No one, not the boys nor Carstairs, would have noticed that the eye of one of the idols had slid open, revealing a glassy lens.

The Chinese boy, his face inscrutable, expressionless, wreathed in narcotic smoke, let the hot stream flow.

"He's here, we're quite convinced, in San Francisco, though to what evil purpose we're as yet unsure."

"But you suspect?" asked Police Commissioner Dermody.

"We suspect," said Sir Adrian Nayland Smith, "that it has something to do with the upcoming election, and with the machinations of a madman who will stop at nothing to rule the globe."

"Reason enough for him to come to San Francisco, Smith. I'll ensure you have whatever resources you need to thwart his evil aims. The police department is at your command. And I have just the man to work under you. His name's Alex Mann—loyal, hardworking, he's been almost like a son to me."

The telephone rang. Dermody picked it up. "It's for you, Smith."

Sir Adrian Nayland Smith's steely gray eyes narrowed. Reaching for the receiver, he said, "I'm surprised anyone but you even knows that I've arrived in San Francisco."

There was a moment of silence at the other end of the phone, a sudden intake of breath, then a guttural voice dripping with contempt. "Ah, my dear Smith, surely you're not surprised that your every movement is known to me? No, surely not, not after all these years. Just as you can be in no way surprised that I would travel to the ends of the earth to defeat you, as I stymied your weakling of a father. No one bearing the name Nayland Smith—not the impotent Sir Denis, nor you, his miserable spawn—shall succeed in foiling my plans."

"You monster!" Smith began. But the phone had already gone dead.

The Englishman hung up the receiver. "Damn him," he hissed. "Damn Fu Manchu!"

Owen Carstairs, his face caked with the heavy makeup the video eye required, stood behind one lectern, his opponent, Charles Rapoport, behind the other. The TV camera zeroed in on Carstairs' patrician face as he spoke.

"It's time to give this city back to us decent San Franciscans, those of us who don't march half-naked in gay pride parades, those of us who don't smoke marijuana or attend orgies," Carstairs said. "We're the men and women who go off to work every day, come home to our families, and lead decent, upstanding lives. And at last we're rising up and shouting out: 'We want our city back!'"

Rapoport, whose reputation for liberalism was well founded, who never missed a chance to march in a gay parade, who had even been known to attend charity auctions held by men in black leather, looked dismayed. The city was changing. Hard economic times and a series of scandals had made many voters long for simpler, more innocent times. And his opponent, once a feeble campaigner, had somehow developed a persuasive, near-hypnotic presence. All the polls indicated the same thing: Charles Rapoport was going to lose. All that stood between him and certain defeat was the city's sizable bloc of gay voters; if they turned out in large numbers to beat back Carstairs' gay-baiting, Rapoport figured he still had a chance.

"And lest anyone feel," Carstairs was saying, "that I'm scapegoating our city's homosexual population, let me now tell all of you something that's been known to a few friends for quite a while. I am, in fact, homosexual myself."

There was an audible gasp in the studio, and the camera caught a disconcerted, startled look on Rapoport's face. "I'm just not one of those self-styled gay activists who dote on victimhood, revel in promiscuous sex, and, their computers full of Internet pornography, cry foul whenever decency and fidelity are mentioned."

In his luxurious lair somewhere in Pacific Heights, Fu Manchu sat before a wall-sized TV and smiled.

Detective Alex Mann was young, ambitious, and built like a football player. Having risen rapidly through the ranks of the San Francisco Police Department, known as an incorruptible cop, he'd been assigned by

Dermody to work hand-in-hand with Nayland Smith in the hunt for Fu Manchu.

"So you think," Mann was asking, "that he's meddling in the upcoming election?"

"I'm afraid it's just his style," Smith said. "He lurks beneath the democratic process, sending forth his tentacles, exerting his fiendish control. Somewhere behind the scenes, Fu Manchu is making sure that whatever happens in next week's election will serve his dastardly ends."

"So we trail Rapoport and Carstairs, then? See if either of them is under his control?"

"Yes," said Sir Adrian Nayland Smith, "that's precisely what we'll do."

It was two in the morning when Owen Carstairs' phone rang.

The voice on the other end was guttural and cruel. "That was an excellent performance tonight. Your confession destroyed what little hope your opponent clung to. We shall win, we certainly shall win."

Carstairs resented and hated it, being under the sway of this megalomaniac. Whatever power Carstairs achieved should be his own by right. He was not the slave of this faceless, unknowable fiend. And yet . . . there was the opium, the boys, and something else as well, as though this voice in the night could burrow deep within his brain and take control. Carstairs would have to play along, at least until he'd become Mayor. After that, when he was in office, things would change. They'd have to.

Carstairs chose his words carefully. "Thank you. I'm glad you're pleased."

"Ah, yes. Very pleased." There was a long pause.

Carstairs, alone in his bed, couldn't help himself. He thought of being possessed by the sweetish smoke, of being humiliated and used by the young, feline boys in the Chinatown brothel. His dick began to swell.

At last the cruel voice spoke again. "And is there something I can do to reward you?"

Damn you! Carstairs thought. But when he spoke, he said only, "Yes, please. You . . . you know what it is."

"Very well," said the voice of the fiend. "A car will be around for you shortly."

Carstairs didn't even have time to ask how long it would be. There was a click, and the line went dead.

"We know that Carstairs went *somewhere* late last night. We just don't know where. My men lost track of the car in the alleys of Chinatown, and by the time they caught up with it, Carstairs was no longer a passenger."

"Chinatown," Smith said. "Hardly a surprise."

Detective Mann winced, a look of pain crossing his good-looking, even-featured face.

"What's wrong?" asked Smith.

"Oh, nothing," said the young detective, "just my calf. I strained it playing racquetball."

"Would you like me to massage it?" Smith's gaze was even and direct.

Alex Mann smiled, pushed his chair back, and extended his legs. "It's the left one," he said.

Sir Adrian Nayland Smith knelt between the young policeman's outstretched legs. Even swathed in flannel, Mann's calves and thighs were clearly well muscled. The Englishman grasped the young detective's calf and started kneading the knotted muscle. "Feel good?" he asked.

"Mmm," said the handsome American youth, tilting his head back and closing his eyes. To Smith's mild astonishment, he felt his own penis becoming erect. His fingers worked Mann's calf, rubbing till the leg of the detective's trousers lifted high enough to reveal a thick woolen sock above a shiny black shoe, then a glimpse of his leg, furry with thick blond hair. Mann shifted in his seat, thrusting his crotch toward the kneeling Englishman. Smith began moving his hands slowly upward, toward the knee, then up to Mann's inner thigh.

"God, that's good," the young man said. "It makes me feel so . . ." And he reached down and gave his own crotch a squeeze. Nayland Smith, emboldened, stroked upward, closer to Mann's groin. Deliberately, he let his knuckles brush the flannel-clad crotch; Alex Mann's cock was hard. Without a word, Sir Adrian Nayland Smith unzipped the detective's pants, revealing a swath of snowy boxer shorts. He looked up. Mann was looking straight at him, smiling.

Smith reached inside the boxers. The swollen flesh was hot. He drew the man's cock out. It was beautiful, perfectly shaped. The head, freed from its generous foreskin, had a shining pearl of pre-cum at its slitted tip. Smith could not restrain himself; he bent and took the velvety head of the penis between his lips.

"Fuck, yeah," murmured Alex Mann. "I keep asking Celia to do that, but . . ."

Smith grabbed onto the detective's muscular thighs and slid his mouth all the way down the swollen shaft, till the cockhead lodged in his throat. His hands kneaded the man's spread upper thighs as the young man thrust his dick even deeper into Smith's mouth.

"Oh, fuuuck . . ." Mann groaned. His cock spasmed again and again, pumping loads of thick cum down Nayland Smith's throat. The Englishman gulped it eagerly. For once, the threat of Fu Manchu was far from his thoughts.

"I won't do it. I'll win or I'll lose, but I refuse to do your bidding any longer." Carstairs could barely believe he was saying those words to Doctor Fu Manchu. The evil mastermind had just telephoned him to congratulate him on his performance at a rally in Union Square, a rally where scores of gay activists had shown up to denounce the mayoral candidate as a turncoat and a threat.

"Ah, but you shall obey me, my friend. You shall. I'll ignore that little outburst of pique; I do understand you've been under a lot of stress. But you and I know what you do to relieve that stress, don't we? You might want to turn on your VCR, Mr. Carstairs, and ponder what consequences any imprudent action might bring."

There was a click, then silence, then an electronic voice: "If you want to make a call, hang up and . . ."

Apprehensive, puzzled, Carstairs reached for the remote, turned on the television and VCR, and pushed *Play*. A crystal-clear image appeared on the screen. It was him, an opium pipe in his mouth, a naked Chinese boy holding a flame beneath the long pipe's bowl while Carstairs inhaled the intoxicating smoke. As Carstairs, dressed in a silken robe, sank back on the cushioned floor, the camera pulled back to reveal two other naked boys in the room, one with an enormous black dildo in his hand.

The naked young man who had lit the pipe straddled Carstairs' head and squatted down, feeding the candidate his butt. Meanwhile, one of the other boys pushed Carstairs' legs up, while the third of Fu Manchu's boys greased up the gigantic dildo and unceremoniously shoved it up Owen Carstairs' ass.

The television screen went blank. Carstairs sat staring into space, the remote control dangling from his hand. The villain was right, of course; release of the videotape would ruin him. He had no choice, really, but to serve the archfiend's purposes. He had no choice.

Dejected, Owen Carstairs didn't even bother to wonder how the tape had made its way into his VCR.

"I'm sorry to have to say this," Alex Mann said, "but I just don't trust the Commissioner."

"Dermody? Your boss?" Nayland Smith sounded genuinely nonplused. "But why not?"

"Think about it. Fu Manchu knew you had arrived in San Francisco. And who else but Dermody knew you were coming?"

"Perhaps he'd told other people in the police department."

"He never told me," Alex Mann said. "Not till long after Fu Manchu contacted you here."

"Well . . ." Nayland Smith hesitated. The word was that Police Commissioner Dermody was dedicated and incorruptible. But Fu Manchu, in his long and evil career, had used many other supposedly upright men. Smith resolved to stay on his guard. "Detective Mann?"

"What?"

Sir Adrian Nayland Smith had spent much of the past day remembering the taste of Mann's cock, the detective's flood of cum coursing down his throat. "I was just wondering . . ."

"Yes?"

"Oh, nothing."

Alex Mann grinned. He stood and walked over to Smith, his crotch less than a foot from the Englishman's face. Slowly, deliberately, he unzipped his fly, reached inside, and drew out his cock. Even soft, it was formidable. Smith stared at the inviting hunk of flesh and licked his lips. "Is this what you were wondering about?" the young policeman asked.

Had he underestimated that simpering sodomite Carstairs? Fu Manchu wondered. The candidate's rebellious gestures of independence had come as an unpleasant surprise. It was nothing he couldn't handle, of course, but it was more trouble than he'd planned on.

The San Francisco operation was supposed to be simple, an easy piece of his master plan. Taking control of Frisco wasn't even particularly vital. He already held sway over the mayors and governors of many states and cities, and more than a few members of the United States Congress answered to him as well. Pundits, too, were under his control; fully three-quarters of the staff of the Fox News Network did his bidding. And several prominent right-wing Christian preachers, the best-known of the televangelists, were in his grip. He had everything in place to initiate his dictatorship. San Francisco was a mere bagatelle. But with its liberal populace and strong gay community, the city had posed an irresistible challenge. Its Chinatown provided cover for his operations, and in Owen Carstairs, Fu Manchu had believed he'd found an excellent cat's-paw. The fact that the candidate was showing signs of independence this late in the game was troubling. Perhaps he should have instructed the proprietor of Wing Ho Lee's brothel to slip Carstairs larger doses of hypnotic drugs, though the side effects could be unpredictable.

Ah, well. With the election in two days, he would simply have to reassert his threat and exert stronger mind control. Nonetheless, a backup plan was advisable. He would order his best San Francisco agent to be at the Golden Gate Bridge tomorrow, in case anything at Carstairs' final campaign rally went awry and the candidacy needed to be . . . terminated. And even if Rapoport should win the mayoralty, he, too, would soon be crushed beneath Fu Manchu's heel.

The wily fiend turned toward the television and pressed *Play* on the remote control. Images of Carstairs and several handsome, naked boys filled the screen. Though sex between men repelled him, he found the images of Carstairs' humiliation, the white man's submission and degradation at the hands of the boys of Fu Manchu, to be irresistibly exciting. Captured by the secret camera's eye, a naked Owen Carstairs, his large cock erect, was being pissed on, then flogged with a vicious cat-o'-nine-tails. As Carstairs writhed in agony, Fu Manchu's right hand, with its long, graceful fingernails, trailed down toward his swelling crotch.

The television crews, disgorged by their remote-broadcast vans, were clustered at the south end of the Golden Gate Bridge, in front of a flag-draped platform. Several hundred Carstairs supporters had gathered for the rally, but the size of the crowd mattered less than the presence of the TV cameras; with the hulking orange icon of San Francisco as its backdrop, this was an event designed for television.

Unbeknownst to the reporters, the enthusiastic crowd contained an unusually high proportion of plainclothes policemen. Sir Adrian Nayland Smith himself wandered unnoticed amongst the spectators. And unknown to Smith, one Chinese-American family—father, mother, and two children—who were walking their bicycles along the walkway of the bridge, hid a sinister secret; the "father" was none other than the diabolical Doctor Fu Manchu.

Carstairs, meanwhile, having received yet another threatening phone call before setting forth for the Bridge, had just arrived in his limousine, his Chinese chauffeur at the wheel. As he reached for the door handle, the chauffeur turned and smiled. "You will be very careful, Sir, will you not?" he said.

As Owen Carstairs made his way through a small throng of reporters, a has-been blues band played onstage, their desultory music carrying a lyric that was either coincidence or threat: I'm your big doctor baby, and you know it's true, *I'm your big ol' doctor baby, and I'll be watching you.*

The song plodded to an end. Carstairs' campaign manager made an overenthusiastic introduction, and, to the sound of slightly lukewarm applause, the candidate strode to the podium. The TV cameramen prepared to tape the first few minutes of his speech, then head back to their studios in time to get their footage on the evening news.

"My dear friends and fellow San Franciscans," Carstairs began, "we've been part of a history-making campaign to put our fair city back in the hands of its citizens, *all* its citizens, and not merely a radical rabble."

Nayland Smith stifled a yawn; so far, nothing new.

"Democracy is, of course, a precious trust," Carstairs continued, looking shaky but resolved. "And so it gives me no pleasure to stand before you today and confess that I came very close to breaking that trust." There was a puzzled stirring in the crowd. "But whatever happens in the upcoming election, it can never be as important as the truth. And the truth, my fellow San Franciscans, is this: Almost since the beginning, this election campaign has been besmirched by a dictatorial force, operating behind the scenes and insidiously determined to take control. That force, in fact, radiates like a spider's web from a single evil man, a villain whose lust for power has no limits. And that fiend's name is . . ."

A single shot rang out. Carstairs pitched forward on the platform, a wound between his shoulder blades leaking crimson life.

"It came from over there!" Nayland Smith cried out. "Let's get him!" And he headed for the walkway of the Golden Gate Bridge, several plainclothes detectives in his wake. Partway down the walkway, a man, his face concealed by a scarf, had tossed a high-powered rifle over the guardrail and was running away. Meanwhile, the Chinese "family," having dropped their bikes in the walkway, started walking briskly toward the other end of the bridge. But Fu Manchu hadn't counted on the small phalanx of policemen who sprang forth to block his retreat.

The masked gunman, sensing himself trapped, ran frantically back and forth, seeming for a moment to contemplate hurling himself among the cars that sped along the bridge, then thinking better of it and backing away. But as he did, he fell over a discarded bicycle, and Sir Adrian Nayland Smith was on him like a shot, pinning him to the metal walkway. Smith reached down and pulled the scarf away from the murderer's face.

It was Alexander Mann.

"You!" said Smith.

"Yes, you old fool," hissed Mann.

And Smith drew back and struck, his fist sending Mann into unconsciousness.

Fu Manchu, meanwhile, was trapped between the police advancing from either end of the bridge. Suddenly, he glimpsed Sir Adrian Nayland Smith sprinting in his direction. For one long moment, Smith stopped in his tracks. The two men's eyes met. Then, the spell broken, the malevolent doctor grinned at Smith, grabbed the guardrail with both hands, and vaulted over the barrier, plummeting into the icy waters of the bay below.

"Well done, Sir Adrian," Commissioner Dermody said, leaning back in his office chair. "Though I can't help but feel that we might have done better, that Owen Carstairs would still be alive if Mann hadn't successfully deceived us. My own detective, one of Fu Manchu's minions. . . . It's startling how a person you thought you knew could be leading a secret life."

Smith couldn't help but think about the hot, rigid heft of the ex-detective's cock. "But at least he's in prison now, Commissioner."

"And let's not forget, Smith, that Fu Manchu, your archenemy and your father's nemesis before you, is no more."

The Briton recalled the many battles his father had fought against the evil doctor. How often apparent victory had turned to ashes! He shook his head. "That remains to be seen, I fear. For the insidious Fu Manchu has cheated death many times, and we can't discount the possibility that somehow, somewhere, the fiend will reappear, obsessed by his campaign to rule the world."

Fu Manchu had barely hit the water when a tiny two-man submersible swooped in. Once through the airlock, the battered but breathing Fu Manchu was ferried out to a waiting submarine that glided out through the Golden Gate, heading for the shores of Asia. He had lost, this time around. But he would live to fight another day.

Somewhere beyond the Golden Gate, the red sun headed toward the horizon.

Never Trust a Pretty Face

Michael Stamp

Being too eager for the Good Life is what did me in. From the minute I stepped inside Fletcher Greenfield's Long Island mansion on that gray, rainy morning, I had dollar signs dancing in my head like sugarplum fairies in the dreams of tots tucked into their beds on Christmas Eve. It was greed, pure and simple. That and the kid. If I'd been thinking straight I would have respected the NO TRESPASSING sign, but when my dick started to lead, good sense deserted me and I followed along blindly. It's a weakness of mine. I've always been a sucker for a pretty face.

Fletcher Greenfield was a name I knew well. Everybody did. I'd be willing to bet there isn't one building in the whole state that doesn't have pipes running through it that came from Bachman Greenfield Ironworks. I just never expected I'd be doing business with the man himself, and especially not in his posh palace of a home. It's an occupational hazard. Guys in my line of work rarely get invited to tea.

I'm a private dick, and even though FDR keeps telling us prosperity is just around the corner, times are hard and money is tight. Considering how bad the times are, you'd think I'd be scrounging for jobs, but I work steady most of the time.

It's been my experience that no matter how much a guy cries poor, when he thinks his old lady's mattress-dancing with someone else, he always manages to come up with my $10 a day plus expenses so he can find out for sure.

Following restless wives isn't much of a living, but when I see guys standing on street corners selling apples, peeping through hotel win-

---

This story first appeared in *Best Gay Erotica 2001* (Richard Labonté and Randy Boyd, eds., Cleis Press, 2000).

Men of Mystery: Homoerotic Tales of Intrigue and Suspense
Published by The Haworth Press, Inc., 2007. All rights reserved.
doi:10.1300/5885_07

dows and taking dirty pictures starts to look real good. So when Fletcher Greenfield called I came running. At least there wouldn't be any haggling over my fee. He probably spent that much on a good cigar.

The man looking at me from across his desk had to be in his fifties, but he was in fine physical shape, which made him appear much younger, despite the generous strands of gray in his black hair. His small mustache was dark except for a large streak of gray, making him look as if he'd forgotten to wipe his mouth after lunch.

What surprised me even more than his wanting me for the job was what he wanted me to do. I'd expected him to ask me to follow his wife or maybe his girlfriend. When you've got big bucks it must be pretty hard to figure out if a dame really loves you, or if she's just calculating your net worth while you're dick-deep in the cooze.

Being rich had to be tough. Given the chance, I knew I could learn to live with it.

But there wasn't any skirt involved. Greenfield wanted me to find some missing designs he thought had been stolen by a less-than-reputable competitor. Almost all my work's as a peeper, so I couldn't figure out how he'd come to think of me for the job. All he'd say was that I'd been "highly recommended." I couldn't help wondering who'd done me such a big favor, but I didn't want to press Greenfield for information, so I just accepted my good luck.

The only problem was, I didn't feel lucky; maybe because I didn't trust the guy. He was a little too polished for my tastes. Call me crazy, but there's something about a guy with manicured fingernails that raises my hackles.

Still, the money Greenfield was going to pay me was good, too good to pass up. I'd have to peep through a lot of windows to make what Greenfield was offering me, and I wouldn't have to worry about getting my face bashed in by some unfaithful wife's burly boyfriend.

"So Korrigan," he asked me, "can I consider you on board?"

Even though a little voice inside me was telling me to cut and run, I told the little bastard to shut the fuck up, and told Greenfield, "I'm your man."

"Excellent. I knew we could come to terms." Greenfield used a silver ink blotter on the check he'd just written, and handed it to me. "This should be enough to get you started."

"It will do nicely," I replied, slipping the check into my pocket. I stood up to leave, but when I offered Greenfield my hand he didn't take it, didn't even stand up.

"You can see yourself out," he said by way of good-bye, and with that I was dismissed. I didn't take offense. It was no less than I'd expected.

I took the stairs two at a time, anxious to be out of the house and back in the fresh air. When I reached the bottom of the staircase I heard an urgent whisper, and turned around just in time to see him coming down the stairs.

Framed between the staircase pillars, he looked like a Renaissance painting I'd seen in the Guggenheim once: soft, gentle features, with eyes such a deep blue I could have drowned in them. That first look was like getting struck by lightning, and my dick had been the lightning rod.

"What can I do for you, kid?" I asked, but the sound of footsteps on the stairs sent him scampering like a scared rabbit. Just as well. Even if he wasn't jailbait he sure looked it, and if he hadn't gone I might have been tempted to do something that would have gotten me into trouble.

All during the drive back to the city I couldn't get the kid out of my mind. My dick was so hard that working the clutch in my 1937 Dodge was almost painful. If I hadn't thought it would cause an accident, I'd have jerked myself off in the car.

My reaction to the kid wasn't surprising. There hadn't been anyone since Frankie.

Frankie was just another Bowery boy when I met him. No mother, and a father who'd crawled inside a bottle of rotgut and came out only to slap his son around. He was living on the streets, doing whatever he had to do to survive. Our introduction wasn't the usual. He tried to pick my pocket. I'd caught him red-handed, but instead of turning him in to the cops, I bought him a bowl of soup and offered him a place to stay for the night. I'd left him on the couch, but I woke up in the middle of the night to find him between my legs with his mouth sliding down my pole like a fireman on his way to a three-alarmer. Frankie never made it back to the couch.

With respect to Fitzgerald, it was this side of paradise, but it hadn't lasted. Frankie had gotten restless, and the lure of easy money had sent him to work as a whore for Blackie McCabe. He'd still come back to my place from time to time and share my bed—on the house, mind you. I should have left well enough alone, but instead I used Frankie to help me on a case, asked him to get information on one of Blackie's regular clients.

Even though six months had passed, I still woke up in a cold sweat from nightmares of his beautiful face with the .38-caliber bullet someone had planted between his eyes. I knew it had been Blackie, but the pimp's alibi had been airtight, so Frankie's death had just been forgotten by everyone. Everyone but me.

After leaving Greenfield's place, I went back to my office and poured myself a well-deserved shot of whiskey while I sorted through the compromising photos I'd taken of the ex-chorus-girl wife of a geezer old enough to be her grandfather.

I turned the radio on, and Lamont Cranston was just about to use his power to cloud men's minds when my office door opened and the kid from Greenfield's place came in. His Renaissance beauty had been marred by a large bruise on his cheek and his eyes were red and puffy from crying. "Mr. Korrigan?" he asked softly.

"That's me," I answered, shutting off the radio. "That's a nasty bruise, kid. Greenfield do that to you?"

His hand went to his cheek. "How did you know?"

"I'm a detective, remember. Finding out secrets is my business." He took the chair opposite my desk, but didn't volunteer anything more, so I asked, "What can I do for you, kid?"

"It's David, Mr. Korrigan. David Bachman."

"As in Bachman Greenfield Ironworks?"

The kid nodded. "My father and Fletcher were partners."

"Were?"

"Yes. He's dead."

"I'm sorry."

"Me, too. I miss him."

"So what were you doing at Greenfield's place?"

"I live there." At my raised eyebrows he explained, "He's been my guardian since my father died."

"So he controls the purse strings," I surmised.

David nodded again, only this time he kept his eyes down. "He's the executor of my father's estate. I have to live in his house and do whatever he says . . ." The kid's words trailed off as his bottom lip began to tremble.

"Are you okay?" I asked.

"I'm fine," he said, but he wasn't fine. He looked pale and shaky and about to come apart like the guts of a Swiss watch, but I kept my mouth shut and waited for him to talk.

When he did he said, "I'm sorry. I shouldn't have come here. I have to get back before Fletcher realizes I'm gone." The kid got up from the chair and would have fallen flat on his face if I hadn't gotten up from my desk just in time to catch him.

"You're in no shape to go anywhere, kid. Now tell me what this is all about."

David Bachman slumped against me and the waterworks started. I picked him up in my arms and he buried his face in my neck.

I kept a couch in my office for those long nights when I was too beat to make it back to my furnished room, and I lay the kid down on it. He wouldn't let go of me, and ended up pulling my bulk down on top of his small, compact body.

Losing myself in his tear-filled blue eyes, I asked, "Greenfield took you into his bed, didn't he?"

The kid blinked, sending tears cascading down his pale cheeks. "It was what I wanted, but then he became possessive, never wanting me to leave the house. I thought he loved me, but when I told him I was moving out—"

"He threatened to keep your father's money from you."

David nodded. "I told him I didn't care about the money, so he said if I tried to leave he'd have me sent to jail."

"For what?"

"For stealing those designs. They're not really missing, Mr. Korrigan. Fletcher hid them away somewhere. He said if I try to leave him he'll tell the police I stole them." It didn't make sense. "Then why hire me?" I asked.

"He knows the police will be suspicious if he doesn't do anything to get the designs back, so he hired you to find them. He knows he'll be safe because there's no way you can find them."

I didn't like being played for a sucker, but I wasn't so sure I was ready to give up the golden goose on the kid's say-so. "So what do you want from me?" I asked.

"I need to get away from Fletcher but I can't do it on my own," David whispered, his lips so close I could feel his breath on my face. "Please help me, Mr. Korrigan."

Knowing I wouldn't be sending him into strange waters, I offered the kid the kind of help I needed as much as he did. "I'm your man, kid," I said, covering his mouth with mine. His lips parted and I slid my tongue inside. He tasted of mint and dark chocolate.

My hands worked quickly as I unbuttoned his shirt. His chest was smooth and boyish, and I ran my hands over it, feeling his tiny nipples harden the moment I touched them. I kissed all the way down to his waist, stopping only to unbuckle his belt and unzip his pants so I could take them off. His silk boxers came off next, revealing a long, slim dick, surprising for a kid his size. I touched my lips to the tip and it saluted like a career soldier.

Sliding my hands under his ass, I cupped his cheeks in my palms as I prepared to swallow him whole. That's when I felt the welts. "Greenfield did this to you?" I asked.

The kid nodded, then turned away, his face flushed. "He likes to play rough. He ties me to the bed and uses his belt on me. It's the only way he can . . ."

Playing rough might have been the only way Fletcher Greenfield could get it up, but I had no such problem. Just touching the kid already had me so close to shooting I was afraid I wouldn't get my dick out of my pants in time.

Greenfield might have been his first, but David Bachman had been a good student. He took my dick out of my pants like a pro, then he turned over underneath me so that he was face down on the couch. When he pulled his knees up under him and raised his ass, I didn't need an engraved invitation. I spit on my dick and sunk it into his hole. The kid groaned, but he took it all, bucking against me until I was buried deep inside him, my balls slamming against his ass while I fucked him. I shot quickly, pumping my jism into him until I'd been milked dry. It wasn't until the kid asked me who Frankie was that I realized I'd screamed out his name when I came.

So I made my pact with the devil, and sealed the deal with my seven inches deep inside David Bachman's ass.

It wasn't difficult to pull off the scam. I learned Greenfield's daily routine, his work habits, his comings and goings, all in hopes of finding the designs he'd hidden away. Each week I turned in phony reports of my progress on the case.

Not that things weren't progressing on my end. I was fucking David Bachman regularly and getting paid to do it. The Good Life didn't seem like such a dream after all. Until I got the wake-up call.

"Artie!"

I was half-asleep. "David?" I asked, still fuzzy. "What's going on?"

"Fletcher found out about us, Artie! He's going crazy! Please come get me before—"

The line went dead. I jumped out of bed and into my clothes. I drove to the Greenfield mansion like a madman, determined to kill Fletcher Greenfield if he'd laid a hand on the kid. But when I got there everything was quiet. The front door was open and I let myself in. I called out, but there was no answer, so I drew my .38 and went upstairs.

There was a light on in Greenfield's study. His chair was turned away from the door. "Where's David?" I demanded. "If you hurt that kid so help me . . ."

When Greenfield didn't answer I went to the desk and spun his chair around so he would face me. Greenfield's eyes were staring straight at me, but he was long past seeing anyone. There was blood dripping down onto his $100 suit from the .38-caliber hole between his eyes.

When I got to David's room I found him naked, tied spread-eagle, facedown on his bed. A silk tie had been tied around his mouth to gag him. "Are you all right, kid?" I asked, putting down my gun so I could untie him. "Greenfield's dead. Thank God whoever did it didn't know he'd left you in here like this."

"He knew very well."

Hearing that voice made my blood run cold.

"Blackie McCabe," I muttered as the dark-suited pimp walked out of the bathroom carrying a leather belt in one hand and a .38 in the other.

"I'm so pleased you remember me, Korrigan." My eyes went to my gun on the bed, but McCabe said, "Don't even think about it." He picked up the gun and put it in his belt.

"Don't hurt the kid," I pleaded.

McCabe shook his head. "You disappoint me, Korrigan. You're such a smart dick, I was sure you'd figure this out right away. Davy likes being hurt." He slapped the belt hard across the kid's ass. David moaned and raised his reddened ass cheeks up for more. "It makes him one of my most popular boys. You'd be surprised how much my customers are willing to pay to beat a rich boy's ass."

"A rich boy?" I asked stupidly.

"Very rich. Davy already has his father's estate. He'll get all of Bachman Greenfield Ironworks now that his dear guardian is out of the way. We just needed someone to take the fall for Fletcher's murder."

The realization fell on me like a two-ton slab of concrete. "You had the kid recommend me to Greenfield."

"Very good, Korrigan." Blackie nodded his approval. "I knew you were a smart dick. I thought you might be too smart to fall for our little plan, but I knew Davy boy would be able to convince you. You always did like the pretty ones, didn't you, Korrigan? Like Frankie?"

"You bastard!" I spat, lunging for the .38 in McCabe's hand. He sidestepped me like Fred Astaire, and brought the butt of the gun down on the back of my head. Everything faded to black.

When I woke up the room was full of blue uniforms and I had McCabe's .38 in my hand. The cops didn't believe me when I told them I'd been framed, especially when they untied the kid and he started talking. David Bachman told them in a small, teary voice how I'd tied him up and forced myself on him, and how I'd shot Greenfield. The kid sounded real convincing, especially with those tears running down his beautiful cheeks.

I'm not in the peeper business anymore. Now I'm getting my three squares a day courtesy of the state. I spend my days making license plates in the Greybar Hotel. And my nights alone in an eight-by-ten cell. I don't mind the solitude. It's given me a lot of time to think.

After lights-out I spend hours staring up at the ceiling. If I look real hard I can see David Bachman's tear-stained cheeks when he asked for my help. I still can't believe what a sucker I was. A pro like me getting conned by a kid like him.

I've never been one to give advice, but this pearl of wisdom is worth taking. Sex and business don't mix. I'm living proof of where a stiff dick can lead you. The Fletcher Greenfield case taught me one other hard lesson. You can never trust a pretty face.

Lions and Tigers and Snares

Vincent Diamond

Mid-afternoon is usually quiet at a big cat refuge, but the lion's roar drowned out Captain Russo's voice on my cell phone.

"Hold on a sec; let me get past Walter Martin." I strode past the lion cage. Flies buzzed over a beef leg at the cat's feeding station; Walter had popped off the ends of the bones to lick at its yellow marrow. The rank odor of rotting meat and lion crap made me wrinkle my nose. The bucket of chicken parts stuffed with Imodion I carried had its own stench. What a job.

"Who the hell is Walter Martin, and what is that frigging noise?" Captain Russo's nasal tone wavered a bit. The signal was never very strong at the Patacoochee Wildlife Refuge in north Florida. Eighty miles northwest of Gainesville and fifty miles south of Tallahassee made it pretty inaccessible—for cell phones *and* visitors. I had the headset on so that if anyone were watching—not that it was likely, but I had to be careful—it would just look like I was talking to the cats. This time of day, the refuge was usually quiet. The cats slept and the humans got out of the heat as much as possible.

"He's a lion that Kendall bought in a Wal-Mart parking lot, believe it or not. Just sounding off, letting everyone know this is his territory." The lion's guttural roars actually moved in my chest; the whump of air displaced by the animal was eerie and affecting. I stepped around a jaguar cage that held a stand of pine trees; it helped buffer Walter's roars. I kept moving toward the cougar habitat. "Better?"

"Yeah, that's better. Update me, Officer Reese."

"They're buying my cover. I must look like a typical dumbass pre-veterinarian summer intern." Russo snorted but let me keep talking.

"There's two main guys here: Ricardo Lopez and Kendall Knight. Ricardo is the money man; he definitely runs the show that way. Kendall is the animal handler; he's licensed, very experienced with Class One carnivores, and he manages all the scut work in the refuge."

"What do you know so far?" Captain Russo asked. The cell phone buzzed a little; I checked the signal—only two bars.

"Ricardo's an asshole: loud-mouthed, aggressive, chain-smoker. He's always showing up unannounced with strangers. Buyers probably. He teases the cats from outside the cages, gets them all riled up. They hate him. Kendall, though . . ."

I hadn't quite figured out Kendall. With his muscular frame, soft brown eyes, and shaved-bald skull, he *looked* like a tough guy, but he was a real softie when it came to the cats. He clearly loved them. The week before, I'd seen him stay up all night with a poisoned cougar somebody had brought in. He changed the cat's IV, kept the cat calm, ran his sturdy hands over its shoulders and back when the heaves came on.

Kendall's hands. I ran a palm down my belly.

"Kendall seems really dedicated to the refuge. He and his assistant keeper, Randy Duboy, are the only paid staff; everyone else out here is a volunteer. Kendall and Ricardo are pretty tense with each other; I'm not sure why. I did the night cage check earlier this week and saw them outside Kendall's office, arguing."

"What were they saying?"

"I don't know; I was too far away. But I could tell by their body language they weren't having a friendly discussion. Kendall was pissed." I had stood in the shadows of a tiger cage and watched Ricardo drive away in his shiny Escalade. Kendall went into his office, left the lights off. I moved closer and saw him smoking in the dark; the acrid whiff of marijuana drifted outside on the breeze. I'd been tempted to go in and see what I could find out. Something made me wait.

He's not ready yet. And neither am I.

"How fast can you get solid intel and evidence out of there?"

When we first planned this detail, I was supposed to have the whole summer to infiltrate the operation and figure out if Ricardo and

Kendall's big cat refuge was a front for moving endangered and prohibited animals in and out of the country. Collectors paid enormous sums for an endangered species in their private zoos. Big game farms needed a steady supply of animals to kill and mount for "trophies." And both markets paid animal dealers and wholesalers big bucks to produce the inventory to do it. The department had investigated for over a year, and we had narrowed it down to a supplier working in the Southeast. Right now, Ricardo and Kendall looked like our perps.

Living animals as inventory. It made my teeth grind.

"I don't know. It's not like I can just go pawing through the office to look for it."

"Find a way!"

"Captain, I—"

"Byron, that's the whole point of undercover. You're in there so you *can* go pawing through the office or get into the house or a computer. Get closer to Kendall and Ricardo, talk to that other kid. See what you can find out."

Get closer? To Ricardo? Not a chance. To Kendall? Chance. And a pleasant one.

"I'll do my best. It's kinda nice to be with the animals again."

I'd actually been a licensed handler until a few years ago. My uncle had a roadside zoo when I was a kid: tigers, a couple of cougars, and bears. Later, I'd volunteered at the Midwest Tiger Refuge. I'm fine with the animals. It's the people that are hard to handle.

"You okay? You keeping your cover?" Russo sounded on edge. He was always hyper about maintaining cover.

"Sure."

"No calling your friends, no checking e-mail, right?"

"Nope. I'm isolated, just like you taught me." That was a key to good cover, immersing yourself in the new world and leaving your real one behind. Not all cops could do it, but I'd managed it. My last lover, Miguel, didn't much like my job. He'd put up with it for three years until having a partner who disappeared for months at a time finally wore him down.

Through the bars of the cougar cage, I saw a bare-chested Kendall come out of his house, a log cabin onsite. Strange; he usually disappeared after lunch. He looked around, spotted me, and waved. He headed toward me.

Shit. What the hell did he want?

"I've got to get off the phone, Captain. I've got company on the way."

"All right. Check back when you have something solid or in a week if you don't," Russo instructed.

"Yes, sir." I bent down to the food slot and slopped out the chicken for the cougar. He ambled over, sick enough to be not all that interested in food just yet. In a couple of seconds I had the headset off, and the phone tucked into a pocket. I heard Kendall approach but stayed down, talking to the cougar. I needed the time to get centered again, to just be Byron Smith, refuge intern, wanna-be veterinarian, just a harmless college kid.

Well, maybe a college kid with a crush.

"Hey." Kendall's voice was deep enough to make you have to really listen to him. He put a hand on my shoulder and I looked up. He wore only cargo shorts, and goddammit if he didn't have great legs to match his solid torso. It wasn't a body you got at the gym; it was a workingman's body—balanced, tanned, and he looked fucking delicious.

"Hey, yourself." When I stood up, I noticed his face had crease marks on one cheek; he must have been sleeping. It made me wonder who he was sleeping with, what it would be like to take a nap in the afternoon and wake up with this man in the bed.

Stop it. Concentrate on doing your job.

"I need your help tonight. Can you work some overtime?"

"Sure. What's up?"

"We've got a big shipment of cats coming in; it'll be late. Probably after midnight. Randy's got food poisoning, we think; he's been throwing up all day. Can you help?"

"Sure. Just let me know what time."

"I'll call you at your trailer."

"Why so late?"

His face closed off a little. "The truck's just running behind schedule."

"What's coming in?"

"Leopards and jaguars, a couple of lions."

"Yeesh, leps and jags. Not my favorite."

"Not mine, either, but that's the gig."

Leopards were the most difficult of all the big cats to manage. All the animals here were wild—and dangerous, of course—but funnily enough, lions and tigers, though much larger, were easier to handle than the leps and jags. You can read lion and tiger facial expressions pretty easily, and gauge their body language to get a sense of what they might do. Leopards and jaguars were harder; their faces weren't as animated as the other big cats, and—worse—they planned ahead. I'd seen a pair of leopards work together once to grab a domestic cat who had wandered into their cage. One of them stalked it from behind; the second deliberately jumped against the fencing, ricocheted off and chased the housecat into its partner's claws. The smartest of the big cats. That made them the scariest.

"Do you need help getting the holding pens ready? I can stick around after my shift."

Kendall touched my arm. "No thanks, I can manage that. Just let me call you when the truck gets in so we can get these animals offloaded." His gaze held me, those soft brown eyes, and now I noticed his thick eyelashes. And his lips were so full and inviting . . .

My arm tingled where he touched me.

"Call me later, then." I said past a swallow.

"Thanks, Byron."

I watched him walk away. His shoulders were wide and brown; he had long legs and a high butt. My cock snaked over inside my pants, just a little.

Geezus, this job was turning messy.

The thunderstorm woke me before Kendall called. A huge crack of lightning snapped close by my trailer, the clock radio flickered, and then went dead. I sat up, disoriented. The dream I'd been having left tendrils of confusion in my head. Did I really kiss Kendall or did I just dream it?

Ten minutes after he called, I was back at the refuge. A semi puffed exhaust into the rainy night. Oak trees swayed in the wind and clumps of Spanish moss and leaves lay on the ground. The rain pounded loud as hail on my little Ranger.

Great. The cats will love this shit.

To my surprise, Ricardo was there. Big-bellied and bearded, he smoked constantly. He used a walking stick, whether affectation or genuine need, I couldn't tell. He wasn't out in the rain, of course, but he barked orders from the shelter of the quarantine barn.

Randy was there, too, looking pale. He and Kendall had the truck's back doors open, and I smelled the cats in the cargo area. The acrid smell of cat piss and wild animal permeated the hold.

I got soaked just running from my truck to the semi. The rain stung against my face and arms. We went to work.

Most animal dealers used steel cages fitted with special load units at the top so you could slide in the metal gripper bars to lift the cages without coming too close to them. We off-loaded a half-dozen of the spotted leopards this way, sliding them out to the gate, riding the noisy ramp down to the ground, then carrying them into the quarantine kennel. The cats growled and spat at us; they would have anyway, but the thunderstorm didn't make it easier. They paced in their little travel cages, knocking us off-balance as they jerked from one side to the other. I slipped and fell once, and we dropped the cage into the mud. One of the big male leopards clawed through the bars, his thick arm reaching out to snag us. My shoulders ached after just fifteen minutes.

Kendall looked pissed. He didn't talk to the cats like he usually did; he just lifted, grimaced against the weight, and kept us moving. We put a black leopard into a quarantine cage, and as we closed the door, Randy bent double, and puked on the concrete floor.

"Oh, shit, I'm sorry. Shit!" He heaved again, grabbing at his belly.

Kendall put a hand on his back. Randy kept vomiting, not bringing up anything substantial. Kendall kept rubbing Randy's back, soothing.

The same way he did with that sick cougar.

"It's all right," Kendall said. When Randy stopped heaving and wiped off his mouth, Kendall stepped to the mini-fridge at the end of the aisle; we usually kept meds in it. He pulled out a Gatorade and handed it to Randy. "Sit down and rest for a while. Drink this. And then you're going home."

"No, I'll be okay."

Ricardo stalked over. "Get moving, girls. Quit pussying around."

Kendall glared at him. "He's sick."

"I don't care. These animals need to be in place and cleaned up by tomorrow afternoon. This is taking too long. Get moving again."

Randy wiped a shaky hand over his face. "I can work."

"No, you won't. Go home and get into the doctor in the morning. Call me if you need help getting there." Kendall looked at him with concern.

"I'll get Melissa to take me. Thanks, Kendall."

Ricardo threw a lit cigarette butt onto the floor and lit another. Kendall pointedly walked over to stamp out the glowing ember. They looked at each other. Some long-standing animosity coiled up between them; it was as easy to see as the cigarette smoke in the air.

"You're not sending him home. We need to get this work done," Ricardo snapped.

"I *am* sending him home. He's my employee and my responsibility. You don't have a say in how I run my people."

"Watch yourself. You're not the only game in town. Remember our deal."

Kendall glanced over at me, his mouth tight and set. He swung back to Ricardo. "Shut the fuck up."

Ricardo smiled and shrugged. "You've got more to lose than I do, Mr. Smartass."

"Get out."

Ricardo flashed yellow teeth again. "Have them ready for inspection by two o'clock. We'll be out then to show the stock."

Kendall's shoulders tightened when he heard "stock." I knew he was like me; he didn't think of these creatures as stock, and it angered him to see them treated like nothing more than a box of soap or a can of soda.

We watched Randy and Ricardo drive away then went back to work.

The rain started to taper off when we had three cats left. By the time we got them settled, we were covered in mud and sweat. Bits of cat fur stuck to us. Cats often shed when stressed, and we both had puffs of leopard and jaguar hair on our arms and faces. Kendall hadn't said much after the scene with Ricardo, and I could see he was both tired and worried by the set of his shoulders and the pinch of his eyebrows.

"They all seem pretty healthy," I said. "Nothing to deal with right away."

"Yeah," Kendall said. He wiped his face with a towel, handed it to me. "But healthy to what end? What a waste."

"What do you mean?"

"Nothing." Kendall turned his gaze away.

"What is it?" This was the time to push, when he was tired and vulnerable and might reveal something he normally wouldn't.

"Not something you need to worry about."

"But *you* need to worry about it?"

He looked at me then. He wanted to tell me; I could read it in his face. He leaned against the wall, arms folded. I mirrored him, a technique I'd learned in an interrogation seminar; mimic the suspect's body language—he might change his attitude. And talk.

I pushed a little more. "Kendall, what's wrong? It seems like something's not quite right about these cats." I leaned a little toward him. Did he lean back? I couldn't tell, but I was close enough to see the pulse-beat in his throat and smell him—sweat and rain and cat all mixed together.

He was silent. Around us, the rain pattered gently on the barn's metal roof. A cat sighed. I heard the jaguar behind us licking itself clean; the rough rasp of its tongue bristling against its damp fur. The mud on my arms itched.

I pressed my upper arm against his solid bicep, almost a nudge.

He wiped his face with one hand, his voice tired. "I'm just as caged as these cats are."

I held my breath. Let the silence make him want to talk.

I pressed his arm again. He didn't lean away. Encouraging.

"Kendall?" I chanced it, put a hand on his dirty forearm and held his gaze. "Maybe I can help."

"You can't."

"Maybe I can."

"I don't think so. But thanks, anyway. You're a good kid." He looked down at my hand, then up. Our gazes locked and the moment caught fire.

"I'm not just a kid."

He grinned and stepped away. "All you college kids say that. Come on. I need a shower, and a smoke, and I bet you do, too."

We showered at his house—in separate bathrooms, to my disappointment. That vibe was between us, the near-certainty that we were going to hit the bed, but there was just enough ambiguity in the air to make me nervous. Maybe I'd misread him; maybe he was just one of those guys who made a lot of eye contact and was a toucher.

I slipped on the clean shorts Kendall had left for me in the bathroom. Music came from the living room, something with saxophones and quiet drums, a slinky sound. The smell of pot wafted through the house—strong stuff. When I came around the corner, Kendall was sprawled on the sofa, a towel wrapped around his waist.

Oh, this looks promising.

His skin had minor tan marks and was dark already, and there was just a hint of browner skin on his arms and lower legs. With his dark eyebrows and brown eyes, he sure wasn't the All-American golden boy I saw every morning in the mirror. Italian, maybe? Hispanic? Either way, caramel-colored skin like his begged to be suckled, licked—appreciated.

Get some intel. I heard Russo's voice in my head, telling me to do my job, but my dick had other considerations. Get some ass, was what it told me.

Kendall waved the joint at me, holding his breath.

"I probably shouldn't. Grass just makes me horny," I said.

"Then you should definitely have some." His grin was wide. He sat back against the leather sofa and spread his legs apart, enough for the towel to reveal one meaty upper thigh.

I swallowed and stepped past the coffee table. The joint's ember glowed in the dim room and it felt like Kendall's eyes glowed the same way. What was he thinking?

I took a hit, coughed a little and then held it down. The smoke filled my lungs, and in a few seconds a quiet buzz of ease moved through my skull. I closed my eyes, and took another toke, letting its soft haze fill me. The sofa cushions squeaked and shifted down as Kendall moved closer. I felt him near me, felt the warmth of his skin. "Take another hit," he said, his voice soft now.

I did. I held his gaze this time, while the smoke curled into me. Kendall eased closer. "Give me some," and he opened his mouth, and I breathed some back into him. He took it in and stayed close, his lips against mine, just breathing each other for a few seconds.

I kissed him first, a real kiss, our lips brushing, then pressing against each other. His full lips were pillowy, softer than those of anyone I'd ever kissed

My cock lifted up and poked out of the flimsy shorts I wore. Kendall's hands were all over me: my chest, my belly, my legs, and finally on my cock, stroking me. I gasped and tightened one hand around his beefy neck. "God, I want to fuck you. Please tell me you've got supplies," I whispered.

"Right here." He leaned over and pulled over a box from the coffee table. Inside were condoms and lube, thankfully.

He pressed me back into the sofa and straddled my lap. I tore the towel off and was thrilled to see his hard cock right in front of me. Its tip glistened, and thick purple veins ran its length. And he was big, two fistfuls of man.

Beautiful.

He put one hand behind my head and guided himself into my mouth. I stretched around him, working the tip until he thrust in with a groan. He was demanding; not that I wasn't willing, but there was a quiet thrill in knowing that he was probably strong enough to keep me pinned down. I opened up my throat and let him all the way inside.

He grunted and started to pump.

I could see his belly tighten with each thrust, feel his thighs tense as he worked over me. His hands moved down to my shoulders. His eyes were closed, his mouth open, his lips wet with my spit. I used one palm beneath his balls, gentle squeezes in time with his thrusts and he moaned, "Oh, Byron, just like that."

I put one finger up to his mouth and he latched onto it. His tongue worked on me, a sensual suckling that made my cock bob up against my belly. When I pulled my finger away, he opened his eyes and looked down at me. I held his gaze, moved my hands over to the box, and squeezed some lube on my fingers.

I worked my slick finger up behind his balls, our eyes locked together. He went still for a few seconds, his thick cock filling my mouth, the smell of him covering me. I didn't wait; I slipped my wet finger into him and he shuddered. His groan filled the room.

I found that little bump inside him and rubbed it with my finger. His grip tightened on my shoulder, so hard that it hurt, but I didn't mind. He suddenly started moving again, a frenzy of motion over me and in me, and I thrust back into him with two fingers now, and he cried out, just an inarticulate groan of passion. And then the taste of him, coming in my mouth, filling me with salty fluid.

I held him; I was in control now. I milked him dry, sucked every drop of semen out of his beautiful cock. It went soft as I held it, limp and heavy. There was a slick plop of sound as I let him go. My hands clenched against his butt, and I kissed his cock again and again.

Kendall's eyes were soft as he looked down at me.

He sagged onto my lap, heavy and thick-bodied. We sat still for a few minutes, rocking together against the cool leather. His belly lay against my cock; the tickle of his pubic hair on me made me smile.

After a while, I couldn't stand it any longer. I sat up, struggling against his weight. He had a light film of sweet sweat on his face, and I wiped it away with my thumbs. "Condom?"

He held up a zebra-striped package and grinned. "Jungle Love brand. What do you think?"

"Too cute. I think you should dress me up and let me get busy."

Kendall smiled as he got me prepped. The condom was slick with lube, and cool, while his fingers were warm. When I was ready, I pressed us sideways. His thick thighs wrapped over my waist. I kissed him a few more times, wanting to thrust into him, wanting to ride him like a demon. Something made me hold back.

"What's wrong?" he asked. His face was tight with yearning.

I'm a liar and a bastard for what I'm doing to you.

"Nothing," I answered. "Just savoring the moment."

"Stop savoring and start fucking."

I pushed his knees back and positioned my cock against him. I couldn't meet his eyes, so I closed mine and slipped inside him. Past that band of muscle and then—*oh, god yes, he's tight on me, oh god, so good*—and my brain clicked off. The smell of his skin against mine, the squeak of the sofa springs as I pumped, the feel of his body pressed to me, his arms tight and strong. We stopped kissing; we were just mouthing each other, with soft cries of encouragement and passion. I felt myself climbing, higher, higher as I pumped harder and harder.

"Come in me, Byron. Give it to me." Kendall's husky voice was enough to send me over.

I cried out and came hard.

When I was back to the real world, he was kissing my neck and shoulders, and rubbing his hands over my back. I pulled back but he kept me close. "Stay here, just for a minute." He grimaced and stretched his legs down; I slipped a little out of him. It felt so warm and sweet to be held this way.

It scared me.

This wasn't what I'd signed up for; I was here to do a job.

After a while we lay front to front on the sticky sofa. Kendall smiled, pushed my sweaty hair back, and kissed me. "A shower, a smoke, *and* good sex. Who knew?"

"You feeling better?" I palmed down his torso, admiring his full chest and broad shoulders.

"Yeah, a lot better."

I leaned up and grabbed the throw from the back of the sofa. We snugged a couple of pillows under our heads and lay back together.

Time to push a little more, I decided. "So, you and Ricardo . . . things seem pretty tense between you two."

"Tense? You could say that." He looked away from me, as if embarrassed.

"You guys exes or business partners or what exactly?"

"Soon to be ex-business partners if I have my way."

"What's the deal?"

Kendall sighed. He ran a hand down my chest and fingered my belly button. "Ooooh, an outie. Aren't you too sexy?"

I touched his chin and made him look up at me. "You don't have to talk if you don't want to. But . . . This could be more than just sport-fucking, ya know? If you let it."

His brow furrowed, but he didn't pull away. He pressed closer and let his fingers run over my face. "Light us another joint, wouldja?"

After a couple minutes, the joint was half-gone, and he was more relaxed. I took a couple hits but didn't want to get too stoned; he didn't seem to notice. He told me how Ricardo had showed up a couple years ago when the refuge was in bad financial shape, how Ricardo had funded a lot of the improvements to be certified as a quarantine facility, that Ricardo paid him a salary that anyone south of Atlanta would blink at. Everything seemed good for the first year; then Ricardo started bringing new cats to quarantine. They'd stay for a couple of weeks, then be gone; Kendall didn't find out where they went until this spring.

Ricardo was supplying the game farms in Texas and Alabama. Wholesale prices weren't very high for some big cats. Hell, you could go to any animal auction in the South and buy an adult tiger for six hundred dollars—but the rarer breeds earned Ricardo real money.

"He makes me sick. What he does with these cats makes me sick." Kendall smacked his palm against the sofa. "That fucker."

"What's his hold on you? I mean, it's not the gay thing, is it?"

"He doesn't care who I fuck."

"So, what's the deal?"

Kendall pointed to a few photos over the fireplace. I got up for a closer look. They all showed Kendall and a dark-haired woman. Older? Younger? It was impossible to tell. She had the distinctive appearance of the retarded: her body blockish and solid, her eyes a little flat, her smile innocent and wide. "Sister?" I asked.

"Yeah, two years older. She's not profound, just moderate. We tried her in a group home but even that was too much for her. So, I've got her in an ALF. She's happy there."

"And having her here isn't an option, obviously."

"Not with my job. Maybe if I were an accountant or something. You know how the cats are; I can't even bring her here to visit."

"Is that where you go on Wednesdays?" He nodded. "ALFs like that are expensive, I bet."

"Four grand a month."

"And how much does Ricardo pay you?"

His dark eyes gazed at me, cold now, a little reptilian. Maybe that was the anger. "Enough to take care of her and the cats."

"You trying to get out?"

He sat up on the sofa, the throw puddled over his legs. He palmed his face, pulling his features back into a grimace. "I'm trying to figure out a way to get out. The refuge can't survive on donations alone; we're too isolated. I'd have to get a fucking job."

I sat down again, close. "Or keep fewer animals."

"Not an option." Of course not, not for Kendall.

"You know for sure that Ricardo's selling these animals off to dealers? And that he's importing them illegally?"

"Yeah. He's got a connection with some old Army buddy of his who's still in Thailand. They fly direct into the country, some kind of military plane that doesn't file flight plans. You can buy anything in Bangkok; hell, you can buy *humans* in Bangkok."

"Does he have any records here? Any invoices or receipts?"

"He keeps some kind of ledger in the office. Plus, he has his Palm Pilot."

"Videos, maybe, of the hunts?"

"He's got some in the office with the VCR, but they're old. Most of the stuff he has coded on his Web site."

"Any other evidence?"

Kendall looked at me sharply. I saw the realization hit him, saw the second that he knew I was after something. "Who the hell are you?"

"I'm not who you think I am." I pressed him back and straddled his thick thighs. I nuzzled at his nipples; his chest hair tickled my lips, soft. Kendall groaned. I pinned his thick arms over his head. His pupils were huge; they made his eyes look abnormal, a little creepy. "Maybe there's a way to get you out of this situation. Are you willing to testify against him?"

His eyes went cold. "Will it put him in jail?"

"In prison. And we'll find a way to save these cats you've got now."

He looked over at the mantel and grimaced. A few seconds ticked by. He grabbed my hands and pulled them to his chest. "What do you need me to do?"

The sun was coming up and the room grayed with soft light. I saw hope in his face, a way out of the mess, a way out for the cats. "Okay, here's the plan . . ."

The plan went fine until Ricardo got hold of the kill gun from Kendall's office.

Most wildlife facilities have a shotgun on-site—for a worst-case scenario. It wasn't something a handler ever wanted to face; killing an animal you were trying to protect felt like the worst kind of failure. But you needed one nearby.

There wasn't time to get Kendall wired, so I made do with a little handheld mini recorder tucked into his waistband. I had Russo and his team in the woods outside the entrance, and when the buyer's truck rolled in, I kept my headset on, and hid in the quarantine barn's office. I could see and hear what went on in the walkway and a little of the cages.

Ricardo and his Texas boys strolled through, Kendall a step behind, glowering.

"Look at these cats!" Ricardo banged his walking stick against a cage door.

The black leopard in the cage growled and crouched down in one corner, unwilling to move. Bored, Ricardo turned to the next cage. The spotted leopard there was waiting for him. When he raised his stick, the cat leaped against the barrier at face level, its claws out. The chain link rattled fiercely as it pawed the metal. Ricardo jerked back in surprise, then recovered. He smacked the leopard's paws from the outside, but it didn't back down.

"Stop it." Kendall's voice was tight.

Ricardo just grinned. "They need the excitement."

"No, they need to be back in the wild. They don't belong in these cages." Kendall stood in the aisle, fists clenched.

"I don't need your candy-ass animal rights crap right now. Shut up."

"You know they're endangered and you sell them. You're helping to destroy the entire population."

"These animals are going to die anyway! If I can make some money speeding up that process, then that's my right."

Good work, Kendall. Get him on tape, get the evidence.

The buyers edged out, looking anxious.

"It's not your right, you lousy fuck. You're not taking these leopards; I'm keeping them."

Ricardo's face went blank, utterly smooth. I had that split second of gut warning and before I could get out of the office, into the barn, Ricardo swung his walking stick against Kendall's head. An ugly crack of sound and Kendall crumpled to the dirt floor, on his knees. He covered his face as blood spilled into his eyes and mouth.

It made my guts twist. Seeing him hurt made my chest go cold. How far to let this go? Should I hold back, wait for Kendall to get Ricardo to say the right words?

The cats went nuts.

They smelled the blood, started yowling. They clanged against the metal cages. The leopard closest to Kendall swiped out with one thick paw, snagged his boot. It actually dragged him a few inches toward the cage.

Kendall kicked back and swayed on his knees. The blood from his scalp wound was bright red, healthy-looking. It turned to copper on the barn's dirt floor.

Ricardo prodded his stick into Kendall's belly. "You are not going to ruin my operation here. You work for me, you little shit."

Kendall tried to rise but Ricardo jabbed the stick into his chest, knocking him back into the dirt. The cats paced in their cages, smelling the blood, sensing a potential victim who was injured, vulnerable. Kendall spoke through gritted teeth. "You're not taking them to Texas to kill them. I'll kill them myself, right now, before I let you do this again."

"We'll see who does the killing today." Ricardo slammed the stick against Kendall's neck, and he went down again, face in the dirt.

Ricardo clumped into the office; even with the walking stick he could move pretty fast. He was in the door and grabbing the shotgun off the wall before I even realized it. He turned, saw me, and his eyes went flat again—dangerously cold. I started to reach for my ankle holster, but he smacked me in the belly with the butt of the shotgun. The air whooshed from my lungs in a sickening wrench; I staggered against the desk, trying to stay up.

Ricardo broke the shotgun, checked the shells and marched back out into the barn.

I sucked for air, hitting the desk with my palms, trying to get my lungs to inflate. Gray speckles of light flashed in my vision.

Oh no, I cannot faint now.

It felt like forever, but it was only a few seconds. I heard Russo's voice in my earpiece say "Are you there? Byron, are you hit?"—endlessly, over and over until I could finally get some oxygen.

"Move in! Move in! He's got the shotgun!" My voice was whispery, dry, but I heard Russo's "10-4" from the other end.

I fumbled in my ankle holster and drew my .45. Frightened as I was, I still remembered to clear the doorway before exiting, to check my line of fire even as I moved toward Ricardo. His back was to me, and he prodded Kendall with the ugly end of the shotgun.

Kendall stayed down.

"Drop your weapon, Ricardo! I'm a game commission officer, and I've got a gun on you. Put it down and turn around slowly. Hands in the air!"

He stiffened. I focused on his broad back, ample target area from just four yards away. The gun was still pointed at Kendall's bloody skull.

"Do it, Ricardo! I *will* shoot you. Drop it!"

It was truly slow motion. His head turned first. I saw his wide eyes, his mouth open and snarling—then his stomach made the turn, his left hand on the stock, and he kept turning and turning, the shotgun swinging toward the cage to my left, then around, its metal glinting, his finger on the trigger—*oh, no, the shotgun, oh no no no no!*

I squeezed the .45's trigger fast—one, two, three, just like on the range—and stopped to check my target. Ricardo dropped to his knees, the blossom of blood on his shirt dark red— heart's blood— and his eyes rolled back up and he took forever to pitch face-forward into the dirt.

The shotgun clattered to the ground.

I kept my gun out and bent to check him. No pulse, just warm flesh, still and silent. My earpiece squawked but I couldn't focus on Russo's words. I walked over to Kendall on my knees.

"Hey, Kendall," I said and rolled him over gently. His eyelids fluttered; he groaned like a bull. "Open your eyes for me, please."

His face was slippery with blood. "What happened?" His voice was raspy, filled with pain.

"Ricardo tried to shoot you. How's your head?"

"Shitty. Really shitty."

"You've probably got a concussion. Just lie still." I pressed my headset. "Russo, tell me there's an ambulance on the way. We need medical attention!"

"Pulling in right now. Ambulance is at the back."

"I've got one suspect down, one with a head wound."

"Are you hurt?"

"No, it's Kendall. He's one of the good guys." I managed a half-smile, put one trembling palm on his slick face. He grasped my hand with his, clutching, tight as a cub. The pain in his eyes made me feel nauseated; he'd taken some hits for his cats, and for my operation.

I heard the trucks barreling up the drive. The cats roared and screamed around us.

I bent down and kissed his soft lips. The blood was salty and sweet at the same time.

He let his fingers trail against my chest. "You stay with me?"

"I'm not going anywhere; don't you worry." I kissed his hand and held it until Russo's team arrived and my vision went fuzzy again—just a little—the adrenaline seeping from my system. The EMTs jogged in with a stretcher, and they pushed me away.

I couldn't stand up; too shaky. I watched them work on Kendall with Russo at my side. He took one look at Ricardo's body, oozing blood into the ground, and just stood with a fatherly hand on my shoulder.

Nine days later, the windows were open to a late-season cool front. We woke in Kendall's bed. The bandage was off of his scalp and fresh pink flesh grew over his lacerations. He'd done a night in the hospital, then a week of rest at home. The department put me on administrative leave, SOP after a shooting. I was fine with the time off. Randy and I managed the cats for the week Kendall was down. Hard work.

Each night Kendall and I soaked in the tub together, and he made me forget my sore muscles.

"Wanna go into town and hit the buffet for breakfast?" he asked.

"You that hungry?"

"Starved." His hand worked between my legs, tugging my testicles in a gentle rhythm. My cock filled with blood and stretched up against my belly. "Maybe I need an appetizer first."

"You do."

He nuzzled down my belly as he straddled my thighs. The heat of his mouth on my cock made me shiver—so soft inside yet insistent. He really liked to suck when he gave a blow job; sometimes it tickled and hurt at the same time. I watched his head bob up and down as he wet me with his spit. He kept one hand between my legs, stroking just behind my balls. The other was wrapped around me, squeezing just beneath the cap, just the way I liked it.

I loved watching him over me: his gleaming skull, his neck muscles that corded as he worked my cock, his shoulders smooth-skinned and solid. His long eyelashes lay against his cheeks, hiding his beautiful eyes. He jerked me faster, and my breathing picked up and sweat prickled my chest and belly.

Close now, so close.

"Look at me when I come." My voice was scratchy. "Make me come, Kendall."

He bent lower, took me into his throat and milked me. The pressured heat ran up my balls and throbbed through my cock. He raised his eyes to mine just as I came and held me with his gaze as he swallowed me down. My fingers gripped his shoulders until the skin turned red, and I bucked up with my hips, wanting to fill him up with more, more, more.

He let me go and kissed up my belly. The breeze carried in the whiff of wild animal and just as he lay his head on my chest, Walter's roar belted through the compound.

A Different Trick

Steve Berman

Tyler West, dressed for another man's fantasy, walked from his black sports car up the sidewalk and to the house's porch. He adjusted the shoulder strap of the tank top he wore—one size too small, so that it bit into his tan skin—and felt rather ridiculous standing there in suburbia in his weekend club clothes on a bright Tuesday afternoon. Impatient and anxious for his "private screening" to begin and end, he pushed the doorbell twice.

Through the stained glass of the door, he glimpsed a shadow. Chilled, air-conditioned air swept over Tyler as his new client opened the door. Tyler guessed the man's age to be mid-forties, at the edge of decline. Wearing a sallow-colored polo shirt over khaki slacks, the john resembled so many other middle-class husbands with the same deep, dark secret. His features had already begun to sag and sink, gaining another stubbled chin, and a stomach eclipsing his belt. In a few more years, the man would be another closeted, gray zombie to Tyler.

"Rick?" Tyler advanced, making sure that a hand rested near his packed crotch.

The man grimaced slightly, making his face look all the more unattractive. "Please, refer to me as Mr. Walsh."

Tyler nodded but inside his head he groaned. Walsh would be another tough one. He had gone into this whole meeting wary, ever since the man had bombarded him with questions even after the e-mail with frontal pictures, rates, and specialties. If not for the promise of an extra hundred dollars to drive out to Santa Monica on short notice, Tyler would have passed. But the money would buy another line of cocaine.

Walsh stepped aside and let Tyler inside the house before closing the door behind him. Then the man turned to Tyler and eyed him up and down for a few moments, while the porn star remained still and allowed his thoughts to drift off and wonder whether his regular dealer had the premium shit.

"Take your shirt off."

Tyler's initial reaction was to demand his fee first. He normally never asked for money up front, but then he rarely ever encountered so much attitude before. He bit his lip, deciding that Walsh was the sort who'd argue endlessly anyway and probably refuse.

With practiced ease, Tyler slowly peeled off the thin cotton tank, revealing inch after inch of ripped abs followed by firm pecs with twin pierced nipples. Just below his neck, in the crevice of his chest, a tattoo of an arrowhead pointed down.

Walsh nodded as if satisfied and started walking down the front hall, turning right at the first open doorway. Holding his shirt in his hands, Tyler followed.

He expected a den with a big, hopefully comfy, sofa in front of a widescreen television with some porn movie already playing. Probably *Summer Fling 2*. The johns always liked that one, especially the scene where Tyler sucked off the blond twink pool boy in the deep end.

But Tyler found himself in a small library. The shelves on the walls were overloaded with tattered volumes. More old books cluttered the floor and a desk. Sheets of notepaper, covered with endless scribbles, were scattered about the room. Tyler picked up the nearest page but didn't recognize the language. It may have been French, but then he had never bothered to pay much attention in high school to anything but Ass. Beneath one long stretch of words was a crudely drawn circle with a comical stick figure spread-eagle.

"That's private." Walsh snatched the paper out of Tyler's hands. The sheet's edge sliced against the soft pad of the porn star's thumb. Tyler sucked at it, barely keeping a curse in his mouth.

The client pushed back the hard wooden chair from the desk, disturbing one stack of books on the seat. Tyler saw titles like *Damballah in Haiti* and *Sympathetic Rites* fall to the floor.

Walsh sat down and motioned for Tyler to come closer. When he did, the man's hands began to roam over the porn star's body, as if smearing paint over a canvas, especially along the ridges of his six-pack abdomen and the hardening lump in his shorts. Tyler moaned as convincingly as possible. Four videos and over a year of escorting had given him a repertoire of grunts and groans to suggest pleasure. He rested his hands on the man's balding head, which felt clammy to the touch. He closed his eyes. In his mind, he saw not Walsh but rather the handsome face of Bobby, his roommate and lover. He thought of Bobby's silly habit of wearing strawberry lip gloss or those startling blue eyes looking up at him, seeking permission before swallowing cock.

Tyler's shorts were tugged down, revealing flimsy European briefs that hid nothing. Fingers groped at the elastic band of the briefs, nearly tearing the silky material in their haste to free the goods within.

Bobby always kissed his dick before taking it in his mouth. A whimsical peck on his pecker, that made Tyler smile. Then warmth and wetness spreading over the shaft until Tyler had buried all seven inches deep and glossed lips brushed against cropped, dark pubic hair.

But Walsh shattered the illusion with his crude technique. He nipped rather than licked, stuffed rather than sucked, barely going farther than the fat vein three inches down. Tyler was forced to open his eyes and regard the man giving one of the worst blow jobs he had ever been inflicted. The scratch of teeth on the delicate underside made him wince and pull the man off his cock.

"What about you?" Tyler asked, trying to change the direction of the affair. Walsh grinned for the first time. The porn star decided the man must be a lawyer or a car salesman or broker or something. No one honest possessed such a sly grin.

He watched as the man stood up and started to strip. He did not offer to help Walsh. The body underneath was starkly pale and matted with reddish hair, becoming unruly around the man's crotch and legs.

An uncut dick, still wrapped by an excessive amount of white, wrinkled foreskin, swayed to its own tune at Tyler. He looked down at the thick and almost grotesque organ and suppressed a shudder.

Walsh threw down his clothes with as much regard as he must have given his books. He groped at his own crotch, offering it with a wiggle to Tyler.

The porn star kneeled down, hearing the crackle of loose papers underneath him, and reached for the offensive dick. With a touch, the foreskin withdrew a little bit, revealing a purplish head surrounded by a corona of smeary white. A pungent odor drifted to Tyler, who struggled not to gag even before he brought his face closer.

"Suck that cock," barked Walsh.

Four hundred dollars, Tyler told himself. Four hundred for just an hour's worth of suffering. He could survive. The sweet promise of getting so high that nothing mattered was there, waiting for him.

With a deft move, his index finger wiped off most of the smegma, and then Tyler went down.

Walsh abused his mouth for what seemed like forever, treating it like a street hustler's rear, each thrust truly a fuck rather than a push. All the while, the man mouthed coarse words, some of which Tyler couldn't even understand. He was too busy trying to suck in air through his nose, keeping his thoughts from the sour taste and odor.

Then he heard Walsh start to gasp out, "Swallow my load. Eat it all." He fell back, the man's dick noisily slipping out of his throat.

"Fuck you. I don't do that shit." A lie, of course, but Walsh didn't know that. Bobby always shuddered and delivered a thick load in his mouth to cap off every lovemaking session of theirs.

Walsh's eyes narrowed and his mouth turned down. "I'm paying you a shitload of money—"

"If you want cheap and easy, go to West Hollywood." Tyler wiped his mouth. He wanted to gargle for hours with industrial-strength mouthwash.

"I'll pay an extra fifty bucks." Walsh reached for Tyler's head, fingers almost clawing at the escort's dark curls.

Tyler shook his head. "Uh-uh." He grabbed hold of the man's cock tightly. "If you want to get off, this is the only way. Otherwise, I'm out the door." He began tugging.

Walsh remained tight-lipped but let him jerk away. A few minutes later, the man shuddered and Tyler's chest was splattered with three smears of yellowish cum he quickly wiped off with the nearest cloth, being Walsh's polo.

The john collapsed in the chair, still dripping. Tyler reached for his clothes. Whether or not sixty minutes had passed since he walked through the front door, he was done. "Leave your underwear," Walsh muttered as he rubbed his damp groin.

Tyler gave him a scathing look. "That's extra."

"How much?"

"You're serious?"

Again that twisted grin.

Tyler shrugged. At this point, he only wanted to leave. "Thirty."

"Fine." Not bothering to put on a shred of clothing, Walsh picked up the escort's briefs and headed out of the room. One smudged page stuck to the bottom of his left foot.

Slipping on his shorts and shirt, Tyler left the library after him. He found Walsh standing in front of the fireplace in the den across the hall. Tribal masks hung on the wall. Walsh began taking bills from a carved wooden box resting on the mantel.

Tyler made sure to count all the money in front of Walsh. Let the asshole know that it was all business. Every dollar was there at least.

Still holding Tyler's underwear, Walsh bent down and started piling up wood in the fireplace. Tyler decided that the man was truly insane to start a fire in August and didn't bother waiting for Walsh to show him out. He stuffed the bills into his pocket and slammed the door shut behind him.

The inside of his car was steaming hot even with the windows slightly rolled down. Tyler wiped at the sweat that quickly beaded on his forehead and upper lip and cranked up the air-conditioning, turning the dial to the maximum, the brightest splash of cool blue on the dashboard. The air blew out from every vent but as he sped off down the street, tires squealing, he still felt too warm, especially his ass on the seat. He shifted about, jerking a bit as he struggled to find a spot on the seat that didn't burn.

He was almost at the highway entrance when he smelled smoke. Not the acrid odor of burning wires or oil, but more of a singed meat scent. A sharp pain tore at his legs and he looked down to see the fine dark hairs on his calves begin to glow orange and burn, shriveling black. His hands instinctively left the wheel to slap at his thighs and the car careened to the side of the road, running up onto the shoulder before he grabbed the steering wheel again.

When his groin caught fire, Tyler screamed, braking suddenly, pitching forward to strike his face against the wheel. But the pain from a broken nose was nothing compared to the agony as the flames spread. Smoke rose from every limb. He felt the heat escape from his open throat and the screams only died down when there was little left of him to burn.

The rough growl of mowers woke Frank Manes from dreams of boys. He blinked at the afternoon sun that snuck through the living room blinds and tried to roll over on the narrow sofa bed to hide from the light, but one of the annoying springs in the old mattress struck a tender spot in his belly. The sharp stab of pain chased away any chance of returning to sleep.

He had to unwrap himself from the many sheets and blankets. His sister kept the apartment bitter cold even though the electric bill threatened triple-digit numbers. He found he was hard, the "morning wood" as porn stories called it, and he idly scratched his boxers down there.

Frank sat up and groped around on the nearby coffee table for his glasses. With them, the world came back into focus. The springs squeaked their displeasure at having to bear his nearly 300 pounds. They groaned again when he rose up, feeling a bit unsteady. He decided his blood sugar must be low and hoped there was enough frosted cereal for a bowl.

The thought of breakfast woke his stomach, which loudly agreed with his diagnosis before arguing with his full bladder over priority. It seemed sure that his stomach would win the battle, when Frank's plodding steps took him past his computer and he stopped to notice that the Caribbean-style screensaver had been interrupted with a flashing red exclamation point.

Frank could never refuse his PC. He sat his bulk down on the folding chair and tapped the keyboard. Immediately the exclamation point vanished, replaced with a box that read *West Update*. The message, a programmed alert of the latest news on Frank's favorite porn star, Tyler West, brought new life to his dick.

He let his hands roam over the keyboard like a blind man's reading Braille. His eyelids drooped, his breathing—nearly always labored these days—became heavier, thicker, almost gasps through a slack jaw.

Working on the computer always had this effect on Frank. He never quite understood how or why he drifted along, barely noticing his thick fingers stabbing at the keys. Windows popped open and closed on the screen in quick succession. Once he had taken an online typing test, curious to see how many words per minute he could achieve. He thought he might reach 20, maybe 25, but the screen had been a shock: 115. He tried taking the test again, purposefully slowing down, barely tapping away, and still 115. Before he even opened his e-mail—which would be only porn pictures from newsgroups, updates on the latest sci-fi movies in production, and the inevitable offer to make money at home stuffing envelopes—Frank clicked the box that promised news on Tyler West.

COURTESY OF ADULT VIDEOS REPORTS
Gay Vid Star *'Flaming Wreck'*

Sammy Rudder, aka Tyler West, died in a car accident Tuesday afternoon July 23. Rudder, 24, star of such hits as *City of Brotherly Love, Summer Fling 2,* and *Whores d'Oeuvres,* was driving on County Road 133 when he lost control of the car. Off the road, Rudder's black Camaro caught fire. Three pedestrians tried unsuccessfully to rescue Rudder. Nearby residents also came out with fire extinguishers to help. All could hear the actor's pleas for help from inside the burning car. Seven minutes later, the fire department arrived, but it was too late.

Rudder enjoyed the attention of the porn industry and raced cars on his off-hours. His partner Bobby Drale once remarked to AVR that his lover belonged behind the steering wheel of a Formula 1 racecar and not in front of the camera. A private memorial service is being held this week.

Frank stared in disbelief. *Not Tyler West,* he thought. In his head, he begged for it all to be a lie. Or better yet, a publicity stunt. He read the report over, twice, three times, not wanting to believe. His hands stayed utterly still, yet smaller windows opened on the screen with pictures of the late porn star and corroborating reports. He felt sick to his stomach and belched, tasting the sour remains of the cold sausage pizza he had devoured as a late-night snack.

Reality had never been Frank's friend. Being 34 and obese was a bitter fact he constantly sought to overlook through the help of television, the Internet, and especially pornography. The joy of being able to watch gorgeous guys have sex right there in front of you satisfied those cravings of Frank's that greasy food and refined sugar could not meet. He had never even kissed a guy and yet, when he watched someone like Tyler West jack off on a Philadelphia rooftop in *City of Brotherly Love,* Frank could believe the performance was just for him.

Now reality had snuck back into the deepest, most private reaches of Frank's life and spoiled that by stealing away his favorite star.

Unconsciously called upon, information on car accidents and the safety record of Camaros flashed across his monitor. A streaming video of a nearly nude West driving a sports car on a racing track began. Frank's eyes tried to take everything in and failed, but somehow his brain caught every bit and byte.

It made no sense, he realized. Tyler West was an excellent driver. A moment later, Frank's curiosity had hacked away and Sammy Rudder's driving record was uploaded from the DMV. No points. No tickets. Flawless, like the guy's tan skin. West—Rudder—was not a careless driver and a brand-new car just doesn't burst into flames after being driven off the road.

Reality was wrong. "Fucking wrong," Frank muttered and scratched at the stubble on his chin with both hands as more information from police and coroner reports flew across his screen. No impact damage on the burnt frame. Parts of Rudder reduced to ashes.

None of it made any sense to Frank. He felt a gnawing sickness fill his gut and he leaned back and whimpered, glad that his sister had not yet come home from her shift at the diner to see him nearly in tears over some pretty guy's death hundreds of miles away. She'd never understand. She had her dates with crummy guys that were little better than eight-percent tips. Frank needed guys like Tyler West. He owed them.

That realization made the screen come alive with travel Web sites. Before he even realized it, the computer searched for cheap flights, booking a round-trip coach class for him later that evening. The funeral. He simply had to attend that funeral and say goodbye properly.

The decision seemed to calm him. Frank rose up from the chair and felt a quiver of excitement. Not some furtive thrill but a new sensation brought on by a plan of action. He would pay his respects, and in doing so, become closer to his idol than he had ever thought possible. He shuffled toward the kitchen. He needed some breakfast, even though it was past 3 p.m.; he needed all his strength to pack and get to the airport.

The skies over the cemetery mirrored Bobby Drale's mood: cloudy, uncertain, threatening rain. Or in his case, tears. So far he had not yet cried. Deep down, he could feel the need, still distant, yet very real. Only, his mind could not keep from being distracted. At every turn, something other than Sammy popped into his head, often the most ridiculous notions. Had he picked up the dry cleaning? Should he call and cancel his dentist appointment on Wednesday?

Someone hugged him from behind. He glanced over his shoulder and saw yet another handsome face, another co-worker of Sammy's. Really a co-worker of Tyler West's, with bleached hair and a bronze cast that looked fake in the dying light of the day.

"How are you holding up?" the top whispered, his voice trying not to be sultry for once.

Bobby nodded an answer. He was sick of being asked that. What could he really say? That he was thinking about whether or not his meeting on Monday at the AIDS Fund office would last over an hour? He'd only seem insensitive, an asshole. They didn't understand he simply could not think about Sammy right then.

He looked away as the rather plain casket was lowered into the ground. His cheek felt suddenly wet and, for a moment, relief flooded him, until he took a hand to his face and discovered it was only a pre-emptive raindrop. He wiped it away with a sigh.

The mourners started to disperse, heading back to the condo. At any moment one of them would come over and tug him along, no doubt offering yet another line of condolences. Bobby glanced at the people getting into their cars. When had so many of their friends become little more than pretty dolls or rich old men who liked to play with them? They all looked alike.

Except there was one stranger. Like Bobby, he had yet to leave the gravesite. The man stood out from the rest. An immense frame that hadn't seen the inside of a gym since high school. Face raw from a cheap razor blade. Nervously shuffling about in the same place, unable to look at anyone directly. Who was he?

Bobby tried to sift through his memories and not the million petty things that begged for notice. Sammy's family these days was a sick mother in a hospice in Florida and a Calvinist sister somewhere in the Midwest. Neither had responded to the news. Unless this was some long-lost cousin.

Perhaps a friend? Doubtful. Poor Sammy barely spoke to anyone who had more than eight percent body fat.

His curiosity now taking over, Bobby walked over to where the stranger stood. The heavy face actually blanched, then blushed, when he came near.

"Are you a friend of Sammy's?" The words came out more accusatory than Bobby had wanted.

The man shook his head no. His eyes, red-rimmed from crying, grew wide and scared. Bobby felt a pang of envy. If wasn't fair that this man could cry over Sammy and he couldn't!

"Family, then?"

Again the same response. Finally, the man licked his lips nervously. "I am an . . . admirer." It seemed to deflate him to say the last word, and even with the large build, he seemed smaller to Bobby, who nodded in understanding. The man was a fan. Nothing more.

Bobby held out a hand. "I'm Bobby Drale."

The other hesitated a moment then took the offered hand in a heavy squeeze. "Frank Manes."

Manes' accent was decidedly East Coast. Bobby looked over the man, saw his rumpled clothing. "You didn't fly out here for this?"

Manes looked away toward the rectangular hole and nodded.

Bobby stifled a laugh, realizing that it was utterly inappropriate but feeling still an odd sense of humor that a fan would come across the country just to see a guy who got fucked for a living laid to rest. "You must have really liked him." The barest of chuckles came out at the end.

"Yeah," said Manes. "Though you were his . . ."

"Boyfriend? Lover?" The guy, Bobby realized, was so out of sorts he could barely function.

One of the pretty mourners called to Bobby from the hearse.

"Are you coming back to the condo?" Bobby asked Manes.

"I wasn't sure . . . I mean, I don't really belong . . ."

Bobby laid a hand on Manes' shoulder. The man trembled beneath him at the touch. "Nonsense. I want you to come back." He was surprised how much he did want Manes there. He needed someone real there. "If anyone asks, you're a friend of mine from college, okay?"

Manes smiled, his grin transforming his face from lumps of clay to something approaching eager art.

Together, the two made their way to the diminishing line of cars on the path that threaded itself through the cemetery. The rain began to fall.

Frank could not believe his luck. Considering he had never been anyplace, somehow natural instincts had guided him through the airport, to a waiting cab, and to negotiate with the Haitian the address of the funeral. That he had made it just as the nondenominational service was beginning seemed like a gift. But for Tyler West's lover to come over and to talk to him, to invite him back to where the two had lived together, seemed almost too much to bear.

He wondered, as he slid into a car being driven by a man who wore more jewelry and perfume than Frank's sister, if Tyler's untimely death had cracked reality and now anything could happen.

The condo was bright and airy, with immense ceilings, the flip side to the cramped apartment Frank suffered in. There were tables with food—not cold cuts but dainty pieces that looked more like tiny sculptures arranged on platters—and bottles and bottles of wine and liquor. If people had been laughing, Frank would have mistaken the affair for a party. When he felt sure that no one was looking, Frank scooped up a handful of snacks and popped them into his mouth. Some sort of fish and cream cheese exploded on his tongue. He washed the food down with a generous sip of a red wine he had never heard of before.

"So I heard you knew Bobby from Penn State?" The question came from an older man dressed in a tasteful charcoal suit. The hair, though, moussed and spiky, seemed a desperate attempt to turn back the clock a few decades.

Frank froze for a moment under the man's stare, before remembering the lie Bobby had offered him.

"What did you study?"

"Computers." The word came unbidden to Frank's lips. It was the only topic he felt comfortable speaking about. Anything else and he'd be tongue-tied.

"Really?" One carefully plucked eyebrow rose on the man. "You wouldn't happen to know anything about Web design, would you? My site's original graphic designer left me in a bind when he dropped everything and flew to the Netherlands to let loose his inner girlfriend."

Frank wasn't sure exactly what the last comment meant, but he nodded absently anyway. "I've done sites before." He didn't offer that the pages, while receiving Internet awards, were filled with fan fiction on the sexual exploits of Star Trek characters.

"I assume because you're here," the man said, motioning with an arm at some of the beautiful men in the room, "that working with porn stars doesn't bother you."

Frank gulped nervously and finished off the rest of his glass of wine. "I love porn," he managed to say after swallowing.

"Excellent." The man's manicured hand slipped inside his jacket to pull out a vibrantly colored card. In rainbow letters was printed HOT PUP PRODUCTIONS, the name HAL CARROLL, EXECUTIVE, and a phone number and e-mail address. "Perhaps we can talk business later." Carroll, smiling, leaned in closer, his lips almost brushing against Frank's ear. "When it's more appropriate."

Frank watched the man walk off to put his arm around a little blonde thing in a silk shirt. He looked back down at the card in his hands, feeling a bit dazed.

"They're always schmoozing, seducing."

He turned around to see a pale Bobby standing behind him, a plate of half-eaten food in his hand.

"It never stops. Sometimes I think the motto is 'The porn must go on.'" He bit his lip. "At least for some it does."

"I'm sorry about Tyler . . . I mean Sammy."

Bobby shrugged. "So is everyone. But I think you're one of the few that really means that. Are you staying in the area long?"

Frank brought up the memory of his travel arrangements. "My flight back's tomorrow night."

"You have a hotel room?"

Frank's mood suddenly crashed. In his mad rush to make the funeral, he had not even considered where he was going to spend the night. Apparently his oversight was legible on his face, for Bobby smiled and offered him the guest room.

"I-I couldn't—"

"Please. I insist. Do you honestly think I want to be alone in this place tonight?" In mid-gesture, the food almost slipped off the plate onto the hardwood floors. "I could use a sympathetic soul right now."

Even after helping to finish off an entire bottle of that wonderful wine, Frank still could not fall asleep. The mattress seemed so soft, the sheets so delicate compared to the cheap sleeping arrangements he had grown accustomed to. He almost yearned for the sound of his sister's snoring coming through the thin walls.

Maybe a snack would settle him. He eased out of the bed and tried to step quietly, not wanting to awaken Bobby, who had been so kind to him that day. He was beginning to believe the lie that they were long-lost friends.

The refrigerator shelves were packed with uneaten remainders and, in the dark, Frank helped himself to his newest discovery: cheese that wasn't served in individually wrapped slices. Between mouthfuls he drank a bit more wine and wondered if such a snack made him "continental" now.

Belly feeling a bit more full, he lightly tottered toward the bathroom, only to be disappointed when he saw the door shut and a line of yellow light showing underneath and through the old-fashioned keyhole. He was about to head back to bed when he heard a light moan and the sound of Bobby's voice whispering the name "Sammy."

Frank eased himself down onto his knees. A brief mutter of shame sounded in his head but the voyeur's voice also there promised more. He brought an eye to the keyhole and saw something wondrous.

Bobby sat on the toilet, his white briefs down around his ankles. He was jerking off, almost violently slamming his grip up and down along the length of a slender cock. Every muscle in the young man was stretched taut, especially along the chest and arms, as Bobby leaned back, his head against the wall, and pounded.

Frank found himself more aroused than ever before. More than he had been while watching the best of porn, even the videos of Tyler West. This was live, the soft grunts, the sound of flesh rubbing against flesh, the smell of sweat rising in the air.

Bobby shuddered and again whispered for Sammy. He stretched out his legs, the toes beginning to curl with the effort.

Frank's own hand was wrapped around his dick, fingers brushing against the damp curls of dark pubic hair.

Then Bobby erupted, his cock spraying out volley after volley of white cum. His stomach began a pool of the fluid as he nearly convulsed.

Frank felt his own orgasm grow near. On edge, he clamped his mouth shut, not wanting to groan in pleasure when he came.

Only, what he saw changed everything. Instead of wiping the cooling cum over his body, like they did in the videos, Bobby began to whimper and finally cry. The sobs grew deeper as the young man slipped off the toilet and fell onto the floor, tears dripping down his face, semen sliding off his body to the tiles.

Frank suddenly felt terrible for peeking, especially after the kindness and hospitality Bobby had shown. He crawled away from the door until he was a safe distance and struggled to get to his feet without making a sound. He went back to the guest bedroom. For all his life he had been envious of the beautiful people. The notion that, even with the right face and body, you could still be unhappy, was new to him. Before he drifted off to sleep, he knew that come tomorrow, he'd have to do something to repay Bobby's generosity.

"You made coffee?" Bobby's voice called from the kitchen. A moment later, "It's good" followed.

"My sister works at a diner. I think it's the only thing she ever taught me."

In the morning, Frank had found a laptop computer in the corner of the living room. Without thinking, he had set it up on the coffee table and begun surfing the net. Though Tyler West was buried, the notion that his death was so unfair, so wrong, had not left Frank. So he had started to explore.

Bobby walked into the room wearing the same briefs from last night and a terry cloth bathrobe. Frank looked up and blushed when he caught himself staring at the obvious basket and returned his eyes to the safety of the monitor.

"So you are a computer wiz."

Bobby's presence was palpable over his shoulder. The young man had a smell about him, the remnant of cologne, maybe a hint of lavender from the bed sheets. It was a bit intoxicating and proving to be a distraction.

"I guess," Frank muttered. He purposefully grazed the keyboard with his fingers, not exerting enough pressure to actually press a key but to give the illusion he was typing fast. Frank did not understand why computers reacted to him, but he did not want to freak Bobby out by seeing him explore without using his hands at all.

What Frank had discovered since 9 a.m. was disturbing. He wasn't sure if he should share the facts, let alone his theories, with Bobby, after seeing how upset the guy had been last night. Yet, he knew that Tyler, if only his own personal eidolon of the porn star, deserved to rest in peace.

"Did you know that Tyler, I mean Sammy, well, he hung out with other guys?"

He heard a sigh from behind him. He glanced over his shoulder and saw that Bobby had moved to the couch.

"Sammy liked to think we had an open relationship."

Frank shook his head. "No, not just sleeping around. I mean . . . well, I think he met other men, older men for money."

For a moment, Frank was sure that Bobby was going to start yelling at him and throw him out. The young man's eyes narrowed and his mouth opened, ready to shout. Then the handsome face fell apart and it seemed ready for more tears. "I listened to every lie he said and wanted so much to believe him that I think I did. Sammy always liked attention. That's why he started working in porn. He loved being watched, being lusted after. Only, once the money came in, he also wanted coke really bad. The problem with fantasies, Frank, is that sometimes you spend so much time with them you never notice they've become nightmares."

Frank felt embarrassed, not for himself like he usually did, but for Bobby. He had no experience comforting others. He turned back to the laptop, to a world he was confident in.

"I've been snooping around. Sammy's death seemed too weird. He was this awesome driver—"

Bobby gave a bitter chuckle. "You really are a fan. You know everything."

"Do I creep you out?"

Bobby was quiet for a moment. "A little. But at least you're honest, unlike most people that knew Sammy. So what did you find?"

"Sammy was escorting regularly. I've read his e-mails back and forth to guys he calls 'clients.'"

"I don't think I want to hear this, after all."

"No, it's important. The last guy Sammy went to see—a guy named Walsh—well, he seems ready for the *X-Files*." Frank tapped the screen with a finger. An image of Walsh from his driver's license appeared.

"What do you mean?" Bobby asked.

"When I dug deeper, I found the guy is into some strange shit. Maybe he's read too much Stephen King, but he's ordered books on voodoo and bought black candles and witchcraft stuff online."

"Wait; this sounds like you're saying—"

"I don't know what to really think, but the guy's strange, really strange. I even found an arrest for cruelty to animals. The guy was torturing a goat."

"So you think he was somehow involved in Sammy's death?"

Frank looked over his shoulder. "Maybe. Guys don't spontaneously combust in sports cars. All I'm saying is that I think you and me should just check him out. In person."

Bobby sat there, apparently thinking about what he had been told. Absently the young man scratched his inner thigh, an act that made him seem even sexier to Frank. "Okay. You find him, I'll go along."

Bobby looked across the street at the unassuming house and wondered what had happened inside, only a few days ago. Frank, who sat cramped in the compact car's passenger seat, seemed sure that the man inside, this Walsh guy, did something. Bobby wanted to believe him—if only to bring some sense of closure to Sammy's odd death—but the notion that black magic had caused the crash and fire seemed ridiculous. But he had listened to Frank, had driven out to the address, and now found himself ready to go in and confront Walsh and find out the truth. *Even if that turned out to be nothing more than some weird old john had paid to fuck his boyfriend who got careless on the drive home?,* he asked himself. He wasn't sure of an answer.

"Are you having second thoughts?" Frank shifted about on the seat, no doubt trying to find some way to comfortably sit his large frame.

"I don't know if I can act like a hustler."

Bobby had watched as Frank had found Walsh online looking for a hookup. Under a newly created screen name, Frank had started a conversation with the guy and in less than ten minutes, pictures had been exchanged, services discussed, and a "date" arranged for that afternoon. Bobby was amazed at the ease with which Frank had handled the computer, as if the clumsiness of the man's size was merely an illusion for a deft interior.

"All you have to do is make sure the door is unlocked for me. Distract him while I look around."

"Distract him?" Bobby looked at Frank dubiously. "I'm not going to fuck him."

"You don't have to. Just flirt with him for a while, lead him on. You have your cell phone with you. I'll signal you from inside when I find something. No matter what, in twenty minutes tops, we'll both be out of there."

Bobby shook his head. It was crazy, he knew, but Frank seemed so sure of himself that the idea was contagious.

He took a deep breath and then turned down the mirror and checked himself out. His eyes still looked a little bloodshot from crying; thankfully he had started last night while trying to relive one last moment with Sammy. But he looked okay enough that Walsh would probably want him.

"Frank, I need this to work," he said getting out of the car.

"We both do," came the reply.

Frank watched Bobby walk up to the front door from the vantage of the damned clown car he sat in, one he was sure the Japanese had built as revenge for World War II. He felt a protective urge to rush out and stop the young man from ringing the bell, to call off the entire crazy scheme. Not that he doubted Walsh was involved, but he worried that he'd never find some way to prove it.

What had he been thinking? There'd be a pile of trophies from the guy's kills? An ugly man opened the door and let Bobby in. Frank swallowed his doubts and squeezed himself out and loose of the car. He felt almost naked while dashing across the street to the house. His hand wrapped around the doorknob and he feared it to be locked tight, but it turned gently in his grip.

He slowly opened the door, mindful not to cause a sound. He heard conversation not far away and stopped. The sound began to fade as Walsh took Bobby deeper into his house. Frank stepped into the foyer and closed the door behind him.

He headed away from the voices and found himself in a den. Graphic porn magazines, alongside a plastic candy dish, littered the table. In the corner of the room, almost hidden from view, was a small mahogany computer desk. The blank flat-screen was an open invitation to Frank.

He merely touched the plastic shell surrounding the dark glass and it sprung to life. He winced at the soft melody coming through the tiny speakers as the computer booted awake. Closing his eyes, Frank could still see, not his surroundings but rather a complex, three-dimensional view of an electronic world of information, details, all registering in some cathode ghost in his brain.

Walsh kept a database of recipes. He paid his bills online. There was a family tree. His address book included fifteen local Chinese restaurants. Nothing helpful, nothing incriminating. Frank's resolve began to falter. He worried that he had been wrong, blinded for his need to prove that something had been amiss, when dumb luck had been the only culprit in Sammy Rudder's demise.

He found a journal. His mind scanned the document entries, not so much reading each and every word, but registering the content as if bringing up old memories. Nothing concise, the writing was barely lucid at times, with cryptic references to "understanding secrets" and the "truth behind events in Haiti and New Orleans." He needed more.

He thought he heard someone shout. Was Bobby in trouble? He began a frantic hunt through every file, every sector, his mind scanning e-mails, links, anything that Walsh's computer had visited, contacted, or touched in weeks, months. The effort made him dizzy, weak, and he felt his knees threaten to collapse.

And that's when he discovered the firewall surrounding the server. He reacted like an enraged bull, heedless of what was behind the obstacle, plunging headfirst. He felt a jolt of pain and his face was suddenly warm and wet. "I'm bleeding," he realized. He tasted the coppery tang of the blood streaming out of his nose. But he pushed through the wall and found the true horrors of Walsh's interests.

The Web site didn't have any recognizable address, just a madcap jumble of alphanumerics—a tactic used by child pornography sites. Diagrams and crude pictures were interlaced with text. But as opposed to the journal, the meaning behind the words was very evident. Voodoo. Something called "sympathetic magic," which Frank's mind cross-indexed with online dictionaries and sources to learn was the basis behind voodoo dolls: taking a personal memento or a scrap of hair or fingernail and working magic through the doll to affect the owner.

But this was no theory according to the site. Frank could see that each and every entry was made by Walsh, recounting his experiments, his failures, but most disturbingly his successes. The latest update, only a few days ago, details the hiring of Tyler West. The entry was written with an obvious angry and haughty tone, with special description paid to Walsh's professed cleverness at getting revenge on the porn star's reluctance to submit by burning his underwear in the fireplace and working a spell that set poor Sammy himself ablaze.

The shouts were definite now and louder. Walsh had killed before and Bobby could well be next. All it would take was Walsh lashing out and ripping a few strands of blond hair from Bobby's head or maybe a scrap of shirt.

Frank couldn't let that happen. Bad enough that Sammy had died, but Bobby was truly the more innocent party; Bobby had come along out of a sense of devotion to someone who cheated on him again and again. Sammy had never repaid that love, but Frank would not abandon the first guy to ever be really kind to him.

He began to delete. Not just the entries and the sick pictures on the site. Everything, every trace of Walsh he could find. The journal. Old e-mails. His criminal record. He went past protected areas in government databanks, knowing that the pain caused by breaking through every ethereal barrier was real and inflicted upon himself. Any trace, any mention of Walsh was systematically hunted down and expunged. Until finally, the last remaining reference, a social security number, was erased digit by digit. The house went quiet, and Frank collapsed onto the floor.

 He woke with a damp coolness on his brow. He looked up and saw a smiling Bobby kneeling over him.

 "Easy; an ambulance is on the way."

 "What happened?" he croaked. He tasted blood in his mouth.

 "Walsh got tired with me stalling and grabbed for me. So I punched him. Bastard leapt at me and was crazy. I think he tried to rip out my hair." Bobby lightly touched the back of his head. "Then he was gone. Just disappeared."

 Frank smiled. Sympathetic magic. Welcome to the twenty-first century, Mr. Walsh, and good-bye.

 "I take it you did that somehow?"

 Frank was too weak to nod. In the distance he heard the sound of sirens.

 "Don't worry. I'll stay with you." One of Bobby's hands rubbed his cheek.

 Frank had never been touched like that before, and he could feel the warmth from the touch spread through his entire body. Whatever pain he felt fled to be replaced by a newfound sense of accomplishment and satisfaction.

Fade to Red

Max Reynolds

Colin Murray woke up cold in the backseat of the Buick that used to feel more comfortable than his own bed. He was naked and trussed, wrists to ankles, like some barnyard animal from his grandparents' farm. He had an immense and inexplicable hard-on and an even more intense headache, and the side of his face was wet and sticky. It was either blood or semen. He couldn't be sure which. All he knew was that he could use an ice pack for his head and someone to jerk off this massive throbbing in his dick.

Colin Murray knew this hadn't been LaVerne's doing. This wasn't her MO; she liked to preserve what she called her feminine side, even as he was pumping her ass full of his dick, riding her harder than he had ever ridden any of the other young men who had come in and out of his life during his ten years as a top detail man for the FBI. Ten years as a G-man, as LaVerne liked to call him. No, Colin would be smelling LaVerne's perfume even as he was feeling her cock, stiff as his own, pressing hard against his stomach. Suddenly her voice wouldn't be as whispery as it was at the club and then she would beg him to slam her, ram her, fuck her into whatever it was they were fucking on. Sometimes she would just spurt against him when he was fucking her, and he would feel her claw at his back and pull him closer, rubbing that hidden cock of hers off against him. Other times he would reach down and take her surprisingly big dick in his hand and jerk her off as he fucked her ass. No, he and LaVerne understood each other. She was a mick from the Lower East Side just like he was and although he was the law and she was breaking many of them daily, they were tuned in to each other. They protected each other in these Commie-baiting, queer-hating days with Joe McCarthy looking for anyone he could get. Down at the Bureau even some of the other agents were worried about the smarmy little senator that everybody hated. No one felt safe with him at the helm. Especially not Colin and especially not now.

No, LaVerne wouldn't have clocked him—not without telling him why. And as he pulled against whatever had him tied up, he knew LaVerne didn't go for kink. Unless you counted being a guy dressed as a girl day in and day out and working in a downtown club as a chanteuse night after night, singing her songs of love gone wrong and the man who got away.

Now LaVerne liked it in the car all right—they'd gone more than a few rounds on this very seat when he was doing stakeouts, her slipping into the car and sliding her hand right into his trousers—but she was always coming straight from her gig singing at the Hot Shot Club, and everybody there knew LaVerne as a woman. In fact pretty much everyone, except a couple of other girlfriends of LaVerne's who were just like her, knew her as a woman.

No, it wasn't LaVerne. She'd been his lover for almost three years now—not the only one, because he liked to be taken down hard by a guy as tough as himself as much as he liked taking LaVerne down hard, but he had a particular fondness for her, even though the first time she'd come on to him at the club he'd brushed her off, not knowing who she really was, thinking she was just another dame with an itch. Then she'd come up to him later—a tallish redhead with a big mouth, green eyes like his own, small breasts and legs that wouldn't quit—when he'd gone to get his coat from the hat-check girl and she'd grabbed his hand and put it right against her, between her legs—right against an amazingly hard cock hidden underneath her slinky silk dress—and he'd been playing with her ever since.

"Best of both worlds, honey," LaVerne had told him the first night they'd gone back to her little Flatbush apartment as she spun around, her dress swirling up to reveal her cock. She'd been wrong about that, though, because he'd never really wanted women. He'd only ever wanted men. And men very different from the man LaVerne might once have been. He liked his men bad, he liked them dangerous, he liked them one step short of being cuffed.

As Colin lay on the plush backseat of his own car, his clothes, his FBI badge, even his shoes, socks, and underwear missing, his dick and head throbbing, he wanted to know who had done this to him. Yet what kept flooding his head was not a list of possible suspects but a flood of sexual images—men he had bedded and been bedded by. Some of them—not many—had been decent guys, guys he had grown up with down on Broome Street; just Irish boys like himself, and a few Italians from over on Mott. In trouble sometimes, but not bad, just a little nicking something here, a little dust-up there. Like Mike Dougherty, the first guy who'd ever taken him, back when he was seventeen. There had been other men, later. Lots of men. Some family guys he passed in a train station men's room or two or a restaurant washroom when he was on the job. But there had been others, too, like whoever was responsible for getting him tied up in his own backseat. Men who had been in worse trouble than the boys he grew up with, men who were very much on the other side of the law from Colin. Men who almost anyone would have thought of as bad. Colin liked that—inexplicably. He had even convinced himself that fucking a man who one day he might end up arresting or see someone else arresting made him better at his job, made him more keen about the criminal mind.

Was that what had happened to him tonight? He was close to passing out again and all he could think of was the Rosenberg case he'd been working night and day and the treasonous guys he'd been trailing. *Spies*. For the Russkies. Of that he was certain. He'd remembered going into that little dive over on—where was it?—to try and use the phone and having a quick stiff whiskey and then—nothing. Had they slipped him something there? Had *they* been following *him?* He shook his pounding head. He could remember none of it.

That's how it had been when he had first started up with guys—he'd go off afterward and have a few and then the memory of the heat and the fucking would recede and he could think of himself as something other than some queer-assed homo aching for dick night and day, for the feel of a morning-after stubble rubbing against his first hard-on of the day as some guy grabbed his dick and stroked and sucked and took it in his ass. His first, Mike, hadn't been one of the really bad guys—at least not then, not when they had first done it. Later it was a different story, but then, Mike had just been a bit of a petty thief. A hustler and a neighborhood tough. The two of them had trained pigeons, beauties—some really nice brown doves, some pretty blue and whites—up on the roof of the seven-floor walk-up where Mike lived over on Orchard Street. They were up there every day, whether they'd gone to school or ditched it.

It had been brisk that day, too early for snow in mid-October, yet it definitely had the feel of snow—thick, heavy gray clouds and a harsh wind that came off the Hudson, wet and sharp. Mike was a big, rough guy whose parents—dirt-poor shanty Irish—had come over from Dublin with him, his baby brother, and four sisters right before the war broke out. Mike had black hair, like his own, but his eyes were amber like a cat's, not the green-glass color of Colin's. Mike was just about his height, nearly six feet. Colin was a little taller and leaner, Mike more stocky and built like his father, a stevedore. His skin was ruddy and his arms and shoulders were tightly muscled from working on the docks with his father on Saturdays. Colin had never understood what he had wanted until that day—why it was that being close to Mike had always gotten his dick hard, the way it never had with girls, even on those Saturday nights in the darkened movie theater making the obligatory move to touch a breast or slip a hand up under a skirt. After that day he understood why being with Mike had always made him have to rush back home and jerk himself off fast in the bathroom before anyone else came in. Jerk himself off thinking of Mike's hands on his dick, not his own.

Colin thought he might pass out again. The pain in his head was excruciating. Nevertheless thinking about that day with Mike made his cock quiver against the soft blue-gray plush of the Buick's backseat, made him ache to have his hands free for more than one reason. If only LaVerne could be passing by right about now like she so often did, to get him untied and give his cock a once-over. He could figure everything else out later.

He and Mike had decided it was too windy and cold to let the birds out that day. They had been sharing a smoke and sitting up against the brick chimney of Mike's building, talking birds and the docks and what was going to happen after this last year of school. Mike was going to work for the Orchard Street boss he was already doing little sorties for, Colin doing the opposite, joining the ranks of the G-men, becoming the guy with the badge and the cuffs and the weight of the law behind him. A gust of wind had blown over them and sparks had shot from the cigarette in Mike's hand into Colin's face. It had stung badly, though not really burned, but Colin had let out a small cry and Mike had leaned over to check his eyes, his hand brushing over Colin's still-smooth jaw. Suddenly he was on Colin, pressing him flat against the tar-paper roof as if they were in a wrestling match. Mike had Colin's arms pinned to the roof and was whispering in his ear as he bit along the earlobe and at his neck. Mike was telling him what he wanted, telling him he wanted to put his cock in Colin's ass, that he wanted his mouth on Colin's dick, that he wanted to watch as Colin took his cock and gripped it hard and jerked it off fast right there, right on the roof, them both watching as he shot into Colin's hand.

Colin had known he should have been protesting, should have been pulling away from Mike's hot breath against his ear, should have been kicking Mike off him and punching him out for thinking he'd do something like that, like some he-she or homo. But Colin had wanted this for months. Every day they had been there with the birds and his dick had ached for Mike, even though he had no idea what it was he wanted Mike to do. He had watched Mike handle the birds, talk to them, stroke them, and it had made his cock swell every time. He had wanted some of that for himself—those strong, tender hands stroking him, stroking his cock, cupping his balls, maybe fingering his ass a bit. That deep, husky voice whispering into his ear just as it was now.

This is how Colin had ended up roped like some County Down heifer in his own car by someone he should have picked up and cuffed and taken away—not to his apartment, but to be booked. He'd crossed a line into danger that day with Mike and he'd never crossed back. Mike whispering in his ear, telling him those things—so illicit, so wrong, so absolutely on the other side of any law he had ever heard about; to do it meant every day after would be rife with danger, every day would put him at risk of being caught.

That was the day Colin had decided a life of risk-taking was for him. He had watched for months as the birds flew out, always wondering if they would come back or if they might get hurt or lost. He had shared those fears with Mike, who had shrugged and told him it was life—lots of risks, lots of danger, lots of not knowing.

Colin's heart had been pounding as Mike had stood up, Colin still on his back on the floor of the roof, his mouth dry, his cock hot and swollen, pressing urgently against his trousers, aching for release. What if someone came up to the roof, like Mike's little brother, Tommy, or one of his sisters, looking for them for some reason? What if they got caught—a couple of homos on a rooftop touching each other's dicks? What if one of Mike's friends came up, or that boss? They might get tossed off the roof. That had happened the summer before to a guy who dressed like a girl and took other guys up there for sex. Thrown off the rooftop of a building near Colin's by someone who decided he didn't like the extra surprise package. And everybody had thought it was the best thing, too, except the mother who had screamed and cried over her son's body, still in a summer dress, one high heel nearby, lying in a deep red current of blood on the sidewalk.

Mike's black wool trousers dropped to the floor, his belt buckle sounding hollow against the wind. Colin saw Mike's massive cock pushing against the white briefs and he stood and walked over to him, heart racing. He ran his hands up under Mike's jacket and shirt, feeling Mike's muscled chest and arms, Mike pulling him tight, running his tongue along Colin's neck. He pulled away a little, then, and unzipped his own trousers, releasing his stiff cock.

The wind was really kicking up and they were both cold. Mike led them over against the wall and pushed Colin against it. He took Colin's thick cock in his hand and ran his fingers along the head, first pulling at the foreskin, then pushing it back. Colin had never felt anything so good, so intense. He put his hand around Mike's and began to move it back and forth over his dick. He could feel Mike's cock hard against him, pushing through the briefs, poking at his thighs. He had a sudden urge to put his mouth on Mike's dick, something he had heard some guys talk about at school, but didn't know exactly what it was. The wind was whipping up and the birds cooed low and sweet behind them.

He pushed Mike away from his own cock and dropped to his knees, reaching into the briefs for Mike's big, red dick. He ran his tongue over the hot head, then down the shaft of it. He pushed the underwear down Mike's thighs and felt his own cock twitch as Mike gripped his shoulders and pulled him closer. He wasn't sure what to do. He closed his eyes and ran his fingers up under Mike's balls and back toward his ass. His skin was surprisingly sleek and smooth and Colin ached to be in a warm bed with him, instead of on the cold rooftop.

It didn't take Mike long to shoot into the back of Colin's throat once Colin got the rhythm of sucking and stroking in sync. Colin had never felt such excitement as Mike thrust his cock into his mouth, Mike telling him how much he loved it, how much he wanted it, how he'd been wanting it for weeks and weeks. Mike saying that he had thought of it every night in his bed and had to jerk off his aching hard-on before he could sleep.

Just as Colin had done.

They slid to the floor after Mike came and Mike leaned over Colin, bending him back against the rooftop, and kissed him—the most frightening thing that happened that day. Somehow the touching could be excused but the kissing was something else and Colin knew it. This was it. He was one of them—a homo; no question, he thought, as his tongue felt the warmth of Mike's mouth and Mike rubbed and pulled and stroked at his cock, pinching the head a little, teasing his tongue along the inside of the shaft and then putting his finger over the opening like he could stop what was about to happen. He was on top of Colin then, rubbing his cock, their skin touching, Mike's own dick hard again and pressing against Colin's smooth, taut stomach, and when Colin came in Mike's hand Mike pressed his mouth hard onto Colin's.

If that day had never happened he wouldn't be in this fix, Colin thought now as he struggled to retain consciousness, struggled to think of something other than the men he had let do almost anything with him in the thirteen years since he had first taken Mike's big Irish cock into his mouth on that freezing rooftop.

If this hadn't been the summer of McCarthy he wouldn't have been in this fix either. And if he had stuck with the sweet and simple LaVerne, instead of walking that dangerous cliff-edge looking for the bad guys in more ways than one, he might be drinking a beer in her little place in Flatbush and getting his dick sucked instead of half-dead in his own car God-knows-where.

He missed LaVerne right now. He had never gone for one of those he-shes before, but LaVerne was sweet, and he liked her, and she knew how to give him what he wanted, whether it was her clever little ass or her soft, hot mouth with the wicked tongue. She would come up to him at the club and kiss him on the cheek, demure, like he was her boyfriend (he guessed he was, in a way), but her hands would always be sneaking straight into his trousers, right for his dick. LaVerne loved dick, as she'd told him more than once as she lifted her firm ass to him or dropped to her knees to suck him off. She'd jerked him off under the table at the club on more than one occasion, he trying not to show any sign of his excitement, she pretending she was looking for something in her purse and then handing him her handkerchief to wipe the come off his dick. She liked that, the danger. He liked it, too. Not that he didn't get enough of it from his job. But he didn't want to go to jail for being a queer. He'd thought he'd been careful about that, fucking guys who had more to lose than he did, and if anyone could put him in the slammer it was LaVerne. But he knew she didn't want that. She liked things the way they were. "I like my G-man in my G-string," she'd quip and flip her dick out into his hand from those silky tap pants she wore.

But now his head was full of fog. Whatever he was tied with was soft, not rough or scratchy. This wasn't rope—neckties maybe? Or the belt of a robe? But how had he gotten here and who had done this to him? He had an idea of why, but not of who. Then he heard the voice from the front seat followed by the little whoosh of a match being lit. A small cloud of cigarette smoke enveloped him and his cock throbbed in time to the pulse in his head. Now he remembered. He was in trouble, deep trouble.

This was the summer of 1953 and all anybody could talk about for months was Communists. It had taken the heat off the queers in some quarters, LaVerne had told him that's what her friends said. (LaVerne knew a lot of queers.) Unless they were Commies, too, of course, like some of those Hollywood types and the New York writers. The Rosenbergs were going to get it any day now and Colin Murray had been stalking some known associates of the couple whom he thought might be the real villains, not this dowdy little pair from Brooklyn with their pencil notations on the Jell-O box and their barely liberal politics. Colin had known a setup when he saw one and that had been one, all right, start to finish.

"They're just Jews, sir," Colin's tone had been close to exasperated when he had discussed the case with his boss. "That doesn't mean they're Communists and it sure doesn't mean they're spies. They're really not . . ." His voice had trailed off before he had said any of the things that had come to mind—"too smart" or "They're just too ordinary, and they spend too much time working and taking care of their kids to have time for espionage."

Colin hadn't been part of the Bureau's original sting of Ethel and Julius, but he had been the guy they'd chosen to do the follow-up because Colin Murray was known at the Bureau for being an ace detail man, the kind of guy who could put all the broken little pieces of the puzzle together to make the big picture stick. But this case didn't have pieces that fit. Every bit of it was broken and stank like three-day-old fish. Colin had talked all the way up to Hoover himself about it, had gone to DC to see the big man in person, he was so worried the Bureau was making a huge mistake that they wouldn't be able to take back—the gas chamber being pretty final. But his boss had been clear: The fix was in on these two. The little guy with the pop-bottle glasses and his tiny wife who looked—except for being Jewish—just like every Irish Mama he'd known as a kid growing up on the Lower East Side with all the other just-landed newly American micks. He could picture Ethel Rosenberg as a spy about as easily as he could his *own* mother—as if there would be time, taking care of the kids, doing the washing and cooking and all. No, he never believed it. Couldn't. It wasn't that he had a soft spot for women—other than LaVerne, and they both knew LaVerne wasn't exactly your everyday gal. He just knew in his gut that this woman hadn't done what she was accused of. And he also knew that after the Commies and the queers, nobody hated anyone as much as they hated the Jews, especially McCarthy, who'd as much as said so.

That's why Colin had been working solo for six weeks now, on his own clock, off the Bureau's ticket. He thought he'd tracked the real spies, the ones who actually had the goods and knew the secrets, right to the little back-office metals company down in the Bowery. It seemed to import and export some very sketchy items on a regular—too regular—basis to places that no one should be shipping anything, while the Russkies were trying to take charge as they had been since Stalin and Yalta.

But Colin needed solid evidence if he was going to trump the case against the Rosenbergs, and more than just a few bills of lading and shipping receipts and suspicious comings and goings. He needed the pieces of the puzzle that would unlock the box the Rosenbergs had gotten themselves shut into when that brother-in-law had made his little drawing on the Jell-O container. And so Colin had been staking the place out, shifting his schedule around at the Bureau to make sure he could watch the way he needed to. Plus he'd needed backup, a shill he could turn to for help for when he had to be back at the Bureau and couldn't weasel out of it. He'd found that person in Sean McGarrity, a bad boy from his old neighborhood who was now an up-and-coming mobster with money-laundering problems and a strip club masquerading as a dance joint down in Bed-Stuy. That McGarrity was also one of those really bad guys he couldn't help getting fucked by, and more than once, made it easier. McGarrity was married with a handful of kids, a pretty little wife who had never let herself go, and a reputation for being tough and a ladies' man on the side; it was an image that he needed to maintain. Plus he was into the Church. McGarrity had more to lose than most and what Colin knew was that one of McGarrity's ladies had been LaVerne's friend Connie and that Connie wasn't the only dick-wielding plaything that McGarrity had dallied with. After all, he and Sean had gone a few rounds over the years and both of them had liked the tumble, changing places tossing each other down and giving it or getting it hard. So Colin had called on McGarrity for help corralling the crew he believed had a hand in framing the Rosenbergs.

They'd met over at McGarrity's dance place, The Swing Low, and sat in a booth in the back, the music and the smoke and the girls swirling around them. The place smelled of cheap gin and cheaper perfume and Colin couldn't wait to get out of there, but McGarrity was in the mood to talk—and he wanted to bargain.

McGarrity had grilled Colin about what was really going down with the job, but Colin wouldn't spill. This had to be as secret as all those times the two of them had gotten to each other. That's what he told McGarrity, and he saw the big man redden in the dim light of the club. Suddenly his legs were kicked apart under the table and Colin knew they were going to go at it again, for old time's sake or to solidify the deal. McGarrity's hand was on his thigh under the table and Colin pulled his cock from his pants and rubbed the head of it against the tips of McGarrity's fingers. McGarrity stood—a muscled six-foot-four with sandy hair and piercing blue eyes. He nodded his head back and told Colin they should head to his office upstairs.

Once there McGarrity had locked the door and then slammed Colin against it. McGarrity had a thing for kissing. His roughly stubbled face, unshaven since the morning, mashed against Colin's and his tongue slid into Colin's mouth as his hands speedily extricated his own and Colin's dicks from their trousers. Colin was hot and swollen and more than ready. He had always liked the rough way McGarrity went for him, holding his shoulders back and kicking his legs wide apart so he could grip his balls and finger his ass, his massive thigh wedged between Colin's leaner ones.

It never took long with McGarrity. It was a wrestling match that sometimes the bigger man wanted to win and other times he wanted his opponent to win. Either way they were on each other—the kissing, then some sucking and then McGarrity, this time the one in charge, bending him over the desk and pumping his ass full of his short, thick Irish cock, his right hand pulling at Colin's longer dick and fondling his balls until Colin pushed the papers off the desk right before he came all over it, pleasure rushing down his thighs and up into his chest. There was something about the men he'd known as boys that always got him better than anything else. Particularly a guy like McGarrity, who'd as soon as slit his throat as slip him some dick.

They washed up in the little sink over in the corner of the hot, dark office and McGarrity pulled out some whisky and a couple of tightly rolled cigars—"Straight from Cuba where they know how to do it right"—and the two lit up and talked about McGarrity's kids and his troubles. Colin made it clear what he wanted—and that the job was dangerous and some muscle might be needed. McGarrity swiveled around in his big chair and grabbed his cock in his trousers and jerked it a little, winking at Colin as he said, "You know I've got the muscle," in the lilting brogue he'd yet to lose all these years after he and his family had come here.

But it wasn't McGarrity in his front seat, blowing cigarette smoke into his face and talking to him like he was a Saturday night whore down in the Bowery. It was Jimmy McAllister and Tony "Whitey" LoBlanco—mobsters in two rival families the Bureau had been watching as long as he'd been there. McAllister ran—no, owned—the dock down where Mike's dad had worked when they were kids. Nothing came in or out of those ships without Jimmy giving his okay. And now Colin's head had cleared enough to see the connection. That little metals company where the real spies were working was part of Jimmy's territory. Jimmy's *and* Whitey's, because LoBlanco covered protection down here, because now Colin knew where he was. He could smell the water and hear the foghorns and the gulls. Jimmy and Whitey had been hooked up for a while and the Bureau just hadn't quite gotten the bead yet. But now it was all falling into place for Colin; the broken little puzzle pieces were now falling into the big picture. Of course the Rosenbergs had been set up. That weasel of a brother-in-law had worked down here with this goombah, Whitey, without even knowing he was involved in Whitey's protection racket. The setup had been so easy everyone should have seen it. But the mobs and the Commies seemed such separate entities to the Bureau—even to Colin himself, who wondered now if, had he been less worried about watching his own queer ass with McCarthy lifting up every rock to see what Commie, Jew, or queer might scurry out, he would have seen the connection before he was trussed up for slaughter in the backseat of his own car.

They had slipped him something when he'd gone in to make that call—a call that never got answered. Jimmy had been watching him for weeks; he just had had someone else doing it for him. McGarrity, of course. Colin grimaced. He should have realized that McGarrity was in deeper trouble than Colin could protect him from when they had talked that day over the whisky and cigars. McGarrity had talked a lot about his kids and the Church. He had said that Father Sheehan was pressuring him about confession and some other things Colin hadn't really paid attention to. Colin had been in that space he was always in after fucking—half-asleep and half-ashamed. If he'd been listening he'd have realized that what McGarrity was telling him was that the priest was shaking him down, that the priest was part of the protection racket run by Whitey. McGarrity was being threatened with something happening to his kids if he didn't offer something big, since he couldn't pay them off because of his money troubles. So what he offered them was Colin.

The back door near his feet opened and Jimmy McAllister slid in next to Colin. "So you're a Commie?" Colin lifted his head a little off the seat to look at Jimmy, remembering games with him and Mike when the three of them raced birds together. Jimmy was a couple of years older than he and Mike, but they had been friends back then. Jimmy—small, wiry, tough, with flame-red hair and a temper to match. He was the prototype of the Irish thug. It was Jimmy who had gotten Mike lined up with the neighborhood boss. Then soon Jimmy himself was the boss and Mike had worked for him until Mike had been killed last year in an accident down at the docks. Colin had thought that accident was because Mike had wanted to leave, was tired of the gangster life, wanted to settle down, get out of the line of danger. Now he was out of it for good, his new wife, Francine, left to raise their little boy alone.

"Not a Commie, Colin, just a businessman. You know, like your friend Sean." Jimmy lit another cigarette, offered it to Colin, who took a long, hot drag.

"That's some action you got there, boy," Jimmy gestured with his cigarette to Colin's dick. "Still just batting the home team?"

Colin swiveled to look at Jimmy, his black hair falling over his forehead. His eyes felt scratchy and bloodshot.

"My job keeps me pretty tied down," Colin responded, suddenly seeing that image of the he-she who had been tossed from the roof back when he was a kid. Was that what Jimmy had planned for him? Had Sean given him that piece of news for his money, too? "There's a girl sings over at a club downtown."

"Yeah, heard about those girls, Colin. Girls up top, boys down below." Jimmy leaned his red face and red hair into Colin's face. "Let's not play games, here, okay? This ain't the birds we're racing here. This is the big leagues and you know that we're playing for keeps. The Rosenbergs are staying put and so, kiddo, are you."

Whitey rustled up in the front seat, turned to look back at Colin and Jimmy. "Let's see what the guy can do, Jimmy," Whitey said, dropping cigarette ash onto Colin's bare thigh. "Let's go back to the office and see what our G-man here has for us except cuffs and a couple a tickets to Sing Sing. Sounded like Sean knew kinda personal-like about Mr. Murray's special charms."

It was raw fear, nothing else, that made Colin's balls tighten and his dick stand to attention at Whitey's words. If he played with them would they let him go or would this be it, regardless? Whitey looked him over. Whitey, with his astonishing Italian good looks. In another few years he would run to fat, his strong jaw would become jowly and his bedroom eyes would just look sleepy in his soft, tanned face. But now Colin saw his sharp black eyes framed with the long lashes of a girl and his pitch-black hair slicked off his handsome face and could only wonder, despite himself, what Whitey's strong stallion body would feel like over him, how big, how hot, how intense his cock would be. If this was how Colin was going to go out—with a wiry little Irish thug and a tall handsome Roman god, then so be it, he was ready. It looked like he was going to beat the Rosenbergs to the other side, much as he had hoped to save them all. The only one he would miss would be LaVerne, but her friends would give her the lowdown soon enough. He just hoped none of the fallout would touch her in the end.

The drive to Little Italy was short and the breeze through the open windows felt good on Colin's sweaty face. Jimmy rode next to him, his arm casually draped over Colin's calves. Whitey drove.

Colin wasn't sure what time it was—1, 2 a.m.—when Jimmy pulled a switchblade from his pocket and sliced through the cord that had kept Colin tied so tight for hours now. Jimmy tossed Colin his white shirt—stained with blood, he noted, gently touching the wound on the side of his head—and his pants. He saw his shoes were on the floor of the car and he dressed quickly. His jacket, badge, gun—all of those remained missing. Jimmy restrained him with his own cuffs before they left the car.

Whitey's cozy little restaurant, the Villa de Roma, had been closed for hours, but the heady smell of fresh sauces and garlic hung in the air. Colin realized he was very hungry. This might be the last crazy risk he'd ever take, so he might as well go for it.

"How about a drink and some food, Whitey? The place smells great. Then I'll suck your dick better than any little Dago gal you ever met." He pulled a chair out from one of the white tableclothed tables and slung himself into it, holding his cuffed wrists up to Jimmy. "How about we take these off, Jimmy? I think we've established I'm not going anywhere, since you have your gun and apparently mine as well."

Jimmy sauntered over and unlocked the handcuffs. Colin rubbed his wrists, which were still smarting from being trussed for so long in the car. He stretched out his long legs and looked around the room. This was it; there was definitely no way out unless someone else came to his rescue. The little restaurant was pretty and pretty hard to escape. He watched as Whitey poured him a glass of Chianti and brought it to the table. When Whitey leaned over to put the glass down, Colin put his hand on Whitey's dick. He felt it stiffen in his trousers.

"Whoa, boy, I almost spilled your wine. I know you're a mick, but how about some nice red to go with your last meal?" Whitey winked at Colin and chucked him under the chin.

The meal came quickly and was just as good as the aromas in the restaurant. If this was the last food he was going to eat, Colin was glad it had been this delicious fare. He wiped his mouth with the napkin, took another swig of the wine and turned to Whitey, who sat on a stool at the tiny bar.

"What's next on the menu, boys?" Colin gave Whitey a wink, then added, "Best meal since the last one my mother made me, God rest her soul. You'll make someone a lovely wife one day." Colin watched Whitey blanch as Jimmy guffawed, then decided to go along with the joke.

Jimmy walked over to the table, pulled out the other chair, and sat down. "What are we going to do with you, boy? I really hate to kill guys from the old neighborhood. It just doesn't sit right with me." He lit another cigarette, took a swig from the whisky he held in his hand, then continued, "But you Feds, you just never know when to quit. We gave you the whole package with that Rosenberg group and you just couldn't let it alone. You had to push it. Now you're into me, boy, and I don't see how I can let you go. It's true—you just know too much."

Colin had no angle left to play. He had been prepared to face death since that first day with Mike on the roof when he had imagined himself being tossed over the edge by guys much like Jimmy. "Just do it quick when you do it, okay? My own gun to the head would be fine. Just don't slander me with some lousy suicide note. I don't want my kid sister and her kids having to take the rap; I've managed to keep them out of everything all these years, and I'd like to keep it that way." Colin leaned over, took Jimmy's cigarette and took a drag.

"I don't suppose I could convince you that if I give you a better fuck than you ever imagined that would be reason enough to let me go— call it a draw. I let the Rosenberg thing go and you leave me alone?"

Jimmy looked at him. Peripherally Colin caught Whitey massaging his dick in his pants. No matter what happened, he was going to have a good time with Whitey.

"Nice try, but no sale. Some risks ain't worth taking." Jimmy stubbed out his cigarette and stood. "I don't care what you two get up to. I'm not interested in screwing any guys. I'll stay here and have another drink. I'll watch if you want, Whitey, but I think this is your ball game, so to speak." Jimmy looked tired and bored. Colin turned to Whitey.

"Where would you like it and how would you like it?" Colin spread his legs out wide, ran his hand along the outline of his cock. He could tell Whitey wanted it badly. For hours his own cock had ached to be let loose as he was tied up in the car. It was time.

Colin walked over to Whitey. They were almost exactly the same height. Colin grabbed the Italian by the hips and pulled him against his own stiff cock and looked into Whitey's incredibly dark eyes framed by the long, girlish lashes. He was a beautiful man. Right out of some Renaissance painting. He'd never been with such a handsome man, such a beautiful man. He ached to take Whitey's cock in his mouth, feel his skin against his own. He could feel Whitey's dick throbbing in his trousers, could feel his dick flush up against Whitey's. They were both ready. Jimmy sat at the table, his hand around his drink, cigarette ash falling to the floor. He looked like he might be sleeping.

Colin put his hand behind Whitey's neck and pulled the beautiful Roman face toward his own. The kiss was surprisingly long and deep and Whitey responded like a girl on a first date—tentative at first, then more than willing. There was real desire here; Colin could feel it. So many men wanted other men; it always shocked him when he discovered another one hiding his desire in a washroom or an elevator.

Whitey took Colin's hand and led him to the kitchen. A big white enamel table stood in the center of the room. At its edges were baskets of vegetables. Whitey moved these to the counter, then turned to Colin. He undid Colin's trousers, awkwardly kissing him as he did so. Colin more expertly lifted Whitey's cock from his trousers. It was large and long and the foreskin had long ago pulled back revealing a lush, velvety head damp already with pre-cum. Colin slid down and put Whitey in his mouth, his tongue flicking up and down the pulsing rod. He ran his hand up under his balls and gripped them lightly, moved his forefinger back toward his quivering asshole and entered it just a little. He heard Whitey gasp with pleasure and pull him in, just a bit. Colin ached to come. His cock pulsed and throbbed. He was so ready to be taken.

He stood up, his hand still lightly stroking Whitey's magnificent dick. He closed his mouth over Whitey's, felt him hesitate, then gasped himself and Whitey took his cock and began to pump it fast in his hand.

Colin liked feeling another man touch him as he touched the other man. It was as if they were touching themselves, but they weren't, and each would pump the other's dick the way they did their own when they jerked off. It added a level of excitement that Colin could never quite articulate. It was a secret revealed: This is how he touches himself, how he's touching you.

Whitey pushed Colin back against the big table. He was unbuttoning Colin's shirt, pulling at his nipples, ordering him to take all his clothes off, to lie back, to touch himself; he wanted to see Colin touch himself. Colin sat at the edge of the table, Whitey standing, half-dressed, in front of him. Colin spread his legs wide, his balls pressed against the chill of the white enamel, his asshole quivering involuntarily. He took his cock in his hand and began to stroke it up and down, to twist it a little the way he liked it all the while looking straight at the handsome face of Tony LoBlanco, with his blue-black hair and his deeply tanned skin and his worker's hands busily unbuttoning his white shirt, then pulling down his trousers, then pushing off his socks and shoes. He stood directly in front of Colin, his finely hewn cock saluting Colin's own. He leaned forward and pulled Colin against him, his arms running the length of Colin's back, his dick brushing against Colin's own. They weren't going to fuck, Colin thought as Tony's mouth lowered onto his—this was going to be the real thing. Whitey might have wanted a taste of something different but Tony the gorgeous Italian man standing in front of him, his long eyelashes fluttering against Colin's cheek, Tony wanted him like a lover. Tony wanted him like he'd wanted a man his whole life and never knew it before this moment.

Colin lay back on the table and pulled Tony down onto him. As they kissed, Tony biting along his neck, leaning down and biting at his nipples, his breath hot and harsh against Colin's skin, Colin took their cocks and rubbed them together, rubbed the smooth soft skin against itself, felt the stiffness and the throbbing as if their dicks were one, not two.

Tony turned on his side, fondling Colin's dick and Colin stroked his. Their legs were entwined, their balls up against each other. Colin lay on his back, pulled Tony onto him. He opened his legs wide and whispered into Tony's ear, asking if Tony wanted to take him in the ass. The quick jolt from his cock was ample answer. Tony slid off the table and went to the counter, returning with a small container of butter. He smeared a little on Colin's asshole, then put a little more on his cock, then licked it off his fingers. Colin raised his legs over Tony's shoulders and held his ass open.

Tony gasped as he slowly stroked his cock into Colin's ass. He was standing at the edge of the table, Colin on his back, pulled down to the edge with him, Tony's cock all the way inside. Tony fingered his balls, tweaked his nipples, and rammed his dick again and again into Colin's ass, the sound of their breathing echoing through the room.

"I'm going to come, come really soon," Tony whispered. "Tell me what to do. Tell me how to get you, make it good for you?"

Colin pulled Tony to him. Now he was fucking Colin hard and fast as they lay on the table, his breath coming in shallow gasps. Tony grabbed for Colin's cock, rubbing it fast between the two of them as he plunged deeper into Colin's ass, telling Colin he was coming, coming hard, coming so hard, unbelievable, incredible, so hard . . . as Colin's dick began to spurt between them, the hot load wetting their hands, their stomachs. Tony leaned over and kissed Colin deep and hard, his breath catching in his throat.

They lay on the table for a while, not talking, legs and arms intertwined, their cocks midway between hard and soft. Colin could feel Tony's long eyelashes flutter against his chest. If this was the last time, at least it had been hot and sweet and with a man whose handsomeness took his breath away.

As they dressed Tony looked at him, awkward, unable to finish a sentence. "It was. . . . There's nothing . . . I'm sorry. . . ." He looked at Colin once more, then kissed him, quick but deeply and walked out of the kitchen. Colin knew this was it. He wished he could talk to

LaVerne one more time. He would ask Tony to get in touch with her after. Maybe LaVerne was what Tony was looking for. A man but not a man.

Colin looked around the kitchen for one last escape hatch to materialize. It didn't. He washed his hands at the sink, slicked back his hair, tucked in his shirt and zipped up his trousers. He wanted to look the best he could for his final appearance anywhere.

Back in the restaurant Tony and Jimmy sat, not talking. Colin asked Tony to look up his friend LaVerne at the Hot Spot, told him to make sure she was taken care of. He looked hard at Tony one last time and then he and Jimmy left the restaurant.

The sky was starting to lighten at the edges of the river. A Maxfield Parrish blue—sharp and deeply azure, with a hint of gold somewhere behind it, where the sun lay waiting to be revealed. Colin took a long breath, smelled the last smell of New York, of his city, his world. He had never thought it would be like this, just an ordinary summer morning, with a case that just was never meant to go right.

Jimmy led him out to his car, told him to lie down on the backseat. "I'm sorry kiddo, but there's no way out for any of us but this."

A single gunshot rang out and Colin felt a heat, a burning sensation, near his right ear. And then there was nothing but the sweet, low sound of the birds, cooing behind him, and the rush of air as he began to fall a very long way into the last of the night, the light beyond his eyes fading slowly to red.

Too Many Questions

Gregory L. Norris

Like a ghost at the window.

That's how I'll always remember Alexi. In this memory, which occurs hours after we meet on the fifty-second floor of the Verano, Boston's famous landmark and one of its tallest buildings, a warm June rain is striking the hotel's windows. One half of the bed sits empty. The sheet shows traces of the body that once rested beside me. Now, like a shroud, I see the impression of an arm, the back of a head, the place where his shoulders pushed into the mattress after I climbed atop him to ride his erection. The wet spot is still there, drying between the reverse bas-relief of his legs. Two spent condoms deflate and cool in the ashtray on the bedside table.

It's dark at 2 a.m. The light of the city can barely reach us forty stories up. It slices through the rain in waves of silver-blue to infuse the room with a strange glow no paint or canvas could ever accurately reproduce. I lick my lips, in this memory, to find the taste of sex still there, a salty, bitter mix of skin, cologne, and the most private regions of a man's body, including his seed. I glance toward the window to see a naked ghost standing there, bathed in the mysterious silver-blue of Boston. Though I haven't known this ghost long, I recognize the familiar contour of his body with a sense of ownership. For now, at least, he is mine.

He stands on big bare feet, Size 12s or 13s, I'm not exactly sure. His expensive leather shoes lie in a tangle of black dress socks and slacks on the floor. His legs are strong and dark with black hair, his ass, muscled and nearly square, like that of a soldier. Alexi's chest is mostly hairless except for the thin black tract that starts just above his stomach and cuts him down to his cock. His dick, his incredible uncut dick, hangs full, not limp but not quite hard, over his balls, which have pulled up close to his root. Lexi's—I can call him that now that we've been intimate—cock is hairy and veiny and thickest at its middle, the head a dark pink helmet with a lush noose of foreskin that captures the city's light. The hair on Lexi's crotch matches that of his legs and the jet-black tufts under his arms. His eyes are an unnatural blue, so rich they verge on cobalt, the raw, deep blue of jay feathers and delphinium flowers and antique glass. He wears a perpetual scowl on his face. He's younger than me, perhaps in his mid or his late twenties. But he's older than my thirty-four years by centuries. His hands are rough and there's a scar on one leg and a puckerish purple circle on his upper right chest.

"Is that a bullet wound?" I'd asked him before this particular memory was imprinted forever on my psyche. His cock would soon enter me for the first time.

"You ask too many questions," he'd answered in a gruff tone made even harsher by the lingering trace of his Russian accent. And then, he pushed that beautiful dick with its moist and musty folds of skin into me, and we made something like love.

If I concentrate hard enough, I can place myself in the back of the limousine right before I met him. The limo pulls into the Verano's underground garage and I hurry out and up to the party up on the fifty-second floor, never suspecting at the time that dark criminal forces are also converging on the very same level deep beneath the building; that briefly, I will meet a strange and handsome young man, and foolishly I'll begin to dream of what sharing a life with this man might be like.

And not long after, that fantasy life will come to an abrupt end.

The limo pulls into the Verano's underground garage and I exit into the raw summer humidity dressed in a black tuxedo shirt under my black linen jacket, black slacks, all in black.

Boston Artists magazine is celebrating its tenth anniversary. The elevator races me up to Sky View, the elegant dining hall on the fifty-second floor, stopping only once to pick up another guest. When I step out into the lobby where the party is taking place, my own face greets me, smiling coyly on the seven-foot-tall reproduction of the magazine's big anniversary issue. BOSTON-BORN, it reads, and beneath the caption, BOSTON-BRED, PAINTER MERRITT LANCASTER STRIKES GOLD.

Huge platters of food are being passed around: scallops wrapped in bacon, cheese and crackers, smoked salmon, fish eggs. An ice-and-fruit sculpture dominates one section of window that looks down on Fenway Park and the Esplanade. The open bar is well-stocked with champagne. I grab a glass, nibble, shake hands. Plenty of hands. The mayor. The conductor of the city's vaulted symphony. *Boston Artists'* editor. I take a seat at the bar after the speeches begin, and as I sit there, waiting to deliver my own words to the crowd, a shadow slides into the periphery of my line of sight. Dark and ominous, it draws my gaze toward it. I unintentionally suck in a breath and smell expensive men's cologne, just enough, and see the profile of a brooding deity.

The young man looks straight ahead, his gaze on nothing in particular, eyes the color of a cold autumn afternoon sky or anemone flowers. He must have shaved that day, but a prickle of scruff is showing through on his cheeks, chin, and neck. I try to swallow, only to realize his stunning good looks have drained all the moisture from my mouth. He catches me looking and glances my way. I deflect my eyes toward the mayor, who is extolling the city's unique art scene in his thick Massachusetts accent. I feel the man's blue gaze drill into me.

"You know," he growls, his voice a deep baritone broken with accent—Eastern European, Russian, I guess. "I've always wanted to fuck a famous artist."

Hot excitement ripples over me. I feel my face flush, fight the urge to laugh. The ludicrous nerve of such a statement, the *balls* of it! Still, I fall into the pull of his eyes. "Oh, really?" I say, trying to seem casual about it.

"Yes," he answers, no apology detectable. Now given license to, I study his body. Under his black sports jacket, he wears a blue dress shirt that matches his eyes decently, but could never truly mirror their cobalt-colored depth. Black slacks, like mine. Black dress shoes. Big feet—God, I love men with big feet. And really big hands, with traces of black arm hair jutting beyond the cuffs of his shirt. He's nursing a mixed drink, not champagne, and chews the red mixer straw with a predator's look in his eyes as he studies me back. "I want to fuck you."

At that moment, the room erupts in applause. Before I can respond to his brass-balls of a statement, I hear my name being called. More applause follows. I turn toward this handsome fucker and he claps, too, his hands striking together like thunder and making my already-drumming heart beat even faster. His eyes lock with mine and never once seem to blink. He's hypnotized me. Somehow, struggling to breathe and with burning coals on my tongue, I make it up to the lectern and deliver my speech. The art scene in Boston, I tell the entire room, has never looked more promising.

Twenty minutes later, I pull free of the crowd and the handshakes and the offers for more of the party's exquisite foods to find the man with the big feet and brass balls seated alone at a table. He's been drawing on the clean white tablecloth with a felt-tipped pen, sketching a portrait of sorts.

"Are you an artist?" I ask.

"If you have to ask, it's obvious I'm not."

I round the table, lean over his shoulder, and see that it's *me* he has sketched into the white linen. My insides ignite. He's sat here all this time, singularly focused on me and drawing my face. "Wow," I gasp, though it hardly seems enough. "That's amazing!"

He drops the pen, extends his large right hand. "Nice to meet you. My name's Alexi. Just Lexi, though, to my friends and to famous artists."

I study that hand, dangerous-looking and strong, yet still precise enough to capture my likeness with exacting detail. Then I shake it. His grip, if he wanted to, could snap bones. But he's an artist, I discover in our brief minutes together thus far. I take a seat across from him. He narrows his cobalt-colored eyes upon me and continues sketching.

"I like the real thing better," he says.

Someone brings me another glass of champagne. I wave them away, buzzed enough, thank you, and both intrigued and giddily aroused, now, too. "So, about this dream of yours . . . "

"You mean about me fucking you?"

"That one, yeah."

He stops sketching and looks up, and once more I surrender to his eyes. The next ten seconds pass in a blur. "Not a dream. It's gonna happen, Mister Lancaster."

"*Merritt,*" I correct. "And what makes you so sure?"

He doesn't answer, doesn't need to. I smile, but inwardly something is telling me to flee. I can't deny him. He already knows this. We are going to fuck.

"I have a limo," I stammer. "And a hotel suite over at the Bixford. Would you like to—"

He tips his head toward the elevators. I nearly trip over my own two feet crossing the distance, which feels like a gulf by this point. I'm also aware of the erection burning in my pants, as it has since before giving my speech. Somehow, on my way out of the festivities, I flag down the waiter and instead of a glass of champagne, I snag an entire bottle. I tuck it under my arm and march past my enormous reflection on the blown-up magazine cover. I show a slight, knowing grin in that photograph, as if I'd known, when it was taken months earlier, of the great and mysterious adventures to come.

Next, we are riding in the elevator, descending over fifty floors toward the limousine parked in the underground garage, and unaware of the danger that awaits us there. Some society woman tries to intrude into the elevator on the thirty-sixth floor. Alexi steps up and says forcibly, "Take the next one, please," and when the doors again shut, our lips crush together. He pushes me against the wall and kisses me deeply, drawing me into the embrace with feral, brutish strength. I sense him keeping one eye on the door, and a siren blares in my thoughts: *He's jumpy for some other reason, not just about people getting on the elevator who might see two men kissing and groping.* I temporarily put this out of my mind when I feel the hardness of his cock push into mine. We are close, so close now, that I can feel something else equally as hard dig into my right shoulder. The siren wails louder, *A gun! He's wearing a shoulder holster under his jacket!*

The first real jolt of panic courses through my insides. Coldness claws at my stomach and cools the sensitive, steamy skin between my balls and my asshole. I remember articles I've read and reports I've seen on the TV about the Russian Mafia moving into Boston. Lexi's accent—it's pure Little Odessa. What the hell have I gotten myself into?

I break the embrace and back away. The elevator glides to a stop in the underground garage. Its doors open, and a billow of hot, raw air cyclones in.

"What's wrong?"

"What is *that?*" I demand, pointing toward his chest.

"That's not for you," Lexi says. "*This* is for you," and he grabs the bulge in his pants, shakes it as the elevator's doors start to close. Lexi reaches out and pushes them open again. "Are we leaving together, or do I not get to spend the night with Boston's most famous artist?"

Every sane thought in my mind tells me not to exit the elevator with him, but I do.

Straight into a hail of bullets.

The memory of those minutes—or were they hours?—travels quickly through my consciousness, as though somehow existing outside the normal parameters of time. The elevator doors open and raw, sour garage air billows around us, smelling of ozone and gas fumes and humidity. Limousines, I know, occupy a special lot not far from the elevator. *To the right,* I am about to tell Lexi when a crackle of thunder erupts through the underground garage. I turn, and a split second before the gun's report deafens my hearing, I see the spark of what I'd later realize was a bullet striking the metal door less than a foot from Lexi's head. Two more gunshots explode, but I barely hear them. My ears ring.

"Get down!" I *think* Lexi barks at me. Suddenly, under the power of his shove, I find myself pushed behind cover of one of the large metal-

and-concrete posts that aid in supporting fifty-plus stories of building weight above us. Behind the post, for the moment, is the perfect place to hide. Lexi's arm grips me protectively, his body covering mine. I press my face against the cold, dank concrete. Somehow still holding the bottle of expensive champagne, I try to make some sense of what is happening. Even though there's a summer storm brewing out there, nobody in the garage could possibly blame the gunshots on summer thunder or the backfire of a car. The echo begins to power down in my numbed ears. I realize Lexi's arm is no longer draped around my shoulders.

I peer around the corner of the support post to see the limousine lot looking impossibly distant now. Worse, coming closer from that very direction are two men ducking in and out of cover of the cars. They move quickly toward us.

I look for Lexi, but he has vanished. The cars parked directly in front of the support post offer some kind of cover and I catch a flash of movement. *Lexi!* He rounds the cars, and soon has positioned himself between me and the oncoming men, the perfect place to surprise them. I take a heavy swallow. My ears pop. I can hear again. An exchange of angry voices takes place; Russian voices, I think.

Both of the men are young, Lexi's age, but like him, toughened far beyond their actual years. One has a shaved head, a trim goatee and mustache, and wears a leather jacket over a white T-shirt, jeans, and laced work boots. The other, a step ahead of the bald guy, is handsome in a dangerous way, a young Turk. He reminds me of Lexi. His hair isn't black, but a dark brown. His eyes are blue and mean. He, too, is dressed well, with expensive shoes on his feet and lots of gold around his neck and on the hand gripping what looks to be a Glock-style semiautomatic. I make the observation in the span of a second, long enough for the space between me and them to lessen significantly.

And then, a surprised shout echoes through the garage as Lexi clocks the bald guy. The gun flies out of his grip and clatters across the garage's oil-stained concrete rampart. The two men struggle. Lexi's fist strikes the flat meat of his opponent's abdomen. But the other thug turns and aims his gun at Lexi, who reluctantly releases his raised fist, lifts both hands, and surrenders. The downed bald man recovers. Together, he and the guy with the gun force Lexi's back up against the passenger door of the nearest vehicle. Cold panic surges through my insides. I know I am about to witness his execution.

"Find the one who was with him," orders the man with the gun to his partner. The bald guy starts toward me.

Lexi protests, "No, Anton, please do not hurt him. You've found me, leave it at that!"

I imagine the one called Anton pushing the muzzle right into Lexi's forehead, flashing a chilling smile as he says, "Stupid move, my friend. Your last, I'm afraid."

Unexpectedly, he touches Lexi's tense, wounded face, strokes his cheek in an action so tender, I could almost believe it. Almost. "You don't leave the Brotherhood, beautiful Lexi, once you're in," he says. "Ever!"

And then he spits in Lexi's face, howling some angry collision of words, all in Russian. This image comes very clearly. I think, in that sped-up confusion of seconds and minutes and hours all blurring together, I must have peered out and seen this clearly. Yes, because now the bald man knows where I am and is sprinting toward me.

Lexi shouts, *"Run, Merritt!"*

But I don't. I won't. Time, running slow, now leaps forward in a blinding rush of action and energy. I step back behind cover of the concrete support, grip the bottle of champagne by its neck, and just as the thug turns the corner, I swing. There is a thunderclap of glass striking bone. My pursuer goes down, his cries of pain quickly powering down to weak moans. The bottle flies from my hands to smash on the floor, its intensity sounding like another report from a gun. Anton turns toward the cacophony. It's all the distraction Lexi needs. He grabs Anton's gun and wrestles it from his hand. Lexi shoves Anton forward, hauls back, and fires off his fist. When I look, Anton lays dazed on the rampart.

"Come on," Lexi growls, grabbing hold of my hand. We race toward the limousine lot. "Where is your car?"

I clamp down on the chaos in my mind and focus clearly. We make it to the car, enter, and slam the doors behind us. Through the glass partition, the driver says, "What the hell's going on out there?"

"*Drive!*" I shout. "Get us the hell out of here!"

Leaving the underground garage seems to take forever. Eventually, we clear the gate and are motoring down the streets of the city.

"We should call the police," I say.

Lexi flexes his hand and winces. "You'll only make it worse if you draw attention to yourself."

"But—"

"No," he says, his cobalt gaze fixing with my terrified eyes. I try to look away, to argue, but can't.

I order the driver to circle the city, just to be safe. Eventually, we arrive back at the hotel. I tip the driver extra, and Lexi and I head up to my suite, neither of us speaking.

We enter the hotel suite. It's big and elegant, and comes complete with a gift basket and flowers. I am shaking. My eyes, I imagine, are wide with disbelief. All the questions I haven't asked suddenly spout from my lips. "What were you doing at that party?" I ask, demand. "And how did you get in? It was by invitation only!"

"I have resources," he says. "Friends."

"I don't care much for your *friends*," I snap.

"That makes two of us, my sweet," Lexi says as he peels off his jacket and scans the room.

There's still some ice floating in the waterlogged ice bucket I'd filled earlier that afternoon. I toss a few melting cubes into a towel and place it over the knuckles of his punch-hand. My terror has turned to anger. I look into his eyes and demand, "What is really going on here? What have you involved me in?"

"Nothing that will come back to you, you must believe me," he says. "I read about you, the big painter, in *Boston Artists* magazine. Doesn't say you suck dicks in the article, but I figure it must be the case. I read about famous *cum-paintings* you do and tell myself I must meet this artist, maybe give him some of my cum to paint with. Magazine says you'll be guest at big party at Verano. And here I am."

Lexi tosses his sports coat on a nearby chair. His gun holster is in clear view. He arches a foot onto the bed and unlaces his shoe before kicking it off. He undoes the other and then peels off his socks. His feet, like his hands, are big and dusted with tufts of black hair. Transfixed by this image, I listen. My rage deflates.

"I can't get this thought out of my mind, artist mixes cum from famous men with paint and paints sperm paintings that sell for big money."

"It was an experiment," I hear myself yammer. "Warhol had his 'piss paintings,' you know—"

"No, I don't," he says, wrinkling his nose, narrowing his eyes. "Paintings of piss?"

"Copper paint. He had some of his male acquaintances piss on the canvas before the paint dried. The piss turned the paint all different colors. Me, I used sperm from two famous ex-boyfriends, my big claim to celebrity."

I realize I've been rambling, still lost in the recent events that have left me shaken. Lexi's holster and gun are gone from sight, tucked under his jacket. He unbuttons his shirt and again my breath falls short at the image of his perfection.

"I think to myself, I must meet artist who comes up with so incredible an idea, for what he has done is immortalize man who gives him the juice. A forever thing, like statue of David, big cock and balls captured in stone, or smile of Mona Lisa, forever smiling . . ."

Lexi's shirt falls open and time again slips from focus. His voice melts me. "Who are you, Lexi? Who are you, really?" I sigh.

"I'm not a bad man," he says. "But I'm trying to be a better man, a man who wants one night with you. And I want to fuck you."

I feel my legs weaken. I drop to my knees in front of him and reach my shaking hands toward his belt. I'm aware of the heat being thrown off his cock even before it emerges from his pants. I glance up and see the tiny, puckerish scar at his shoulder.

"Is that a gunshot wound?" I ask.

He then reminds me that I ask too many questions.

I haul down his zipper. The black, skin-tight briefs he wears beneath follow his pants to his ankles. I study them, lying draped over his bare feet. His toes flex contentedly, like a cat's. Lexi steps out to stand completely stiff, his uncut member thickest at the middle and the head. I tug on his heavy, hairy nuts while opening wide to accept him. Lexi cups the back of my head with one of his giant hands to steady himself as he rides my face. Silence fills the room, throbbing only with the drumming beat of my heart and his breathless grunts. His balls slap at my chin, heavy with the seed he'll soon spray across my tongue. I consider holding it in my mouth, spitting it out into the ashtray on the bedside table, saving it for future use like I once did with the famous actors-turned-movie-stars whose sperm helped launch my career to its current commercial success. But Lexi tastes so good, so powerful, I swallow him down, absorb his power. Like him, his cum is raw and primal, intoxicating. I look up to see sweat streaking his forehead and the barest trace of a smile crack through the perpetual scowl on his handsome face.

He stands at the window, looking like a ghost, trapped in thoughts that only I can guess at. It's 2 a.m. Lexi said he wanted to fuck an artist, and he has now. Twice.

For a brief and blinding instant, a wave of emotions rushes over me. I imagine being with Lexi in my home and studio in the mountains, sweating and screwing from room to room, and perhaps something even more. Something tender, deeper, and longer lasting.

"Do you want to come home with me?" I ask. "You'd love the Berkshires."

"Can't."

"Will I see you again?"

"Unlikely," he says without turning to face me, his gaze buried in the city's pulsating light.

I realize I am asking questions again, too many of them, and turn over in the bed, not sure of what I am feeling, or what I should be. The wave of emotions passes, burying me in exhaustion. Lexi has milked two orgasms out of my dick to the three I've given him. I fall asleep and wake just before sunrise, alone in my hotel suite. He is gone.

I eat breakfast, masturbate, pack up all the trinkets from my stay, and ready to head down to meet the car that will whisk me home. I wear the same clothes as I wore to the party and still feel shaken by the previous night's events, still find myself jumping at sounds and looking over my shoulder. On my way to the door, I spy two filled condoms lying in the ashtray, looking like bloated garden slugs, thick and juicy on the insides. They're full of Lexi.

I carry them over to the bathroom, plan to dump them into the toilet and flush, but at the last second, I rescue them, tie them both at their sticky tops. It takes some effort. Lexi's stale load coats my fingers. I pocket the condoms in my linen jacket and catch myself sniffing my hands on the ride to my home in the mountainous green of Western Massachusetts. His smell is forever imprinted upon my psyche.

Later that morning, I mix paints—obsidian black, silvery flesh tones, and cobalt, the color of his eyes. I begin to paint and realize I've gotten hard again. I often paint this way, with a boner, with the TV on in the background, the canvas slightly angled toward the tall windows that show the Dome, the nearest and largest of the mountains.

This is what I remember: The news is playing. It catches my attention. "*. . . unidentified man, believed to be in his mid-20s, shot to death in what police are calling a revenge killing linked to the Russian Mafia . . .*"

My brush stills. I freeze. Questions fill my head. I fight them, paint. Soon, the newscast ends. Hours, maybe days, later—it's hard to tell, because I work without further interruption—Lexi is staring back from the canvas. I have immortalized him, just as he wanted.

This ghost, however, may haunt me forever.

Hollywood Blvd.

M. Christian

This isn't one of those nice Hollywood stories. You know the kind, where the hero—usually the guy with top billing—rides off into the sunset. Not this time. Not this story.

I guess you could say it did have a happy ending, if you look at it the right way. All I ever wanted was a nice place, like one of those great big houses on the 10,000 block of Hollywood Boulevard. A place with a nice big hot tub.

Well, I got it. But not the way I wanted it, of course.

There's just been a murder in one of those big Hollywood houses. The homicide squad's on its way there now, sirens wailing down that famous street. A guy's been killed: two bullets in his back, one in his stomach, his body left soaking in one of those room-size tubs.

You should hear this story from someone who knows, before those big Hollywood columnists get their hands on it, turns it into something cheap and sleazy.

Look at me, bobbing there, blood staining the expensively treated water. Poor dope, all I wanted was a hot tub. Unfortunately the price was just a little too high.

I was one of those journalists you don't hear about. You know the kind—the one whose name always seems to escape being tied to a headline. Definitely not one of those columnists who get to turn tawdry into sleazy. I'd had a couple of good scores. Remember that big piece a couple of years ago, that old heartthrob that people almost forgot all about, until he got linked to that cute little high school jock? No, I didn't get the scoop, but I proofed it for the guy who did. I was that kind of journalist.

The only thing I had to my name was the cheap furniture in my cheap apartment, an ancient laptop, and my car. It wasn't much, it wasn't anything at all, but it was my life. The problem was that things were tough: my money was almost gone. I'd had to hock whatever I could and it still wasn't enough. My landlord was a nice old queen who I knew I could stall for at least another two months—but my car was another matter. The finance company was getting more and more nasty: if I didn't pay, they'd come and drive it away.

Can you imagine being in LA without a car? It was a cruddy car, but it got me around. I was driving it that Thursday afternoon, going from one paper to another, trying to get someone to give me something on spec—anything, I needed anything, to keep the repo man away—when the thing sputtered and died. I managed to pull into an alley off Hollywood Boulevard, down where those big old houses haven't been torn down to make way for cheap apartments like mine. The place was really overgrown, tangled weeds and vines covering the front gates and the tall brick walls all around it, but you could see that at one time it had been fantastic, all deco and style. Now it was just dirt, dust, and weeds, but once it had been grand.

I noticed that the huge iron gates were ajar. I don't know why I went in; maybe part of me was curious. It was part of old Hollywood, from the era of roller disco and platform shoes. I wanted to see what was left.

Inside the gates, the place was big—really big. There was a pool, empty of water, but full of leaves. There was a big Cadillac in the drive, once pink and now deep red with rust, sitting on four flat tires. I was just starting to walk up to the big front door when it opened.

"You're late," he said. "He expected you hours ago." When you're older, drag just doesn't work. It's just a man's cross to bear, I guess; put on a wig and you're suddenly five years older. Sometimes it's pathetic, other times it's just tragic. But he . . . or she . . . was old, maybe in his middle fifties, and yet somehow on him it worked. He wasn't Cher but he could almost have been Bette Davis. He wore curls as red as that rusting Cadillac, a simple white dress, and just enough makeup so he didn't look like he'd been hit by an explosion at Max Factor. His incongruous voice was a deep rumbling bass, with a hint of a German or Hungarian accent and no attempt at femme tones.

I went in. White shag, pink leather sofas, mirrors everywhere. A disco ball in the living room. A huge television on one wall, and on the other, movie posters. Some I'd seen, others I hadn't: *Backroom Boys, Disco Dynamite, Roller Leather,* and the like.

"This way," Bette said, leading me toward a brass and marble staircase winding upstairs.

"Excuse me," I started to say, "but I just came to—"

Then someone from upstairs called: "Maxine! Maxine! Is that him? Bring him upstairs this instant." Bette turned, looking down at me from the first step, and said. "He is waiting for you. This way."

So I went up those stairs, following behind "Maxine," noticing as I walked that the brass was green, and the marble deeply cracked.

He must have been a special hamster, maybe related to some famous hamster, though I couldn't think of any. He was lying there, on a velvet pillow, his little feet stiff in the air.

It took a few minutes to get it straightened out. No, I hadn't come from the vet; no, I hadn't come to take the little creature away. I was just in the neighborhood when my car broke down, and I just wanted to use the phone.

I answered his questions, trying not to stare. I knew him from somewhere. The moment Bette brought me upstairs, opening the door to the big master suite and ushering me in with a gravelly "He's here," I realized that something about him was familiar . . . but from where?

He was handsome. There was no denying that. Standing by the huge round bed surrounded by gold-veined mirrors and floodlights, I was instantly struck by his beauty. It had faded, certainly; skin that had once been clean and smooth was now rugged and deeply tanned, a body that had once been strong and broad-shouldered was now stooped and softer. "Well, what are you doing here then if you're not going to take little Manuel away?"

His voice was marvelous, deep and rich with a purr that reached down and tugged at me. It was another piece of the puzzle, another clue to who this man was, but my mind was still not putting it together.

"I was just in the neighborhood. My car broke down. I just came to use the phone."

"The phone?" he said, that powerful voice slipping into a glass-breaking screech that made me wince. "You came into *my* house, disturbed me, over the *phone*?" Without waiting for my response, he turned and bellowed to Maxine, standing in the doorway. "Show this gentleman out."

Then it hit me. As Maxine reached for my arm, I turned and blurted it straight out, without a clue in the world where it was going to lead me, what was going to become of it: "You're Norman Desmond. You used to be in porno. You used to be big."

"I *am* big," he said, his voice ringing with injured pride, thundering with a vigor that defied the stooped shoulders. "It's *porno* that got small."

Eventually it came out that I was a writer, and that changed everything. Blue eyes sparkling like new rhinestones, he took me by the hand and pulled me past a sneering Maxine and into the hall. "Ah, a writer! Just the kind of man I need to see. Just the man—"

The hall was more white shag, more gold-veined mirrors, and rows of tiny white lights where mirrors met shag. He took my hand in a firm grip and pulled me along, our reflections becoming an endlessly duplicated couple, striding into infinity.

Norman Desmond . . . there was a name that took me back. One of the greats, if not the greatest. Before Norman Desmond, queer porn was all greasy-mustached plumbers or pot-bellied sailors. Loops long on cock-sucking but short on plot. Sure, they would get you off, but they didn't stick in the mind beyond the mechanics that happened between the plumbers and the plumbing. Then came Norman Desmond: handsome, strong, virile, but more than that, a presence. Norman Desmond filled the screen with attitude, with charisma. You didn't look for one of his flicks to see where his impressive cock would go, what he did with it, or who he did with it, but because of who he was.

Now I remembered those films—*Backroom Boys, Disco Dynamite, Roller Leather,* and all the others, the movies those posters downstairs belonged to. They were some of his greatest. The best of the best. I was in shock, I was in awe.

But more than that, I was hopeful. Norman Desmond, *the* Norman Desmond—alive and well and living in that great big house full of memories and stories, right off Hollywood Boulevard. It was just what I needed. It was a story, what could be a kick-ass story, and he wanted to tell it to me.

The backroom looked like a set, something straight from *Hollywood Hustlers or I Love the Big Life*: crystal chandeliers, a big leather sofa, mirrors, mirrors, and more mirrors, and right there, a hot tub. Not just any hot tub, mind you, but rather *the* hot tub. Sure, some may call *Hot Water* derivative; I mean, how could you not, considering the plot was stolen from an old 1940s' film. But for me it was pure Norman Desmond. I stood and stared at it, running the flick over and over in my mind. The bubbling, steaming water where Norman took Roger Biggies from behind, his muscular ass driving Biggies till he screamed, his cum mixing with the churning water in simple cinematographic genius. The water where he splashed with Tumescent Dan, taking his impressive tool down his throat in one awe-inspiring swallow. Looking at the water I felt my own cock stirring, aching for a touch, any touch.

"Here," Norman said, retrieving a thick manuscript from a table next to the sofa. Five, six hundred pages at least. It felt like a phone book. *Salome: The Norman Desmond Story,* it said. I looked up at him. "You're a writer; you'll be able to help. I'm not really so good with . . . words. Now the pictures, that I'm good at. But this, this is something

I could use some help with. I want to tell my story, to remind everyone of who Norman Desmond was. Yes, yes, to show them all that Norman Desmond is still here, just waiting for the right chance to get back up there on top where he belongs."

I held the manuscript in my hands. "You want to make a comeback?" I said, my voice catching somewhere from throat to lips.

"No. I hate that word. No, I'm going to return—that's the word—return to the thousands of people who have never forgiven me for deserting the screen."

I didn't say anything. I just stood there, weighing the heavy book in my hands. Older, there was still a power about him—something beyond the crow's-feet and thinning hair, the gentle pot belly—something remaining of the legendary Norman Desmond. I also weighed my tiny apartment, and my even tinier life.

I said something, probably "Yes" or "I'll do it," but to be honest I don't remember. All I remember is his hand on mine, piercing blue eyes looking straight into me, filling me with some of his boundless determination, looping me into his dream of returning to the movies, and tugging at my memories of the great Norman Desmond.

So that's how it happened, the very first step. I had no idea at the time where it would lead me, or just how far it would go.

At first I only came by the grand old place on Hollywood Boulevard a couple of times a week, but quickly I realized how empty my apartment was compared to the grandeur of Norman's house. My old laptop and knock-off furniture just couldn't compare to the hundreds of films, the thousands of fan letters. Being back at my place reminded me how small I was, how pathetic. One day I was sitting at a huge steel coffee table in Norman's living room while he was upstairs watching and re-watching his films in the tub room. Maxine was puttering around, dusting the furniture and polishing the mirrors. Looking over Norman's manuscript, I guess I muttered something, commenting to myself on some detail of his fantastic life as one of the true legends of the porno screen. Maxine must have overheard, because he stopped polishing and walked over to me. "He was the greatest of them all," he said. "In one week he received seventeen thousand fan letters. Men bribed his hairdresser to get a lock of his hair. There was a prince who came all the way from England to get one of his jocks. Later he strangled himself with it! You are privileged to be here, privileged to be allowed to work on his return to the screen."

Eventually I was living in a tiny room above the garage, spending most of my days going over the book. At first occasionally, then frequently, Norman came by to check on my progress.

It wasn't all work, at least not on Desmond's part. Not by a long shot. The fragile ego that was Norman Desmond required constant feeding. First there were the fan letters that arrived every day, brought to Norman by Maxine on a silver salver, opened and gushed over with great enthusiasm. "Wonderful," he would warble in his melodic voice (the very same voice that had demanded "Suck my cock" in *Alley Tails* and "I'm going to fuck you long and hard" in *Beachfront Property*) as he opened them.

Then there were the movie nights. He'd escort me upstairs to the tub room and we'd sit and watch movie after movie. The steam from the water made clouds, catching stray fragments of light from the old projector. I'd seen a lot of them before, of course, but having Norman there was like a personal tour through the heyday of Hollywood queer smut. I heard all about the stars, the directors, the gossip, and the dirt. It was fascinating, and I began to look forward to those nights more and more.

Then everything changed.

I'd been working on the book, finally starting to realize what a mess it was. The heart was there, the passion that was Norman Desmond the legend, but it was lost, polluted by bitterness, delusion, and outright fiction. I had to be careful, very careful, about what I cut and what I didn't. It was starting to be a problem, with Norman screeching in a piercing falsetto—a tone that made me realize the commanding Norman Desmond of *Army Brats* might be done—over any suggested change.

Then Norman walked in. Readying myself for what I expected to be the usual fight over the book, he shocked me by putting a hand on my shoulder and saying in his good voice, his purr of firm masculinity,

"You look tense. Why don't you come up and soak in the tub for a while?"

The tub. To be honest, I'd never really thought of Norman as someone who'd have any interest in me. Not that I'm a troll—I never had to look hard to find a date on Saturday night—but I was simply not in his league. I worked out just enough, I took care of myself just enough, but I definitely could have done more. And yet here he was, the legend of 8-mm loops, of *Backdoor Romeo,* inviting me up for a soak.

I felt like I was walking into a loop myself, standing in front of that famous hot tub. I realized it was just like the one I'd always wanted, wanted because I'd seen it, this very tub, in one of his movies.

Norman stripped quickly and efficiently, as if performing some kind of magic trick they taught in porno movies. It was as if he was in one of his old loops, clothes simply vanishing from one scene to another. I sat on the edge of the tub, dimly aware that the bubbling, steaming water was soaking my pants and shirt, but I couldn't continue. Norman Desmond was a very handsome man. Very. Age had come on him slowly. He had all the evidence: wrinkles, sags, that little belly, the thinning hair, a few liver spots on his arms, a few rose marks on his chest. But these insults were restrained, at least for a while, by his overwhelming determination to remain an idol, to freeze himself at the height of his career.

My cock was instantly hard, and Norman was instantly aware of it. He still projected in the flesh what he'd delivered so many times on the screen: a tremendous sexual presence. Part of the arousal, too, was that I was getting naked for the man who had been part of my sexual dreams for so long. Wrinkles couldn't take that away; in fact, I doubted anything could.

Naked, hard, I stood in front of him, bubbling waters of the tub behind me, adding to the heat that rose and kept rising in my body. I was sweating, gleaming, but only partially from the steam.

He reached out and wrapped his hand around my hard cock. He held me that way for a good long time, never once looking at anything except my eyes. Locked on me, rigid, he slowly smiled as he looked deep into me. Then, never taking his hand from my cock, he led me into the hot, churning water.

It was good, as good if not better than I thought it would be. But there was something else, something that skated over the surface of my mind, refusing to come together until much later when I'd cooled down. He took my cock in his mouth, and brought me close to tears. I touched him, amazed by the noises he made, the way he played his body like a fine instrument. He stroked me, working my cock like a master—which he was. I felt self-conscious returning the favor, but he seemed to truly enjoy himself and when his cum followed mine into the steaming water, I smiled at his deep, rumbling growls of pleasure.

We spent a long time in the water. The heat of the tub added more and more steam to our play. My fingers wrinkled, and my head started to swim from too many bouts of near overheating, but we kept at it. I remember details of it, captured crystal clear as if on one of Norman's old reels: the pebbled texture on the bottom of the pool; the white, almost translucent plastic; the moment when Norman playfully took a deep breath, vanishing into the wildly boiling water to take my cock in his mouth; looking up and catching myself and Norman reflected back and forth in the mirrors, seeming to superimpose us like actors in one of his films.

Finally he started to tire and we climbed out, toweling off. I worked back into my clothes as he slipped on a big terrycloth robe held out for him by Maxine.

As I walked the long, mirrored hallway back to my room—the intimacy of actually sleeping with Norman Desmond never occurring to me—he called my name. I turned, seeing him at the far end of the corridor, silhouetted against the wavering light from the hot tub room. "You see," he said, his voice breaking slightly, "you see, I can still do it! I still have it! Soon it'll just be me, the cameras, and those wonderful people out there in the dark!"

Suddenly chilled, I gave him my best smile and returned to my little room over the garage.

We quickly settled into a nice little routine. I continued to work on the book, and Maxine continued to dust and clean and deliver, every day, a new stack of fan mail for Norman. At night, it would be me and Norman in the tub, me in awe of the great porno star, he needing my fresh, new admiration. It was good, at times very good, but there was also something else there; a vague feeling that hovered, like something you can just barely see out of the corner of your eye, but can't define.

Sometimes Norman would be sucking my cock as I stood in the burbling water and I'd look down to catch him gazing off into the distance, playing for the cameras—the audience—that wasn't there anymore. Others he'd prance a bit too much, or work too hard at sucking or stroking me, acting for the director in his mind.

His comeback began to obsess him more and more. The world could have burst into flame and shrunk down into ashes and all he'd have cared about would be that there wouldn't be enough fans left to send him mail. I started to stand in front of the window, stare out at those high walls and their dead creepers, and wonder about the world. Sure, it hadn't been a great world—at least not to me—but it was real. It was a world that revolved around the sun, and not Norman Desmond.

I started sneaking out at night, rather than returning to my little room over the garage. Exhausted from Norman's tongue, lips, and hands night after night, I tried to walk as far as possible just to prove to myself that the world hadn't ceased to exist.

One night, Maxine was waiting for me at the door. The Master was asleep, but he was waiting for me all the same. At first I was ashamed of leaving the all-encompassing light that was the great Norman Desmond, but then I felt a stab of anger. "What is it, Maxine? His highness miss my adoring presence for ten minutes?"

He glowered at me through his thick black lashes, hands clenched. "You are not worthy of him. He is Norman Desmond and you, you are just a distraction. He is great, one of the greatest that ever lived."

"Take it easy, Maxine," I said, seriously wondering for a moment if the old drag queen was going to have a stroke. "I just needed a breath of fresh air. No harm done."

"You do not realize how important he is. How carefully I have maintained him for the moment when he returns to his rightful place on the screen. I will not have you ruin him for that great time when he is accepted back as the legend that he is."

I was getting very tired of the "worship Norman" game. I had taken my walk, I had seen evidence that, even at night in the dark, there is more in the sky than The Great Norman Desmond. "He's a big boy, Maxine. He can take care of himself."

"Do you really think so?" He answered, stepping back and starting to close the door, leaving me to tramp around to the side entrance. "Then I suggest you check the handwriting on those fan letters."

The next night that feeling that had been lurking at the edges of my mind was right there in my face, obvious and more than slightly grotesque. It happened after a worshipful showing of *The Plumber Rings Once,* after Maxine floated through the flickering lights of the tiny 8-mm projector to hand us our martinis. Norman stood with a flourish, saying, "Maxine, you may go. We want to be alone."

There we were: me, Norman, the hot tub, and the precious myth of the famous porn star—a myth that was more important, and more real, to Norman than anything else.

We got into the famous tub. Norman was in fine form, and for a long time the suspicion and depression were in abeyance. It was just Norman and me. He kissed me, something he hadn't done before. Standing in the hot water, bubbles nibbling against my balls and my quickly hardening cock, he gently bent forward to touch his lips to mine. His lips were soft, something I knew very well from having them attached so often to the head of my cock, but with that kiss I realized they were almost too soft to feel. Cautiously, his tongue touched mine and time seemed to stop. We stood there, water teasing our hard cocks, and just kissed. It was good. It was just very, very good.

Soon we really started to heat up, and only partially because of the steaming tub. As we kissed I gradually became aware of his cock touching mine, an unconscious dick dual in the gurgling water. Then he broke the kiss and smiled at me. Norman. Not Norman Desmond, just Norman, I thought, I wanted, really and truly, to believe.

Then he pushed me back against the edge of the tub. Before I could say or do anything, his lips were on my cock, the water smoking and boiling around his tanned shoulders. Good before, fantastic now. I knew he was older, that he had his share of wrinkles and gray hairs, but none of that mattered. Yes, he was fantastic.

He worked me for what felt like hours, maybe even days. Finally when I was ready to explode, he released me, a thread of saliva vanishing into the steam. He stood, facing me. Then he said it, and it all fell apart: "Jerk off for me."

It took a few minutes for the words to reach the part of my mind that was actually capable of thought. It was an uphill battle, struggling through all that lust, long minutes with my hand wrapped around my cock; stroking myself slowly, then faster, the water like a thousand hot little tongues on my shaft and head. I was close, so close, when those words hit me. Not just those words, because I'd heard those words before, but rather the way he said them, the way he was standing, the look he gave me—looking for the camera again. *The Plumber Rings Once.* Action for action, word for word, a performance. On stage, always on stage. I had been wrong. Norman wasn't there, probably had never been there; it was all Norman Desmond, the great, the legendary, Norman Desmond.

Cold water. Not hot. No, not hot at all. Cold. Ice cold. I stopped, with a pearl of pre-cum just forming at the head of my cock, which slowly dropped into the hot water. I stood stock-still. Anger flared through me, my body rock hard with fury and tension. I climbed out. He might have said something, standing there looking lost and alone in the bubbling water, but I didn't hear it.

"Darling, come back, darling!" I finally realized he was imploring me as I furiously thrust on my discarded clothes.

"No," I finally said. "No, Norman; I'm going. I have to get out of here. I have to get out of this damned museum. I have to breathe real air, not this dusty celebration of who you used to be."

"No!" he screeched. "You can't leave me! I'm Norman Desmond. You have to love me, just as all my fans love me."

I stopped, looked at him. I was angry, but seeing him, careful hair mussed by lust and hot water, face scarlet with emotion, I was also sad for him. I was sad for the lies he spun around himself, the fantasies that had become more important than reality. "Do yourself a favor, Norman. Look at the handwriting on all those letters, and talk to

Maxine about it." Then, and I really did mean it: "I'm sorry, Norman. I really am."

"I'll kill myself," he said, those perfect blue eyes unhinged with fury. "I will, you watch! You watch!" He walked over to a small table, opening a drawer. The pistol was small, like a toy in his big hands. I knew what it was and what it could do, but seeing it in his hands only reinforced the sadness of him—how far down someone so talented, so hot, had gone.

"No, Norman, you won't. Wake up. There wouldn't be anyone to appreciate the gesture. It's just you and Maxine in this empty house."

"This isn't over," he said, his voice slipping back into the thunderous command of those long-ago loops. "I'll be back, you'll see. I'll be back up there on the screen where I belong. I'll be back. I swear it! I'm Norman Desmond!"

"No," I said, "you used to be Norman Desmond."

Then it happened: Three shots. Two in the back, one in the stomach. There wasn't a lot of pain, which surprised me. The bullets hit and spun me around, slamming me facedown into that famous hot tub, maroon blood unfurling in the bubbling water.

This is where we came in, at that famous tub, the one I always wanted. It's morning now, and everyone's here: police, photographers, and those trash-talking columnists, too. But don't believe them. Believe me; I was there. After all, who are you going to believe? Them, or the corpse himself?

Like I said: Not exactly a happy ending. I got my pool—but not in any way I could really enjoy it.

Norman? Norman put on quite the show as they led him away in handcuffs, as the flashbulbs popped and the hacks called for statements. He may have gotten the best deal of all—walking out into infamous celebrity, the star of tabloids for years to come. It may have been his last close-up—but he was more than ready for it.

Bruised

David-Matthew Barnes

For Courtney Love

Anthony placed a palm to the brick wall, flattened against the cool-to-the-touch masonry so that his knuckles relaxed. The alley next to the bar smelled like piss and rape and the sweet fruit of suicide. It was a place for sudden deaths, backbreaking sex, and hushed transactions involving stolen money, lewd propositions, or mind-altering drugs.

Anthony lowered his head in the dark, sucked in the bone-chilling February air, and welcomed the city stench into his lungs as if it were a kick to his stomach. He started to gag and his body tensed with eager anticipation. He wanted to puke. He closed his eyes, focused on the sour stink that swarmed around him, hoping it would induce vomiting.

Anthony's left eyelid twitched as the music caught his attention. It was low and muffled, like a voice in a library. At first, Anthony assumed the sounds were spilling out of the bar. He titled his head toward his right, leaning closer to the allure of the words. It was a woman's voice that was singing; raw and angry, desperate. His eyes fluttered open and he saw the light, red and glowing. It started to blink with an erratic rhythm. In pulses, it flashed in a dead-end corner of the alley. At first, the radiance throbbed off and on every two seconds. Anthony counted the moments under his breath, mesmerized by the movement. The blinking became faster, like a strobe light. Suddenly, there was a buzz of electricity and the light maintained, weaker and more subdued, but steady. On instinct, Anthony pulled his hand away from the wall, clenched his fists, and felt fear tickle the edges of his spine.

A figure, tall and lean, stood beneath the light, dancing in slow-moving circles. Beckoned by the hum and glow of the red brilliance, Anthony inched closer, moving deeper into the alley. He looked up, realizing the red light was crawling down the brick wall from a neon sign above, posted on the roof of the bar like a beacon for those who were looking for ice- cold beer and white-hot sex. The sign spit and hissed and struggled to stay alive, but the red light in the alley kept breathing. The stranger, who was bathed and illuminated in the red shine, suddenly stopped dancing, sensing Anthony's presence. The figure stepped further into the light, as if he were an actor on stage, and his face was revealed. Anthony felt his breath catch in his lungs, his fingers uncurl. He recognized the sweet, angelic features of a man that Anthony himself had once described as being too pretty for his own good. The dancer slid a pair of silver chrome headphones off of his ears and said, in a soft voice that contradicted the sharp edges of the cobblestone alley, "Life despite God."

"Excuse me?" Instantly, Anthony felt the warmth of the dancer's infectious charm. He tried to resist a smile, but it was a failed attempt.

"What's so funny?" The voice, like the face, was young and exuded a bittersweet tenderness, a naiveté that was simultaneously arousing and nurturing.

Anthony felt his smile brighten. A giddiness crept into his dark eyes, a feeling he had no words for because it was the first time he had felt it. "Nothing. I'm not laughing."

The dancer was playful and tossed the words back to him. "You look like you might."

Anthony then realized that the dancer was three or four inches taller than him. Anthony touched his own face, stroking the underside of his goatee, feeling the softness of the skin and hair below his chin. It was a nervous habit; something he did when he was unsure of himself. As it was his self-imposed rule to never let down his guard, Anthony straightened his posture and the firmness of his words and declared, "I know you."

The dancer took a step back, his face shrouded again by darkness. Only his scuffed Adidas and the front of his legs could be seen in the red light. "No, you don't." The words seemed like punches, futile swings at an intruder.

"No, we've never met before."

"Then, how do you know me?"

"I know you from the bar. You're a go-go dancer. The guy in the cage. You wear the white thong."

The words were shot back to Anthony, strident. "You know my face, my body. That's all."

Although he wasn't sure what he was apologizing for, Anthony felt the urge to do so. "I'm sorry. I didn't recognize you at first."

"Because I'm dressed?" The dancer took another step, forward into the light. An oversized olive-green sweater reached down to his fingertips and a pair of beige Bermuda shorts hung loosely from his hips. His hair was a California melody of toast brown and platinum streaks, overgrown with thick strands shrouding his deer-brown eyes when he moved. All he needed was a baseball cap and he could have been the poster boy for every fraternity in America.

Anthony fished in the front pocket of his tan leather coat, searching for his pack of Marlboros and his Zippo. He said with a casual shrug, "You look different."

"I look normal." The dancer smiled and it was at that moment that Anthony felt a sudden need to protect him. He looked up as a two-car subway train rattled on wooden tracks above them. Silver, purple, and orange sparks pirouetted like tiny flecks of light to the cold, wet ground of the alley.

Anthony waited until the train had passed before he said, "What are you doing out here? Alone?"

The dancer's left hand moved up gently. His fingertips toyed with the gold crucifix that hung around Anthony's neck on a paper-thin chain. Just as quickly, he pulled his hand away. "You here to protect me? You and Jesus?"

"I don't know," Anthony replied, pulling the Zippo out of his jacket with one hand and his red and white pack of cigarettes with the other. "Do you need to be protected?" The flame from the lighter illuminated their faces with a quick flash as if a photo had been taken of the two of them.

"Maybe I was waiting for you," the dancer offered, watching the cigarette go to Anthony's mouth as he took a second drag.

Anthony revealed his Brooklyn roots when he replied, "I don't think so." He had struggled for years to rid himself of that terrible accent. Silently, he hoped the dancer hadn't noticed it. He didn't want to be known as just another Italian from Brooklyn. People in this city didn't seem to like him much and his accent only agitated them even more.

The dancer folded his arms across his chest. "No? No one's ever waited for you before?"

"No one like you."

"I'm not your type?"

"I don't have a type."

The dancer's eyes widened. They were sincere and warm, genuine fondness shining through. He winked and said, "Well, I do."

Feeling the power in the situation slip away from him, Anthony was intent on getting it back. He moved close to the dancer, the front of his faded jeans brushed against the dancer's bare legs. He leaned in and whispered in the dancer's left ear, "I just killed a guy in the bathroom in the bar."

Anthony waited for the response. In truth, he expected the dancer to pull away. He waited to hear some lame excuse about how the hour was growing late and that the dancer needed to go home. Instead, the world spun on him when the dancer leaned even closer to him and whispered back, "I know." With ease and precision, the dancer slid two fingers between the waistband of Anthony's skin and his boxers. Beneath his jeans, Anthony felt the dancer's fingers rub the tip of his pelvic bone, teasing him with a sudden sensation. Anthony ached for the dancer to touch his cock, as he felt the head of it start to swell. The dancer pulled his hand away and spoke again, his words falling onto the side of Anthony's neck, causing him to close his eyes momentarily. "Did you like it? Murder?"

Anthony answered quickly, still trying to intimidate. "I've done it before."

The dancer was intrigued and aroused. For a quick second, he squeezed the tip of his own cock through his Bermuda shorts, as if he were trying to pinch away his desire. "Why did you kill someone?"

Anthony's words were hushed. "I can't tell you that. You don't need to know."

The dancer looked him over again and surmised, "I can tell you didn't want to do it. That's why you were out here. You were about to be sick."

Anthony wiped his mouth with the back of his left hand and took another drag on his cigarette with his right. "I don't feel sick anymore."

The mood suddenly shifted as the dancer shoved his disc player and headphones into a black and white duffelbag that was perched on a pile of wooden crates. "I think you should know, I'm not looking for a boyfriend or a lover or whatever you want to call it. And just because I work in this bar doesn't mean I go home with every dumb fuck who asks me to." He zipped the duffel bag closed, then, "I do it for the money."

On instinct, Anthony took the duffel bag from the dancer in a silent gesture of chivalry. He looked the dancer in the eyes and answered, "So do I."

The dancer seemed nervous, anxious. "The cops will be here soon."

Anthony leaned forward, his Italian lips brushing against the dancer's cheek. His voice dripped with temptation when he asked, "Wanna be my alibi?"

The restaurant was nothing more than an open-all-night hole in the wall. Gyro meat on an upright spit twirled in the front window, glazed by an orange-red heat lamp. The place smelled of salt, lard, and heavy-duty pine-scented cleanser. An overweight woman with a head full of damaged, frizzy hair greeted customers from behind the canary-yellow counter. She looked older than she was and barely moved her mouth when she spoke. She habitually wiped her hands on a knee-length, permanently stained apron that she wore around her neck, untied and loose fitting. "Order's up!" she barked, her lips frozen and her jaw clenched.

Anthony and the dancer sat across from each other in brown plastic chairs, their elbows resting on the chrome edges of a shoddy table coated with smudges of grease. A faded poster of a Greek island was hung, crooked, on the wall beside them.

The dancer leaned forward, the front of his cable-knit sweater hanging only half an inch above his plate, the puddle of ketchup he had flooded his fries in. "I'll do anything," he declared.

"Oh yeah?" Anthony reached for his cup of black coffee, noticing the faint stain of lipstick around the lip of the mug.

"I don't mean sexually. I'll do anything to get out of this city."

"Where are you going?"

"I don't know, but I'm going tonight."

"I'm confused."

The dancer pushed the sleeves of his sweater up to his elbows. His eyes flashed with an inner excitement. "I quit my job tonight."

"What did you do that for?"

"Because I had to. I can't stay in this city anymore."

Anthony lowered his voice to a cautious whisper. "Somebody looking for you?"

The dancer shook his head. "Not anymore. My parents were for a while. I split when I was seventeen. Got a fake ID. Got a job. Waited things out until I turned eighteen."

"And now?"

"I turned twenty-one yesterday. I've worked in that dump for three years too long."

"So you're just going to take off?"

"Yeah, so?"

"So, why *now?*"

"I was living with this guy."

"A boyfriend?"

"He thought so. He was three times older than me. I couldn't do it anymore." The dancer stopped for a moment and took a sip of his banana milkshake. "The fucker was crazy and he smelled. It was all bullshit. I just needed a place to crash, so I could save up some money."

"To escape with?"

"I wasn't dancing in that place for my health. Letting every sleaze fuck barfly feel me up like they were shopping for vegetables in a supermarket."

Anthony fell silent for a moment, trying to recall the first time he had noticed the dancer at the bar. New Year's Eve? "Did I ever come on to you before?"

"No, but I caught you checking me out once or twice. You come and go alone. Never leave with anyone. You're a mystery to me."

Anthony cracked a smile then reached for his coffee cup, careful to avoid the lipstick stain when he took a sip. "You've been spying on me?"

"I can see everything that goes on in that place when I'm up in the cage. I have the perfect view."

Anthony glanced over to the counter, watched the woman behind the cash register run her swollen fingers along the sides of her legs, smearing flashes of mustard across the dingy apron. He turned back to the dancer and explained, "I was there for a reason."

"I don't believe you," the dancer threw back at him, confident. "You've been coming there for three months."

Anthony was firm, defensive. "I had a job to do."

"The guy in the bathroom?"

"I was just waiting for the word to do the deed. I went to that bar to prepare. It's necessary to know the outline of a place."

"In case something goes wrong?"

"It never has," Anthony said, his right hand moving up to his goatee.

"Never?" the dancer challenged, toying with his straw around his mouth, his shiny white teeth.

"I don't make mistakes. That's why they hire me. I'm the best at what I do."

The dancer took another swallow of his milkshake, licked his lips. "Who was he?"

"The owner of the place," Anthony responded. "Your boss."

The dancer didn't flinch. "Good." He shifted in his chair, leaned back a little. "I hope you did it slowly. That son of a bitch always wanted me to suck his dick. He was a fat bastard who stole money every chance he got."

"I thought you already knew who I had killed. You said you knew—"

"I lied. What are you going to do, kill me?"

Anthony cracked a smile and the shine in his dimples nearly reflected off of the top of the table. "No."

The dancer returned the smile. "No?" He paused a moment, pushed his bangs out of his eyes. "What are we doing here, Anthony?"

"This place was your idea."

"We're wasting precious time."

"I didn't realize we were in a hurry."

"I figured we needed a little foreplay."

"We're just talking."

"Conversation can be the ultimate turn-on."

Anthony's volume dropped down to a seductive purr. "As long as you know how to keep quiet when the time comes to shut up."

Their eyes locked. "Try me."

Anthony's gaze fell to the dancer's mouth, imagining. "I'm planning on it."

"You seem awfully sure of yourself," the dancer decided, then added, "Must be a Brooklyn thing."

Anthony's shoulders tensed up. "You got a problem with that?"

"No, I don't got a problem with any of this."

"Even though you know what I do for a living?"

"Who am I to judge?" The dancer reached for his duffel bag, ready to go. "You wanna walk around for a while?"

Anthony shook his head. "I'd rather take you home with me."

"That would mean I'd have to postpone my plans. My getaway."

"There's a bus leaving this trash city every second of the day. Twenty-four seven."

The dancer took a long stare at Anthony, silently understanding. "Sounds like you've thought about it, too. Running away from all of this."

"I'm planning on it."

The dancer fell silent for a moment, studying Anthony's hands. "When?"

Although Anthony had been battling with the idea, he had never talked about it. When he said it aloud, it felt as if his decision was suddenly put into motion. "I've got one more job to do. Then I'm out."

It seemed like the dancer was taunting him when he said, "Oh yeah? Where are you gonna go?"

"I don't know yet. *You* tell *me*."

The dancer stood in a corner of the living room of Anthony's cramped apartment. He flipped through a blue milk crate of record albums, Anthony's prized collection. "Mono," the dancer read from the front of a cover. "Some of these are real old. They're classics."

Anthony stood in the kitchenette, pouring white wine into two black coffee cups. "You said something to me in the alley. When we first met. Something about God. What did you mean?"

"Life despite God," the dancer repeated. He moved away from the records, his duffel bag on the floor, and looked around the claustrophobic apartment. There was a single window, above the asthmatic radiator, that over looked the city street five stories below. The dancer moved to it, lifted the window open and welcomed the icy, wintry air on his face. He noticed a family of pigeons, huddled together on the fire escape trying to keep each other warm. "It's the name of a song. I was listening to it on my headphones when we . . . met."

"Never heard of it."

"It's by Courtney Love."

"I've never been a fan."

"I have. I live by her words. She and I understand each other."

"Yeah, you know her?"

"Not personally. But she's my kindred spirit." The dancer turned away from the window and looked across the room to Anthony. "She used to dance, too. She knows what it's like. This life."

Anthony moved toward him, offering him a cup of wine. "These are the best glasses I have."

"No offense, Anthony, but I figured you lived in a nicer place than this."

"I've been saving my money, too. I don't need to live like a porn star."

"I'm sure you get paid well, for what you do."

"Why spend it all on a house? I like my apartment."

"It's the size of a shoebox."

"It serves its purpose."

"Just a place to put your head down, right?"

"I don't have much company. I'm not worried about impressing anyone."

The dancer took a sip of the wine and then said, "I know. That's what I like about you."

Anthony glanced around the room, seeing it for the first time with a pair of fresh eyes: the water-stained ceiling, the marred hardwood floors, the walls yellowed with layers of tobacco and years of occupants who had lived hand-to-mouth, paycheck to paycheck. He often wondered how many people had lived there before him and where they had ended up in life, in the world.

The apartment was decorated with bits of furniture that had been found, left behind, or given away by neighbors who were fleeing an eviction notice. There were no personal touches; no photographs, college degrees, or family heirlooms.

The dancer's words cut through Anthony's observations. "Why do you do it?"

"Live alone? I'm not much of a people person."

"No. I'm talking about your vocation. Are you Mafia? An assassin? A hired gun?"

"Is this a multiple-choice question?"

"I'm just curious."

"I've killed eleven people."

If the dancer was nervous or scared, he didn't show it. He responded with "Only eleven?"

"The world is a better place without them."

"If all of them were like my boss, then I would have to agree with you."

"Despite the stereotype, my family is not affiliated with the Mafia. The fact that I'm Italian was not a requirement for what I do."

"Then how did you get into this line of work? I'm sure you didn't have to fill out an application."

Anthony smirked, amused. "Some things are better left unsaid."

"You'll have to forgive me. I've never gone home with a professional killer before."

"Let's just say that a friend of mine recommended me for a job. I accepted the challenge, pleased the people in charge, and they were impressed enough to put me on the payroll."

"They had my boss killed because of the money he stole, didn't they?"

"You're too smart for your own good. Pretty, too."

"Never underestimate a go-go dancer."

"I'll remember that in the future." Anthony reached for the dancer, wrapping an arm around his waist, pulling him closer to his own body. He could smell the sweet wine on his warm breath. "No more questions. I'm not proud of what I've done."

The dancer looked up, deep into Anthony's eyes. It was a crucial moment for them as they understood each other without speaking. The bond between them was sealed, their fate. "Neither am I," the dancer confessed.

Their mouths inched closer, drawn together by lust. Anthony closed his eyes as he felt the dancer's tongue slide gently into his mouth. He shuddered a little. The dancer pulled away, concerned. "Are you cold?" he asked. "I could close the window."

"I've got a better idea," Anthony decided. He took the dancer by the hand and led him toward the bathroom. He reached into the darkened room and flipped on a dull, yellowish light. "This is why I took the apartment," he explained.

The dancer stood in the doorway, glancing over Anthony's shoulder. "I love it," he agreed, marveling at the antique claw-foot bathtub.

Anthony turned to him, pressing him against the doorjamb so hard that the wood dug into the dancer's back. Immediately, he unbuttoned the dancer's shorts, tugged them down around his knees. The dancer protested a little, grabbing Anthony's hands with his own. "I don't want this to be typical." Anthony looked at him, puzzled, as desire flashed in his dark eyes. "We don't have to rush. I want to enjoy every moment with you that I can."

"What?" Anthony stammered.

The dancer leaned forward, pressing his weight against Anthony, who fell back against the opposite side of the doorjamb. He suddenly felt the dancer's mouth on his neck, breathing and licking and sucking. The intensity of it caused Anthony to moan a little.

"If we're gonna do this," the dancer panted, "then we're going to do it right."

Tendrils of hot steam rose up from the bathtub and clung to the walls like secrets. Shadows danced around the room, projected by the glow of seven vanilla-scented candles. Anthony stood in the water, his left hand braced against the plastered wall. The dancer was beneath him, on his knees, his sweet mouth lowering down on Anthony's cock. "Suck it," Anthony instructed, as the dancer's tongue wrapped around the huge head.

With his left hand, the dancer reached up and ran a hand over the dark hair on Anthony's stomach, pulling at it. With his right, he cupped Anthony's balls, massaging them. "Oh fuck," Anthony whimpered, his cock twitching from the pleasure. He placed his hand behind the dancer's head, guiding him down, deeper.

The dancer reached down to his own long, hard cock and began stroking it with a passion. He looked up at Anthony, his lips sliding up and down on Anthony's thickness. Anthony glanced down and watched as his dick disappeared further into the dancer's mouth with each thrust of his hips. His low-hanging balls, smooth and hairless, smacked against the dancer's chin and neck. "That feels so fucking good," Anthony breathed, fucking the dancer's face, ramming his cock in until it banged against the back of the dancer's throat.

The dancer suddenly stopped. He looked up at Anthony and whispered with urgency, "I want you inside of me."

Anthony kneeled down in the water. The dancer turned over, offering his round ass up in the air, his face only inches above the water. Anthony spread the dancer's ass cheeks apart and gazed at his pink hole, puckering with anticipation. Anthony placed the tip of his index finger against the hole, pressing and probing. The dancer moaned and began to grind his hips, his hard cock slashing the surface of the water like a knife as he fucked the air.

Anthony lubed up his cock, paying particular attention to the enormous head of it. The dancer reached behind himself, spread his ass open even further, inviting Anthony inside. Anthony rubbed the knob of his cock against the dancer's taut hole. "Give it to me," the dancer begged. "You know I want it."

"You wanna get fucked?" Anthony asked, his Brooklyn heritage cutting through his words.

The dancer groaned with ecstasy as Anthony's cock slid inside of him, slowly entering his body. "Oh my God."

"You like it?"

The dancer wrapped his hands around the edges of the bathtub, his knuckles paling with tension. "Come on. Fuck me."

"Yeah?"

"Do it."

Anthony pressed harder, feeling his cock slide further inside of the dancer's tight hole. They fell into a rhythm of their own as Anthony's hips slammed against the dancer's ass. Anthony looked down at the dancer, running a hand across his back, his shoulder blades, his spine. He bent down, kissed the back of the dancer's neck, smelling the heat in his skin.

Anthony wanted to stay there forever; inside of the dancer, just the two of them locked together. Anthony struggled to dismiss the sudden wave of emotion he felt sweeping across the stage of his soul. The physical attraction between them bordered on savage. Never before had Anthony felt such pleasure, such a sense of completeness. He knew he was falling fast for the dancer, despite the fact that he knew they would never have a future together.

The dancer closed his eyes, muted by the sensations that were spinning through his body. In his mind, he heard music, the lyrics to one of his favorite songs, the voice of his idol. Water splashed up and into his face, over the lip of the bathtub, trickling to the floor beneath them.

Moments later, Anthony stood at the pedestal sink, facing the wall mirror. He was fully dressed, wearing a pair of old jeans and a tight-fitting black T-shirt. He wiped the layer of steam off of the glass and glanced at his own reflection. The dancer stepped out of the bathtub and wrapped a white towel around his waist. Their eyes met in the mirror, both nervous and furtive. There was a strange tension in the air. It was palpable. The dancer's hands trembled as he slipped on his boxers and pulled his T-shirt and baggy sweater over his head.

"I guess you'll be going soon," Anthony said, although he knew the dancer would never leave.

"The sun will be up soon," was the dancer's response.

The tickling of fear that Anthony had first felt in the alley beside the bar quickly returned in a flash flood. He had been in enough situations that his instinct was sharp, and he always trusted it. He was suddenly filled with a sense of dread and suspicion. It was evident in how the dancer avoided Anthony's eyes, now that he was nearly dressed, zipping up the fly of his Bermuda shorts.

Anthony's voice sliced the heavy, humid air in the bathroom. "I know what you did." His words hung in the space between them.

"What are you talking about?"

"I'm on to you," Anthony informed him.

The dancer fought to maintain his composure, his cover. "I don't know what you're talking about." He moved toward the doorway, but Anthony stepped in front of him, blocked him.

"You helped yourself, didn't you?"

"I think we both wanted this to happen, Anthony."

Anger fused Anthony's words. "I'm not talking about us. I'm talking about the money."

"If it's money you want, I don't have any."

"Bullshit. That guy you were telling me about, the one you said you lived with. The old fucker. You were talking about your boss, weren't you?"

The dancer licked his lips, ran a hand through his wet hair. "Aren't you the clever one?"

"You were fucking the guy I killed tonight?"

"I wouldn't exactly call it fucking."

"There was ten grand missing from the safe in his office. I know. I checked. I had the combination."

"Did you check his pockets? They were always filled with money. Not that I ever saw a dime of it."

"I'm not buying this."

"Well, I'm not selling."

"You said so yourself. You do it for the money."

The dancer appeared insulted. "I was talking about dancing."

A vein in Anthony's left temple began to throb. "Where in the fuck is the money?"

"It doesn't belong to you."

"Did you take it, Shane?" The words, the name, had stumbled from Anthony's mouth.

The dancer's face paled with fear. "How did you know my name?"

Anthony faltered, tried to recover. "Everybody knows your name at the bar."

"Bullshit," the dancer fired back. "I don't use my real name there. I never have."

"You told me your name. In the alley."

"The fuck I did." Shane's furtive eyes dashed around the bathroom, as if he were looking for something. An escape? A weapon? Suddenly, a realization crept into his mind and the brevity of it flashed across his baby face, made his bottom lip quiver. "You said you've killed eleven people."

"I need that money. I don't know what kind of bullshit you're trying to pull—"

"You said you only had one more job to do." Shane's eyes began to swell with tears.

"What about it?"

Shane's voice quaked as he asked, "Who's number twelve?" Anthony smiled in response. Shane tried to hold his ground, raised his voice. "Who's number twelve?!"

A look of regret swam deep in Anthony's eyes before he answered, "*You* are." Anthony lunged for Shane, his hands wrapping around his neck, shoving the breath out of him with force. Shane stumbled back, his bare feet sliding out from underneath him, trying to find some sort of traction on the wet tiled floor of the bathroom. He felt the middle of his back slam against the edge of the bathtub. Anthony's weight was on him, pushing him toward the water, struggling to shove Shane below the murky surface to drown him. The fingers, the grip around Shane's neck were tightening. Tiny black dots strutted and shimmied in front of Shane's eyes. He started to panic, realizing he was on the verge of losing consciousness. On instinct, he lifted his left knee, ramming it into Anthony's crotch. Anthony bellowed in pain, his grasp on Shane loosening momentarily. Shane rolled away from the bathtub, hitting the cold floor with a thud. He scrambled to his feet, half-crawling toward the door. Breathless, Anthony pursued him, following his victim.

As Anthony entered the living room, he heard a zipper. His eyes moved to the source of the sound. Shane stood in the corner, near the record collection and his duffel bag. In his hands was a gun. It was aimed with perfect—even professional—precision.

"What the fuck?" Anthony squeezed out of his throat. "You were packing a pistol this whole time?"

"It's my job," Shane responded, his composure intact.

Anthony lowered his eyes, accepting defeat. "Oh fuck," he muttered.

"I'm a cop, Anthony. Undercover."

"Yeah, you usually sleep with all of your suspects?"

Heavy emotion floated behind Shane's words. "Only the ones I could fall in love with."

"What are you going to do, kill me?" Anthony asked, throwing Shane's own words from earlier in the evening back at him.

They both turned at the sound of heavy footsteps on the stairs outside of the apartment. The sound of a police radio could be heard; voices melded with static.

"Fuck, are you wired?!" Anthony demanded.

"No. I'm not," Shane insisted. "I don't know why they're here."

"Don't fucking lie to me. Not now!"

Their eyes locked, spoke to each other silently. Finally, Shane broke the mutual silence between them. "I really liked you, Anthony."

"Yeah, I can tell," Anthony fired back. "I feel like an idiot. I can usually spot a cop at ten paces."

"Why *me?* Why did you get an order to kill me?"

"Because you knew too much."

"I was just a dancer in a bar."

"I followed you out to the alley. We met on purpose."

Shane tightened his grip on the gun, repositioned his aim. "Was this whole thing a big fucking joke?"

Anthony looked away, his eyes burning. "No," he answered. "Under different circumstances, you and I—"

"Under different circumstances?" Shane repeated. "You're a professional killer. I'm a cop."

"Is that why you took the money? Was I going to take the fall for it?"

"You're wrong, Anthony."

"Am I?"

"You were wrong about the money. It wasn't ten grand that was missing," Shane said. Then he quickly added, "It was a *hundred* grand."

"You set me up, you son of a bitch."

"I did," Shane admitted. "At first."

"What's that supposed to mean?"

"God forgive me, but I trust you."

"Well, you shouldn't."

"I know." The tenderness that Anthony had found so alluring returned to Shane's eyes. "But I can't help myself."

Anthony returned the same sentiment. "You think it would have been easy for me to kill you?"

"I want you," Shane breathed.

"Then why do you have a gun pointed at me?"

There was a knock at the front door. Their eyes moved in unison, darting to the door and back to each other. Shane's words were quick. "I have a plan."

"I'm listening."

"I'm giving you ten grand." Still holding the gun, Shane lowered his left hand to the ground, to the inside of the duffel bag. He pulled out a clipped wad of cash. He tossed it in Anthony's direction. The money fell with a thump at Anthony's feet. "Find a place to hide for a few hours. There's a bus leaving for El Paso at 12:12 this afternoon."

"El Paso?"

"Just a hop, skip, and a jump away from Mexico," Shane explained. There was another knock at the door, harder and angrier. "If you meet me at the bus station, we'll disappear together."

"If I don't?"

"Then I'll know it was never meant to be. You can take this money and leave me behind or—"

"I'll be there," Anthony promised.

Shane gestured to the open window with the gun. "Go. Now."

Anthony reached down for the money, still keeping his eyes on Shane. "Can I kiss you good-bye?"

"Only if that's what this is."

Anthony shook his head, stepped into a pair of athletic shoes, grabbed a coat, his wallet. "This isn't good-bye." He moved across the room, ready to make his exit. He lifted a leg, put it through the window. He looked back, straddling the windowsill. "Life despite God," he told Shane. "Kindred spirits, right?"

"Mr. Visconti, this is the police department," a rough voice said from the other side of the apartment door.

"You have ten seconds before I open that door," Shane whispered to Anthony.

"And you have a lifetime to make this up to me," Anthony replied. He pulled himself through the window and started his descent down the fire escape.

Shane watched from above, waited until Anthony was safely on the ground. He turned to the door of the apartment, moved toward it. He took a breath, reached for the brass knob. The door creaked open and Shane faced two officers with eager looks on their faces.

"Hey boys," he greeted. "There's nothing here. Looks like he slipped away." Shane managed a faint smile, his mind already on a bus to El Paso. "He's a tough one to catch."

Augury

Mark Wildyr

AUGURY: (ô-gye-rē) n.—*The art or practice of divination from omens or signs* (Random House *Webster's College Dictionary*)

I first saw him on a street corner as I left my attorney's office on a glowering August day when New Mexico's monsoon season threatened to cut loose at any moment. I don't know why I noticed him, because I was totally wrapped up in my hometown after a long absence. Maybe it was the way he held motionless while humanity washed around him. Or perhaps it was because he was observing me across the broad intersection.

Although I'm a reasonably attractive and fit thirty-five-year-old WASP, handsome strangers do not often stand and stare at me with such intensity. He was too far away to discern his features clearly, but I knew he was young and handsome with the same certainty I knew I was the object of his interest. That he was well put together was obvious even from this distance.

Intrigued, I stepped to the intersection. When the traffic light changed in my favor, I fought my way through the downtown Albuquerque noontime rush of attorneys, bankers, and government workers, all of whom chose that moment to cross Central Avenue. When I reached the far curb, he was gone. Vanished! Poof! Unreasonably frustrated, I looked up and down West Central and Third streets. There was no dark, mysterious figure. How could he have disappeared so quickly? Mentally shrugging, I reversed course and hurried off to lunch at Eulelia's in the historic La Posada Hotel.

John Hoar, an old friend and former lover, was already seated, but stood with a big, happy smile on his face to wave me over. He was still a handsome man, I noted with pleasure.

"Ted Oxley!" he roared, holding out a big hand. "Methuselah was a babe the last time I saw you!" Not satisfied with a handshake, he pulled me into an *abrazo*, the Latin embrace of men in a manly way.

"John, you old Hoar," I fell automatically into the teasing ways of our brief affair before I left for graduate school at Columbia University thirteen years ago. To be honest, I felt a flicker of interest, the first in some time.

"Teo, Teo," he reverted to style as well, using the initials for Theodore Ellis Oxley. In fact, that's the way most people knew me, thanks to him. "God, it's good to see you! How long has it been?"

"Ten, twelve years, I guess. I hear you're a successful real estate developer now."

"Developer, yes. Successful? That depends on the month. The day. The hour! It's a demanding business."

"What isn't?"

"I see you've come back from restoring the Sistine Chapel."

I sat opposite him and accepted a menu from the waiter. "Assisi, not Rome," I replied. "Worked with the team restoring the St. Francis frescoes damaged by the earthquake. Learned a lot, especially about computer restoration."

"Is it completed now?"

"Oh, no! It's a long, slow process. It'll take years yet. Although the computer program they're using to position broken pieces has cut that time in half. It's ingenious!"

"How long were you there?"

"A bit over a year. Then I was at the Duomo in Florence for a while. That's where I got the call."

"The San Pedro Mission in Alma Pura," John nodded, looking like the frog that ate the dragonfly.

"I thought you might have something to do with that." I smiled at the attractive man opposite me. "You wouldn't be on the board of the Hixton Trust by any chance, would you?"

"Guilty."

"Now I know how the name of an obscure art restorer came up in the discussion of some old frescoes in northern New Mexico."

John took a sip of water and held his tongue until we ordered. "It didn't come up casually, old son. I checked you up and down and backwards and forwards. You've been investigated, my friend. Seriously investigated. And you measured up. You're a good, competent art restorer specializing in murals and frescoes, as well as a native son. You've built a solid reputation, Teo. I wouldn't have proposed you solely on the basis of friendship . . . or past relationship. This is too important to the Trust and to the people in the area."

"I appreciate that. And thanks for the vote of confidence. Have you seen the frescoes recently?"

"Yes. A few of us made the rounds of all the projects. The Hixton Trust is financing the repair of approximately a dozen artworks in danger of being lost. Some are in churches; some are not. One is a mural in a former bank building right in this town."

"The old Albuquerque National headquarters," I nodded, referring to a building a block from where we sat.

"Right. But wherever they are, they're a part of our past." He grinned impishly, one of the few forty-year-olds of my acquaintance capable of doing so. "But I made sure you got the challenge of the lot."

"How bad are they?"

"Pretty sorry shape, I'm afraid."

"Natural or forced?"

"Beg pardon?"

"Is the decay from age and neglect, or has there been some other cause, like an earthquake or a crumbling structure?"

"I'd guess neglect and age, but there are some cracks that may come from a four hundred-year-old building simply getting tired and sagging a little. Although it's difficult to imagine four-foot walls sagging."

"Settling," I corrected automatically. "Well, I'm anxious to get to work. I just signed the contract at my attorney's office. You do realize it's going to take some time, don't you? More importantly, do the authorities on the site, the priests, realize it?"

"They're likely inured by now. The mission recently underwent a structural restoration, but they didn't touch the artwork. The santos and the old crucifix have been removed and taken to a wood restorer. There is one main fresco of Saint Peter on the wall behind the altar, and a smaller one of the Patron Saint in the narthex. That one will be more difficult because it's so damned busy. It's got a whole host of figures, some you can hardly make out."

"Have there been problems with the work?" I asked.

John immediately understood that I was talking about interference. "No. Have you ever visited the mission?"

"Not since I was a teenager."

"Well, it's not staffed permanently. They hire a local man to see to the daily tasks such as locking and unlocking the place, cleaning up, and the like. A priest, Father Hidalgo, travels weekly from the cathedral in Santa Fe to say mass and conduct any other rites that are required. They've suspended all services during the restoration."

"I see. So the only one likely to be breathing down my neck is the caretaker?"

"Probably not even him. He's a young fellow. Lives at the Teuano Pueblo and drives in every day."

"An Indian?"

"Yes. Most of the congregation, and to call it a congregation is a stretch, are Indians, mixed-bloods, and the Spanish in the area."

"And the trust is spending a lot of money to restore the place?"

John frowned. "It's just the thing old Charlie Hixton had in mind when he set up the trust. He always said big, well-known pieces of art will be taken care of; it was the lesser-known works that needed his help. Besides, the mission is an important piece of northern New Mexico's heritage, Teo. It deserves to be rescued."

I held up a protesting hand. "You don't need to convince me! I believe *all* art merits salvation."

Our orders were delivered, and I caught up on this dear friend's life while we ate. John lived openly with his significant other, a man whom I did not know. Despite his protestations, he was one of the more successful developers in the city. He had a hand in most of the major renovations in the downtown area. Of course, he soon discovered I was alone, prompting a review of mutual acquaintances, who was available and who was not. He didn't quite buy the claim I had time for nothing but work. He was also a little put out that I could not provide risqué tales of studly young Italians I'd seduced.

"You're not claiming to be celibate?" he asked suspiciously. "You haven't converted and become a priest, have you?"

I laughed uneasily. Knowing John, he wouldn't quit until it came out. "Converted? No. Neither in faith nor in orientation. Celibate? That pretty well describes my life for the past couple of years."

"Why?" he asked in his blunt manner.

"Long story. Not sure I'm up to telling it yet," I put up a final, half-hearted resistance.

"Nonsense! Surely a man of letters like you knows confession is good for the soul. At any rate, I need something to fill my busy afternoon."

We left the dining room and found a couple of comfortable chairs in the magnificent, rustic lobby that magically transports a person a hundred years back in time. After we snagged a couple of drinks, I started down a painful road.

"I was with someone for three years, John. A wonderful man with similar interests and a hyper, quirky sense of humor. We complimented one another perfectly. Don't know why, because he was as macho as I am, but it worked. Our biggest trouble was fighting off women when we went anywhere together." I swallowed hard at the memory. "Leo—his name was Leonard—was an art historian."

"Leo and Teo? That's pretty neat," he interjected.

I didn't react; I'd commenced and needed to finish. "We were at Columbia together, but were just friends for the first couple of years. Got together almost by accident, but when we did, it was everything it was supposed to be. All the bells and whistles. Everything from knock-down drag-outs, to long peaceful moments of enjoying each other, to the most perfect lovemaking imaginable.

"Too good to last, I guess, because he got mugged in Washington Square one afternoon by three goons. Being the man he was, he took them on. Mistake. Ended up in the hospital. They did all kinds of tests and assured us he was mending well. For a few weeks he complained of occasional headaches and a lack of energy. Then one day he didn't get out of bed. I don't know how long I slept beside him after he died," I continued, my voice breaking. "He was clasping my arm when I woke." Blinking rapidly, I took a swallow of the drink, choking on the liquor.

"Jesus, Teo. I'm sorry."

"I went nuts, John. After I buried him, I went stark raving mad. I retained just enough sense to realize if I turned to liquor, I'd never crawl out of the bottle. So I started fucking instead. I'm amazed I'm not dead of AIDS or some other STD. I fucked everything that moved! Got a hell of a reputation . . . of another sort. It all came to a head one night when two other libertines and I decided to hire some call boys, you know, young studs. I ended up with a novice, a young kid from Wyoming who didn't know what he was getting into. He was seduced by the money and got talked into it by a buddy who was a pro."

I dropped my head before his gaze. "Damn, what I did to that kid! He'd probably had a blow job before, maybe even given a few, but that's about all. I fucked his face and his ass all night long. By morning, the guy was used up. The look in his eyes when I paid him probably saved me. He was hurt, not physically . . . at least not too much . . . but deep down where he lived. I likely put the nail in his coffin when I gave him a thousand dollars out of pure guilt. I suffered for that, John. I tried to get in touch with him a couple of times to apologize, mentor, hell, who knows? But he was gone. Left town. It bothered me so much I went to a clinic, got tested, and haven't touched anyone since. I left for Italy shortly after that and figured I'd be lured out of it by those hot Italians, but I wasn't even tempted."

"Be damned," was all John could come up with. "Have you continued to be tested?"

"Yeah," I nodded. "Went to a hospital every three months for two years. Everything's clear."

"Don't know what to say, Teo. You were lucky. Doesn't even sound like you. You were so damned careful when we were together. A regular pain in the ass about it, as I recall." He chuckled at the double entendre.

"I wasn't kidding, John. I went crazy!"

He inspected me carefully. "Doesn't show. You still look as fresh and unsullied as the day I met you. Damn, you're a handsome fellow."

I gave a grudging grin. "You're taken, so cut the crap." I turned back to business. "Where will I stay while I'm working up there? As I recall Alma Pura is sort of remote. In the mountains, right?"

"Right. Actually, the church is outside of town a few miles. There's a small, rundown adobe a couple of hundred yards from the mission. You're welcome to use it during the project. Don't know how suitable it will be, but it's yours if you want it."

"Great! I don't care what kind of shape it's in; I'll take it. The job will involve some equipment, and that will save a lot of trouble hauling it back and forth."

"I had them leave the scaffolding from the structural work," John added. "It's lightweight metal, portable. And I had them deliver a gasoline generator—two, in fact. One for the church and one for the shack."

"Do I need camping gear?"

"A fart sack might not hurt, but there's a bed and some broken-down furniture. It gets cold at night up in those mountains. I don't know if you remember, but August is the rainy season up there."

"Yes, and the humidity will be a problem. But the diagnosis will take a lot of time, so the rains will likely be over before that's finished."

"Featherbedding already? Remember, it's a fixed-price deal!"

I laughed as John's practical side surfaced. "Yeah, but this is slow work, my friend. There's an old saying: 'People without the patience to do art restoration take up searching haystacks for needles to make a living.'"

John rolled his eyes. "Oh, man! Well, I'm going back to real estate development work and leave this artsy-fartsy stuff to you." He hesitated before rising. "Tell me something. Do you guys really use *bread* to clean old paintings?"

I smiled. "Sourdough is best. You knead it into a ball, roll it against the surface, and it lifts dirt right off. Have to be sure to remove all the bread, or you'll attract insects."

I refused his offer to drop me off at my car parked a few blocks away and left La Posada by the Second Street exit. I was grinning with pleasure at seeing my old lover again when I suddenly halted and looked behind me. A man in black waited across the Tijeras intersection half a block away. Eerily motionless, he was peering intently in my direction. No . . . *at me.*

I made a snap decision and walked straight to the intersection. The figure stirred uneasily. A city bus almost clobbered me as I attempted to cross against the light. Jumping back onto the curb, I impatiently let it pass before dashing across the street.

There was no one there!

The first big raindrops of the monsoon season pelted my head and shoulders as I stood mystified on the empty corner. It made no sense. There was an unimpeded view for a solid block in every direction, and no convenient doorway into which he could have slipped. So where was he? The fucker was there two seconds ago! Had a car picked him up and whisked him away? Had there been a vehicle at the curb? Maybe there was, but if he didn't want to confront me, why the hell was he *watching* me? A chill independent of the soaking I was suffering gripped my entire body.

I encountered no mystifying wraiths over the next few days as I looked up old acquaintances and assembled the equipment I needed for my trip north. On a thunderous Sunday afternoon I loaded everything into a leased Toyota four-by-four and drove up I-25 through intermittent rainstorms. I stopped by the cathedral in Santa Fe to pick up a key to the old mission church that was my destination, dined in one of the City Different's excellent restaurants, and then drove the remaining forty miles to the mountain community of Alma Pura, a village that Richard Bradford could have been describing in his hilarious and touching *Red Sky at Morning,* although the film based on his novel picked Truchas, New Mexico, which lays several mountain peaks distant.

There was nothing to the rustic hamlet except for a dilapidated general store, a café, a farm and ranch supply house, and, of course, the ubiquitous corner garage and filling station—except there was no corner. Or traffic light. Or even a stop sign. Pausing only to top off the gas tank, fill up a couple of jerry cans with fuel and water, and ask directions, I headed up a narrow mountain track east of the village as quickly as the weather and road conditions permitted in order to arrive at the Misíon del San Pedro de las Lomas before darkness fell.

The little church might have been called St. Peter of the Hills, but it was located in a small valley smack-dab in the middle of the *mountains*. The rain that pestered me virtually all the way ceased as I entered the little glen. My first view of the mission in twenty years was through a wispy fog in rapidly failing light.

Although this House of God was small as such structures go, it loomed large above the Toyota as I sloshed to a halt before it. The color of mother earth with two stubby campaniles that had never seen bells, it could have been a monolithic, cross-crowned boulder hurled from a long-forgotten volcano. It looked half-natural, half-manmade, as if some gargantuan Michelangelo had abandoned an unfinished masterpiece. A campo santo spread out to the side and curled around behind the building. Obviously ancient, the cemetery appeared well-tended.

The only other structure in the valley was a small adobe shack not far to the west of the church. With sinking heart, I realized this was my home for the next few months. Ignoring the unnatural, damp chill of the rain-soaked mountains, I set to work making my quarters habitable. Thank God for John Hoar's gasoline generator! It was the only thing that made the place livable, providing heat as well as light. Before I moved a single piece of equipment, I swept and dusted the place thoroughly. When I finally went for my personal luggage after everything else was put in its place, I froze with the car door half-open. The rain had started again, gently plastering my hair against my skull. My flesh puckered. A chill swept down my back and gripped my testicles.

Frantically, my eyes roved back and forth. Someone, *something* was there. There by the church. In the deep recess sheltering dark, crudely carved doors. A shadow. A black shadow. The Indian caretaker?

"Who's there?" My shout echoed hollowly through the sodden twilight. "I'm here for the restoration!" I called foolishly, my voice falling away at the end.

The thing stood mute. Motionless. Could it be a mere shadow? Grabbing a heavy flashlight out of the glove box, I walked slowly around the car, my eyes never leaving the dark outline. If the thing was going to disappear, this time I was damned well going to see it! I covered fifty yards. A hundred. Nothing changed, except the outline of the shadow grew clearer. It was no natural thing! Fifty yards away, my nerve failed. I stood in the rain, water rolling off my shoulders, trembling from cold and fear. Yes, fear! As I watched, the shadow edged out of the recessed doorway and slipped around the corner of the building. Its flight released me from my paralysis.

"Hey!" I yelped, my voice reverberating eerily off the hillside. "Come back here! Are you the caretaker? Hey, I need some help here!"

I knew before reaching the corner he would be gone. I was right. There was nothing there. No *thing* and no *one*. Spinning awkwardly in the mud, I splashed back to the adobe, my soaked back tingling with an apprehension that refused to leave even after I closed the thick wooden door to the shack behind me.

Despite my eagerness to examine the frescoes, I lost the desire to visit the mission church that night, telling myself it would be better to wait until morning when there would be natural light. What a load of bullshit! The building would be dark and gloomy with small clerestory windows that admitted little daylight. During services, the mission would be close with the scent of a hundred burning candles and human bodies. I fixed something to eat and retired. Forgoing the sleeping bag, as it was something I could not exit in a hurry, I opened it up and made a heavy comforter out of the thing.

As I lay waiting for sleep to claim me, I reviewed what I knew of northern New Mexico. The most Spanish, as opposed to Mexican, part of the state, it bore a reputation as clannish and closed. This was the land of *machismo* and *mirasoles, palo altos* and *moradas,* the very heart of *Los Hermanos de Luz,* the Brotherhood of Light, New Mexico's secretive Penitenties. For all I knew, San Pedro de las Lomas was a chapter house for these self-flagellants with a passion for Christ's Agony. The sect was not just the stuff of colonial legend; it existed today. Would they welcome a chestnut-haired, hazel-eyed, homosexual, Anglo-Saxon Protestant in their midst? Probably not. Would they act on their prejudices? Probably not. But who knows? I certainly didn't. I grew distinctly uncomfortable in my new environment before a restless sleep came for me.

Stealing in on the night, the specter crossed unknown dimensions to take advantage of my slumber and claim my unconscious. The Stygian presence roiled the swirling mists of my dream. Cold, prickling fear drew me halfway out of my sleep, but my tormentor remained subliminal, insubstantial, permitting only swift, fragmentary glimpses of himself. Dark, sharply planed features. Midnight black hair leaking from a rough, brown cowl. Bottomless eyes as dark as the pit. I cowered before him, lying naked except for my briefs. My nose stung with the hint of something in the air. Despite my terror I became hopelessly aroused by the *varón*. How did I know he was a man in his prime? My cock knew; it strained to escape its cotton sheath in an erection surpassing any I'd achieved in two long, dry years. My ethereal visitor took on substance as he sought to commune, but the dream Theodore Oxley, the pitiful, excessively stimulated creature shivering at his feet, gradually put aside his terror and surrendered to the overwhelming sexual excitement that suffused the dream.

I shifted, fearing to move, but *needing* contact. The shadow that was not a shadow threw back the cowl covering his head, revealing long ebony locks. The shimmering face steadied and took on form, drawing my breath from me. A sigh echoed through the dream and became a word. "Beauty!" Beyond handsome, beyond comely, but an abject beauty never before beheld! Yielding to a long-denied, pent-up, suffocating desire, I timorously reached for him, but he escaped my grasp, losing some of his definition. I did not care. I callously masturbated while he watched, the expression on his face neither revulsion nor desire. As I spilled my seed, he faded from the dream, his disappearance rekindling a vague sense of fear as I realized he had failed to make the reason for his presence known. *He would return!*

I woke to a sticky wetness and found my belly awash in a sea of cum. I had not ejaculated in over two years, so my system spewed semen lavishly. Much of it slid down my sides to soak the mattress beneath me. I lay as I was, suffering the discomfort, afraid that to move was to lose the last vestiges of the dream. Able to reconstruct only bits and pieces, I finally rose and scrubbed my person and my bed clean of the mess. Then I slept deeply for what remained of the night, untroubled by whatever lurked out there and in the fringes of my mind.

Daylight filtering through thick, fast-moving clouds dispelled little of the old mission's mysterious atmosphere. The damp morning virtually cried out for an *alba,* that sweet, haunting Spanish paean to the Virgin raised by chanting voices of padres and Indian neophytes. But the hulking church remained silent, its adobe exterior slightly out of true, its walls sloping inward as they rose. The only adornments were a simple cross at its apex and a rude cinquefoil above the flat, segmented arch of the entryway. A fresh, earth-brown wash covered the building, effectively concealing any work the architectural renovators might have performed, at least on the outside. The doors, less crudely carved than I'd imagined last night, portrayed events in the life of the Saint. The world was totally silent when I turned the big key in the old lock. Just as I moved into the narthex, a single squirrel set up a noisy chatter in the nearby woods.

The first fresco, the busy one, spanned the wall above the entry to the nave. Inspecting the mural by the half-light of the open main doors, I was dismayed by its condition. Faded colors were expected, but a leak in the ceiling had allowed water to stain the plaster and bleed the paint. Even in the gloom, I spotted a large crack running diagonally across the piece.

I passed through the narthex into the sanctuary, a large, open chamber bare of pews or furnishings of any sort. Low-ceilinged aisles on either side held the Twelve Stations of the Cross in carved stone. The large mural behind the altar above the open chancel was arresting even in the dim, musty light despite its state of decay. The Saint, Catholicism's first Pope and my denomination's Rock, surveyed his New

World converts through the large, liquid eyes of an Indian. This was not Italian art, but was painted in the flat style we now term "Primitive," relying upon the clever use of color to bring the painting to life. Zia sun rays haloed the Sainted One, who was surrounded by the cloud and rain and rainbow symbols of his Native faithful. Even faded and cracked and in need of help, the fresco was awesome, a worthy challenge.

While I was inspecting the disassembled, stacked scaffolding, my butt suddenly puckered. Turning, I beheld a black figure at the far end of the nave. Obscured by gloom, silent and foreboding, he struck me dumb. Slowly he came forward in a curious gliding motion. He had covered half the cavernous room before I discerned it was caused by the swaying of a cassock. My specter genuflected before the altar and then stood to face me, taking the form of a handsome, hawkish, Hispanic man with an air of authority. I judged him to be about my age.

"You must be the art restorer," he said in a voice that would carry well throughout a church much larger than this one.

I closed my mouth with a snap, realizing this was not my stalker from Albuquerque. Nor was he the material manifestation of my dream habitué. Or . . . was he? Had I masturbated last night in the presence of a priest? A wave of shame swept over me as I replied.

"Ted Oxley, at your service. I was taking my first look at the job." I instantly regretted my choice of words as demeaning.

Dark, fanatical eyes scanned the mural above us. "Father Hidalgo," he said absently. "I have the privilege of serving this mission." The deep-set gaze moved to me. "Are you of the Faith?" he demanded.

"Not *of* the Faith," I replied carefully. "But I have a deep respect for the Faith. I spent the last two years at Assisi and the Florentine Duomo."

"I see," the man breathed. It was impossible to fathom his attitude toward me, but his next words betrayed distaste for his forced reliance on a mere mortal. "Can you save it?"

"Yes. I can restore the frescoes."

"You have a holy task. I trust you will measure up to it," he proclaimed ponderously, making his way to a door that exited the chancel. He paused. "Rodrigo will help. You may consider him your servant in this matter."

"Rodrigo. Is he the caretaker?"

"Yes," the priest nodded and spread his hands, an unconscious gesture that was oddly sexual. "He will be here later this morning. He can assist with the scaffolding."

"Thank you. I'm sure he'll be a big help." But I was talking to an empty doorway. The strange, sensual cleric had moved out of sight. Shaken, I shook my head to clear it. Was I lusting after a priest now? Maybe he *was* my vision.

Turning back to the painting, I noticed the *retablo*, which normally rests behind the altar, was missing. Likely it was an elaborate wooden carving that had been taken with the crucifix and the santos. Too bad. I would have liked a shot at restoring those, as well.

I had erected a skeleton scaffold before the main fresco and was teetering at ceiling height to take the last in a series of photographs when I heard a noise below. Startled, I almost fell. Clutching at an unsteady upright for support, I glanced down. When viewed from this perspective, the church did not appear so small. A child stood before the altar gazing up at me.

"Hi!" I said as brightly as my lurching heart would permit. "I'm finished with my picture taking. Be right down." Why it was necessary to explain this to a boy, I wasn't certain. When I reached the stone floor, I discovered it was no child standing there, but a young man. A young Indian. A handsome, young Indian. Recovering, I held out a hand.

"You must be Rodrigo," I said. "I'm Teo Oxley."

The child-man extended a slender, muscled arm and accepted my hand, allowing me to do all the gripping. "Meet you," he almost whispered in a throaty voice. I gathered there had been a "Glad to" in there somewhere.

"I'm the restorer. You can call me Teo. Father Hidalgo said you'd be willing to help me from time to time?" It came out as a question more than a statement.

The dark head bobbed once. The youth seemed painfully shy around gringos, at least around this one. He dropped his huge brown eyes before my curious examination. Here was another who could have populated my dream, although my impression of the mysterious watcher was of a taller man. Rodrigo was short, like many of the Pueblo Indians of my experience, but his five-seven frame was packed with muscle. Red-brown skin, fleshy nose, a face broader than the priest's. Features put together in an earthy, handsome way. He must have been around twenty, yet he radiated the aura of an adolescent. But there was nothing childlike about his build. Wide shoulders fell away to a ridiculously narrow waist and trim hips. My cock stirred as I regarded him.

"Would you like to help? Perhaps learn something about how to care for the frescoes?" I asked, more to break the silence than for any other reason.

He raised his gaze to meet mine briefly before sliding away to the side. God! This youth's soul wept from his eyes! If he ever actually looked at me, I stood in danger of losing control. No one had made such an impact on me in a long time . . . except possibly the priest. I began to perceive the Misíon del San Pedro de las Lomas as a dangerous place!

"Yes," the youth answered quietly, his Adam's apple bobbing with his words. "I would like to be able to take care of *El Señor*." It startled me that he spoke of the Saint as he would the Lord Jesus.

"Great!" I enthused falsely, seeking to shake the lusty image of this youth forming in my mind. And in a *church* yet! Fortunately, it is a cultural trait for these people to avoid staring directly at another person, or he would have read the lascivious thoughts painted across my face.

"Well, you can start by helping me take down this scaffold and reassemble it. I don't think I did it right the first time. Too rickety."

Rodrigo scampered up the shaky structure, further inflaming me with a good view of his exciting backside. It took almost an hour, but we tore down and reassembled the thing so that it was much more secure. It would serve my purposes nicely.

The youth hovered at my side on the scaffold as I set about examining the mural in detail. I prattled constantly, probably out of nervousness over his disturbing presence.

"This is going to take a little time, Rodrigo. It's slow, painstaking work. Actually, it's four jobs. First you have to diagnose the situation. Find out what the problems are, like what caused those cracks, for instance. And how deep do they go? Do they radiate? What materials were used to create the work? How was the paint made? It was ground up, you know. The paint ingredients, I mean. And then they were applied right onto the wet plaster. That's the difference between a mural and a fresco. Anyway, I have to determine things like that."

I took a breath as I continued to scan the Saint's face up close. "And then there's the job of cleaning. Removing centuries of accumulated dirt and smoke can be tricky. This painting should have been cleaned every generation or so. What's a generation? Twenty years? That means Saint Peter should have taken a bath twenty times since he was created. Probably hasn't been cleaned once."

The silent young man conducted his own inspection, obviously thrilled to be so close to his Saint. I went on pontificating.

"The third step is to repair the mural. Correct any damage, fill the holes, mend the cracks without losing any more of the original work than necessary. And then comes the biggie . . . the retouching. That's what takes the longest. We'll actually re-create the fresco using paints and colors as close to the original as possible." I glanced at the young man at my side, taking a moment to appreciate the way his clothing hugged his form. Nice!

"Do you know anything about painting, Rodrigo?"

He shrugged before answering. "I do some pictures. You know, draw them. Paint them."

"You ever painted old Saint Peter?" I made it a jocular question, but he took it seriously.

"Yeah," he replied, flushing a shade darker. "Once or twice."

"May I see them?"

His eyes flickered over me and then returned to the face of San Pedro. "Maybe. Someday."

I almost laughed at his endearing shyness. "I'd like to see them, Rodrigo. Really."

"Donno. You're a real painter. I'm not. They say you painted for the Holy Father in Rome."

I did laugh then. "No, but I helped restore Saint Francis of Assisi and did some work on the Zucarri frescoes at the Duomo in Florence."

Out of the corner of my eye, I saw him swallow a host of questions that leapt to his lips. Smothering this spark of real interest, he turned stolid again.

"Promise me you'll show me some of your work, Rodrigo." Seeking to overwhelm his reticence, I put the force of authority in my voice. "I want to see it. I need to judge just how much help you can be to me. I'd like to know if I can hire you as my helper."

The surprise showed momentarily before he got control of himself. "The priests pay me."

"They pay you to take care of the premises. I would be paying you to help with this job. You can perform your duties to them and earn something extra for yourself . . . and your family," I added as a clincher.

"I donno. Maybe."

Judging it best to leave matters at that, I returned to my minute examination of the fresco, explaining to the young man what I was looking for and what I was finding.

The threat of rain was heavy that night as I prepared to go to bed—with some trepidation, I might add. Would my specter visit tonight, disturbing my rest with that curious mixture of fear and excitement? Had I met him today in the flesh? Was it the haughty, aristocratic Father Hidalgo who preyed on my mind in the darkness of my dreams? But would the bold Hidalgo shirk a physical confrontation after traveling to Albuquerque to see me? He would most likely have marched straight up to me and made his presence known. Or was it gentle Rodrigo, he of the dark beauty so akin to my spectral visitor? It could be either. It could be neither.

No. The mysterious figure who watched from across the chasm was not Hidalgo or Rodrigo. He was similar, but not identical to either of these darkly handsome men.

My thoughts turned to my reaction to each of them. After two years of sexual denial, why was I responding to these particular males? Was it as simple as the chemical affinity of pheromones? I had long ago come to accept my homosexuality. I saw nothing wrong with it. Love was love was love. Praised as man's ultimate achievement throughout the entire world, why should it be wrong when applied to mature adults of the same gender? Simple. It shouldn't. My love for Leo was not sick or dirty or disgusting. It was beautiful and fulfilling and right for the two of us. And our libidinal activities were merely the physical expression, the customary outlet for the natural lust kindled by that love.

I accepted, of course, that there were limitations. Early on, I had created my own absolutely inviolate limits. I would not accept the love or the attentions of someone who was bound by a vow. Any sort of a vow. A vow of marriage, a pledge of love . . . a priestly oath. Then why had I reacted to the powerful presence of Father Hidalgo? I met a host of handsome, lusty priests in Italy and had been tempted by none. But had this magnetic cleric offered himself, I would certainly have violated a personal rule and fallen victim to my libido.

And Rodrigo! Oblivious to his own sexual prowess, the young man exerted an appeal that was difficult to ignore. I sensed there was danger lurking beneath his innocence, and found myself wondering about his sexual partners. Had there been any? Of course there had! A handsome, healthy male does not achieve the ripe old age of twenty or so without finding physical expression for his desires. Had he been with a man? Or were they all women? Was he pledged? Married?

And then there was that third presence. The mysterious shade that eluded both my tangible and my ethereal touch. Perhaps it was the mystery surrounding this dark stranger that made him the most frightening and desirable of the three. After all, he had watched me stroke myself to an ejaculation. A real one, not an illusory one. At least, the hot, sticky cum was real. Slowly, I succumbed to slumber and slept peacefully through the night.

Rodrigo brought samples of his work the next morning, and I was pleasantly surprised by what I saw. His drawings were well proportioned; his colors, good and strong. The flat primitive figures in his work were well balanced with complementary and contrasting colors in interesting ways. The kid had talent! Hiding his pleasure behind a handsome, stolid face, he nodded somberly when I praised the work and agreed to hire him as my helper. He was not quite so bland when I named a salary; the brown eyes widened fractionally.

The boy was a great deal of help and well worth his wages. He saved me time in immeasurable ways, but it was his mere presence that was most comforting. In truth, the gloomy old mission church spooked me. There were countless sightings of shadows that should not be, of a *presence* in remote corners, occasional assaults on my olfactory senses even though there was no discernable odor. The impression of being observed. A few times, even the placid Rodrigo exhibited an unaccustomed uneasiness.

Concerned about the leak in the ceiling over the fresco in the narthex, I went up to make certain our daily rain showers were not adding to the problem, but the structural restoration had repaired the leaky roof. I set up some lights to dry the damp plaster. Rodrigo was weeding the graveyard, so I worked alone this morning. Sensing him behind me, I turned to explain I had to be careful not to dry the spot too quickly, as that would cause the plaster to flake and peel.

There was no one there!

Yet there was! I could sense him. In the far corner, a darkness too deep to be natural stirred as I grew aware of it. The hair on my neck and arms rose. My flesh pimpled like a goose's. Fear dried up my throat.

"Who are you?" I croaked. I was answered by a sigh, the same as in my dream. "What do you want?" My voice took on timbre, strength. "Why are you doing this to me?"

The shadow undulated, as though in agitation. Was it angered by my interference? My very presence?

"Look," I said reasonably. "I won't be here long. I'm just repairing the ravages of time. Then I'll be gone, okay?"

A gust whipped through the closed narthex. My nose itched fearfully. My body chilled, and then heated as I responded to an overpowering rush of sexuality. Lust swept my entire body, weakening my knees, engorging my cock, fevering my mind. What was *happening?*

Even as I responded physically, even as my turgid cock pressed against my trousers, the presence retreated. The shadow weakened, but before it faded away completely, I glimpsed that handsome face of my dreams twisted in anguish, in frustration! Then he was gone.

Giving way to my own fear, I rushed out the heavy, carved doors into a weak sunlight, crashing into Rodrigo on the steps.

"What's the matter?" he cried, concern written across his handsome, beardless face. *"Patrón! Qué pasa ?"*

"I'm . . . I'm going to the house for a few minutes," I gasped, pulling from his grasp and staggering across the muddy distance to the adobe. I did not realize he had followed until he entered behind me.

"Are you all right?" he asked in the deep voice that couldn't possibly come from that young larynx, yet did.

"Sorry. I just felt . . ." My voice died away as I turned to face him. Not a yard away, he was almost lost in the gloom of the place. He stood, as my apparition had stood, watching me through old eyes set in a young face. His unconscious masculinity robbed me of my senses, gave me the audacity to match my sudden surge of strength.

Still in the grip of the *presence's* sexuality and the strange scent that had no odor, I touched his smooth, dark cheek. My thumb traced the line of his chin. His eyes widened in surprise, but he held still. I placed my hands on either side of his head and drew my thumbs over the fine, curved arch of his eyebrows. I touched his silky lids, endured the tickle of long, curled lashes.

Slowly, I moved my hands down his neck to his shoulders. He made no sound or movement. His mouth was parted, his breath light and feathery on my wrists. My hands roamed of their own accord, exploring the hard biceps, enjoying the satiny flesh of his forearms. Then I clasped him below the armpits and moved along the flared ribs to the waist.

Rodrigo was frozen, muscles tense and trembling. The buttons to his cotton work shirt were undone in an instant. My fingers touched the hot flesh of his smooth chest. He remained silent as I slid my hands down his belly, detecting hidden muscles. He flinched when I reached his groin, but permitted me my way.

Caressing his manhood delivered me into the power of this mystifying, overwhelming sexuality permeating the atmosphere. I fell to my knees and fought open his fly, revealing a flaccid cock built to Rodrigo's own scale, its flesh darker than that of his flat belly. Without hesitation, I gently sucked him to an erection. I clawed his clothing down to his knees; my hands cupped the smooth cheeks of his buttocks, clasped the full balls, played in the hair of his bush as I worked on him. In time a sigh filled the room, not a ghostly gasp, but a worldly expression of pleasure from the comely, sculpted Indian in my grasp. A thick, musky stream of semen hit the roof of my mouth. Rodrigo grunted as his orgasm impacted him, but otherwise he remained as motionless as a statue. I sucked that exciting organ until it began to soften. Only then did I move away from him and tear open my trousers.

The boy stood with his pants around his ankles and watched me masturbate. I came quickly, excited by this beautiful innocent watching my self-abasement through wide, wondering eyes. With ejaculation came shame. I had used him. I turned away to clean and cover myself. When I looked again, he was gone, leaving me to wonder if he had merely acquiesced to my demands or willingly participated.

I found him in the nave setting out the materials we would need for the day, acting as though nothing had happened, but avoiding my gaze. It was an hour before I could behave naturally around the achingly handsome youngster.

As August passed into September, the monsoon season weakened, bringing only intermittent thundershowers. My diagnosis completed, I started cleaning the main fresco. Rodrigo worked at my side, unknowingly stoking my passion as he moved about his tasks with a natural, manly grace. I took small liberties I am not even certain he understood. A hand on the shoulder as we stood contemplating something. A lingering touch on the arm as I made a point. A finger on his broad chest to emphasize that point.

Hidalgo appeared a few times, moving almost as silently and mysteriously as my shadowy wraith. His presence continued to disturb me, and when he left, I would look hungrily at Rodrigo, who did not appear to notice.

Other than checking on the drying of the plaster, I did not work on the fresco in the narthex. I first wanted to finish the restoration of the one in the nave, the major work. Normally, I would have tackled the minor piece to learn the peculiarities of a job, but for some reason I was reluctant to take on that one. Perhaps it was because, as John Hoar had said, it was so busy. It was also in greater disrepair. The large one in the nave was less of a challenge; therefore I reversed the learning process.

The cleaning went surprisingly well. Rodrigo's plodding patience paid off in spades. The tedious care demanded by the work did not bother the youth as much as it did me. Working closely beside him made the tedium infinitely greater.

I went into Santa Fe one Friday for supplies and tarried over until Saturday morning in order to pick up some of Rodrigo's paintings I had had framed as a surprise. They looked terrific.

When I handed them over, he appeared more embarrassed than pleased, but I was beginning to understand the boy and knew he was appreciative.

"Do you ever sell them?" I asked.

"Sometimes," he admitted reluctantly. "At powwows."

"Great! I'll give you a hundred dollars apiece for these two," I said, pointing out my favorites, one of which was San Pedro himself.

"Give them to you," he mumbled.

"No you won't. You sell your art; you don't give it away. Deal?"

He ventured to look me in the eye fleetingly. "Deal."

"Good. I'll add it to the paycheck next Friday, okay?" He nodded. "Right now, I'm going to go hang them in the shack. Give me a hand?"

He hesitated briefly before nodding.

I don't think it was a ploy on my part, but it might as well have been. As he stood in front of me straightening a picture after we hung it, I put my hands on his trim hips. He froze.

"Rodrigo," I gasped, pulling him against me. He leaned quietly against me as my hands encircled him, roving his body freely. "Oh, God, I want you!" I whispered raggedly. "You are so beautiful!"

The youth allowed me to strip him naked and study his perfectly proportioned body. Rodrigo remained soft, unexcited. I tore off my clothes, pushed him onto the bed, and fell on him. He moved his head slightly, causing my lips to brush his smooth cheek, but I turned him to me and thrust my tongue into his mouth. His entire body stiffened, but he suffered this, too. The kiss struck me senseless. I went wild, as mad as I had been after Leo's death. I kissed and bit and sucked the dark, roseate flesh over the whole of his body. But only when I took him in my mouth did he respond, his thick, uncircumcised cock growing full length down my throat.

I drew him almost to climax. When his legs went tense and his testicles began to draw up, I released him and sucked the balls back down into place. Mad for him, I rolled over and raised my legs so that he fell against my fevered ass. When his prick jabbed at me, I locked my ankles behind him and pulled him into me. Rodrigo entered my channel in one long thrust. Only then did he permit an emotion to cross his handsome features: surprise! Clearly, he had never done this before. Once the astonishment passed, something else flickered in those big eyes. He thrust at me tentatively, and then gaining confidence, he fed the thing growing in him. Desire. Carnal desire.

Once his switch was thrown, Rodrigo fucked like a savage, throwing himself into it with everything he had! He beat against me frantically, as though frightened of what he was doing, but helpless to prevent it . . . as if in terror of discovery and interruption.

"Easy," I whispered.

Immediately, he turned amazingly sensitive, brushing my lips with his fingertips, my nipples with his soft lips, pressing my erection against his belly. He settled into a strong, rhythmic thrusting that drove me wild. Long before he was ready, I reached the point of no return. His hard stomach rubbing against my cock brought me home. I grunted, groaned, and spewed. The youth picked up his pace, delivering long, slashing lunges. Soon, his lids dropped slowly over his eyes, and he came, sowing his seed with the first audible noises of our lovemaking, strange sounds in his native tongue. He could have been calling me a son-of-a-bitching, pansy queer, and it wouldn't have mattered. The words were beautiful to my ears.

The boy shyly avoided my eyes as he drew out of me and rose to clean himself. Nonetheless, I saw him dart a look at my nakedness as I directed him to a basin of water. When he was dressed, I stopped him with a hand on the arm.

"Stay the night with me, Rodrigo," I whispered.

He dropped his gaze to the floor. "Can't," he mumbled, and was gone.

With his departure, I sensed something, felt something. My nose tingled. Tremendously aroused, I fell back on the bed and masturbated, holding desperately to the image of the boy laboring above me. But as I came, the vision altered, and the formless beauty of that shadowy specter replaced the gentle features of my young lover. The eerie sense of being watched eased, and I knew the shade had departed.

The *presence,* as I came to regard him, lurked at a distance, remaining in the shadows as work on the main fresco progressed quickly. At night, he teased my dreams on occasion, and even entered them once, but when I became instantly stimulated, he withdrew, fading away in obvious distress. I had lost my fear of him now, although on occasion his appearance would raise the hair on my neck. It was apparent he wanted something, but was unable to communicate it.

As for Rodrigo, dear, sweet, even-tempered Rodrigo, he worked at my side, learning a lot about art restoration in a short period of time. He never initiated anything, but once or twice a week I would grasp his arm, and he would follow me to the adobe shack to fuck me so competently I would be sated for the next few days. He did nothing he would consider "unmanly," and only reluctantly jerked me to orgasm with his hand when I got into the 69 position while sucking his hard, fat cock. Ejaculation was never a problem when he fucked me. His cock stroking my prostate always brought me to the brink, and his belly rubbing against the underside of my cock finished me off. Beautiful!

When Father Hidalgo brought a bishop to review our progress, it reawakened my inexplicable hunger for the priest. He appeared in mufti one day and condescended to help me move a piece of equipment, revealing strong, corded arms and a wisp of black hair at his neckline. Poor Rodrigo had to fuck me twice that night to ease my black longings. Not only that, but I believe the boy had an inkling of my attraction to the churchman.

Upon completion of the work on the fresco in the nave, I stood with a gathering of church officials and received their approval. The job had gone well, I had to admit. The mural looked much as it had when the unknown painter first applied pigments to the fresh plaster almost four hundred years ago. I contemplated that long-departed artisan for a few minutes, trying to see St. Peter through his eyes.

A high, keening sigh filled the sanctuary, causing me to whirl around, finding no apparent source. At that moment, the Archbishop and his entourage entered the nave. A tall, reserved man of considerable natural authority, his fresh, Irish face at contrast with the darker countenances of his court, the prelate halted several times during his progress into the auditorium, almost as if he were saying the Twelve Stations. By the time he knelt at the altar to give thanks for the rebirth of his Saint, approval and gratitude were clearly etched on his face. Over his cloaked shoulder, I saw Father Hidalgo glance up with reluctant admiration in his eyes. Instantly and inappropriately, my groin ballooned.

Once congratulations had been offered and accepted, the hierarchy of the See of New Mexico departed. Hidalgo lingered only enough to incite me nearly to the point of approaching him openly. The gleam in his dark eyes told me that he understood my attraction. Expecting condemnation, I was surprised to see wry amusement in his eyes as he took his leave.

Rodrigo went to work moving the disassembled scaffolding from the nave into the narthex while I considered the second fresco. If anything, it was more dynamic, more dramatic than the larger painting. In the foreground, San Pedro, still exhibiting obvious Indian blood, suffered his martyrdom in the traditional manner. His cross was inverted; his agony, tangible. Priests and soldiers and Indian shamans and sheep and horses stood at a respectful distance to suffer with their Saint. Above them all, a distant, gentle Jesus looked sadly down upon the crucifixion of his Apostle.

A scrabbling in the corner heralded the puckering of my flesh and the tickling of my nose. The *presence* was back, as always stronger in the narthex. Momentarily unable to confront him, I fled into the nave and steadied myself by enjoying the sight of Rodrigo gathering pieces of scaffolding. Hurrying to his side, I grasped the end of a long segment he was struggling to lift and reluctantly helped carry it into the narthex. The phantom had retired restlessly to the far corner. Warily, I helped my young assistant erect the gigantic tinker toy that would support us as we worked, my need for him growing by the moment.

I became distracted and allowed Rodrigo to slip away that evening. Anguished, I considered chasing him down in the Toyota, but resisted the urge, realizing as I did so this would be a difficult night. The priests had been here. Accolades had been given, and even Hidalgo had allowed his approval to show. I pictured him as he stood in shirtsleeves that one day, black hairs casting shadows on his forearms, an ebony curl at his chest. His long, lean legs encased in trousers and open to my view for the first time. Immediately, I ached.

My fears were fulfilled. Agitated, aroused, I tossed and turned on my bed, lonely and wracked by a forbidden desire. *He* appeared the moment I slipped over the edge of tortured sleep. The dark, amorphous presence from another dimension took on definition and light. The cloak and cowl were thrown off. The white of his cotton shirt glowed eerily, unnaturally. Rude cotton trousers were held at the waist with a strong cord. His feet were shod in *huaraches,* open-toed sandals. His being took on the color of the earth and then lightened with a tinge of rose. For the first time, the face clearly appeared in all its manly strength. I gasped, astounded by his incomparable male beauty. The scent without odor assailed me.

He stood before one of Rodrigo's framed paintings, a ghostly hand moving across the surface and coming to rest in a corner of the frame. Blind to all but my uncontrollable lust, I threw off my covers and lay naked and exposed before him. My hot, erect cock beat the air. Sensing something different about this dream, about this night, I did not rush to masturbate myself. He paused, his finger on the painting; I waited, pulsing with desire. At length, that strange, echoing sigh filled the hut, and he turned to me. Slowly, reluctantly, as though surrendering to inevitability, my specter drew off his rough shirt. The expanse of bronze chest took my breath away. When the pantaloons dropped to the floor, I cried aloud. He was magnificent! Without imperfections! A long, heavy cock hung between his legs, covering full testicles.

The phantom caressed my side with a feathery touch. I reached for him . . . and encountered nothing. Sobbing aloud, I realized I had not the ability to touch him, to enclose him in my arms, to caress him. But he could make contact with *me!* An insubstantial hand teased my chest, disturbing the hair and raising my nipples. He lay beside me with his head in the hollow of my neck. There was a subtle pressure along the length of my body, a modest heat at the groin where that great cock rested. As the ghostly hand roved my body, I moaned and writhed from ecstasy denied. My engorged cock strained as his spectral fingers closed around it. That non-odor, that heavy, overpowering dose of pheromones overwhelmed me! Disbelieving what was happening, even as a dream, I shot my excited seed all over my torso. A single drop seemed to hang for a moment on his diaphanous flesh before slowly penetrating it to drip onto my side.

Deliriously happy, I stretched and began the journey back into the real world. Frantically, he gestured toward the wall, to the painting. I surfaced from the land of dreams, exposed and shivering in the cold night, drenched in cum, and unable to hold onto the fading images. I lay awake the remainder of the night fretting over something beautiful that had escaped me.

I remained abed so long the next morning that Rodrigo came looking for me. I pulled him inside, and lay on my belly with my butt raised for him to assault while I desperately sought to recall my dream. When the boy came far up my ass, I spewed semen all over the covers. We lay for half an hour with his warm body covering me before I made him do it again.

Given the lessons learned on the first fresco, work on the second progressed faster than I had hoped. Things were relatively quiet until the final phase of the work in the narthex, the retouching. Even this, I believed, would be expedited because I had existing supplies of the paint elements from the first fresco. As I carefully worked on an agonized St. Peter hanging upside down on his cross, I sensed a presence on the scaffold with me other than Rodrigo, who was carefully retouching the background. *He* was here, suffering with the Saint, experiencing the pain of the nails, the horror of approaching death. My God! Could my shade be the Saint himself?

A sudden spasm seized my right hand, causing me to drop my brush and cry aloud. Rodrigo rushed to my side, concern written across his man-boy features.

"It's okay," I said, rubbing my hand vigorously. "Had a cramp, that's all. Think I'm going to call it a day."

"Can I stay and finish this part?" the boy asked, indicating a small area in the upper left corner.

"Yes, but don't go beyond that point," I warned. He nodded his understanding as I walked across the scaffold to start down the ladder, assessing what remained to be done as I went. I paused before some of the minor figures and noticed a faint blur of color in the extreme right near the bottom. Adjusting one of the lights so I could see better, I made out the form of a man, but there was not enough left of the original paint to indicate who, or even what, he might be. Was he a soldier? A religious figure? One of the Indians proliferating the scene? I could not tell. I'd have to use my imagination on that one, virtually the only part of the original fresco that could not be accurately interpreted.

I did not ask Rodrigo to tarry that evening even though I was sexually restless. A stirring in the woods, the ominous atmosphere in my shack, a hint of odor warned me of the *presence* and fueled my excitement. After bathing out of a basin and listlessly eating something tasteless, I studied sketches of the fresco for a few moments before turning off the light and going to bed.

"Why don't you stop screwing around and just tell me what you want?" I said into the darkness. I immediately rued my words. What if it *were* the Saint himself? Impossible! He had died half a world away.

He came to me that night, determined to make me understand. It took time for him to find form and definition, and as usual, I became so besotted during the process that I could think of nothing except my desire. He went to one of Rodrigo's paintings and turned toward me, his shadow luminescent from emotion.

"I've looked at the painting!" I wailed, unable or unwilling to concentrate because of my simpleminded lechery. "I don't understand!" I added, exposing myself and revealing my excitement.

A whirlwind shook the interior of the tiny building. The painting went crooked on the wall and crashed to the floor. If he sought to frighten me, he succeeded. I lost my erection as my skin puckered from a sudden chill. Chastised, I regarded my ghostly visitor through eyes that were unclouded by lust. I crawled from the bed and went naked to pick up the fallen picture. Suddenly curious, I snapped on a flashlight and turned it on the painting. He shrank from the sudden light as I examined the lower-right corner where the protoplasmic finger often rested.

"It's just Rodrigo's signature. That's all," I said impatiently. But a small mark beneath his name caught my eye. "Wait! There's something else. I can't make out what it is."

Ignoring the nighttime chill that had descended upon the hut I rummaged around in my things until I found a magnifying glass. Using that, I could make out several brushstrokes that took the form of a small, stylized man tucked just below the lettering.

"What the hell is that?" I asked aloud, moving to the boy's second painting. The tiny figure was there, as well. "I'll ask Rodrigo tomorrow," I said, not knowing whether I was talking to myself or my phantom.

He knew. That skin-puckering sigh filled the room. The figure without form molded against my back, exerting a gentle, comfortable pressure against my naked skin. Contentedly, he held me to him, inflaming me again. Wispy tentacles grasped my rapidly rising cock, and somehow I came in a mighty orgasm without once touching myself. This time there was no fight for consciousness; I realized with a start I was awake, and had been for some time. I remembered it all, everything that had happened, clearly, in minute, delicious detail. And with that realization, he slowly evaporated from the room, leaving me sated but aching with loneliness. On some level, I recognized this strange shade had attended my need in repayment for my one, brief sincere effort to understand *his*.

As soon as Rodrigo appeared the next morning, I dragged him into the shack and surprised him by failing to rip off his clothing. Instead, I handed him one of the paintings and pointed to the small figure below his signature.

"What is that?"

"Me," he replied.

"What?" I asked, a glimmer of understanding flickering across my brain.

"Me," he repeated. "I put that on all my drawings. I sign it like you're supposed to, but that's the white man's way. You know, his alphabet and all. But that's the real signature. That's me!"

"I love you, Rodrigo," I said, giving him a pat on the back and confusing him completely. "Come on, let's go to work." I was suddenly anxious to be back on the scaffold again.

Thoroughly confounded, he gave the bed a quick look before striding out the door. I trailed him to the church, thoroughly enjoying the manly sway of his butt as he walked.

I spent the morning completing the retouch of the crucifixion of St. Peter. I suffered through an impatient lunch, during which Rodrigo sent me strange looks, because of my uncharacteristic silence, I suppose. Once we finished eating, I rushed back up the scaffold and grabbed a clean brush. I again surprised my young companion by ignoring other major figures and going directly to the faint outline in the extreme-right corner. Rodrigo held his tongue, but was clearly curious. I ignored him.

Cleaning dust from the faint impression of color, I took up my pigments and lovingly began to paint. I had to fight the impulse to do a two-dimensional portrait, but that would have been horribly out of character with the rest of the fresco. Instead, I followed the outline my augury had clearly revealed to create a figure of substance out of what had been illusion. As I finished, Rodrigo put aside his brush, stretched his back fetchingly, and sauntered to my side. He suddenly froze. Holding my breath, I waited him out.

"It looks just like him!" he breathed in awe. "You've seen him, too?"

"Yes. Daily. He wouldn't leave me alone. I wasn't certain you knew about him."

"For a long time, he scared me to death. I almost quit working here the first day I started, but finally I understood he didn't want to hurt me. You know who he is?" he asked.

"Yes, but I didn't until this morning. You told me who he was."

"Me!" Rodrigo exclaimed in confusion.

"He's the artisan who painted the frescoes," I replied. "He's the Indian who created all of this beauty."

"Why . . . why did he stay around and . . . bother us?"

"Haunt us, you mean? Because he wanted to be remembered for what he did. But every time he came to me, I'd get so sexually excited I couldn't think of anything except finding release! I was so thick-headed, I didn't understand until you told me about your unusual way of signing your work. Then I knew that's all he wanted. He wanted his image reproduced so it was recognizable. It was so faded I might have turned it into anything—or erased it entirely."

Rodrigo gave a shaky laugh. "I thought I was the only one who could see him. Except maybe Father Hidalgo. I think he knows about him."

I studied the handsome youth as he spoke, and saw him glance at me briefly. Knowing he would never ask the question on his tongue, I answered it anyway.

"Yes, I was obsessed," I admitted. "I was sexually stimulated by a ghost, someone from another dimension, another time. He came to me in my dreams, but I would never pay attention to what he was trying to communicate. I'd just get excited and the whole thing would turn into a wet dream!"

"You . . . you did it with a ghost?"

"In a way, Rodrigo. But once I knew what he wanted, I came to my senses. You can't really have sex with a phantom. Not truly," I said slowly, not entirely believing my own words. "But he led me to you, and that is a wondrous thing! Rodrigo, I said something back there in the hut this morning. And I meant it. It wasn't just a meaningless expression."

"What?" he played dumb, most likely embarrassed to speak his mind.

"I love you."

"Can't!" He paused. "Can you?"

"More than you know, Rodrigo. You'll never feel about me the way I do about you, but when our work is done here, I hope you'll come with me. I've accepted another restoration in a church in the western part of the state. I'd like you to help me with it. I'll pay you a living wage, and we can . . . be together."

He looked me fully in the eye for the first time. "You want me to keep . . . doing it to you?"

"Yes," I chuckled. "I want you to fuck me, Rodrigo. Make love to me. Touch me. Be with me."

His eyes fell to belt level. He'd had enough of direct confrontation for the moment. "I thought you wanted Father Hidalgo," he said quietly.

"I was confused for a while, but that's over now. I just want you to tell me you'll stay with me, at least for this next job."

"Think about it," he mumbled. Then his eyes snaked back to mine for just a moment. "But we can go do it now . . . if you want."

I wanted. Very much!

Breakfast in the House of the Rising Sun

Caitlín R. Kiernan

Out here on the tattered north rim of the Quarter, past sensible bricks to keep the living out and the dead inside, weathered-marble glimpses above the wall of St. Louis #1, and on past planned Iberville squalor and Our Lady of Guadalupe. Hours left till dawn, and the tall man in his long car turns another corner and glides down Burgundy. Almost dreaming, it's been too long since he slept or ate, so long since he left Matamoros and the long Texas day before of sun and gulf-blind blue. All that fucking coke sewn up in the seats, white blocks snug in plastic wrap beneath his numb ass, and he checks the Lincoln's rear-view mirror, watching, watching in case some Big Easy pig doesn't like his looks. The fat veins in his eyes are almost the same shade of red as the little crimson pills that keep him awake, keep him moving. But there isn't much of anything back there—silhouette and streetlight shadow of a crazy old black man in the street, and he's pointing up at the sky and falls to his knees on the asphalt, but he's nothing for Jimmy DeSade to worry about. He lights another Camel, breathes gray smoke, and there's the House, just like every time before. Gaudy Victorian ruin, grotesquerie of sagging shutters and missing gingerbread shingles, slow rot of time and Louisiana damp. Maybe it's leaning into itself a little more than last time, and maybe there are a couple of new dog or gator skulls dangling in the big magnolia standing shadowy guard out front. Hard to tell in the dark, no streetlights here, no sodium-arc revelation, and every downstairs window painted

---

This story first appeared in *Noirotica 2: Pulp Friction* (Thomas Roche, ed., Masquerade Books, 1997).

black as mourning whores. Jimmy DeSade drives on by, checks his mirror one more time and circles around to the alley.

Rabbit opens his door a crack and watches the trick stagger away down the long hall, the fat man that stank like garlic and aftershave, fat man that tied Rabbit's hands behind his back and bent him over the bed, pulled down his lacy panties and whacked his butt with a wooden hairbrush until he pretended to cry. Until he screamed stop, Daddy, stop, I'll be a good little girl now. They still give him the creeps worst of all, the call-me-Daddy men, and Rabbit eases the door shut again, whispers half a prayer there will be no more tonight, no more appetite and huffing desperation, and maybe he can have a little time alone before he fixes and falls asleep.

Let's not count on it, he thinks and kicks off the black patent pumps, walks the familiar five steps back to the low stool in front of his dressing table, sits down and stares at himself in the mirror. Every minute of twenty-two years showing in his face tonight—and then some—a handful of hard age shining out mean from beneath powder and mascara smears. Rabbit finds his lighter, finds the stingy, skinny joint Arlo slipped him earlier in the evening, and the smoke doesn't make it easier to face that reflection; the smoke makes it remotely possible. He pulls a scratchy tissue from the box, something cheap that comes apart in cold cream, and wipes away the magenta ghost of his lipstick, sucks another hit from the joint and holds the smoke until his ears begin to buzz, high electric sound like angry wasps or power lines, breathes it out slow through his nostrils. And those gray-blue eyes squint sharply back at him through the haze—Dresden blue, his Momma used to say—pretty Dresden blue eyes a girl should have, and Rabbit licks thumb and forefinger, pinches out the fire and stashes the rest of the joint for later. Tucks it safe into the shadows beneath one corner of a jewelry box; later he'll need it more than he needs it now.

Rabbit restores the perfect bee-stung pout, Cupid's-bow artifice, a clockwise twist and the lipstick stub pulls back inside its metal foreskin. No point in bothering with the eyes again this late, but he straightens his dress, Puritan-simple black as if in apology for all the rest. He also straightens the simpler strand of pearls at his throat, iridescent plastic to fool no one lying against his milk-in-coffee skin, skin not black, not white, and there he is like a parody of someone's misconception of the mulatto whores of Old New Orleans. Bad romance, but *this* is real, this room that smells like the moldy plaster walls and the john's cum drying on the sheets, cheap perfume and the ghosts of tobacco and marijuana smoke.

This is as real as it gets, and you can sell the rest of that shit to the turd-for-brains tourists with their goose-necked hurricane glasses, Mardi Gras beads, crawdad T-shirts, and pennies for the dancing nigger boys with Pepsi caps on the soles of their shoes. Rabbit closes his eyes and makes room in his head for nothing but the sweet kiss of the needle, as if anticipation alone could be rush, and he doesn't move until someone knocks on the bedroom door.

Arlo works downstairs behind the bar, and he sweeps the floors and mops the floors, scrubs away the blood or puke and whatever else needs scrubbing away. He sees that the boys upstairs have whatever keeps them going, a baggie of this or that, a word of kindness or a handful of pills. Sees that the big motherfuckers downstairs at the tables have their drinks, empties ashtrays, takes away empty bottles, and washes whiskey glasses. And Arlo isn't even his name. His real name is Etienne, Etienne Duchamp, but no one likes that Cajun shit up here, and one time some mouthy, drunk bitch said his hair made him look like some old folk singer, some hippie fuck from the sixties. *You know, man, Alice's Restaurant*, and *you can get anythang you waaaaaant* . . . and it stuck. Good as anything else in here, and in here beats selling rock in the projects, watching for gangbangers and cops that haven't been paid or might not remember they've been paid.

Arlo pulls another beer from the tap and sets it on the bar, sweaty glass on the dark and punished wood, reaches behind him for the pissyellow bottle of Cuervo, and pours a double shot for the tall man across the bar. The man just passing through on his way back to New York, the man with the delivery from Mexico City, the man whose eyes never come out from behind his shades. The man who looks sort of like a biker but drives that rusty-guts land-yacht Lincoln. Jimmy DeSade (*Mr.* DeSade to Arlo and just about anyone else who wants to keep his teeth, who wants to keep his fucking balls), so pale he looks like something pulled out of the river after a good long float, his face so sharp, lank blue-black hair growing out of his skull.

"Busy night, Arlo?" he asks, icicle voice and accent that might be English and might be fake, and Arlo shrugs and nods.

"Always busy 'round here, Mr. DeSade. Twenty-four, seven, three hundred and sixty-five." And Jimmy DeSade doesn't smile or laugh but nods his head slow and sips at the tequila.

Then a fat man comes shambling down the crimson-carpeted stairs opposite the bar, the man that's had Rabbit from midnight till now, and Arlo sees right off his fly's open, yellowed-cotton wrinkle peekaboo careless between zipper jaws. Stupid fat fuck, little eyes like stale venom almost lost in his shiny pink face. And Arlo thinks maybe he'll check in on Rabbit, just a quick *You okay? You gonna be okay?* before the two o'clock client. He knows the fat man wouldn't have dared do anything as stupid as put a mark on one of Jo Franklin's mollies, nothing so honest or suicidal, so not that kind of concern. But this man moves like a bad place locked up in skin and Vitalis, and when he hustles over to the bar, ham-hock knuckles, sausage fingers spread out against the wood, Arlo smells sweat and his sour breath and the very faint hint of Rabbit's vanilla perfume—Rabbit's perfume like something trapped.

"Beer," grunts the fat man, and Arlo takes down a clean mug. "No, not that watered-down shit, boy. Give me a real beer, in a goddamned bottle."

Not a word from Jimmy DeSade, and maybe he's staring straight at the fat man, staring holes, and maybe he's looking somewhere past him, up the stairs; there's no way to know which from this side of those black sunglasses, and he sips his tequila.

"Jo knows that I'm waiting," Jimmy DeSade says, doesn't ask, not really, the words rumbling out between his thin lips, voice so deep and cold you can't hear the bottom. Arlo says yes sir, he knows, he'll be out directly, but Arlo's mostly thinking about the smell of Rabbit leaking off the fat man, and he knows better, knows there's nothing for him in this worry but the knot winding tight in his guts, this worry past his duty to Jo, past his job.

The fat man swallows half the dewy bottle in one gulp, wet and fleshy sound as the faint lump where his Adam's apple might be rises and falls, rises and falls. He swipes the back of a porky hand across his mouth, and now there's a dingy grin, crooked little teeth in there like antique cribbage pegs. And "Jesus, sweet baby Jesus," he says. "That boy-child is as sweet a piece of ass as I've ever had. Mmmm." And then he half turns, his big head swiveling necklessly round on its shoulders, to look directly at Jimmy DeSade. "Mister, if you came lookin' for a sweet piece of boy ass, well, you came to the right goddamn place. Yessiree."

Jimmy DeSade doesn't say a word, mute black-leather gargoyle still staring at whatever the hell the eyes behind those shades are seeing, and the fat man shakes his head, talking again before Arlo can stop him. "That's the God's honest-fucking truth," he says. "Tight as the lid on a new jar of cucumber pickles—"

"You done settled up with Rabbit? You square for the night?" Arlo asks quickly, the query injected like a vaccination, and the fat man grows suddenly suspicious, half-offended.

"Have I ever tried to stiff Jo on a fuck? The little faggot's got the money. You think I look like the sort'a cheap son-of-a-bitch that'd try to steal a piece of ass? *Shit*," and Arlo's hands out defensively, then, No, man, that's cool, just askin', that's all, just askin', and the fat man drains the beer bottle, and Arlo has already popped the cap off another. "On the house," he says.

Behind them, the felted tables, and one of the men lays down a double-six (no cards or dice, dominoes only in Jo Franklin's place, and that's not tradition, that's the rule), and he crows, answered with a soft ring of grumbled irritation round the spread of wooden rectangles the color of old ivory, lost money and the black dots end-to-end like something for a witch to read.

His hair not gray, cotton-ball white, and even in the soft Tiffany light of his office JoJo Franklin looks a lot older than he is, the years that the particulars of his life have stolen and will never give back. He closes a ledger and takes off his spectacles, rubs at the wrinkled flesh around his eyes. Rows of numbers, fountain-pen sums scrawled in his own unsteady left hand because he's never trusted anyone else with his books. He blinks, and the room stays somewhere just the other side of focused: dull impression of the wine-red, velvet-papered walls, old furnishings fine and worn more threadbare than him, the exquisitely framed forgery of Albert Matignon's *Morphine* that a Belgian homosexual had tried to pass off as genuine. He paid what the man asked, full in the knowledge of the deceit, small talk and pretended gratitude for such a generous price, then had the Belgian killed before he could cash the check; Jo forgot the man's name a long time ago, but he kept the phony Matignon, the three beautiful morphinomanes, decadent truth beneath Victorian delusions of chastity, and this fraud another level of delusion, so worth more to him than the real thing could ever be. The value of illusion has never been a thing lost on JoJo Franklin.

And now Jimmy DeSade's outside his door, waiting to do business, the simple exchange of pure white powder for green paper. JoJo puts his glasses back on his face, wire frames hooked around his ears, and the three ladies in the painting swim into focus, gently euphoric furies hiding one more deception, the counterfeit bills just up from Miami, stacked neat in his safe, company for his ledgers and the darker secrets in manila and old shoeboxes; good as gold, better.

The topmost drawer of his desk is open, and the little pistol is right there where it should be, tucked reassuringly amid the pencils and paperclips. Just in case, but he knows there'll be no ugly and inconvenient drama with Jimmy DeSade, creepy fucking zombie of a man, but a sensible zombie; no more trouble than with the Haitians the night before, the Haitians who are always suspicious of one thing or another, but these bills so goddamn real even they hadn't looked twice. Jimmy DeSade will take the money and carry it northwards like a virus, no questions asked, no trouble. In a minute or two, Jo Franklin will push the intercom button, will tell Arlo to send the smuggler back, but he's thirsty, and something about the pale and skinny man always makes him thirstier, so a brandy first and *then* the intercom, then the zombie and this day's transaction.

Jo Franklin rests his hand a moment on the butt of the pistol, cold comfort through fingertips, before he slides the drawer shut again.

Four knocks loud on the door to Rabbit's room, four knocks heavy and slow, reckless sound like blows more to hurt the wood than get attention, and he blots his lips on the cheap tissue, quick pout for the mirror before, "Yeah, it's open," and it is, the door, slow swing wide and hall light spilling in around them. Rabbit sees the men reflected without having to turn his head, and he sits very still, seeing them. Both dark, skin like black, black coffee and both so fucking big, and Rabbit can't really see their faces. Silhouettes with depth: one much thinner than the other and wearing sunglasses, the other bald and built like a wall. Concrete in a suit meant to look expensive. Pause, heartbeats, and "Come in," he says and wonders if he said it loudly enough because the men don't move, and his voice grown small and brittled in an instant. Christ, it's not like he hasn't done doubles before. Not like Arlo would ever let anyone come up those stairs that was gonna be a problem. Speaking to the mirror, scrounging calm, "Please, he says. "You can shut the door behind you."

A low whisper from one or the other, and the bald man laughs, hollow, heartless laugh before Rabbit breathes deep and stands to face them. The tall man first, his face so slack, his bony arms so limp at his sides, torn and dirty Mickey Mouse T-shirt and rattier pants, no shoes on his knobby feet. Movement underwater slow, sleepwalker careless, like those four knocks, and the bald man follows after, shuts the door, and the lock clicks very loud.

"Three hundred and fifty for the both," Rabbit says, cowering rabbit voice that wants to be brave, that wishes for the needle and sweet heroin salvation; the bald man smiles, hungry-dog smile and one silver tooth up front catching the candlelight. *"Ou chich,"* chuckled Creole and Rabbit shrugs, street-smart shrug even if he doesn't feel it. "Whatever. We're priced to sell round here," and the ice not breaking even though the trick laughs again, every laugh just that much more frost in aching veins, laugh and "You're a funny *masisi,* funny faggot," Caribbean-accented bemusement, Jamaican or Haitian or something; the tall man stands behind him, back against the door and doesn't smile or laugh or say a word.

Just part of their turn-on, trying to flip you out, and *Don't you let 'em fuck around with your head,* he thinks, trying to hear those words in Arlo's voice, or Chantel's, Chantel three doors down who never gets cold feet with weirdoes. But it's still just his own, small thing rabbit whispering from tall bayou grass. And a fat-ass roll of bills comes out of the bald man's coat pocket, rubber band snap loud, and he's peeling off two, three, four, laying them down like gospel, like an exclamation point on the table by the door, the table with plastic lilies stolen late one night from a St. Louis vault. Sun-faded plastic lilies in a dry vase.

"Gonna fuck you till you can't sit down, funny *masisi,*" and Rabbit looks to the money for strength, four one hundred dollar bills, crisp new paper, bright ink hardly touched, and there's an extra fifty in there, fifty free and clear of Franklin's cut. "Yeah," he says. "Whatever you want, Mr. . . ." and the customary pause, blank space for an alias, your name here, but the bald man is busy getting out of his jacket, too busy to answer, or maybe he just doesn't want to answer. The tall, still man takes his jacket, drapes it gently across one thin arm, nightmare butler, and the bald man reaches for his zipper.

"What about him?" Rabbit says, trying to sound hooker tough but almost whispering instead, sounding scared instead and hating it, motioning at the man with his back pressed to the bedroom door. "He doesn't talk much, does he?"

"He don't talk at all, and he don't fuck. So you don't be worrying about him. You just gonna worry about *me.*"

"You paid enough, for both—"

"*Fèmen bouch ou,*" and a sudden flicker like lightning in the man's dark eyes, flickering glimmer down a mine shaft so deep it might run all the way to Hell. Rabbit doesn't understand the words, but enough meaning pulled from the voice, from those eyes and the hard lines of his face to know it's time to shut up, just shut the fuck up and play their game by their rules until it's over.

"Stop talking and take off that ugly dress," the man says, and Rabbit obliges, unzips quick and lets the very plain black dress fall around his ankles, pool of black cotton around his heels to step out of, reluctant step closer to the man. His pants down, gray silk trousers to match the jacket but no underwear, uncircumcised droop, bizarre and fleshy orchid, organ, but he's getting hard, and Rabbit knows he'll probably be using hemorrhoid pads tomorrow, shitting a little blood as well. The pants hung on the tall man's arm now, too, and still no emotion in that face, every movement past slow or efficient, pared to jerky last stop before coma paralysis. He makes Rabbit feel cold inside, more naked than can be explained by the discarded dress; the bald man makes a satisfied sound in his chest, mumbled approval, and Rabbit glances at himself in the dresser mirror. His thin body like a teenage girl's, almond skin, legs and underarms shaved smooth, and he's wearing nothing now but the black lace and satin, bra and panties trimmed with scarlet, naughty somber contrast, matching garter belt and thigh-high net stockings on his long legs: nothing to mar the cultured illusion of his femininity except the subtle bulge at his crotch and the flatness of his chest.

"Sure you a boy?" the man asks, and this is nothing new, this question and the answering so routine that Rabbit can almost relax a little, and he hooks a thumb into the front of his panties, pulls them down enough to reveal his own sex, sex of his flesh, and the man nods, one hand rubbed across his hairless, glinting scalp. He mutters, "Leave them on."

"Sure, if that's what you want," and the man's big hands on him then, sweat-warm palms and fingers over his cool skin. Hard kiss like something desperate, something forced that isn't but needs to feel that way, faint cigar taste, tongue pushing past Rabbit's teeth and inside him, exploring teeth and palate and his own tongue. And then their lips parting, string of spittle between them to cling to Rabbit's chin.

"Bend over, bitch," the bald man says, and Rabbit bends over, hands on the bedspread, ass to Heaven, and he feels his panties coming down, draws a deep breath before two wet fingers shove their way inside him, probing, working his asshole, and he closes his eyes, braces knees against the sagging bed as those strong hands grip his thighs, purchase found, strong fingers to leave bruises behind, and there's the smallest whimper from Rabbit's lips as the bald man's cock pushes its way inside.

The very last door at the sunset end of a hall that is all doors, six choices with antique crystal knobs to ease decision, and that last door is Chantel Jackson's; been here longer than anyone, any of the boys, longer even than Arlo. Her end of the deal upheld after JoJo Franklin paid for her trip to Brussels, money she'd never have to resolve the quandary between her legs, and money he'd never miss. In return, she's the House specialty now, this one all the way, not just a pretty boy in frilly drawers, no shit, wanna know what it's like to fuck pussy that used to be dick? And she's got no complaints, so many ways things might have gone so much worse and that resolution all she ever really wanted anyway.

No complaints except that magnolia right outside her window, and there's a few minutes before her two-fifteen so she sits on her bed, smokes and watches that scary old tree, the sash down and locked, smudgy glass protection between her and those crookedy limbs, big leaves like the iridescent green shells of a thousand gigantic beetles. Nothing good about that tree, and mostly she ignores it, keeps the blinds down and tries not to notice the shadows it makes on her walls day and night. But sometimes, like now, when the demons inside are worse than the demons outside, she tries to stare it down, make it blink first, make *it* flinch. She imagines that magnolia shriveling the way movie vampires do if the sun gets at them, all those leaves turning brown and dropping off, gone to dust before they even touch the ground, gnarled trunk husk laid bare like a guilty heart, and wood cracks and splits, and the earth opens to take it back down to Hell. Or, maybe it bends itself over, pulls up its roots, tired of the masquerade if some tranny hooker bitch has its number, anyhow, and it shamefully drags itself back to the swamps, move over Mr. Catfish, move over Mr. Snapping Turtle, and it'll lie waiting in some black pool until everyone's forgotten it again.

"Silly fool," she whispers, knows it's goddamned silly to be scared of an ugly old tree when there's plenty enough else to be scared of in this city; silly bitch, but there's her church-neat line of charms and candles, anyway, painted saints and plastic Jesus and Mother Mary on the windowsill. Her careful shrine just in case it's not so silly to be afraid of ghosts after all, ghosts and worse things than ghosts.

They used to hang pirates from that tree, someone said, and thieves and runaway slaves, too. *Just about everyone got hung from that tree,* depending on who you happen to ask. And there's also the tale about the Storyville lovers: impossible and magic days a hundred years ago when hooking and gambling were legal, Storyville red-light before the whole district was razed for more legitimate corruption: a gentleman gambler from Memphis, or St. Louis, or Chicago, and he fell in hopeless love with a black girl, or a mulattress, under this very tree, except she was a *loup-garou,* and when she finally showed him her real face he went stark-raving bugfuck mad. *You can still find their initials carved in the trunk,* name-scars trapped inside a heart, *if you know where to look,* can still hear her crying if the moon and wind are right. Can still hear the green-stick snap of his bones between her teeth.

None of that shit even half as bad as the bleached animal skulls and little skeletons wired together wrong ways round, charms the voodoo women still leave in the limbs when no one's watching, the things JoJo won't ever cut down, won't even let Arlo get near them, never mind the awful racket they make whenever a storm blows up.

And tonight it just stares right back at her, that magnolia and all its guarded secrets, truths and lies and half-truths, steadfast, constant while the world moves around it. *Not tonight it ain't gonna blink for you or for nobody else, not a chance,* and Chantel Jackson crosses herself, then, reaches for the dangling cord to lower the blind, and down there in the always-shadow that grows beneath a tree like this tree she sees the men coming, the dark and confident men on the overgrown walk to the front door nailed shut. And one face glances up, and maybe it sees her, small and haunted in the frame of her window, and maybe it doesn't, but it smiles, either way, and she hears the wind, and the bones in the tree, like champing teeth and judgment.

The door bursts open, cracking splinter-nail explosion, door years sealed and boarded but off its rusted hinges in one small part of an instant and split straight down the center. Arlo doesn't wait to see, one hand beneath the bar and right back up with the shotgun Jo keeps mounted there, twelve-gauge slide-action always loaded, and he levels it at the bad shit pouring through the shattered door. Men huge and black and hard enough they barely seem real, skin like angry, living night, the flat glint of submachine-gun steel and machete blades; the domino players cursing, scatter of bodies as Arlo levels the Winchester's barrel at the Haitians, white tiles flying like broken teeth, tables and chairs up for shields before the thunder. God of sounds so loud and sudden it wipes away anything else in the buckshot spray, and he blasts the first big fucker through the door, and he also hits a man named Scooter Washington, slow and skinny shit into JoJo for almost ten thousand dollars, and Scooter falls just as hard.

Jimmy DeSade is moving now, scrambled vault uninvited over the bar and something coming out of his jacket but no time for Arlo to see just what as he pumps the shotgun again, empty shell spit, and he makes thunder one more time before the Haitians are talking back, staccato bursts chewing apart the room, wood and plaster and flesh all the same. Hot buzz past Arlo's left ear, and the long mirror behind the bar comes apart, razor-shard rain as he drops to the floor, and it seems like every bullet ever made is hitting the bar, punching straight through the oak and finding the steel plating hidden underneath.

"Shit," he says, can hardly hear himself over the Uzis, but "Shit, shit, *shit*" anyhow, and Jimmy DeSade doesn't say a word, big-ass revolver in his steady white hands, six-shot cylinder flipped open, chambers full, snapped closed again, careful man double-checking; the glass still falling on them, downpour of glass and whiskey, rum and all the sweet and sticky liqueurs. And then silence as harsh and sudden as the gunfire, heady quiet weighted at the edges with the choking stink of gunpowder and spilled alcohol.

"Sonofa*bitch*," and Arlo knows how scared he sounds but doesn't care, and then the booming, pissed-off voice from the other side—"*Hey there, Mr. JoJo Franklin!*"—alligator-bellow voice pounding air still shocky from the guns. "*Where are you at, Mr. JoJo Franklin?*"

"You *know* these people?" and a full moment passes before Arlo realizes that the question is meant for him, Jimmy DeSade and his shiny black Smith and Wesson crouched back here with him, and he wonders if his chances are really that much better on this side of the bar. "Yeah," he says, yeah, I know them, "They were around last night, business with Jo, but I don't know what, honest. A bunch of Haitians from the other side of the river—"

"*I say, I done come to talk to you, Mr. JoJo Franklin!*"

Arlo swallows, fever-dry swallow, closes his eyes and digs down deep for calm, anything to make his hands stop shaking. "That one talking, he was with the Tonton Macoute, I think, before Duvalier went down."

"That's some reassuring shit, Arlo," words sizzling out between clenched teeth, and Jimmy DeSade stares up at the place where the mirror used to be.

"I don't know his name—"

"*Going to have to start shooting again if you ain't gonna talk,*" the Haitian shouts, and Arlo can hear the impatient, grinding sound of their boots on broken glass. "*Going to have to start killing some of these fine people out here, Mr. JoJo Franklin!*"

Jimmy DeSade bows his head, the tip of his sharp nose resting against the shark-fin sight at the end of the pistol's long barrel; he sighs, and that's another bad sound to make Arlo's stomach roll. "Stupid bastard's probably halfway to Baton Rouge by now," Jimmy DeSade whispers. "Wouldn't you say that's a fair enough guess, Arlo?"

"Yeah, probably." Not like he's gonna disagree, and not like he has any fucking idea *where* Jo might be at the moment, just wishes he was there, too, and it was somewhere far away, wishes he'd taken Rabbit and hit the road a long time ago. "We're absolutely fucked," he says. And Jimmy DeSade looks at him, and the sunglasses have slipped down his nose a little ways, far enough that Arlo gets a glimpse of the gray-blue eyes back there, almost the same eyes as Rabbit's, *wolf* eyes, and he thinks maybe he's going to throw up after all.

"Everybody's fucked, Arlo," Jimmy DeSade says calmly, resolutely, as he thumbs back the revolver's hammer and stands up.

After the bald man's cum, and Rabbit lies on his stomach on the bed, squeaky springs finally silent again and his asshole on fire, forget the witch hazel, he's gonna be wearing fucking maxi pads on his butt. Semen-wet, sweat-damp down there, blood, too, but he lies very still while the man puts his clothes on again, zips himself up, and Rabbit only clenches his fists a little because it hurts, and he wants to be alone. Wants to fix and go to sleep and forget these two ever happened.

"Good fuck, *masisi*," the man says, satisfied grunt like Rabbit's stepfather pushing back from the dinner table after a big meal. "A shame that I have to kill a pretty piece of ass like you," and the words not quite registering, threat too many steps removed from here and now, as unreal and far away as the tall, death-quiet man standing at the door, but Rabbit's rolling over, turning so he can see the big bald man and his rumpled clothes and the machete in his right hand.

"It is nothing personal," he says, sour hint of a smile at the thick corners of his mouth. *"Je suis un pauvre Tonton,* Miss Chantel, and I just do what my boss say to do, and he says it will teach JoJo Franklin a lesson if we kill his special whore."

Rabbit's mouth open and the words jammed in his throat, *I ain't Chantel,* words dead as corn in fear-dry fields, spit gone to paste. And the bald man's arm rises like proof of guilt and penalty being served.

"I ain't Chantel," ugly croak across Rabbit's lips, not his voice, but those were words, words this man should understand, even this man with an arm that ends in that long, dark blade. "You got the wrong room—"

Abrupt apocalypse, then, downstairs cacophony and Hell coming up through the floorboards, everything there but the trumpets; Rabbit moving, belly scramble across the bed, and he can feel the shudder of shotgun blasts, one, two, before the machine-gun tattoo begins, and by then he's off the other side of the bed, falling like this was the edge of a flat world, no sound as he hits the floor because there's so much sound already. Blood in his mouth because he's bitten the tip of his tongue, and one hand's pushing in between the mattress and box springs, frantic grope, and it's there somewhere, it's always fucking there so why can't he find it? *I don't give a shit if it scares you,* Arlo said, *You're gonna take it and put it someplace you can get to it fast if you ever have to, okay?* And this isn't fast enough, not nearly fast enough.

Downstairs, the gunfire stops, and now there's just his heart and the bald man's footsteps coming round the end of the bed, the bald man cussing the stupid little faggot on the floor, and Rabbit's hand closes around the cold butt of the pistol.

"I can make it fast for you," the bald man says, "if you just be still for me," and then he's looking at the gun in Rabbit's trembling hand, Rabbit scooting backwards across the floor, hard bump into the nightstand, and something falls off, breaks loud and wet. The bald man is laughing now. "*Oh,* you gonna shoot me, eh? You gonna shoot poor Charlot with that silly—" And Arlo says so calm and patient, *Squeeze the trigger, just point it and squeeze the trigger,* so Rabbit squeezes, winces expectantly, but it's not such a big sound after all, bottle-rocket pop, firecracker pop, and then that hole opening up like magic in the bald man's neck. Neat little hole barely big enough to put a pinky finger in, just a little blood for him to look so surprised as the machete clatters to the floor and his big hands fumble for his throat.

Rabbit squeezes the trigger again, and the man stumbles, sinks slowly to his knees, and there's still nothing much on his face but surprise. Grin wide and white teeth bared, mouth open to speak but there's only more blood, a fat red trickle from the corner of his mouth and down his chin.

"Fucking *die,* goddammit," Rabbit growls, but it's like someone else said that, someone in a movie, and the next bullet hits the bald man square in the face; there's lots of blood this time, a warm and sticky mist that gets Rabbit before the man tumbles over on his side and lies dead on top of the machete. Quick glance at the tall man, almost-forgotten accomplice, Rabbit's adrenaline-stiff arms pointing the pistol that way but he hasn't moved, slack face as blank as before, the dead man's jacket still draped across one arm.

"Whatever this shit's about," says Jimmy DeSade, speaking so calm to the big Haitian, "it doesn't have anything to do with me." And Arlo's still crouched on the floor with the shotgun, wondering if he can make the stairs without getting killed, maybe even make it all the way up to Rabbit's room, and then the both of them could duck down the rickety backstairs to the alley and then get the fuck away from here, just as far and fast as they can run.

"Who the hell are *you*?" says the big Haitian, and Jimmy DeSade replies, "Nobody. Nobody that wants any trouble," and then he kicks Arlo hard in the hip with the sharp toe of one of his sharp black boots.

"All we *got* here tonight is trouble," says the Haitian and he laughs, laughter rumbling around the room like reckless desolation. "So you in the wrong damn place, Mr. Skinnybones White Man, if you don't want no trouble." And then Jimmy DeSade gives Arlo the boot again, and *"Fuck you,"* out before there's any stopping himself.

"I don't work for JoJo Franklin," says Jimmy DeSade. "Whatever he's done to you, it's got nothing to do with me. And I don't give a shit what you do to him. He probably has it coming."

Silence for a moment, like maybe the Haitian's thinking all this over, and Jimmy DeSade may as well be marble as flesh and bone, may as well be carved out of fucking ice, standing there with his finger on the trigger and the long barrel pointed straight ahead.

"But maybe I *don't* care 'bout that, Mr. Skinnybones," the Haitian rumbles. "Maybe I'm so pissed off tonight I just want to kill me all the ugly white motherfuckers I can find."

Copperhead words from Jimmy DeSade's pale lips, then, whisper-hiss dripping down on Arlo's ears—"Get the hell up here, Arlo, or I'm gonna shoot you myself." And because there's nothing left to do, because he doesn't have the guts to run, doesn't have the guts to stay put, Arlo stands up slow. Slow as a man can move, slow as dawn at the end of the world's longest night. He clutches the shotgun to his chest, crucifix of steel, gunpowder rosary, and the two men are talking again, but there's no room in his head for anything now but the meathammer sound of his heart.

And the sudden, clumsy thump and thud of footsteps on the stairs.

It's not like the movies, not at all, slow-motion painful so everything makes sense even if there's nothing he can do to stop it; no time for regret and pointless dot-to-dot foresight. Time for nothing but scalding adrenaline and the Winchester coming down, pumped and both barrels emptied before Arlo knows it's Rabbit, Rabbit half-naked on the stairs and the tall black man trailing behind, tall man in a Mickey-the-fucking-Mouse T-shirt and *Can you* believe *that shit?* Tall man there to catch the body, all that's left after the iron shot is done and only the crimson-black hole where Rabbit's belly was and the empty look on his pretty face that isn't surprise or accusation or pain or anything else Arlo's ever seen before.

A cold pearl sun almost up and the eastern sky turning oyster-white off toward Biloxi and Mobile; Jimmy DeSade hunched behind the Lincoln's steering wheel, trying not to notice the muddy, dark waters of Lake Pontchartrain, the waves rough and sleek as reptile skin beneath the long bridge out of New Orleans. He lights a cigarette and keeps his eyes on the road, stares down the car's long hood, the tarnished ornament like his pistol's sight and his foot on the trigger.

Nothing he could have done back there, nothing else at all but what he did; twelve fat kilos of primo coke to the Haitians for his skin, and they let him walk away, luckiest fucking day of his shitty life, and there ought to be relief burning him up from the inside out, but there's just Arlo kneeling over the ruined body of the dark boy in women's underwear. Arlo screaming, tin and gravel man-scream, a sound to keep the dead awake nights, and everything so ridiculously goddamn still as the shotgun turned toward the Haitians. The cartoon sharp *bang* when Jimmy DeSade put a bullet in Arlo's head, *bang*, and the Winchester clattering to the floor. He knows it was the bullet that saved his life, not the fucking dope; that's a stone-cold fact, and there's nothing he can ever do to change it.

Jimmy DeSade stares out at the stark and brightening world from behind his tinted lenses, and his big car rolls east, and the sun makes no difference whatsoever.

Above All the Lights

Patrick Califia

Hollywood is corrupt from the ground up, but it's the world's largest (or at least the best-documented) playground. So you should just close your eyes to the game's wicked ways and play, play, play. Or so they say. "They" being people I've never met, those who are actually in charge of everything. I'm not sure what scares me more: the nefarious heartlessness of "them" or the possibility that *nobody* is in charge.

I was too far away from the epicenter of Movietown, USA, to be a major player anyway. My office did not look down upon Mann Chinese Theatre and its forecourt of stars' names and handprints, or the offices of a major studio. Instead, it looked down upon a high school where the rich and famous sent their progeny. These were kids who did not have to raid dad's liquor cabinet, steal mom's cocaine, or wreck their parents' automobiles. They had plenty of booze, drugs, and cars of their own. I should know. I used to go there.

Who was I to interrupt the law of supply and demand? Nobody special. Maybe that's why I was hell-bent on picking up litter along a highway that was strewn with broken bodies. I focused the telephoto lens on my camera and took another picture of a car that had just pulled into the parking lot. It was lunchtime, and the car was not driven by a student, a teacher, or an employee of the school. Nevertheless, it was there every day, punctual as the Malibu tides.

I made sure I had thoroughly documented the license plate, then took leisurely flip-book photos of the driver and his customer, who brazenly handed over a large stack of cash and pocketed fistfuls of tiny plastic bags that were probably not filled with pea-sized lumps of bathroom cleanser.

Last week's photos of these transactions had already been sent to the police. Nothing had been done, which I had expected, so I had retained the ugly receipt the post office gives you when you send something by certified mail, just in case the men and women in blue wanted to claim they weren't getting their deliveries in a timely manner. This week's pictures would go to a couple of local newspapers along with a copy of that receipt. Maybe nothing would happen again. In which case, there was always the Associated Press and *The New York Times*.

What did I think of the War on Drugs? Not a hell of a lot. What did I think of someone who sold drugs to kids, even if they were kids his own age? Ditto. Silly, I know, but in these days of economic downturn with few paying customers, a man's got to have a hobby. Consistency being the hobgoblin of et cetera, et cetera.

Speak of the devil. Here comes honest work. The door to my reception area had just opened and closed. That anteroom would not delay my caller long because there was no receptionist. I wondered, and not for the last time, from whence film noir detectives got their buxom and irrationally devoted secretaries. (From the pool of starlets who had not yet learned to give blow jobs as good as Marilyn Monroe's—I know, I know.) But the last thing I wanted was a blow job from a buxom blonde, and wasn't that part of my problem?

If anybody knew that better than me, it was not the guy who barged through the door to my inner sanctum and then fell into the chair across from my desk as quietly as an autumn leaf descends to become part of Nature's mulch heap. He's one of those big guys who are honestly not fat, who move on the balls of their feet like quiet hunting cougars. I think he has to pretend to be as noisy and bluff and hearty as the men he does business with. Mama, don't let your babies grow up to be realtors. It was my old classmate Sheldon Fawn. He has everything that his daddy once had and then some. That would include his daddy's last mistress, who is now Mrs. Sheldon Fawn.

Her last encounter with the paterfamilias had resulted in a fatal heart attack or something very much like it. I had been summoned to keep that mess out of the papers and off the police blotter. That had cost me my job on the force, which was quite a blow, considering that the job had cost me an inheritance. But Sheldon believed in trickle-down economics, so I got invited to way too many of his stag parties. Okay, so I *can* get it up for a hooker who charges five grand for a night of her time. All men are dogs. Say woof and swallow that cheese.

"Shelly!" I said, full of bonhomie but unable to pronounce it. "How's life among the slumlords, Bambi?"

"Shut up," he said, and helped himself to a cigar. The only reason he'd given me a humidor full of them in the first place was to make sure he'd have access to them when he came to the office. Unlike his wife, who had no reason to be prissy about other people's oral fixations, I let him smoke it. I liked seeing that fat brown cylinder in his overprivileged puss. White man sucking up carcinogens. Geronimo's revenge. Oscar Wilde's too, because sometimes a cigar is *not* just a cigar—as Sigmund Freud knew perfectly well.

"Are you working hard?" he asked, eyeing me through blue smoke and eyes I wished I did not know were a sultry blue as well. "Or hardly working?"

"Can't be hard and work at the same time," I said briskly.

"That's not what I heard," he said, and we went *haw haw* together. Nobody here but us testicles. My stomach was tense. The worse the joke, the nastier the job a client is about to hand me.

"So," he said, blowing smoke at the ceiling, "we've got a little problem, Harris."

"Do *we*?" He was oblivious to my sarcasm. My position in his life was one of delicate ambivalence. I had (sort of) weathered the scandal that got me kicked out of school, but because I had been accused of letting one of the school's top jocks suck my dick, I was a safe person to come to with the indiscretions of other members of our class. But I was no longer really a member of the club. If I were, my reception area would not be furnished with plastic patio chairs from Wal-Mart, perfect for al fresco blue-collar dining. I suppose I could have gotten something that was still cheap but not so god-awful ugly. But that was what my business was all about: ugliness.

"Smitty has been videotaped in compromising circumstances," he said bluntly.

"They say compromise is the basis for all lasting relationships," I mused. Shelly gave me a bland look that said, *You're crazy but I could still get you to buy a condo.* I tried to recall when Smitty Martingale had been elected to the city council. Did you know that Martingale is short for Goldfarb? Good; you're not supposed to.

"Do you want his money or not?" Sheldon Fawn demanded in the same tone of voice that he used to tell me to put his dick into a whore.

"Yes," I said, as I had so often before, and pulled out the keyboard tray on my desk. "What did he do?"

"He got videotaped with a he-she and now he's being blackmailed by its pimp."

"It?" I was suddenly all business as well, showing my teeth and raised hackles. Nobody comes to the defense of the criminal element more quickly than someone who is supposed to apprehend and punish them for their evildoing. Shelly gave me an affable but apologetic smile and even waved some of his own smoke away. Boundaries had been drawn and mutually acknowledged.

"So you want me to get the tape back," I hazarded a guess. Sharp as Occam's razor. Which, come to think of it, would make a damned fine name for a detective agency. If really smart people ever needed bottom-feeders like me.

"That would be nice. For a start."

I raised one eyebrow. Banks give away toaster ovens to new customers. I distribute quizzical facial expressions to all comers. Because your first impression is your last impression, or so they told me in charm school.

"Some people don't know how to play by the rules," he explained. "I don't deal in chicks with dicks, but if I had fucked up as bad as this pimp has, I'd be run out of town on a rail no matter what was my stock in trade. You get my drift."

I rolled my eyes, having last heard that idiom in a John Wayne movie. I resisted the impulse to say, "I used to be Snow White, but I drifted" in my best Mae West. Forcing my voice into the bass register of a porn film, I thundered, "You want me to find the blackmailer, retrieve the tape, and get him to leave town."

"The further away he goes, the better," Bambi said, and put out his cigar. He tossed a fat envelope on the desk, and while I was still staring at its thickness, trying to estimate how many hundred-dollar bills it took to make a stack that high, he got up, adjusted the waistband of his slacks in a vain attempt to camouflage a fart, and left.

I stuck my face in the cash and fanned it like a deck of cards. The air quality suddenly improved. There was way more there than the price of a plane ticket to New York City. Or Paris, for that matter. Did Shelly (or Smitty) imagine this was the price of a broken leg or a bullet to the head? If so, they had overpaid street value and underpaid downwardly mobile little old me.

My mendacious school chum also left me a typed list of some other information that might help me to track down the blackmailer. There was a head shot of the hooker as well, a pretty woman who was one of those unique-to-California ethnic combinations: black and Japanese, shaken up with the aristocratic offspring of the lost Aztec empire and Spanish conquistadores. As they say in Kyoto, *domo arigato,* Charles Darwin, and pass the salsa verde. I gave Bambi's cheat sheet a read, feet up on my own desk, then clambered onto those same size twelves and shuffled off in quest of a hamburger patty with no bun and a salad. After that, I would come back to the office and take a nap on the cracked but still comfortable leather sofa. I would have to wait until after dark to really go to work.

If you'd like to know what will be on the Paris runways next spring, take a postprandial walk with me along the ho stroll of West Hollywood, otherwise known as the TV Channel. This year, the girls-of-color-who-used-to-be-boys were congregating along Hydrangea Boulevard between Camellia and Rhododendron Streets. It was a few months until another election would roust the police, who would simply chase them into a new locale a few blocks over. Sort of like a dog trying to catch a seagull. But to complete this metaphor, we'd have to find a seagull that is paying off the dog to leave him alone. And a dog that liked to fuck seagulls.

Every one of these girls looked like a supermodel. But the fashion industry has room for only one or two black stars per year. I was a little overwhelmed by the profusion of miniskirts; fishnet stockings;

halter tops; black patent leather, high-heeled boots; gold lamé; elaborately styled wigs; cat's-eye makeup; dangling earrings; and short-shorts. They were underwhelmed by me. Foot traffic is never welcome. A man who can't afford a car will try to get his head at a bargain rate. Doing the nasty in the great outdoors would be a big step down for these front- and backseat fillies. Only the lowest crack whore will forgo the mean shelter of a windshield. Whenever I approached a group of them, they turned their backs and walked away, asses swaying invitingly, shoulders stiff with disapproval.

I took out a twenty and held it on top of the photo I was trying to match to an actual person. That got me a little more respect. "Why do you want to find this girl?" the first hooker I came up to demanded.

"She's my long-lost sister," I replied.

"Bullshit," she snapped. Her head began to bob and weave upon a neck like a black swan's. This is the African-American woman's way of giving warning, much like the rattlesnake's ominous buzz. I was in no mood to be dressed down like a boyfriend who had bet the rent money on a pit bull who'd lost his balls. "Can the righteous indignation," I said. "Do you know the sister or not?"

"Not!" She snatched at the twenty.

"So who might know her?" I asked, clamping my thumb down on the cash.

She threw her head back and tossed a quick look at a girl in a red kimono that covered more of her body than the outfits of the girls she was apparently supervising. "Taneena," she said grudgingly. "Her old man likes slant-eye bitches."

"Tch-tch. Where's your respect for diversity?" I chided, handing over the twenty bucks.

She pocketed it and snapped her fingers at me three times, tracing a Z in the air. "For this chump change you don't get to lecture me about multiculturalism, white boy," she declared. There was not a trace of the ghetto in her voice. She sounded like a college English literature professor. Then, when she was sure I had gotten the point, she reverted to the cant of the street. "Get outta my face."

It was actually the twin cheeks of her high, perky, and utterly salacious butt that I had to turn my back upon. I did so rapidly, before the impulse to spend all my cash on a chance to fuck her up the ass got the best of me. Fucking smartasses doesn't discourage them. They just learn to mouth off when they want to get screwed. Ask Shelly.

Taneena didn't try to avoid me. With the composure of an experienced First Lady in charge of her old man's stable, she took the photo and said, "This girl is one of my family all right. You want to date her or somethin'?" The veteran of several busts, she knew perfectly well that I was no undercover vice cop. Or client.

"Yes," I replied. "I'd like to talk to her."

I expected to get a little bit of a runaround, but Taneena only pretended to be hurt. "I'm not pretty enough for you?"

"Baby, you're so pretty that your old man has got your booty locked up tight, doesn't he? The only part of you I could have is your mouth."

She laughed at me, licked her lips sensuously, and laughed again. "You want to fuck Lotus, you going to have to pay a lot more than twenty dollars," she warned.

"I got three hundred in my pocket just for twenty minutes of her time."

"Ooo eeee, twenty minutes! We got Marathon Man here with us tonight. Marathon Man is in the house. Give it up!"

We shared a giggle and I waited patiently while she chastised a plump girl in translucent lingerie to get off the curb faster when a car slowed down. "I want to see those big titties of yours fly through his window the minute he roll it down," she declared. "Work what you got for your birthday, Delanya, or Daddy gonna want his implants back."

"So what corner is Lotus prowling tonight?" I asked, getting Taneena back to the business at hand.

"She in the crib," Taneena said, as if any child should have known that. "Knox says if you go on the street with your face all beat up you won't get nothing but the freak trade. So he keeping her home."

"But she'll still see me?"

"Call him up and see. 1-800-FORT-KNOX." She sprang into the center of her little pack of trainees and administered a slap to an ass encased in copper-colored silk. "What you mean, you won't date that man, Sugar Bear? You here to make money, girl, not find somebody to marry. If he got his dick and his wallet out, you best try to take that money away from him. I don't care if he's an old man. Old men got more money than young men anyway. Sugar's no good if it stays in the bowl, bitch."

Realizing I was in the way, I dragged my attention away from this psychodrama and stumped back to my car. There I had a swig of bottled spring water, which presumably came from the same sort of spring from whence our tap water is derived, and dialed the toll-free number. "Fort Knox," somebody growled. The voice was as deep and musical as Barry White's, but more menacing than seductive. Some girls just like it rough, I guess. Unlike me, of course.

"Taneena told me to call you about Lotus," I said.

"Lotus," he repeated flatly, not helping me along.

"Yeah, I saw a picture of her and I'd like to talk to her," I explained. What a lame story. What street-corner girl has a portfolio in circulation?

"Three hundred is a lot for a conversation," he said. Of course Taneena would have called him about the weirdo who was snooping around.

"Yes," I said. "It is. But I understand the lady is indisposed."

He abruptly told me an address and hung up. I wasn't sure why he had decided to let me make this unorthodox appointment, since I had not identified myself as Smitty's go-between, but I committed the digits to memory and got out my *Thomas Guide*.

"Knox?" I asked when a gentleman answered the door. He looked like he went with the voice on the phone.

I got a look of pity and disgust. Bodyguard, then. Of course Knox would not open his own door. A pimp with as many women as Taneena had jumping would be top drawer, and he'd be able to afford hired muscle. He'd need it too. The Ten Commandments tell us not to covet our neighbor's wife, but they don't say anything about his cash. Or his cocaine.

Not sure who I expected to meet, I shouldered past the bodyguard and went down a short hallway to yet another door. There were compartments cut in the wood paneling of the hallway. Guns or other weapons ready to drop if war was declared and battle came down? The place was also monitored by a security camera. Somebody had invested money in setting up his headquarters.

"Harris," a voice inside the main room said, and I almost threw the door shut and ran back down that hall. It was a voice from my past that filled me with fear and shame. We all have some dirty secret that we desperately hope will never be exposed to anyone else's view. This was mine.

But I had a client. I'd taken his money and promised to do a job.

And, may all the gods of pagan Greece assist me, I was horny. My barely repressed curiosity about what the transsexual prostitutes' panties contained had me itching for something larger and more familiar.

"Mojo," I replied heavily, and went to confront my disgrace.

He didn't weigh an ounce more than he had in high school. But he'd added a grown man's muscle. That football uniform wouldn't fit anymore, but the tailored Armani suit he wore fit goooood. It looked as natural and fine as a fox coat does on a fox. He was a color that reminded you why they called his people black. He was Zulu black. Yoruba black. Africa's child and yet as American as the Scotch-Irish mutt I was.

"Knox," he corrected. "Everybody knows me as Knox now, Harris."

"What are you doing here?"

"I could ask you the same question." He held out his left hand, and a woman I had not noticed before poured something that smelled like very old Scotch into a glass, and put the glass in his hand. I spared a glance for her, reluctant to drag my eyes away from my long-lost scapegoat and lover. She was Lotus. And someone had beaten her up with professional care. Recently too.

Mojo drank a sip of expensive amber Scotch, smiled at the liquor's aroma, and gestured me into a chair. "Go on out now, honey," he told her. *Honey*. I felt a pain in my chest that reminded me I'd never started taking the once-daily baby aspirin I'd bought a month ago. She left walking proudly despite the livid marks on her face, without a pout or a backward glance, obviously confident in his ability to handle her business. The memory of her small, high breasts barely covered by her spaghetti-strap violet dress disturbed me.

"Cocksucker," he said evenly as soon as the door was closed.

It had been ten years. I still wanted him. Would this sad story never end? I bowed my head, acknowledging his authority as I never would a preacher. Mojo got to his feet, came around the desk, grabbed me by the front of my shirt and my tie, and slapped me. Like Lotus, I let him do whatever he was going to do. Did she love him as much as I once had loved him? Did I love him now, or was I just so guilty I was willing to let him do whatever he wanted to me?

"Does your family know you're a pimp now?" I asked, surprised by my sudden desire to hurt him.

"What did you expect me to do? Getting caught in the shower with you ruined any chance I had of a football scholarship. Unlike you, my family wasn't prepared to pay cash up front for a crack at the Ivy League. But I heard you were stupid enough to throw your admission to Yale away."

"Yeah," I said, and he slapped me again, harder this time. "If this doesn't stop pretty soon, people will think Lotus really is my sister," I jibed. My attempt at a wry chuckle didn't quite work because I had a fat lip. The inside of my mouth had gotten cut on my own teeth. The taste of my own blood was sickening.

"You God *damned* fool," he said, pronouncing each word with heartfelt care. Then he grabbed me in a rib-cracking embrace, and kissed me. My body responded instantly to his tongue slipping between my teeth. I returned his kiss with all the care that my wounded mouth allowed. Then I remembered that he was tasting my blood along with my spit and tried to wrench my mouth away. He wouldn't let me escape. My struggles subsided and I had to just stand there and let him rape my mouth. As if you can rape the willing. All he had to do is stick his hand in my pants, and he'd know instantly how much I wanted him. Just the way he had always known.

He loosened my tie and took it off over my head, then unbuttoned my shirt. "You going to keep my secret?" he asked, brushing his lips over my nipples. His hands clasped my waist lightly but with so much erotic authority I wanted to faint.

"You kept mine," I choked. "Why did you do it, Mojo? Why did you tell them it was you who was the queer and not me?"

"Secrets," he mused, baring my torso and unbuckling my belt. "We all got 'em, don't we, Detective Harris? All the cops are criminals, and all the thieves are saints. Here you are guilty as sin, trying to catch bad guys, while I just pander to their worst tendencies. But we're done with secrets now, aren't we, Harris?"

When he pushed me toward the desk, I struggled again, and this time he got me in a headlock and took me down, bent forward over its cool surface, as glossy and smooth as a mahogany-colored glacier. He kept one hand on the back of my neck while he used the other one to tug my trousers down. I wore a jockstrap underneath because that kind of underwear works better for my purposes. Normally it helps me to hide. But this afternoon it was exposing me.

"I didn't tell them," he said, parting the cheeks of my ass, "because I could let them think I was queer, but they'd still think I was a man, Harris. Remember the first time we fucked? You'd come into the locker room to photograph me for the yearbook, and I teased you into taking some nude shots. But I wanted you to undress too. And you said you wouldn't because you were afraid that if you took your clothes off I would think you weren't a man. I promised you that I didn't care what you looked like naked, that to me you would always be a man."

The length of him slid into me, so thick I thought I could not bear it, and then so long that his girth was wiped out of my mind. The world's most perfect cock was inside of me. I couldn't allow myself to enjoy him; I didn't deserve it. And I was angry with him for wrestling me onto the desk. My body tried to escape, but there was no place to go. "I always loved the way you would wiggle," Mojo said. "Do you know how good you look with my dick in you? It feels so fine when you struggle on my cock. I could just stand here for an hour and make you do all the work. 'Specially if I slapped your big white ass."

"All day? Slapped my ass? Oh! Please!"

"I never break my word, Harris. And I never keep any of my bitches waiting."

Then he fucked me good and proper. I no longer cared if I was betraying myself by crying out. Let the bodyguard know he was screwing me. Let Lotus hear my guttural cries for rescue from peril that fed my very soul. No more hiding. No more bogus medical excuses from taking gang showers with the other boys in my gym class. No more visits to the doctor in Baltimore who photographed the shame between my legs. I am that photograph in medical textbooks of a rare and horrible creature, the perfect hermaphrodite. Except that my cock is too small to penetrate anyone. Out of concern for their reputation in polite society, my parents would not bow to the doctors' pressure to castrate me and raise me as a girl. No more tucking a prosthetic in my jock strap every day before I went out into the world. No more avoiding public bathrooms and carefully calculating just how high Bambi and his latest call girls were before I joined in the fun with an artificial prick that would never knock anybody up or give them the clap.

"You're one in a million, Harris," Mojo said, and it was literally true. "Do you know why I collected this little family of he-shes, brother? Once you've had a boy with a pussy, and you can't find another one like him, it's not that big a reach to chicks with dicks. Is it? *IS IT?*" And there came the blows from his huge hands that finally set me free. I came from the pain, crying with joy and shame because he was finally giving me the punishment that I deserved. Only someone who has tortured himself very nearly to death can appreciate the bliss of finally being hurt by the person who has the right to injure or kill him. I almost wished he would kill me. Except that he'd made me feel so good, I realized I could no longer be insouciant about my own life expectancy.

"Let me up," I demanded. He had one arm bent behind my back. He let go of it and laid forward on me, toying with my tits.

He paused. "Naw," he said, as if he had seriously thought it over. "I gotta get what's coming to me." The fuck that he threw me then was purely selfish. I couldn't get my breath, he slammed into me so hard and fast. My hips were taking a beating on the wooden edge of the desk. I'd have bruises tomorrow. The tweaking at my nipples was another fiery challenge to assimilate. He was deliberately making me sore inside. "You don't have to walk tomorrow, do you?" he asked once. I could hear the sneer on his face, imagine the way he twisted up his eyebrows when he asked me that question.

"I don't have to walk tonight," I affirmed. What is it about getting fucked that makes you get off on your stud's pleasure? The thought of him coming inside of me was so exciting that I couldn't keep track of my own needs anymore. I would happily have postponed any climax of my own to intensify his. Instead, he squeezed my throat and ordered me to close my muscles down on his dick, to milk it for him as it clawed its way in and out of me. My cunt is smaller than a woman's, and having a small penis as well was no compensation. I couldn't penetrate anyone else, and it was difficult to allow them to penetrate me. But Mojo was ignoring the limits of physiology, and when I clamped down on his cock, he hurt me in a whole new way before he finally came, and thrust so hard at me that it felt as if his cock had broken through to my guts.

"Bastard," I said, feeling sweat cool between us. His arms around me felt like coming home.

"Get up," he said, and dragged at one of my arms. But he wouldn't let me stand up. Instead, I was shoved onto my knees. "Suck it," he said, swiveling his hips. I could see the sheen of sweat on his curly black public hair. "Clean my dick off. If you can get it up, I'll let you have it again. But this time I'll fuck you like a real boy, Peter Pan."

I swallowed his cock a half-inch at a time, partly to tease him and partly to help myself remember how it was done. Oh, right—you just stopped caring if you could breathe or not. Simple. My throat was just one more hole that he could use, but wouldn't it be nice if every asshole or cunt had a tongue in it? He couldn't seem to decide if he should be sweet to me or cruel. Sometimes he stroked my hair lovingly and sometimes he fucked my skull with deliberate brutality, his hands clamping my face to his groin until I saw a black mist and knew I was about to pass out. I didn't fight him, and for a second, I did wink out. I think that scared him because he was marginally nicer after that, allowing me one breath per ten thrusts. It was enough to sustain life, but barely. Soon his cock was hard again and leaking salty trails wherever it went. The extra lubrication was welcome.

"Get on the couch," he whispered, and herded me there with his foot. I crab-walked, not daring to rise all the way to my feet. He stripped off his shoes and slacks, stretched out on the black leather on his right side, and motioned for me to put my back side up against him. He lifted my left leg and slid his slobbering cock up my ass. "How'd you get so tight?" he asked. I didn't bother to reply. "Jack yourself off while I fuck you," he said tersely, and I put my hand upon the cock that he had protected with his lie.

"Do it nice for Daddy," he whispered, nuzzling my neck. My leg up in the air allowed him to get into me as deep as a bucket hitting the bottom of a well. Only it felt like this bucket was a hell of a lot bigger than the shaft it plumbed. "Let me see how much you like getting pumped," he encouraged, looking down at my hand. "Red little boy cock," he whispered. "Jerk it for me, sweetheart. Is Daddy fucking the come out of you? Tell the truth. I'll know if you lie to me. Don't you ever lie to me."

"No, Daddy, I'll never lie to you," I gasped, my hands a blur. My dick might be small, but it felt so good to manipulate it while he filled my ass that it brought tears to the corners of my eyes. "Oh, Daddy, you are fucking the come out of me. Yes, you are. Oh, please don't stop."

His cock was a reassuring presence, in and out, in and out, unfailing in its steady rhythm. "Daddy will always be here for you," he said in his deep, honeyed voice. "You can come on Daddy's big cock as often as you need to, honey. But you better not come unless I tell you that you can."

"Please! Let me, please!"

"Now?"

"God, yes, now."

"It's awful soon."

"No, Daddy, it's not soon; it's been a really long time. I've had your dick up my ass for a really long time and I need to come now, Daddy, I really do, oh please, I'll do anything you want."

"I've heard that before," he chuckled. But his thrusts in my ass sharpened, sped up. "If I let you come are you going to make it a good big one?"

"Yes!"

"Do it for me, Harris. Let me see you shoot. Else I'll have to take this big thick dick away from you and slip it into some other boy. You wouldn't like that, would you?"

"Oh, Daddy—oh, you can put your cock wherever you want. But I need it now. I do. I'll come like you say. I'm going to shoot. Only let me now—now? Now?"

"Of course you can," he said, like it had never been in doubt. And my wrong-ass body did indeed ejaculate at his command. The thick liquid spurting out of my hole made me dizzy with its smell of warm honey and sex. The sight of my orgasm made Knox lose control as well. He turned me onto my belly and fucked me up the ass while I begged for mercy and begged for more cock with no pride or copy-editing for inconsistencies. He got a big thick load up me. I could tell by the number of shudders that accompanied his orgasm, and the fact that the upper reaches of my ass felt heavy and hot even after his cock softened and slipped out.

Lotus came in the door with a pile of warm, wet towels on a tray. She went to Knox first and bathed the lower part of his body, receiving a loving kiss as her reward. Blushing, she came to me next and shyly put me to rights. She'd also brought a couple of cotton men's kimonos with her, and after she belted them, Knox drew both of us into the circle of his ebony arms.

Then we went into another part of the house, where there was a living room that opened out into a dining room area and kitchen. Lotus brought us food and sat close to Knox. He fed her from his own plate, and I was too happy to be jealous. I let her sit nestled close to him and took our dirty dishes into the kitchen myself, rinsed them and loaded them into the dishwasher. There was more Scotch on the counter, and I poured some for all of us. Three cut-crystal tumblers on a tray. I worried for a bit that Lotus would want a pastel drink with an umbrella and some fruit in it, but she tossed back her Scotch quicker than I could.

"Are you going to help us?" she asked me as the fumes from the Scotch made me suddenly very tired.

"Help you what? Lotus, I'm supposed to buy back the videotape and run you all out of town."

Knox shook his head. "You aren't buying any tape from me, man. That's evidence. See, if we go to the police and tell them that prick of a politician beat up my girl, he's going to claim that he didn't know she was pre-op, and the jury will let him walk. But what we got on that tape is him quizzing me about her, saying he won't take her into the bedroom if she isn't 'fully functional.' Plus a little something to prove that he wasn't talking about wanting a pussy. All a these rooms got cameras in them because I'm sick of my girls getting hurt. Sick fucker thought he could suck dick and get fucked and then fuck her up. No way that plays in Fort Knox, baby."

"Do you know how dangerous it is to go up against a councilman?" I asked. "Smitty's family has got more money than my family ten times over, Knox. He'll crucify you."

"Well, that's where you come in," he said, and toasted me with a half-empty glass. "You know where all of those pricks have the skeletons in their closets. You can walk us through the system. Once we've made our point, I don't mind leaving town."

"There's no place in America where you can hide from the Martingale clan," I said.

"Yeah, but I doubt they got connections in Thailand. We're going to bag us a crooked politician's ass, then we're gonna get enough money out of him to take my entire family to Southeast Asia and buy all a these girls a box. Except Taneena. She's a top."

"What about me?" I asked. He was asking me to break faith with a client. I had taken Smitty's money and given Sheldon my word that I would do a job. My life had been such a series of fuckups. Disappointing my family by being born somewhere between male and female. Betraying my lover. Dropping out of college without even trying to make a go of it. Humiliating my family more by becoming a cop. Fucking up being a cop. Becoming a PI. Now was I going to mess that up too? Where was my honor? Where was my honesty? And what kind of a man could I be without those two things?

In ones and twos, girls began to come home. Each of them handed Mojo a roll of cash and got a kiss, a grope, and a few endearments in her ear. One of them claimed Lotus, greeting her with romantic intensity, and the two of them went into the kitchen to neck and pet. The bodyguard also came in, and he was greeted by two of the girls, who ordered Chinese food and turned on the television. Some of the women regarded me with speculation, and Knox had me slide over to sit where Lotus had been. When he began to fondle me, one of them pointed it out to the others, who shrugged and went to pay for the food delivery.

"Hollywood nights," Knox said, and his stubble brushed my face as he kissed me. "Right now you're thinking what your choice is going to be. And I'm telling you that you got no choice. Now that I have my hands on you I am not letting you leave again. This is your home." He took my hand and put it on his bulging crotch. "All you got to do is give me the money you brought to pay for a chat with Lotus. Tomorrow we'll go back to your office and you can give me the rest of Shelly's money."

The idea of letting Knox manage my life the same way he managed his stable was too appealing. I reached for the inside pocket of my jacket, which I'd retrieved from his office on our way to the living room. It would be humiliating to give up that cash, partly because every female eye in the room was riveted on me, to see if I really was one of them. A moneymaker for the Pimps Up/Hos Down Savings and Loan.

Never forget that everyone in Hollywood is a player. I wish life could be like it is in the movies, but in real life, there are no whores with hearts of gold, and no love affairs between handsome black pimps/reformers and downwardly mobile, repressed and depressed, intersexed, haole detectives. The outed high school boyfriends who were once the affronted talk of the town do not reunite and pledge their eternal love across the barriers of race, class, and gender. And this high school boyfriend had not taken me to the drive-in movie, bought me a strawberry malt, or even asked me nicely before he introduced me to the painful and squalid, if effective, delights of wriggling on the end of his prick like a speared fish. There will never be a movie about any of these people either, by the way, so don't waste your time writing a screenplay.

I brought out cash, all right, and the very tiny gun that was hidden behind the bills. While Knox's attention was distracted by the thick bundle of bills, I snugged the barrel up to the base of his skull. "Get up," I said in his ear. "Don't make me embarrass you in front of your ladies."

He muttered something about putting the cash away in his safe. We rose to our feet and went back toward his office. There I had him sit down with his hands behind his back, and used my necktie to firmly secure his hands to the slats of the chair back. The bodyguard was stoking up a hookah with a couple of Knox's working girls. He wouldn't be able to stop me before I was out the door and gone. While Knox watched me in fury, I stepped over to the control console for the security system and removed the tape that had captured our encounter. It went into my coat pocket as silently as sorrow too great to allow for noisy tears.

"Don't you want the tape of Lotus too?" he asked, eyeing me with hate but with admiration too.

"There's nothing on that tape," I said. But I picked it up anyway, curious to see what was really on it. Maybe some decent porn from one of the girls' bedrooms. "There never was. Bambi just got tired of me holding his father's death over his head. This was all a setup to get you to take me out of circulation. The only person who was going to be blackmailed is me. You're probably the one who beat up your girl, and she let you because you promised her something she's always wanted. That operation in Thailand, probably. Shelly figured I wouldn't be able to resist a reunion with you. But you know what, Knox? You never really asked me if I wanted you to fuck me. You just assumed that you could. And I won't say I didn't like it. Because you know that I did. But there was never any love between us. You didn't give it up to protect me. Everybody in our school administration just assumed it was a case of the driver raping Miss Daisy. They were glad to get rid of a troublemaking black man who was screwing too many white girls and making their paleface boys look bad on the ball court."

"Shelly did come to me," Knox confessed. "But I was going to double-cross him. Don't *do* this, Harris. Don't walk out on your second chance for happiness. *Stay* with me, baby. We can still do all the things I promised you."

I couldn't afford to listen to him. "There was never any love between us," I insisted, and walked out with that lie ringing in my ears.

The corrupt people who run this playground are alive enough to reach for what they want. They still believe that life has something sweet enough to offer that it's worth any betrayal or robbery to grab. You couldn't accuse me of being corrupt, could you? Because I'd do the job my client had told me to do even though he was crooked as San Francisco's Lombard Street. But you couldn't exactly accuse me of being alive, either, could you?

There is no statute of limitations on murder. It was time to hold Sheldon Fawn responsible for what he and Mrs. Bambi had done. I could probably wangle a deal that would let me walk away without serving time, despite obstructing justice by withholding evidence. Either way, it was time to get off this merry-go-round. People with machine guns and grenades would be watching the swing set and the tetherball pole once I opened my she-he mouth. If Mojo really meant to double-cross Shelly and Smitty, maybe I'd find out if he liked Thai food as much as I did. Lotus could stay. I'd always wanted to be a big brother to some beautiful girl. Or several. More players just makes for a much more interesting game.

Afterword: What If . . . ?

Was it as good for you as it was for me?

Having been tainted early on in life by several crime noir writers—such as the late great Jim Thompson—I've always been most impressed with writers who keep the bad guys front and center and don't feel the need to *pretty* them up, or to clean up the messy loose ends and make the ending safe and happy. I love the bad guys, the losers, the down-trodden, the rough, tough, dangerous men from the underbelly of society, from the *wrong* side of the tracks, the *other* side of town, the ones you should know to run away from but can't.

And while I do enjoy a well-written love story—and there are several in one form or another in this tome—what is most striking to me, what gets me most *hard,* are writers who have characters, even mean ugly ones, that I care about. Or better yet (gulp!), that I want to fuck, no matter how awful the dirty deeds they do.

I completely identify with the men and women who fall for them: who should know better; who deep in their hearts know they shouldn't do whatever they're going to do; who can't help themselves because the danger of the "man of mystery" is part of what makes them so irresistible, so sexy, so worth everything that might happen; who know that even though some bad things are more than likely to follow, the chance to feel and taste and experience the dark ride with a stranger—basically letting your boner overrule the danger alarm in your head—makes it all seem worthwhile.

And in the end it doesn't always turn out okay, does it? Sometimes it turns out to be a much darker ride than expected, and the fuck turns out to hurt a hell of a lot more than you thought it would.

But it's all fantasy, isn't it? While most of us *would* probably listen to our built-in warning at the first glimpse of the tall, dark, handsome, and obviously Mr. Wrong, or run at the first sign of trouble, we all *do* fantasize about the danger and the *what if*. What *would* it be like to be involved in some wild mystery adventure that involves personal danger and intrigue? What *would* it be like to get swept off our feet by a handsome but very, very bad man we'd normally steer way clear of?

Would it be worth the trouble?

And how *fucking good* would the sex be?

I've had a blast working with Sean and all of the wonderful authors on *Men of Mystery*. I truly enjoyed meeting all these mysterious and often not-so-nice characters. And I thoroughly enjoyed the dark tasty rides they took me on. It *was* worth it. The sex was fucking amazing! Thank you all.

Greg Wharton

ABOUT THE EDITORS

Sean Meriwether has been published in *Lodestar Quarterly*, *Best Gay Love Stories 2006*, and *Best of Best Gay Erotica 2*. In addition to his nighttime career as author, he is managing editor of the online e-zine *Velvet Mafia: Dangerous Queer Fiction* (www.VelvetMafia.com). Sean lives in New York with his partner, photographer Jack Slomovits. Stalk him online @ penboy7.com.

Greg Wharton is the author of *Johnny Was & Other Tall Tales* and the editor/co-editor of numerous anthologies including the Lambda Literary Award-winning *I Do/I Don't: Queers on Marriage*. He lives in Oakland with his brilliant and sexy husband Ian.

CONTRIBUTORS

Patrick Allen currently lives in Southern Ontario, Canada. He spent a very instructive eight years in Los Angeles where he first read and began writing gay erotica. As a lover of mysteries it seemed natural to try to write a mystery with an erotic slant. Why not? Sleuths like to fuck too, right? The result is "The Rubens Gamble."

David-Matthew Barnes is the author of more than forty stage plays, two collections of poetry, and the novel *The Common Bond*. In addition, he is the writer and director of the coming-of-age film *Frozen Stars*. His work has appeared in more than 100 literary journals and anthologies. His stage plays have been performed in eight countries and twenty-five states, and have been featured at over a dozen nationally recognized festivals. He graduated magna cum laude from Oglethorpe University with a degree in communications and English. He is currently earning an MFA in the low-residency creative writing program at Queens University of Charlotte. He is a member of Alpha Chi, the Dramatists Guild, and the Theatre Communications Group. For more information, visit his official Web site at www.davidmatthewbarnes.com.

Steve Berman thinks that sex is like a good mystery: things suddenly come to a head while working undercover. When not thinking up awful puns to include in biographies he is hard at work writing queer speculative fiction stories. His work has been published in many anthologies and annuals *(Best Gay Erotica, Country Boys, Sex in the System)* as well as in the virtual pages of *Strange Horizons* and *Velvet Mafia*. In 2007, he has two books from Haworth Press: a young-adult novel, *Vintage: A Ghost Story,* and an anthology of queer fairy tales, *So Fey*. His Web site is steveberman.com.

Patrick Califia is the author of *Hard Men,* short stories about gay leathersex, and *Mortal Companion,* a vampire novel. He lives and works and plays in San Francisco. Well, mostly works.

M. Christian is the author of the critically acclaimed and best-selling collections *Dirty Words, Speaking Parts, The Bachelor Machine,* and *Filthy*. He is the author of the novels *Running Dry, The Very Bloody Marys,* and many others in the works. He is also the editor of *The Burning Pen, Guilty Pleasures,* the *Best S/M Erotica* series, *The Mammoth Book of Future Cops* and *The Mammoth Book of Tales of the Road* (with Maxim Jakubowski), and more than fourteen other anthologies. His short fiction has appeared in more than 200 books, including *Best American Erotica, Best Gay Erotica, Best Lesbian Erotica, Best Transgendered Erotica, Best Fetish Erotica, Best Bondage Erotica,* and . . . well, you get the idea. He lives in San Francisco and is only some of what that implies.

Vincent Diamond is a Central Florida writer whose work is slated for *Best Gay Romance 2007, Country Boys,* and *Hot Cops* (Cleis Press), and *Love in a Lock-Up* from StarBooks Press. Diamond's stories have also appeared in *Best Gay Love Stories 2005* and *2006* (Alyson Publications), *Feathers* and *Play Ball* from Torquere Press, and online at *Clean Sheets* and *Ruthie's Club.* Time away from the keyboard is spent riding horses, gardening, and pondering the inestimable beauty of tigers. More info is at www.vincentdiamond.com.

Fiona Glass lives in a pointy Victorian house in Birmingham (United Kingdom) with one husband, one visiting cat, and too many spiders. She writes short stories (published in *Velvet Mafia, Sigil: Volume 2,* and Torquere Press's *Fresh Starts*), and her collection of gay love stories, *One Degree of Separation,* is now available from Torquere Press. She is also seeking a publisher for her first novel—all sensible offers considered. In her spare time she edits the online homoerotica magazine *Forbidden Fruit* (www.forbiddenfruitzine.com). Her Web site, Through a Glass Darkly, is at www.tavaran.pwp.blueyonder.co.uk.

Trebor Healey is the author of *Through It Came Bright Colors* (Haworth Press, 2003), which was awarded both the 2004 Ferro-Grumley Fiction Award and the 2004 Violet Quill Fiction Award. He is also the author of a poetry collection, *Sweet Son of Pan* (Suspect Thoughts Press, 2006), and a short story collection, *A Perfect Scar and Other Stories* (Haworth Press, 2007) due out in the fall. His short fiction has appeared in *M2M, Quickies 3, Best Gay Erotica 2003* and *2004, Best of Best Gay Erotica 2, Best American Erotica 2007, Law of Desire, Out of Control,* and *Pills, Thrills, Chills and Heartache,* as well as the online journals *Lodestar Quarterly, Blithe House Quarterly, Ashe,* and *Velvet Mafia.* Trebor lives in Los Angeles. His Web site is www.treborhealey.com.

Caitlín R. Kiernan is the author of six novels, including *Silk, Threshold, Low Red Moon,* and *Murder of Angels.* Her short fiction has been collected in *Tales of Pain and Wonder, From Weird and Distant Shores,* and the forthcoming *To Charles Fort, with Love.* She is a three-time recipient of the International Horror Guild Award, and has also received the Barnes & Noble Maiden Voyage Award. Born in Ireland, she now lives in Atlanta with her partner, Kathryn Pollnac, and her cat, Sophie.

Jeff Mann's work has appeared in many literary journals and anthologies, including *Rebel Yell, Rebel Yell 2, Kink, Best S/M Erotica 2,* and *Best Gay Erotica 2004.* He has published two collections of poetry, *Bones Washed with Wine* (Gival Press) and *On the Tongue* (Gival Press); a collection of essays, *Edge* (Harrington Park Press); a novella, "Devoured," in the anthology *Masters of Midnight: Erotic Tales of the Vampire* (Kensington Books); a volume of memoir and poetry, *Loving Mountains, Loving Men* (Ohio University Press); and a collection of short fiction, *A History of Barbed Wire* (Suspect Thoughts Press). He teaches creative writing at Virginia Tech in Blacksburg, Virginia.

Gregory L. Norris is the nom-de-porn of a full-time professional writer who works for a number of national magazines and has several books under his belt, as well as episodes of a popular Paramount TV series. He lives a very happy life with his man of mystery, Bruce, and their two cats in a very safe house somewhere, courtesy of the Witness Protection Program.

Max Reynolds is the pseudonym of an award-winning East Coast journalist who deeply enjoys questing for social justice by writing class-conscious porn. Max divides his time between writing for various national straight and queer publications, teaching writing at a major East Coast university, and writing and filming porn. Max's erotic vampire novel, *Touches of Evil,* will be published in 2007 by Haworth Press. His stories have appeared in anthologies from Alyson, Haworth, STARbooks, and Suspect Thoughts Press. He is currently working on a collection of noir porn tales.

Thomas S. Roche's literally hundreds of published short stories have appeared in such anthologies as the Best American Erotica series, the Best Gay Erotica series, and the Mammoth Book of Erotica series. His own books include three volumes of the Noirotica erotic crime-noir anthology series as well as several short story collections. After editorial and marketing jobs with GettingIt.com, Gothic.Net, Libida.com, GoodVibes.com, GMPass.com, and 13thStreet.com, he is currently the editor of Eros Zine (http://www.eros-zine.com), a pansexual Webzine of news, events, and erotica. His personal Web site is www.skidroche.com.

Simon Sheppard is the editor of *Homosex: Sixty Years of Gay Erotica* and the author of *In Deep: Erotic Stories, Hotter Than Hell and Other Stories, Sex Parties 101,* and *Kinkorama: Dispatches from the Front Lines of Perversion.* He's also the co-editor, with M. Christian, of *Rough Stuff* and *Roughed Up,* and his work has appeared in well over 200 anthologies, including many editions of *Best Gay Erotica* and *The Best American Erotica.* He writes the column "Sex Talk," and lurks in the shadows at www.simonsheppard.com.

Michael Stamp's earliest influences were the writings of Gordon Merrick and John Preston, so it's not surprising that the New Jersey-based author's own erotica, including the S/M tales, has a decidedly romantic bent. Stamp's stories can be found in the anthologies *Best American Erotica 2002, Best Gay Erotica 2001* and *2002, Best S/M Erotica, Casting Couch Confessions, Daddy's Boyz, Friction 6, Sex Toy Tales,* and *Strange Bedfellows,* the e-book *Y2Kinky,* and magazines like *Inches* and *In Touch.*

Mark Wildyr was born and raised an Okie, and now lives in New Mexico, the setting of much of his fiction, which explores sexual discovery and intercultural relationships. More than thirty of his stories and novellas have appeared in works by Companion Press, Alyson Publications, Arsenal Pulp, The Haworth Press, STARbooks Press, *Men's Magazine,* and a pending Cleis Press anthology.

Order a copy of this book with this form or online at:
http://www.haworthpress.com/store/product.asp?sku=5885

MEN OF MYSTERY
Homoerotic Tales of Intrigue and Suspense

_____ in softbound at $15.95 (ISBN: 978-1-56023-663-4)

274 pages

Or order online and use special offer code HEC25 in the shopping cart.

COST OF BOOKS_____	☐ **BILL ME LATER:** (Bill-me option is good on US/Canada/Mexico orders only; not good to jobbers, wholesalers, or subscription agencies.)
POSTAGE & HANDLING_____ (US: $4.00 for first book & $1.50 for each additional book) (Outside US: $5.00 for first book & $2.00 for each additional book)	☐ Check here if billing address is different from shipping address and attach purchase order and billing address information. Signature_____
SUBTOTAL_____	☐ **PAYMENT ENCLOSED:** $_____
IN CANADA: ADD 6% GST_____	☐ **PLEASE CHARGE TO MY CREDIT CARD.**
STATE TAX_____ (NJ, NY, OH, MN, CA, IL, IN, PA, & SD residents, add appropriate local sales tax)	☐ Visa ☐ MasterCard ☐ AmEx ☐ Discover ☐ Diner's Club ☐ Eurocard ☐ JCB Account #_____
FINAL TOTAL_____ (If paying in Canadian funds, convert using the current exchange rate, UNESCO coupons welcome)	Exp. Date_____ Signature_____

Prices in US dollars and subject to change without notice.

NAME_____
INSTITUTION_____
ADDRESS_____
CITY_____
STATE/ZIP_____
COUNTRY_____ COUNTY (NY residents only)_____
TEL_____ FAX_____
E-MAIL_____

May we use your e-mail address for confirmations and other types of information? ☐ Yes ☐ No
We appreciate receiving your e-mail address and fax number. Haworth would like to e-mail or fax special discount offers to you, as a preferred customer. **We will never share, rent, or exchange your e-mail address or fax number.** We regard such actions as an invasion of your privacy.

Order From Your Local Bookstore or Directly From
The Haworth Press, Inc.
10 Alice Street, Binghamton, New York 13904-1580 • USA
TELEPHONE: 1-800-HAWORTH (1-800-429-6784) / Outside US/Canada: (607) 722-5857
FAX: 1-800-895-0582 / Outside US/Canada: (607) 771-0012
E-mail to: orders@haworthpress.com

For orders outside US and Canada, you may wish to order through your local sales representative, distributor, or bookseller.
For information, see http://haworthpress.com/distributors

(Discounts are available for individual orders in US and Canada only, not booksellers/distributors.)

PLEASE PHOTOCOPY THIS FORM FOR YOUR PERSONAL USE.
http://www.HaworthPress.com   BOF07

Dear Customer:

Please fill out & return this form to receive special deals & publishing opportunities for you! These include:
- availability of new books in your local bookstore or online
- one-time prepublication discounts
- free or heavily discounted related titles
- free samples of related Haworth Press periodicals
- publishing opportunities in our periodicals or Book Division

❏ OK! Please keep me on your regular mailing list and/or e-mailing list for new announcements!

Name _____

Address _____

STAPLE OR TAPE YOUR BUSINESS CARD HERE!

*E-mail address _____
*Your e-mail address will never be rented, shared, exchanged, sold, or divested. You may "opt-out" at any time. May we use your e-mail address for confirmations and other types of information? ❏ Yes ❏ No

Special needs:
Describe below any special information you would like:
- Forthcoming professional/textbooks
- New popular books
- Publishing opportunities in academic periodicals
- Free samples of periodicals in my area(s)

Special needs/Special areas of interest:

_____

_____

_____

_____

Please contact me as soon as possible. I have a special requirement/project:

_____

_____

_____

_____

The Haworth Press, Inc.

PLEASE COMPLETE THE FORM ABOVE AND MAIL TO:
Donna Barnes, Marketing Dept., The Haworth Press, Inc.
10 Alice Street, Binghamton, NY 13904-1580 USA
Tel: 1-800-429-6784 • Outside US/Canada Tel: (607) 722-5857
Fax: 1-800-895-0582 • Outside US/Canada Fax: (607) 771-0012
E-mail: orders@HaworthPress.com

GBIC07

Visit our Web site: www.HaworthPress.com